TEN-YEAR-OLD JAMES CANN
AWAITS HIM AND THE PRI
NEXT TO HIM ON THE INFAN.

MW00795328

"Fine writing and character insight by a master storyteller. Not since reading *Power in the Blood* by Greg Matthews have I found a study of Americana that's as compelling as *The Orphan Train*. Brigman has quickly established himself as a new novelist with a superb, coarse-grained voice that makes you want more. *The Orphan Train* is based on a history that was cold-hearted, sometimes tender, and extremely embarrassing for the Eastern U.S. between the years of 1859 and 1929. He takes the rich power of Dee Brown and mixes it with Thomas Berger's sprawling easel to paint a portrait of what it was like to hack a life out of the Ozark wilderness. Brigman is the Ozark's new narrator who will stand with Alan Le May, A.B. Guthrie, and of course, the above-mentioned Greg Matthews."—*Reavis Z. Wortham, author of the Red River Mystery Series.*

"Gripping from the first sentence to the last—I could not put this book down! I'm not sure I've ever read a story that kept surprising me with so many unexpected twists and turns in a plot that kept me guessing the entire length of the book. This one's got movie potential written all over it! An outstanding debut novel from author Steve Brigman."—*Diane Moody, author of "Of Windmills and War" and "The Runaway Pastor's Wife."*

"Brigman is an excellent writer. I could see the characters vividly in my mind as I read the story."—*Rolland Love, author of Blue Hole and River's Edge.*

THE ORPHAN TRAIN

STEVE BRIGMAN

Moonshine Cove Publishing, LLC

Abbeville, South Carolina U.S.A.

FIRST MOONSHINE COVE EDITION MARCH 2014

ISBN: 978-1-937327-41-5

Library of Congress Control Number: 2014932097

Book design by Moonshine Cove; cover from original artwork by Deborah Wilson, used with permission.

Acknowledgments

My sincere gratitude goes out to my friend and author, Reavis Z. Wortham, who took the time to go page by page through the first draft and lend badly needed advice and encouragement. My wife, Kathy, is a tireless supporter as coach, critic, proofreader, and lives the stories I write just as I do. I wouldn't accomplish much without her. I would also like to thank the staff at Springfield History Museum for their valuable help in my research.

Dedication

This and everything I write is dedicated to Kathy, my perfect bride of 39 years.

And I also dedicate this novel to my dear sister Claire, who is always there for me.

Also By Steve Brigman

Somebody's Gotta Do It

Our Season of Glory (forthcoming)

The Old Wire Road (forthcoming)

"The joy in life is his who has the heart to demand it."

—Theodore Roosevelt

THE ORPHAN TRAIN

Prologue

A slight chill washed over me when the words registered in my mind, *Orphan Train Reunion.* I stared at the envelope before opening it, wondering how on earth they were able to find me after all these years. Increasingly unsocial in my later years, gatherings with people I didn't know were usually out of the question, but a twinge of curiosity landed the invitation on the counter, where it remained until I picked it up a couple of weeks later for directions.

There were about a dozen vehicles in the lot when I pulled into the senior's center. A chubby woman named Beth greeted me inside from behind a registration table. Putting a checkmark on her list, she pasted a nametag to my sweater and ushered me into a large room where the other attendees were gathered. Most were at the back of the room, examining the memorabilia set out on long tables.

"We're so happy you came." Beth patted my shoulder on her way to check in more guests. I wandered over toward the others.

One of the older, sepia-stained photos made me smile, reminding me of the knickers we wore back then. There was a newspaper article from recent years that described one of these reunions, mostly about a local guy who had been a prisoner of war in Germany. An older report on yellowed newsprint described the arrival of an orphan train in the flowery language reporters used back then. The photograph of frightened faces peering through train windows held my attention. I recalled how terrified some of them were and wondered how many had been lucky, found decent homes, survived. But the small, battered suitcase at the end of the table transported me all the way back. It was exactly like the one that carried my meager possessions from one life to another. I could feel the plastic handle in my trembling hand and hear the murmur of the crowd on the depot platform.

"Is it like the one you brought with you?" I hadn't noticed a younger woman step up next to me.

"Exactly."

"Hi, I'm Linda Baker." She extended her hand. "We're so honored you joined us here today."

"Thank you, it was nice of you to invite me."

"You were smiling. Was yours a good experience?"

"For the most part. When you've logged as many years as I have, you've had your share of ups and downs."

She nodded approvingly. "Can I borrow you for a minute?"

At the other end of the room, people were coming together. Linda escorted me to the front, where she addressed the group. It turned out I was the oldest of the handful of orphan train survivors in attendance, which earned me a plaque. We posed for photos, and then a pair of polite little girls served me cake and punch. As I finished eating, a small circle of people collected around me, asking about my experiences. I was at first reluctant to go back, but certain of their inquiries touched things that felt good. Uncharacteristically chatty, I went on as one recollection unearthed another.

Tiring quickly in my old age, I was among the first to leave. On the drive home, I went back to the memories, sifting through chapters in my life I hadn't revisited in decades, the best of times dominating my reminiscing. I hadn't shared the worst parts at the reunion.

The snap of the screen door startled me back into the present.

"What you doin' out here, Grandpa?" No surprise, it was Ashley; we were the closest. She eased into the porch swing, wrapping her sweater tight against the chill. "Aren't you cold?"

"Feels good to me."

We rocked, taking in a sunny but brisk Thanksgiving afternoon.

"Get a deer?" she said.

"Shot a doe for the freezer ... passed on a decent eight-point."

"I didn't get to go ..." She cut off her sentence when I nodded. We were spending precious little time together since she took her first job as a reporter, and it was a sensitive subject between us.

"I saw your plaque."

"A dubious honor."

"Mom told me about how you came to Missouri, but I never heard you talk about it."

"It's not very interesting."

"Do you remember much about the orphanage?"

"Oh sure. I was there 'til I was ten." I paused to collect my thoughts. "I was happier there than I should have been. Ignorance is bliss, I guess. It was all I'd ever known. The priests weren't like parents of course. There were too many boys for that, but they cared about us and did the best they could. Father Vincent encouraged my reading. I loved the stories about the Wild West in the papers and magazines he scrounged up for me. The tales from the frontier captivated me."

"So what about the orphan train?"

"We were shipped out west to be adopted. A reasonable idea, but it turned out a lot of folks were more interested in extra farm hands than the pitter-patter of little feet. I'd read about it and figured at some point I'd be traveling out west. I was excited, and in a hurry."

"So you remember the day you left?"

"Like it was yesterday. They told us a few days before, so I had time to consider the prospect of being in a family, and the more I thought about it, the more the idea appealed to me. When the priests came in with the little suitcases, it was like Christmas. We also got new clothes. It all came from fundraising drives, I'm sure most donors happy to see us headed out of town."

"Did you have any idea where you were going?"

"No. I knew some had gone to Kansas and Indiana, but in my mind, I'd built it up to be Montana or California. I pictured myself a cowboy on some sprawling ranch, busting broncos, riding fences, fending off grizzlies."

Ashley's cute snicker hadn't changed since she was a little girl.

"They lined us up at the station, along with the girls from another home. I remember one of the sisters working her way down the line of boys, pulling knots from their hair with a big comb. I still remember the vice grip she put on my jaw as she raked my scalp." The image in my mind made me chuckle. "I wasn't interested in girls at that point, or at least not before we boarded the train. I'd never even talked to a girl."

"Yeah?"

"But there was this precious little angel ... red hair, big dimples, bright blue eyes ... struck me like a bolt of lightning."

"Grandpa! You still think about a little girl from way back then?"

"Yeah, I still think of her ... every day."

Chapter One

If the priests put me at the front of the line to encourage the others, they got what they wanted. I hopped on the train, ran down the aisle, slung my suitcase into the overhead bin and hung out the window. Fascinated by the bustle around the depot, I made a game out of guessing the baggage carriers' tips, finding humor in their faces when they were disappointed. Each person who hurried down the platform was a mystery, solved in my imagination, assigned important professions and exotic destinations, of which I'm sure each would approve. I hadn't noticed the car quickly filling. On my knees with my legs folded behind me, the spot next to me was among the last to be taken.

"May I sit here?" A delicate voice stole my attention.

I'd seen the girls from another orphanage lined up and assumed they were heading out west like us, to be adopted. I'd never spoken to a girl in my life, and I got off to a bad start. "Huh?"

"Is anybody sitting here? It looks to be about the only vacant seat left on the whole train."

"No," was all I could muster

"No, it's not taken, or no, I can't sit here?"

"You can sit here."

I settled down into the seat, but she remained standing. "I wonder if you would be a gentleman and help me up with my luggage. I don't believe I'm tall enough, and besides, a proper lady shouldn't stand on the seat in a dress anyway."

Her suitcase was quite a bit lighter than mine. For many of the children, they were but empty props. She sat and folded her dress primly around her legs before turning to address me.

"My name is Veronica. I'm traveling out west to join a new family." She had a funny formality about her, with a hint of Irish accent. "I suppose we all are. I think it's mostly a good thing, but I *am* a little nervous."

I nodded. Conversation, a skill I had always enjoyed in abundance, suddenly abandoned me, but Veronica was suffering no such inhibition.

"Sister says the best thing for a child my age is to be in a family. It would of course be wonderful to have a mother. She could brush my hair before I go to bed each night, and we would talk about boys who wish to call on me. I would also very much like a sister, but I'm not so sure about a brother. A baby brother would be wonderful to care for, but he would probably grow up and punch me in the arm."

Having also given considerable thought to what it would be like to be part of a family, it never occurred to me that someone might punch me in the arm.

"What's *your* name?"

"James."

"James is a nice name of course. He was a disciple, you know. I knew a boy once whose real name was James, but they called him Jimmy. That's a fun name. May I call you Jimmy?"

I nodded.

"Then Jimmy," she held out her hand, "I'm pleased to make your acquaintance."

I was horrified when she pulled it back and wiped perspiration on her sleeve.

"How old are you Jimmy?"

"Ten."

"I'll be nine next month, but Sister says I'm mature for my age. We should get along fine. Where do you think we're going?"

"Don't know, maybe Montana."

"Montana! It's freezing there, and there's grizzly bears, wolves and Indians."

"Montana's beautiful," I said, finally able to find my voice. "A wonderful country with big mountains, clear streams and wide-open prairie. Buffalo and elk and antelope are everywhere. Sunsets fill the sky with beautiful colors. I like to imagine myself fishing in a cold mountain brook, catching trout for dinner for my family ... I read all about it. Father always found me stuff to read."

"I suppose when you put it like that, it does sound okay. Wherever we end up, we just as well make the best of it, because we can't do anything about it ... so then, you're already planning to be married are you?"

"I guess."

"I'm not so sure. I'm just eight years old. But I'll start considering that soon. Sister says I have thoughts beyond my years."

"It'll be a long time ... I guess I wouldn't know exactly how to go about it."

"Well, you have to be in love first, and that takes a good deal of courting. You have to give flowers and candies and stuff, maybe take walks or sit on the front porch. Writing a poem helps. If you start kissing, it means you're falling in love ... a man has to get on his knee to propose, so you just as well get ready for that."

Her grasp of the subject amazed me. I'd never lent a single thought to writing poetry.

"If you're real handsome and have a high-paying career, then you will marry a beautiful woman, but not every woman is beautiful, so they marry the men who are not so handsome. But they don't care because they're in love."

13

"Huh."

"You're a decent looking boy, tall; that helps. But you could use a little meat on your bones. I suspect by the time you are old enough to call, you will be an acceptable suitor."

I couldn't have hoped for higher praise.

Veronica continued to expound on a range of subjects as I clung to her every word, nodding and grunting occasional acknowledgments. The conversation eventually landed on the countryside streaking past the window. She was also advanced in geography and maintained a running commentary on where she imagined we were. We shared a special moment: spotting the first cattle either of us had ever seen.

"We'll eat more beef where we're going," she explained. "That will help you fill out more. Ranch work will help develop your muscles."

"Maybe buffalo meat."

She crinkled her nose in disapproval.

It was getting dark when the sisters collected our dinner napkins. Veronica was still talking, sharing a detailed history of her life at the orphanage. She had something to say about most of the other girls, none of it terribly malicious, but nothing in her narrative suggested she was particularly close to any of them. Her stories put her to sleep before they did me.

An eerie silence settled over the car as most of the children slept. I stared out the window, a thousand thoughts bombarding me. A ghostly moonlight defined the hills, the occasional stream gleaming from the blackness when we passed over a bridge. Every few minutes, I glanced back over at Veronica, each time more beautiful than the last. When a curve in the tracks caused her head to roll over against my shoulder, I froze, terrified my trembling might wake her. She mumbled something, and I listened carefully, wishing badly to know what she was dreaming, but I never made out any of her words. It was about thirty minutes before one of the sisters came up the aisle, and tapped her on the shoulder. "Let's give this young man some room dear." Without fully waking up, she rolled her head over and fell back to sleep. I was oblivious to the possibility that the sister's suggestion was something other than her unfortunate misreading of my comfort.

The moment Veronica opened her eyes, she picked up right where she'd left off the night before, lecturing on a wide range of topics. As the miles melted beneath us, I remained glued to her every word and expression. The changing landscape, which would have normally fascinated me, passed with hardly a notice.

Just past St. Louis, the priests announced we would be stopping soon and some of us would likely be adopted. They reminded us to be on our best behavior and gave each a number on a piece of cardboard to hang around our neck. It struck me as I handed down Veronica's suitcase that I might not see her again. I tried thinking of something memorable to say as we stood in the aisle waiting to disembark, but I just couldn't muster the words.

Most of the people on the platform were just nosey onlookers. Several of the boys were inspected, like livestock, teeth being a common interest, and a boy a year younger than me but more physically developed was taken. A skinny, sun-baked farmer felt my bicep and shook his head in disgust, but nobody else even glanced at me. Veronica was the only girl to garner much attention. When it was time to re-board the train, she was still in the clutches of a finely dressed woman who stroked her hair and argued with her husband. I imagined him to be a lawyer, pleading some important case. By the time the priests began herding us back onto the train, her future still hung in the balance.

Among the last to board, I was horrified to discover there were no empty seats. If Veronica got back on the train, I couldn't save a place for her. I agonized, settling finally next to a bashful girl younger than me, my eyes locked desperately on the door. Though I understood that being adopted by the couple was likely the best thing for her, I could hardly breathe as I waited.

Finally, she came bouncing up the aisle. Perhaps the man wanted a son, I considered. There was also the possibility Veronica talked too much for their liking. She was quite satisfied to be back on the train but not at all pleased I hadn't saved her a seat. After I explained, she worked to remedy the problem. Her initial negotiations fell through because the boy next to her didn't want to sit with the girl beside me, but she was able to pull off an arrangement where we ended up across the aisle from each other. Those few feet were no barrier; she immediately began a detailed analysis of the couple that considered adopting her. My infatuation continued to grow as I listened.

Our next stop was early the next morning. The depot sign said we were still in Missouri. Tiny puddles lingered on the platform boards, and the sun burned hot, the air thick and steamy. Down the tracks, a rainbow reached across the sky into a dark cloudbank. A few folks stepped out from under the awning, but like before, there were many more sightseers than those interested in adopting.

One of the youngest girls was singled out immediately and smothered into the chest of a hugely obese woman. The boy next to me, Michael, caught the attention of a gentle-spoken couple that by all appearances made their living in the field. I eavesdropped as they became acquainted.

"How was your trip?"

"Fine."

"Are you excited about being with a new family?"

"I s'pose ... don't quite know what to make of it."

Despite Michael's limited interviewing skills, the couple was determined to adopt him. Soon they had one of the priests over, scanning his list. As I watched, there was a gentle tap on my shoulder.

She was the most beautiful lady on the platform, younger than any of the others inspecting the children. I was thrown off guard by some of the same emotions I experienced when Veronica first spoke to me. "Hello. We're the Crawfords. What's your name?"

"James."

"Well, it's nice to meet you James." She held out her hand, and I shook it firmly like the priests taught us. "I'm Clara, and this is my husband Joshua."

He stepped up with a disapproving squint, his grip limp and insincere.

"We have a farm southwest of here in some beautiful hills. A lovely stream runs just below the house, a wonderful place to swim and play. We have cows and chickens, fresh eggs every morning. I'm sure you'd just love it there. Do you think you would like to come live with us?"

"Yes ma'am, I think I would," surprising myself with such a quick answer.

Clara commanded the attention of one of the priests while her husband stood with me, staring off at the horizon. After completing paperwork, she fought against the tide of children being loaded back onto the train, a frantic expression on her face until she located me. Hurrying over, she took my hand, raised it to her lips and kissed my fingers. "Let's go home."

When I noticed the conductor collecting one of the stepstools, I panicked. Searching the platform, I realized Veronica was not among the children being adopted. The train was easing slowly away before I finally spotted her; face pressed to the window, tears streaming down her cheeks. She managed a sad wave, and I waved back. Our eyes remained locked until she disappeared down the tracks.

Chapter Two

The wooden crate was wet, but I sat as instructed, almost falling off when a slap of the reins jerked the wagon into motion. Despite a thousand unfamiliar sights and sounds, my curiosity focused on the people who had adopted me. Clara seemed the perfect angel, but Joshua's cool disinterest was frightening.

Just outside of town, Clara turned and began to describe my new home. "The Ozarks are a wonderful place. The hills and forests are beautiful, and the streams are clear and full of life. In the evenings, the deer come out, and in spring turkeys strut and gobble. We see otters and mink all the time on the river. On summer nights, the whippoorwills sing to us and fireflies fill the air. There is always some owl hooting, or coyotes howling off in the distance. In winter, you can hear the ducks quacking all night down on the river ... the trees are so beautiful in the fall."

I didn't know what a whippoorwill or firefly was, but I was spellbound. It sounded like some make-believe land in a fairy tale.

As we bounced along rocky wagon ruts through a green, flower-splashed meadow, a curious rabbit monitored our progress. I kept a keen eye on the surrounding forest, hoping for a glimpse of a bear or Indian. The trail wound through lower country for the most part, the whisper of running water never too far out of earshot. Twice we splashed through shallow streams, the muffled crunch of hooves in the gravel a fascinating new sound. When we came up onto a high, open space, hills rolled infinitely on, dull blue beneath a hundred shades of warmth in the late afternoon sky. At the bottom of the hill, Clara tapped my shoulder and pointed ahead to a doe and her two white-speckled fawns. They studied us carefully before bolting into the trees. I watched in awe, white tails bouncing after the rest of their bodies had vanished into the shadows.

We arrived at the farm just after dark, my bottom sore from hours of bouncing. In the moonlight, the house looked more sturdy than attractive. The barn was built of the same rock-and-log construction as the house with a connecting corral of split rails. Down below, out in the darkness, the river hummed a soothing welcome. Clara ushered me into the house while Joshua put the mule and wagon away. In the dim light of a single grease lantern, the cabin appeared roomier than it looked from the outside, decorated simply but neat and well kept. A door led to the one room off an open space consisting of the kitchen, dining table and sitting area around a fireplace. My eyes were drawn to a set of deer antlers above the mantle.

"I'm hungry," Joshua growled as he came through the door.

I sat at the table watching Clara put dinner together, pieces of venison cooked with beans, bread and onion slices. I had never tasted coffee and found it bitter. Clara continued to extol the glories of the Ozarks as we ate, as though she was trying to sell me on it, which wasn't the least bit necessary.

My bed was in the loft, accessed by a ladder up the side of the wall. The feather mattress sewn especially for me was far more comfortable than the cots at the orphanage, but the heavy blankets were too much. Exhaustion allowed me to sleep as deeply as I ever had. It says something important about a place that you sleep well there the first night.

I woke to an angelic humming. Accustomed to the obnoxious bell ringing at the orphanage, it took a few moments to recall where I was. Peeking over the edge, I saw Clara tending the stove. The aroma of bacon was as pleasant a treat as my nostrils had ever experienced. I didn't even know what it was. Breakfast at the orphanage consisted of the same porridge every morning. I hurriedly squirmed into my trousers and climbed down.

"Good morning darling," Clara greeted me in the sweetest voice I'd ever heard.

Joshua backed through the door with three eggs in each hand. "Get washed up," he said.

"There's a bucket of water on the porch," Clara said without looking up from the stove.

At breakfast, we began to take the first few steps of our journey together, but not until I devoured the scrambled eggs, bacon and biscuits, the best meal I had ever tasted. And this time the coffee didn't seem quite as harsh. I allowed Clara to pour me a second cup.

"What should I call you?" I eventually got the nerve to ask.

"You will call us Mother and Father. We're family now."

"I'm riding down to look at that bull the old man has for sale," Father pushed himself away from the table.

"We can't afford it Josh."

"Lookin' don't cost nothin'."

"We'll need another riding horse."

He ignored her and gathered his hat.

"Take James?"

"I best not."

"You and I will take a walk along the river," she said after he left. "Go out and take a look around while I clean up. I'll be right out."

In the golden light of morning, the house took on a more noble appearance. Above a rock foundation, the walls were constructed of well-manicured logs, laid with obvious craftsmanship. It sat at the edge of a small glade in the shade

18

of two gigantic oaks. Across the opening, the land dropped off sharply to the river. The barn was a little larger than the house, taller to accommodate a hayloft. A handsome, brown horse watched me over a fence rail while the disinterested, sway-backed mule stared off through the other side of the corral. Beyond the barn and a patch of chest-high corn, a black cow stood like a statue near the trees on the other side of a pasture, nursing a calf.

A few steps into the barn, a frenzy of flapping and squawking startled me breathless as a half dozen chickens bolted from their boxes. The gang of angry hens gathered on the hay-strewn floor and strutted indignantly out the door, clucking their displeasure as they passed me. I giggled at the way they bobbed their heads, and noticed that a couple had left eggs behind. Having just discovered how much I enjoyed eggs, I was delighted with the idea of just going out to the barn and picking them up, but it occurred to me that my intrusion might have interfered with the process. I gave the chickens a wide berth on my way back to the house.

Mother stepped out onto the porch, changed into pants and a shirt. "Ready." The spring in her step reminded me again of how she appeared too young to be the mother of a boy my age. In those earliest days, I had a crush on her, like a schoolboy on his teacher.

"Come on." She waved, and I followed her down a path through the trees, the sound of moving water growing louder as we hiked through the cool shade. We emerged atop a vertical, rock bluff a tree's height above the river. Mother stood right at the edge, hands on hips, staring out as if seeing it for the first time. "This is one of my favorite places."

The view warranted such an honor, rolling hills stretching as far as you could see. Just below, the river plowed through a rocky shoal before emptying into a deep, aqua pool, as clear as I could imagine water being, almost invisible in some places. I could barely make out silhouettes near the far bank, small fish resting in the shade of a low-hanging sycamore branch. Finally Mother sat, dangling her legs over the ledge, and motioned me to join her, reaching out for me after recognizing my apprehension.

"We own down to just past that bend." She pointed. "It ends around the corner right where the shoal begins ... but only on this side of the river." She looked the other direction. "It goes about a quarter mile that way, a little beyond that big rock."

"How much land do you own?"

"We," she stressed. " *We* have fifty-six acres."

"Are *we* a ranch?"

She laughed. "No, we only have three cows ... but two of them with calves."

I had read enough about cattle ranches to understand something was missing. "How do you have calves with only cows?"

"A neighbor lets us use his bull, and we furnish him with eggs now and then, and corn if we have it. We did have over a dozen head, but Josh sold to buy more acres. We'll build the herd back up someday ... and grow more corn now that you're here to help."

She glanced down at the river. "You can swim any time you like. The water is spring fed and very cool. You'll appreciate it on a hot summer day."

I'd never been in water for any reason other than to bathe. "Is it okay to get my cloths wet?"

She cackled. "You don't wear your clothes ... you wear your birthday suit."

I didn't understand.

"You swim without any clothes ... naked."

Thoroughly embarrassed and confused, I wondered if she would also be swimming without her clothes? How much privacy did a guy have to sacrifice to join a family?

"There's never anybody around but Josh and me." She grinned at my discomfort. "Just let me know when you want to swim, and I'll stay up at the house."

Mother stood suddenly, urging me to follow her down another trail. At the edge of the river, she introduced me to skipping rocks. When a big, yellow grasshopper was blown onto the water, squirming to take flight, she pointed and whispered: "Watch this." A fish twice the size of those in the shade glided up and sipped the insect from the surface.

"A bass. We have wonderful fishing. Have you ever been fishing?"

My headshake made her giggle at how silly the question was.

"Then we'll go fishing tomorrow."

We could hear up above that Father had returned, so we climbed the trail back to the house.

"How did it look?" Mother asked as he wrestled the saddle from the horse.

"Too much."

At dinner, I made the mistake of throwing my two cents in on the family cattle business. "Why don't we just buy cows if we can borrow a bull?" Father glared down at me, then shot a hostile glance at Mother. Joshua Crawford was driven in his desire to build a large ranch, and I didn't understand the symbolism of having a herd bull.

I was going to find out too soon how Father's grand ambitions would alter my life, but I was spared another day. He rode off again the next morning, this time offering no explanation of where he was headed. Mother came out in the same pants and shirt, this time wearing a tattered, straw hat. She fetched two long willow branches from the barn, each with string tied to the smaller end. In her other hand, she carried a glass jar with a leather thong to hang over her shoulder. I followed her down the trail to a wide gravel bar, where she slipped off her moccasins and waded into a shallow finger of still water just below a rockslide. Bending over, she studied the bottom. After a few seconds, she eased her hand into the water and struck suddenly, like a snake, holding up the small crawfish for me to see before putting it in the jar.

I waded in, the pea-size gravel melting around my feet, crawfish and minnows darting in every direction. Catching one looked impossible, but Mother was soon depositing another in the jar. I bent down, mimicking her technique, and finally spotted the granddaddy of them all in the shade of a large rock. I slipped my hand within inches of the unsuspecting victim. I hadn't really gotten a close-up look at Mother's crawfish. Neither had I taken notice of their pinchers.

My initial stab was at first a success, and I proudly hoisted a small lobster into the air. Mother's smile turned into laughter when I yelled and tried to shake the creature from my thumb. After a few violent jerks, it flew loose and plopped back into the river. When Mother finally quit laughing and caught her breath, she explained. "We don't want the big ones. And you have to grab 'em behind the pinchers."

Determined to make her proud, I developed the art of catching bait the hard way. I had a couple of crawfish and twice as many welts on my hand when she waved me down the bank. Instead of choosing the pool where the big bass had come up for the grasshopper, she waded out into the fast water a few feet from where it emptied into a pool. I watched carefully as she ran a hook through the tail of one of her crawfish and slung it upstream. The current swept the line quickly past, over a gravel slope vanishing beneath deeper water. When it tightened directly downstream, she eased the bait to the surface before slinging the line back upstream, the whole sequence lasting about thirty seconds. On her second drift, she lifted the pole suddenly. A fat, brown fish took a waist-high leap. I watched, enthralled, as Mother let the bass tire itself with short runs and jumps. Finally, she held the pole high above her head, reached down and lifted the fish from the water by its bottom lip. Removing the hook, she reached around for a cord in her back pocket, fished it through the gills and tied it to the rope that served as a belt.

It took me a while to get the hang of fishing, losing several of the hard-earned crawfish by jerking them from the deep water before the current pushed them to the top. I was paying little attention to my own fishing, instead watching Mother fight her third bass, when the pole was snatched from my hand. I dove with a loud splash, managing to get a hand on it, but as I tried to stand, the gravel washed from beneath my feet and down I went on my behind. Mother grabbed me by the collar before I was swept into the deeper hole. After regaining my balance, there was still a throbbing pressure on the pole. When I pulled back, the fish broke the surface in an angry somersault. I held on with both hands as it ran a wide circle around me and leaped again. My bass was twice the size of the ones Mother caught.

After adding my fish to the stringer, she asked: "Can you swim?"

"I don't know," I shrugged. "I never tried."

That night I was introduced to the taste of fresh fish, immediately joining eggs and bacon as my favorite foods.

Chapter Three

I enjoyed a week of fishing and exploring before Father put other business behind and announced at dinner that I was to join him the next day clearing brush. He'd said little to me that first week, but I was learning that it was just his way. The few words he spoke were usually about expanding the farm, converting the entire property into pasture, fencing it and purchasing more cattle. His pithy utterances often referenced his determination to buy more acres. Father's ambitions were spectacularly beyond his resources.

That first morning, before the sun peeked over the hills, I followed proudly in his footsteps, axe in hand, brimming with excitement. I had no understanding what lay ahead. It made me feel grown up to be helping with the farm chores, but I was a skinny ten-year-old who had never done a minute's labor in my life. Father left it to me to watch and learn, glaring over when I wasn't sawing or chopping. I didn't accomplish much the first day, suffering an exhaustion I had never known and returning that evening with my first blisters.

"They'll form calluses," Father mumbled as Mother treated them. "He ain't gonna amount to much help," I heard him tell her after I went up to bed.

"He's just a little boy, Josh."

"Well, he's gotta grow up. Might as well be now."

In the days ahead, Father called me lazy for kneeling down to catch my breath. At one point, his frustration drove him over to a small tree where he stripped the leaves from a thin branch and whipped me. I struggled to sleep that night, listening to them argue about the marks on my back. Mother was vicious in my defense, but the exchange concerned me since I was again going to be out the next day clearing land with Father, well beyond her protection.

He didn't beat me after that, but he still drove me as hard as he did himself. When Mother brought water and lunch out to us, the two of them often bickered about how hard he was pushing me.

"He's just ten years old," she argued almost every day.

"When I was his age, I did a good day's work or I was beaten."

"Well, you were raised by a son-of-a-bitch. We're not treating our son like a draft horse!"

The hardest part of working with Father was that he never took a break. When I was forced to rest, his disapproving glare bothered me, but my greater disappointment was in my inability to keep up. I wanted to feel like a man, help build the kind of ranch I'd dreamt about. Each day, I pushed myself harder, and each night I returned freshly thorn-scarred with more insect bites and a darker sunburn. Cramping muscles robbed me of badly needed sleep, adding to the next day's exhaustion. My frail body was being pushed to its limits, and there were evenings when I worried I wouldn't survive it.

Eventually my strength and stamina grew, but I was having no such luck adjusting to the heat. It was fortunate Mother arrived with lunch one day just as it was turning serious. When she saw me semi-conscious, leaning against a tree shivering, she threw me over her shoulder and sprinted down to the river, laying me in the water and cupping water over my head with her hands. She may have saved my life that day. As I began to gather my wits, I noticed Father up on the bluff, shaking his head in displeasure.

The three days I was allowed to recover, Father pressed on, working from sunrise until dark, not wasting even a second to check on me. Mother's pampering was a new and appreciated experience, well worth what I'd been through. Each time she blotted my forehead with a wet cloth, she promised things were going to get better. What I'm sure she didn't understand was that I was anxious to get back to work. I was determined to please Father one day.

I returned to work feeling stronger, determined to jump right in and carry my load, pleased over my growing contribution and impressed with how quickly we were carving pasture from forest, but Father never seemed satisfied. The work was physically draining, but I enjoyed it because I was living, where before, at the orphanage, I had merely existed. We continued to cut trees and burn brush throughout the summer, oftentimes late into the night. By the first cool breezes of September, we had cleared over five acres.

One October morning, the chilliest of the early fall, we stepped out onto the porch to the sounds of migrating geese. In the early light, I was barely able to make out the long Vs heading south. Father stared skyward with me, demonstrating an uncharacteristic interest in his surroundings. Just as odd was the satisfied tone I had never before heard from him. "We'll start putting back wood today."

Sawing, splitting and hauling firewood turned out to be as tiring as clearing brush. Mother began joining us a couple of days a week once the weather cooled, and she was a workhorse. Father, in one of our rare conversations, said she was able to work like that because she only does it for a few days a week, in cooler weather. It seemed a lot to expect her to be stacking firewood at all. She did the cooking, cleaning, fed and cared for the animals, and was always sewing something to expand my wardrobe. In those early days, I dreaded holding my tired arms out for a fitting after a day of swinging an axe.

We lit the fireplace a couple of days before topping off an enormous woodpile. On the first day of November, Father threw on the last piece and sighed. "There." It marked the beginning of his hibernation. He despised cold weather and didn't work in it, sulking around the fireplace all winter, carving everything from serving bowls to turkey calls. He was a gifted craftsman.

Father wasn't much of a hunter. He took a trip up north with his brothers for a week each fall, declaring that it was to put back venison, but he took obvious pride in the antlers that hung over the fireplace. He had no interest in hunting turkeys, but his cedar box calls were quite sought after by local hunters. He was able to buy another cow with all the items he carved that winter.

But late fall and winter became an extraordinary time for me.

It was Mother who first took me hunting. We snuck through the woods one brisk afternoon and sat just inside the trees at the edge of a small meadow. My butt was numb by the time the sky began fading into a gray twilight. The first two hours of deer hunting had been a terrible bore. I was studying a small bird that landed a few feet away when Mother nudged me. Across the opening, a large buck was easing out of the shadows, cautiously scanning his surroundings. Leaning over to pluck a mouthful of grass, he raised his head high again, pivoting nervously as he chewed. When he ambled behind some dense brush, Mother motioned for me to get ready. I raised the rifle and held it on the spot I expected him to re-emerge. The sights danced wildly as I fought to steady the rifle, the trembling worse with each second the buck waited to step out, but just as it was becoming unmanageable, he simply appeared, like an apparition, statue-still, right where I was aiming. I closed my eyes and reminded myself to squeeze the trigger like Mother taught me. The recoil bloodied my nose, but she didn't notice, whooping like nothing I had ever heard. She celebrated my first deer like it was one of life's greatest events. Straddling its massive back, she held the antlers up. They spread the width of her shoulders. After a congratulatory hug, she handed me her knife, and talked me through the bloody field dressing. I almost threw up at first, but once finished, I took great pride in having gutted the deer myself.

Father heard the shot and was rigging the wagon when we got back. He didn't share Mother's passion for hunting, but meat was meat and he was happy to help bring it in. I was elated to learn later that he was perfectly happy to butcher the deer. We hung the carcass in the barn to age. Mother said the buck was in rut, so its meat wouldn't be as tasty, and a good aging would help. I regretted asking about this "rut." It was the first of many embarrassing life lessons Mother was too comfortable delivering.

During the week, a couple of neighbors rode over to take a look. My head swelled as they gushed over my trophy. When Father butchered it, Mother took the antlers to a man who mounted them on a walnut plaque for three dozen eggs.

That's pretty much how things went those first couple of years. We worked until it got cold, and then Mother and I started hunting. And the more I hunted, the more I loved it. I was spoiled to the point that I was often allowed to set aside my studies, or my few winter chores, in favor of hunting. I had thousands of acres to roam and was determined to cover every inch of it. In those days, neighbors were happy to let you hunt on their place. Mother also used the winter months to concentrate on my education. Those were special times, not only because the backbreaking work was over for the season; I cherished my time with her. I enjoyed reading and discussing the books she made Father buy in town. He shunned these discussions. I only learned that he couldn't read after he was gone.

I don't remember feeling lonely without other children around. Mother dedicated much of her time to me, often walking around the property sharing her considerable knowledge of the trees and animals. We once hiked a couple of miles up the river to a fishing hole, lugging backpacks loaded with all the necessary items to cook lunch over a fire. At her urging, I took my first overnight camping trip on a gravel bar a few hundred yards from the house that next spring. I remember lying next to a small fire, terrified a bear might charge from the trees at any time. But soon I was spending at least one night a week out until it was time to start clearing land again.

Mother continued to hand down directives to Father about my treatment. It was music to my ears, as I lay awake hearing her say things like: "He needs time to be a little boy." But it was unsettling how often I was a source of conflict between them. On a few occasions, while out working together, Father slapped me for questions he deemed sass. Without coming out and actually reporting it, I made sure Mother knew he hit me, and it always ignited an argument. It was a source of comfort that Mother did most of the yelling. Father ignored me for several days after their quarrels, which was better than the hitting, but it still bothered me.

Emboldened by Mother's protection, I began to steal a few hours here and there to sneak off fishing when Father was away. I was off neglecting my chores the morning he died.

He was to be gone for the better part of the day, so instead of taking tools from the barn, I came out with my fishing pole and the crawfish jar, planning to fish most of the morning before returning to my duties. The bass were in a feeding frenzy. I caught one after another, loosing all sense of time. It was nearing noon when a cool breeze came up. A nearby crack of lightning caused me to flinch. So absorbed in my fishing, I'd failed to notice the dark, angry clouds rolling in from Kansas. But the rain wouldn't hit for several minutes, so I swung my line back into the stream one last time, and another bass grabbed it. As I fought the fish, the first hailstones drove waist-high fountains from the river. When a jagged piece of ice hit my shoulder, drawing blood through my shirt, I was sure it was broken. I scrambled beneath a thick juniper just in time to escape the downpour. The ground was covered with ice within minutes.

The hail ended as abruptly as it had begun, so I made a run for it up the trail, slipping on gravel, tearing my trousers and bloodying my knee. When I peeked over the last few feet of the climb, I was struck with the full force of a powerful wind. Throwing my arm up to shield my eyes against a cloud of leaves, I was barely able to make out the house in the blowing dust. The roar was deafening, wind whipping the trees, debris slapping the barn like rapid gunfire. Fear paralyzed me, rendering me unable to manage even a step. I could barely make out my parents holding on to porch columns, Mother yelling inaudible instructions and waving me in. Even Father was shouting something I couldn't decipher.

Just as I was mustering the courage to take off, I spotted something emerging from the dark sky: a ghostly white tentacle hanging from a low cloud, dancing vulgarly back and forth as it stalked within yards of the barn. I'd read about tornadoes and knew I was face-to-face with one. Instincts propelled me to sprint the short distance and dive behind the rock wall surrounding the well.

Mother became so desperate that I finally heard her.

"Come on James ... run! ... hurry!"

I didn't understand why they didn't take shelter. It looked liked I was a goner. They needed to save themselves.

"Come on boy!" Father hollered. "Now!"

One of the biggest oaks snapped like a rifle blast, the huge limb landing just feet from me. It was swept away instantly, rolling like a giant tumbleweed. I huddled as close to the rocks as possible, eyes closed, praying. Bracing for the end, I was startled by Father's strong grip on my arm. He jerked me up and threw me over his shoulder.

The barn exploded before he could take but a few strides, a fence-post-size splinter finding his temple, a loud crack like a baseball on a bat just a few inches from my own head. I probably survived because he fell on me.

In the eerie aftermath of the storm, we discovered that the blow had clubbed the life from him. I was immediately overcome with excruciating guilt. Father died saving me because I hadn't obeyed him. I at first feared Mother would hate me for it, but that was of course not the case. I never shook the guilt.

Besides a few cuts and bruises, Mother, the house and I survived relatively unscathed, but the rest of the farm was in ruin. All the chickens and both horses perished, and a healthy beginning to a corn crop wiped out. The cows survived because they were grazing across the field from the barn, and I'll never figure out how that old mule survived, right in the middle of it all. Mother said it was just too stubborn to die.

We dug Father's grave a short distance behind the house. Mother had me read Psalm 23 before we shoveled dirt back into the grave. She never shed a tear. She just wasn't a crier, but it was easy to see that her heart was broken. I'll never understand how she loved that man so much. I believed she grieved until she died. And for reasons I don't fully understand, I still miss him.

Chapter Four

After the initial cleanup, Mother set her sights on a new barn. Neighbors offered to help, which seemed especially generous to me. I was appalled when she graciously declined.

"We don't need a church barn," she told me. "They say they want to help, and I'm sure some do, but what they want mostly is to be seen helping. They'll throw up the quickest thing they can and then pat themselves on the back, but you don't end up with much of a barn. We'll do better on our own."

One very friendly man insisted on lending a hand, and even came out with a wagon loaded with tools, nails and lumber. Unusually cool to his generosity, Mother later told me he had interests beyond building a barn. I was to become accustomed to the attention paid my mother by the men of the region.

She wanted to duplicate the original construction to match the house, so first we had to gather stones for the base. The ones she wanted were down along the river. After a single trip up that hill, I was discouraged to the point of giving up, but watching Mother exhaust herself alongside me, I dared not complain. Thank goodness, after a couple of days of backbreaking work, she dipped into our scant savings and bought a pack so the mule could carry up four stones at a time.

Mules have a well-deserved reputation for stubbornness, but ours had a particularly foul disposition. He was mean as a snake, the scar on my hand a permanent reminder of the day I found that out. But Mother wasn't going to take any more crap off that animal than she had from the other men in her life. It was going to haul rocks whether it wanted to or not, though it remained in doubt for a while. We expended a considerable chunk of one morning just trying to get the pack secured. The mule had been around long enough to know that nothing good could come from it, and he wasn't going down without a fight. I was convinced there was no way we would get the delinquent creature to haul rocks, but Mother came up with a way to coax him up and down the trail with sugar cubes. He eventually caught on to the treat-at-the-end-of-each-leg pattern, and became moderately manageable. One night during my studies, Mother challenged me with an equation to determine whether the price of sugar was worth the time gained by using the mule instead of hauling the stones ourselves. I didn't need math to answer that question.

After the base was complete, we started taking logs from the next logical patch of forest to be turned into pasture. Again, we used sugar to get the mule to drag each log to the construction site. Mother hired a couple of drifters to help with the upper section of the barn. They were lazy, but without their strength, we couldn't have managed to get certain logs in place. When autumn arrived, we were finishing off the inside with a couple of horse stalls. It was a handsome building, just as Mother planned, except one of the corners where the log fittings were a little sloppy. But it was sturdy, and its flaws were not visible from the house, so we took no shame in it. It was on to the next project.

The let-me-be-a-little-boy days were in the past. Not satisfied with simply rebuilding what we had, Mother was obsessed with growing the place as Father had dreamed, and I was expected to do my part. She had no qualms about working in the cold, which was a problem during hunting season. We got started late on firewood, and I suffered the indignity of watching two large bucks lock horns with nothing but an axe in my hand. Then a big wind came through, and we had to repair fence in the snow. I don't honestly know that Mother slept every night. She was usually sewing when I dragged my tired muscles up to the loft, the next morning's progress suggesting she'd been up quite late.

We were allowed a brief respite during the Christmas season. For the first time, Mother had me cut a tree for inside, and she actually spent a little money on decorations. She baked all kinds of goodies, and much to my chagrin, made me join her caroling around town with a group from the church. Under the tree on Christmas morning, I found an expensive bamboo fly rod she mail-ordered from Chicago. Christmas was always a big deal after that.

In the spring, Mother purchased twice the amount of seed corn we usually planted. When it came time to prepare the ground, you could see it in the mule's eyes; he was too familiar with the plow. It was a battle getting him harnessed that first time, but after a lengthy stalemate, we lured him in front of the plow and broke ground with Mother in the lead, rope in one hand, sugar cubes in the other. I was always afraid a neighbor might ride up and see our ridiculous little parade. It took all my strength to manage the plow, and the patch of earth we were carving seemed to grow as slowly as the base of the barn, but like the barn, its completion was a great source of pride for us both.

The sky opened hours after the last kernel was in the dirt, and stalks shot from the ground. We were able to borrow money against the crop and got the best prices in years for a very successful harvest. It was a significant windfall. Mother used some of the money to buy me a double-barrel shotgun. The family guns had always been communal property, but she wanted me to have one to call my own. All I had to do was find time to use it.

Besides being a tireless worker, Mother had a real knack for business. She found buyers for the timber in areas she wanted to convert to pasture and hired a woman to help with the growing demand for her sewing. She was shameless in negotiating the price of land, cattle or anything else we purchased, angering a few who had to lower their price to do business with her.

Eventually, I began to get breaks from the farm chores with trips to town, excursions Mother felt important to my overall development. She sent me to the bank, post office and the general store. Many assignments were hardly worth spending the better part of a day away from the farm, but I was fine with that. Mother was also determined that we become increasingly involved in community, dragging me to weddings, holiday celebrations, church socials and dances. I was fifteen when she taught me to dance. Her sighs at my initial effort planted seeds of insecurity that haunted me my first time on the dance floor, but she saw to it that I eventually became a good dancer and developed all the other social graces. I shot up that year like a weed, to just under six feet, and filled out, much of it muscle earned on the farm. Along with the physical development, my confidence grew, and I began paying closer attention to the young ladies in town. It wasn't long until it was me dragging Mother off to church socials and dances.

She was by a long shot the most beautiful woman at whatever gathering we attended, graciously spreading her dances among the many who sought her company, careful to show no favorites. She appreciated the attention of men, but never anyone in particular. I don't know if she just didn't want to marry again, or if there were no suitable husbands in the area, but I felt, though I really didn't understand why, from very early on that she wasn't going to re-marry. When a handsome lawyer moved to town, he did all but refuse to take no for an answer, and Mother agreed to see him long after she would have ended it with another suitor. That he and I got along so well was likely part of it. But in the end, it ended abruptly, one of the few things she refused to talk to me about.

At first, Mother found my blushing admission about a crush on a certain girl in town charming, but I was only sixteen when it began to cause trouble between us. She heard from some gossiping neighbor that I was seen in the company of a young lady whose mother practiced a less-than-honorable profession. Actually, the poor girl was ashamed of her mother's prostitution and was something of a prude. She wouldn't even let me kiss her for quite a long time. But I wasn't extended the opportunity to explain that to Mother, whose order to not see her was final and not open to debate. When she heard that I ignored her edict, she greeted me on the porch with a slap to the shoulder intended more to express her displeasure than cause pain, but it left a bruise. The issue worked itself out when the girl unexpectedly left town. Mother and I went out of our way to patch up our differences after that, and she was elated when I began to show an interest in Melissa, the minister's daughter.

Now Melissa we could agree on. She was a knockout, a doll's face framed with long, chestnut hair and a very womanly figure for her sixteen years. I'd seen some of the men in town staring lustfully at her, and even caught myself doing the same on a few occasions, but my wandering eyes weren't greeted with

31

the disgust she flashed at the old men. At first, when she smiled at me, I was rendered speechless, but she had a way of putting me at ease, and we quickly became friends. My head-over-heals crush was almost immediate, but I was careful to bury those feelings. I knew I wasn't in her league and didn't want to threaten my time with her by doing something stupid like trying to kiss her.

Along with her physical charms, Melissa was full of mischief, with tomboy tendencies. Stealing a watermelon was our first crime, and she sometimes stole a cigar from her uncle for us to share. Mother once sniffed me and crinkled her forehead suspiciously, probably aware of what I'd been up to, but smoking wasn't the taboo it would become later. In the beginning, our shenanigans were pretty innocent, but you could sense a time coming when Melissa was going to push the envelope.

That day came when one of her girlfriends told her you couldn't get pregnant if you did it in the water. Though I had no insight into such a claim, it struck me as a ridiculous notion. But this was a force I was helpless to resist. We planned our rendezvous with all the secrecy of a bank heist, the pool below the house an obvious choice. Mother almost never went down there any more, and her weekly trip to town was good insurance against it.

I arrived first, trembling so badly I feared not being able to move when she showed up. The best-looking girl in town was about to see me without my clothes, which oddly dominated my thoughts over getting to see her naked. But I hadn't long to fret, catching a glimpse of her reflection off the water, just upstream, wading across a shoal with her shoes in hand.

"Hi," she greeted me in a matter-of-fact tone, no hint at the monumental event about to take place. "Sorry it took so long. It's a couple of miles, even down the creek."

"That's okay. I just got here."

"Did your Mom go to town?"

"First thing."

She glanced back at the pool and then turned with an impish grin, "You ready?"

"I guess."

"Well I hope you're more excited than that."

"I am."

Her smile told me it was all right.

Stepping back to make sure I was paying proper attention, she pulled the dress over her head and tossed it on the gravel, and then, grinning up naughtily at me, slid her underpants off. It hit me like a jolt of electricity. I had never seen a woman naked.

"Come on," she waded in. Waist deep, she turned to watch me undress. "You are excited!" she cackled when I dropped my trousers.

32

I knew my rising enthusiasm was natural, and in fact necessary for the task at hand, but still, it was incredibly embarrassing. I hurried into the water. Melissa wasted no time stalking me to the still corner of the shoulder-deep pool. When she reached down to take the lead, my knees almost buckled at her touch. I thought I'd explode before she was able to guide me into her. It was incredibly awkward, more like a couple of bear cubs wrestling, but we were without question accomplishing the mission. With her arms and legs wrapped around me, she breathed into my ear, sending a shiver through me with each sound. When something akin to a gasp echoed off the bluff, I instinctively glanced up.

There was Mother's unmistakable silhouette locked in an angry pose, glaring down from the ledge.

At my gasp, Melissa stepped back to see what was wrong.

I looked back up and she was gone.

"Mom."

"What! Did she see?"

"She saw."

"Oh my God! ... Oh my God!" Her eyes danced about wildly. "But wait, your Mom 's not a gossip. She wouldn't say anything."

"She'll have plenty to say to me."

"It can't be all that bad. The boy never gets in trouble."

"She's not going to be waiting up there to *congratulate* me ... nobody will find out, unless she tells your parents."

"Oh God, James, please tell me she wouldn't do that?"

"I don't know ... I guess I ought to go."

It seemed appropriate to kiss her, and as I held Melissa against me, it stirred us to blot out the impending storm long enough to complete what we'd started, which didn't take long.

"Did you like it?" she said before I caught my breath.

"Yeah," I wheezed.

She chortled a throaty approval. "Me too ... I want to do it again."

"I better get up there."

"I didn't mean now, just again ... sometimes."

She hurried out of the water, and I followed more slowly.

"Let me know what your Mom says." She pulled her dress down over her hips.

"You may be able to hear it in town."

"Surely it can't be all that bad. It's not like you're a girl."

"I don't know." I glanced back up. "But I'm about to find out."

"Well okay, good luck ... see ya." She pecked me on the lips.

I watched her wade through a riffle and scamper down the bank, growing smaller, until right before fading into the shadows, she stepped out into the sunlight, waved and vanished into the trees.

Mother was waiting on the front porch. I couldn't have walked any slower once I spotted her.

She started right in on me. "You're sixteen years old for God's sakes! If that girl is pregnant, you'll have to marry her!"

At least I had the good sense not to explain why Melissa couldn't be pregnant.

After a lengthy screaming session during which she planted a bruise on each of my arms, she began to cry, bemoaning her skills as a mother. She kept after me until I escaped to bed early, "disgraceful!" and "irresponsible!" echoing in my head.

Sulking around like a wounded puppy wasn't going to help this time. A week passed in silence, except for some distasteful chores Mother handed down, and then there was another week of hourly scoldings. But things started to thaw after that, which I felt was pretty soon considering those first few hours.

Sometimes Mother was hard to figure out. I was absolutely perplexed that she didn't forbid me to see Melissa. In fact, she seemed to be suggesting I not avoid her, asking often if I'd talked to her, as if nothing had happened. Maybe at that point she thought Melissa might end up her daughter-in-law. I'm sure Mother was anxious to find out if she was going to be a grandmother. In town several weeks later, she pointed out nonchalantly: "There's your friend. Be a gentleman and go over say hello."

We acted out our greetings, careful to not stand too close. After a few pointless pleasantries, Melissa's attention shifted to Mother, who was examining a store-window display. I must have looked satisfied, because she scowled: "She's watching in the reflection."

With gossip the favored pastime in the region, the three of us sweated our secret, all aware Melissa was the most likely to let it out. It turned out that we were well justified in that fear. She couldn't resist sharing the news with her closest friends, and with the odds of adolescent girls keeping a secret like that somewhere near impossible, the story soon filtered up the nosey-old-lady grapevine. Before that, I got the impression Mother couldn't care less what people thought of her, but when the stares and snide comments about my misbehavior greeted her in town, it opened up a whole new round of wrath.

"The preacher's daughter, for Christ's sake!" she bemoaned about a dozen times a day for another week.

I ran into Melissa not long after that, and she proudly confirmed that she was not pregnant. I was so naïve that she had to explain how she knew for sure. Mother got past my indiscretion pretty quick once she learned there wouldn't be a shotgun wedding. I was always forgiven. That's one of the ways I was spoiled. Melissa was probably right about a boy not getting in as much trouble. Actually, it wasn't long after before Mother's interest in girls my age rivaled my own. She began urging me to call on certain ones whose parents she thought highly of, but mostly found fault with those who caught my eye. After Melissa, I had little interest in the skinny daughters of my mother's friends.

I wasn't a bad looking kid, but I have to credit Melissa with some of the popularity I enjoyed among the town's teenage girls. I thought the rumors would have caused them to shun me, but it had the opposite effect. Daughters of the town's most prominent citizens sought out my company, always keeping a sharp eye out for their parents. But Melissa was avoiding me. In a rare slip of the tongue, I mentioned it to Mother, and she assured me it had more to do with her father than with me. I never knew for sure whether he found out, but whenever I saw him in town, I ducked out of sight. I wasn't much of a churchgoer after that.

I eventually refused to even discuss my social life with Mother, which she begrudgingly respected to the best of her ability, which was limited.

Chapter Five

Between the farm and her sewing, Mother had little time to herself, but there was nothing else she would rather be doing. Though I didn't share her zeal for work, I was enjoying life and found our accomplishments rewarding. I was now running most of the errands in town and overseeing work projects on my own. Mother was particularly proud when I fired a lazy worker for his constant complaining, and she was surprisingly unfazed that I almost had to fight the guy to make him leave. I gained a lot of respect from the boys that day.

But Mother continued to insist we always share the evening meal and scheduled her life around it. She tried her best not to discuss business, which was going very well. The sturdy shirt's she designed, with a handsomely cut pocket flap, became popular with the men in the area, selling so well she had to put on another woman to keep up with demand. We continued to purchase cows, and eventually, instead of borrowing a bull from the neighbor who was happy to let the beautiful widow use it for free, paid a high price to rent a bull from a ranch in Oklahoma with one of the top Angus bloodlines in the west. Mother also bought four heifers from a nearby ranch whose Angus herd was of note. Our first bull would put us on the map. At first, the men at the auction barn ridiculed Mother's calculated approach to the cattle business, but they retreated into respectful resentment when Bellringer grew into the best bull anyone had ever seen in those parts. He was enormous. It wasn't long until ranch owners were stopping by to inquire about "Bellringer Angus."

When the size of the herd lagged behind demand, Mother sought out a rancher in Texas to add more mother cows, and I took my second ever train ride to see them back safely. We purchased acreage as profits allowed, especially when adjacent property became available. When a greedy speculator beat us to a piece of land, Mother dug in her heels. Even after a year, when he dropped the price to reasonable market value, she refused to even entertain his offers. Finally, he was forced to let us have the property for a steal. We eventually bought another particularly beautiful tract from neighbors who had not shared our success. It stretched the ranch farther down the river with a mix of grazing and timber, including a grove of mature walnut trees, half of which Mother sold for a very handsome fee. She stayed out in the hot July sun for days supervising their harvest. Her selective cutting left a shady, park-like setting where enough sun leaked through to grow grass. There would also be a significant walnut harvest from the remaining trees.

She finally turned the shirt-making business over to the ladies who helped sew them. Cattle was our business, and there was little time for anything else. We abandoned corn farming, instead purchasing enough from neighbors to feed steers for personal consumption. When prices were low, we fed more animals. Mother loved to entertain, showing off Crawford corn-fed beef.

Despite the demands of the ranch, she never lost her determination to see me educated, making sure I always had an abundance of books and a few hours a week to spend with them. We sat out front on warm evenings where she loved to hear me talk about what I was reading. She always picked out something to discuss involving history, science or geography. It was a game we both enjoyed playing. But the lion's share of my education was in business. Mother saw to it that I was by her side when she conducted her more important affairs. She spoke in a way that suggested I was a partner in the negotiations, always asking my approval before finalizing any deal. I doubt anybody really believed I shared any real voice in the decision-making, but she wanted everybody to know I would be handling some of these matters in the future. When I turned seventeen, she pulled me aside and opened the books, explaining the business with numbers. I was astonished at how much we had accumulated, but had no desire to be involved in the bookkeeping.

Mother eventually put on enough hands that it wasn't necessary for me to work as many hours, but I usually did. I liked the work, and I liked being around the boys. She worked alongside us whenever she had time, setting a pace that prevented some of the newly hired help from returning for a second day. You could depend on her being out there when we had a new man starting. To those who hung with it, she paid the highest wage in the region, and we built a roomy bunkhouse out away from our home on a beautiful hillside that was the envy of men from other ranches. Everybody on the place was invited to Sunday lunch, where we discussed ranch affairs as if all the hands were partners. Mother gave an extra week's wages at Christmas for those who had been with us throughout the year, while the others received one of her shirts. There was little turnover despite the backbreaking pace of the work, though occasionally we lost someone to marriage. Mother allowed only single men in the bunkhouse, and wanted all the help onsite.

In five years, we built the finest ranch in the region, and could properly be called wealthy by local benchmarks. And Mother was growing into one of the most influential people in the western Ozarks. But through it all, the priority remained her son, and she was proud of the job she had done raising me. I was a stylish young buck about town, popular with the young women, respected by the business community and envied by more than a few.

We were enjoying a bowl of stew one evening when the sky opened up, and we had to raise our voices over the pummel of rain on the roof. It had been a particularly wet couple of weeks and more rain wasn't welcomed. As the din grew, a sudden gust flung debris against the window. I pushed myself away from the table and hurried over to look outside. A small stream was already carving a path next to the house; tree limbs whipped violently in the flickering light. I jumped back at a nearby explosion, its blinding flash washing out everything. As the world faded back into darkness, I stepped back up to the window and spotted a small flame through the trees.

"It got a tree."

"Doesn't sound like any hail, though."

"Nope," I turned back toward the table. "Thank goodness."

I hated the look she gave me. At that age, I didn't care to have my phobias acknowledged. A near-death experience with a tornado is certainly just cause for a fear of violent weather, but Mother looked at me as if I had some pitiable affliction. Fearless in all aspects of her life, she had little understanding of my feelings. We ate without trying to talk over the storm until a pounding on the door startled me off my chair.

"Good Lord," Mother yelled as she hurried over to answer it.

Ben, our top hand, stepped inside, out of breath, a small lake forming around his boots. "Calf stuck! ..." Mom held up her hand to calm him and pushed the door shut. "The river's coming up fast," he managed a modicum of composure. "It slipped in the mud and got stuck down in the brush. I'm scared we're gonna lose it ... it's one of the Angus."

Aggravated at Ben for not handling it, Mother grabbed her coat and hat and charged out into the deluge. I followed.

The little fellow looked doomed, tangled in a matt of roots and vines, the muddy water rising rapidly a few feet below. The river was as violent as I had ever seen it with entire trees rushing by, twisting eddies whipping up foam. The roar was deafening. Shallow banks across the river had surrendered to the flood, water stretching into the trees, boiling over jams. After ordering Ben back to the barn for a rope, Mother tested the footing for an almost vertical climb.

"Don't!" I yelled.

She held her hand up to silence me.

The calf bawled in terror as its mother peered anxiously over the edge. Ben was back in a few minutes. We tied the rope to the base of a small tree as Mother threw off her coat. My heart sunk when she slipped on the mud stepping over the edge, but she grabbed the rope to keep from falling. With an astonishing strength and agility, as if she had done it dozens of times, she rappelled down and secured the rope around the calf's midsection as its legs flailed at the water. On her signal, we hoisted the traumatized youngster up and released it to a grateful parent. When we threw the rope back down, the water was lapping over her boots. She grabbed it in one hand, and tested a tree root with the other. Waist-deep in the woody mesh, she had to lift a leg high to extract it. When she pushed at her supporting foot, it slipped, and she fell through the tangle as if it wasn't there.

Clinging to a thin root with one hand, she struggled unsuccessfully to bring her other arm around against an impossible torrent. I hadn't moved a muscle when it broke loose, and she was swept downstream. I sprinted down the high bank, trying to keep up. She was a good swimmer, but no match for the power of the river. Her frenzied strokes were getting her no closer to safety. Some-where inside, I had to understand what I was witnessing, but I ran anyway, stopping briefly at openings in the trees, and then frantically trying to beat her to the next one. When the trees opened up over a long stretch, we locked eyes. She quit swimming, as if resigned to the inevitable. With my attention fixed on her, I tripped, skidding face first. From my belly, I searched in panic, spotting her just as she was vanishing into the darkness.

I never saw her again.

Chapter Six

Long after authorities gave up looking, I wandered distant riverbanks numb to the reality that Mother was gone. And just when I was about to abandon my search, the hat she'd wore that night was found downstream. After exhausting even the faintest hopes, I moped around in a dysfunction, avoiding trips to town and shunning interaction with even the boys on the ranch. I was actually relieved when they left. Citing a late payroll, it's more likely that they simply saw no future in the place with Mother gone.

She had seen to it that her will was in order, the estate handled by a lawyer who held back an obscene fee. It had been important to her that I understood all aspects of the business, and I was reasonably prepared to carry on with the ranch. But I was desperately unprepared to be alone. It was a blessing the depression manifested itself into sleep. For weeks, I spent much of the day in bed. Reading helped a little, but sleeping was the only way to totally escape. I seldom cooked and ate little, not venturing outside for days on end except to check on Bellringer, one of the few things I tended properly. I'd developed a deep affection for the old fellow and found comfort in his company. I forced myself to go hunting in the fall, but it amounted to little more than roaming around the woods. When the first really cold snap hit, I shivered in my bed, having neglected to put back firewood. Just before Thanksgiving, I became ill and spent the holiday in bed with a fever. Christmas was just as difficult. I was becoming dangerously apathetic.

It took a long time for the despair to give way to numbness, and then the first fleeting feelings of normalcy were still weeks away. But as the days grew noticeably longer, I began to stir from my torpor, and in small doses began to lend thought to the future.

About the time I began to get the itch to get out and move around, a late March storm dumped a foot of snow. When I was little, Mother loved taking me out to look for tracks. It never failed to astonish me how many animals moved about without us ever seeing them, like ghosts. I loved those walks and was drawn outside by their memories. The cloudless sky was a deep sapphire, the snow blinding, a silence challenged only by a stout north wind ripping through naked branches. The cold provided a pleasant sting to the cheeks. Pulling my coat collar up around my ears, I headed off toward the river. At the bluff, I stood for a good while, staring out over a snow-blanketed landscape. Directly below, a foursome of mallards dabbled in the still water behind a gravel bar, chattering blissfully between bites. The aroma of a burning fireplace rode the wind from a neighboring ranch, a reminder that I hadn't seen anybody in weeks. I headed down the bank before trudging along a distant fence line. A huge limb had fallen across it, and there was another breach farther up.

The snow melted quickly, and I got busy. My neglect left plenty of repairs undone and a good part of the herd roaming about the countryside. I tackled the work with vigor. It felt good to be back on a horse. A couple of neighbors were kind enough to help me round up most of the strays, commenting a couple of times about such fine animals running around loose. Exhaustion helped restore my appetite, and I began to gain back some weight. Things began to seem somewhat normal when it warmed up enough to sit on the porch in the evenings. I felt better everyday, having settled with my grief, but a new and different sort of challenge was emerging; I was lonely.

Despite trying to shame myself out of it, shunning loneliness as an unmanly frailty, it grew worse every day, most acute at night as I lay awake in bed. Well aware it wasn't healthy to live like a hermit like I had done for the better part of a year, I forced myself to ride into town more, but I ran into an awkwardness I'd never suffered before, bashful and tongue-tied around people I'd known for years. I wondered briefly if my year of isolation had driven me a little crazy.

Standing at the corral on a warm afternoon, foot on the bottom rail, scratching Bellringer's forehead, I finally said out loud what I had been pondering for some time. "Bell, I may just have to find me a wife one of these days." That I talked to my bull about it was cause enough for consideration, and perhaps concern. I guess ol' Bell helped me decide to move on with my life.

A fresh haircut, shave and the nice clothes Mother insisted I have buoyed my confidence as I rode into town. At first, I strutted down the boardwalk like a spring gobbler, but found little interest among the young women with whom I had once been popular. Some avoided me like I was inflicted with some ugly contagion. Even Melissa was nervous about being seen with me. I was dumbfounded, and deeply hurt. Rejection from the area's young ladies was new to me, and I was ill prepared to deal with it. After just a few trips into town, I withdrew to the ranch, only Bellringer to keep me company.

In town a few weeks after setting aside the wife hunt, I ran into Melissa. We stepped behind the blacksmith's barn to talk. I felt strangely at ease sharing my feelings of rejection with her.

"Jesus, James, give it some time," she consoled. "You're the best catch around. You don't want to end up with one of these girls anyway." She brought her hand up to my cheek. "Come on now, don't look so sad. I can't take it."

Realizing I was sulking as I had so often with Mother, I muttered: "I'm okay," and went my way.

Two days later, Melissa rode up as I sat on the porch. Even though she was engaged to marry a handsome, young lawyer, she came out to be with me anyway. Her fiancé was out of town on business, and she had extra clothes in her saddlebag.

She stayed two nights, cooking and cleaning the place during the day, pampering me like a baby brother. But there was nothing sisterly about our nights in bed together. Her passion for making love to me, the intimacy of our conversation and how happy she seemed throughout our time together was deeply confounding. Though she was to be married to another man, everything about our time together suggested she wanted to be with me. Finally, just before dosing off on our last night, I got up the nerve to ask her what had been on my mind since she'd come out.

"Would you consider marrying me instead?"

Her pitiful expression crushed me before she even spoke a word.

"Oh James," tears forming in her eyes. "That is so sweet. You're the most wonderful boy I've ever known. You're my best friend."

That she called me a boy, and friend, explained too much.

"Some girl will be the luckiest one on earth to marry you, but it's different between us, don't you think?"

"Oh, sure. I just thought maybe you wanted to."

"Ahh," she purred sweetly. She kissed me, and we made love again.

I couldn't have been more confused, crying like a baby the next morning after she rode off, not speaking again until we danced at her wedding. She rescued what was left of my ego, whispering that I was a wonderful lover and some girl would be very lucky one day. Even though Melissa broke my heart, she helped me through a depression from which I may have never recovered.

My other saving grace was Luke Lancaster. He showed up one day looking for work, and I hired him as much to have somebody else around than for any pressing business purpose. But I soon discovered that his knowledge of cattle rivaled Mother's, and he possessed a strong work ethic and uncanny business acumen. I had the good sense to name him foreman, deferring to him on all ranch decisions. He earned his pay from day one, managing the herd with skill and putting on some men to help with the growing amount of work. He didn't hesitate lending suggestions on matters beyond his responsibilities, and I gratefully reaped the benefits of his advice. Luke quickly grew to care about the place as if it were his own, preferring to take a lead role in its management, a burden I was all too happy to relinquish. He wasn't bothered at all when I left him to look after things while I went off fishing.

Besides being good for the ranch, Luke was great for me. I'd never had a male friend, and we quickly grew close, spending most of our evenings together on the porch talking about everything from work to women. That fall, we hunted together, both killing large bucks. It was one of many things we shared. Luke had been hunting since he was a kid, and I had already developed a reputation as a skilled woodsman.

I was also getting another reputation. Rumors of my leisurely lifestyle had been vastly exaggerated, becoming favored fodder on the gossip circuit. "And to think how hard his Momma worked so that he can just fish and hunt all day," some complained. "He's gonna let that place run down to nothing," another predicted. But the criticisms were easy to ignore. The ranch couldn't have been in better hands, prospering under Luke's management.

It was scandalous news when I purchased one of the first automobiles any of the locals had ever seen. There was this industrious fellow who would drive a new Oldsmobile from St. Louis, sell it at a handsome profit and take the train back to repeat the process. When I first laid eyes on the car, I knew I couldn't live without it, paying what I learned later was an outrageous price of $2,500. But that didn't matter. I loved that machine, a black Palace Touring Car, a four-seater open like a buggy. Not everyone in town looked upon my new toy with disgust. Our enterprising blacksmith began to order fuel to sell me. The price was high and availability spotty, but I was happy to get it. When I had him order a new tire, he took the initiative to order extras that I would soon be purchasing as I discovered how poorly matched the Ozarks' roads were to an automobile.

It seemed fitting that Luke and I take a road trip. Despite his reluctance to leave the place without either of us around, and perhaps an understandable concern for his safety, I convinced him that a few days off would be good for us both and one afternoon we headed north to Joplin.

We had just turned out of the front gate when we came across a gray-haired black man standing next to a wagon with a thrown wheel. When we pulled up next to him, he offered a tentative wave. A trio of frightened children peeked out from beneath a canvas covering.

I came around the hood to take a look. "Where y'all headed?"

"Texas ... wheel's in bad shape."

"I bet this fella can help you." Luke was already on his back, examining the damage.

A reassuring gesture from the old man coaxed a girl and two younger boys from their hiding. They joined us in a semi-circle around Luke, watching him push and tug at the wheel. He named off a short list of tools, and I drove back to the barn to fetch them. When I got back, the children's mother had mysteriously appeared. She was tall, her thin dress clinging to her shapely contours. I'd seen few black women in my life, and she was the only one who I'd found attractive. Her hands draped over the boys, whom I now recognized as twins. With the old man helping Luke, I attempted some small talk.

"So what's in Texas?"

"It ain't Missouri," the woman scowled. "We just figured warmer would suit us better than colder."

"What's wrong with Missouri?"

"They're hangin' black folks up in Springfield."

"What! ... Why?"

"Cause they're black ... they say that man raped that white woman, but everybody knows it ain't true. White folks even know better ... it's gettin' too dangerous. Three boys was lynched over at Pierce City, and I heard one was kilt in Joplin. All the black folk I know are moving out."

"Ever been to Texas?"

"Nope."

These travelers hardly looked prepared for such a journey, with only a few boxes of provisions in the wagon. Once Luke had the axle repaired and the wheel back in place, I offered to let them camp on the ranch until they were rested and ready to continue on their way, telling them to help themselves to water and anything in the barn they needed. The woman assured me they had food, but they gratefully accepted the invitation to stay the night.

"Better tell the boys," Luke warned under his breath.

"Oh yeah."

We drove back in and told the guys at the bunkhouse about our guests. When Luke added that they were black and were to be left alone to help themselves to whatever they wanted, the men's expressions confirmed the need for Luke's stern instructions.

We passed the wagon on our way back out.

"Looks good so far!" I yelled over the car engine.

"Thanks again. We'll be on our way as soon as we get a little rest."

"Take your time."

Luke told me he had little confidence that their wagon could make it to Texas.

We started with an expensive steak dinner, and then strolled down Main Street. Joplin was a center for the considerable lead mining in the region, its rowdy personality appealing to me. We stopped into a saloon, and it wasn't long before we were exchanging laughter with a group of intoxicated mine workers. After a couple hours, we stood to leave with them. I had no idea where we were going, depending as always on Luke as my compass. He seemed quite happy to go along, so I followed, somewhat excited, but not sure why. When I stepped out into the warm night, I realized how drunk I was, obviously worse off than the others.

We walked several blocks before turning onto the walkway of an enormous, two-story house. A heavy-set, middle-aged woman in a silky, black gown leaned seductively against one of the porch columns, smiling like she was especially glad we were stopping by.

"Hi darlin's, I thought we might just see you back here before too long. Come on in. The girls missed you."

Even as we followed her through the front door, it still hadn't registered where we were or what we were doing there.

"It's his first time," Luke shoved me to the front.

"Well, well, do I have a little sweetheart for you ... Darcy?"

The youngest of the women seated on the couch stood timidly as the others giggled and pushed her forward. She wore a knee-length, shiny, red dress, cut low and a little big on her. Her pale skin looked like it had never seen the sun. Despite her girlish thinness, her feminine curves were not completely hidden through the ill-fitting clothes. She had a cute face with a tortured expression.

"It's her first time too, so to speak," all the other women snickered.

Darcy blushed, but forced herself over and took my hand. "Come on good lookin'." The women cackled again. Ignoring them, Darcy led me upstairs. She couldn't have been seventeen, and looked as terrified as I was.

"It's okay," I offered up in the room. "We don't have to."

"You don't want to?" she sounded offended.

"Sure I do."

"Then help me out of this dress," she turned her back to me.

She was passionless at first, making me feel I wasn't doing a good job, but the alcohol stretched it out long enough that finally a barely audible purr made her at least seem alive. When we returned to the lobby, my companions had vanished into other parts of the house. Darcy offered me a whisky in a formal tone, as if memorized from a script, and suggested we sit outside.

From a bench at the end of the porch, we sipped our drinks and watched the heavy-set woman greet a fresh pair of patrons and usher them inside.

"Was that really your first time?" Darcy said.

"No."

"Why did that man say it was?"

"He just figured it was, I guess. I'm the youngest."

The longer we sat without the others re-emerging, the more it concerned me that perhaps I hadn't understood something. After a while, Darcy took my glass and returned with two more whiskeys.

"You seem like a nice boy. Why do you hang around with those hooligans?"

"Luke and I work together. We just met the others tonight."

"That short one hit Sally. If they'd been much drunker, Mama wouldn't have let 'em in."

"Mama?"

"That's just what we call her. She ain't nobody's real mama or nothin'."

Darcy caught me glancing at her modest cleavage. "Wanta go back up?"

Even though our first time lacked enthusiasm on Darcy's part, she had potential for being good at her trade. She was attractive enough and demonstrated a talent for knowing how to treat men. She grabbed the whiskey bottle before heading up, whispering at the door: "I wanted to come back up too." She was a good enough actress to convince me that she enjoyed it the second time.

Afterward, we lay in bed having another drink until boisterous voices boomed up the staircase. When I stood, the room spun, and as I reached for Darcy's hand, I could see in her bloodshot eyes that I was likely her last customer for the evening.

The next thing I remembered, Luke was driving through the darkness. With the money we spent on the girls, he decided against a hotel room. His first driving attempt would have likely been a sobering experience, but I passed out and slept all the way back.

A faint, peach-colored blush was just beginning to define the horizon as we pulled up to the house. The wagon parked next to the barn didn't register, but I wasn't going to concern myself with it. Nothing was going to interfere with me collapsing into my bed.

Chapter Seven

Sometime in the afternoon, I managed with great effort to roll my legs over the side of the bed. My mouth felt like I'd been eating ashes, the corners of my eyes crusted shut. When I pulled the door open, sunlight seared through my pupils, doubling the intensity of my headache. Sitting on the steps, face in hands, swearing I would never drink another drop, I heard footsteps. Luke was heading my way, the black family trailing behind him.

"You look like crap."

"That's how I feel."

"Well, Henry here is looking for work. We sure need help."

"What about Texas?

The woman stepped forward. "I could tend to the house, cooking and cleaning and such ... wouldn't take much pay. The children are well behaved."

"We're not really set up for families," recalling how Mother would have handled such a proposal.

"We could set 'em up in the barn," Luke suggested. "We need to build another house anyway."

I was astonished. These folks show up because we offered them a respite from a long journey, and after one day, Luke was ready to build them a house? How much help could an old man, a woman and three kids be anyway? The three youngsters looked to be in that eight- to ten-year-old range.

"Henry here is a carpenter," Luke patted his shoulder.

"As good as there is," he said with a nod.

My temples were pounding, making it difficult to resist what sounded like an absurd arrangement. "Okay, I guess Henry can sleep in the bunkhouse, and ..."

"Sarah." She stepped forward.

"Sarah, you and the kids can use the loft in the barn for now, 'til we figure something else out. Can the kids climb the ladder okay?"

"Yes sir."

"Okay, get 'em settled in, Luke."

"Come on," he pivoted toward the barn.

"Thank you," Henry smiled before turning to follow.

Sarah added an appreciative nod and ushered the kids along. I went back inside to lie down.

It seemed I'd been asleep only a few seconds when I was startled awake by a pounding on the door. Mike and Pal, our two ranch hands at the time, were standing on the porch, Luke behind them at the base of the steps.

"We need to talk, James." Mike always did the talking.

I didn't care for his tone. "What is it?"

"We ain't stayin' with no nigger in the bunkhouse."

I was shocked. I hadn't considered that. It took me a few seconds to respond.

"Okay, Luke, pay 'em and get 'em the hell out of here."

Mike pushed at the door before I could swing it shut. "Wait a minute! We been good hands. You can't just cut us loose like that."

"It was your choice ... be off the place by sundown."

Sinking into Father's old chair, I agonized over what had transpired in the previous 48 hours. I trusted Luke, but running a ranch with the two of us, an old man, a woman and three kids struck me as ludicrous. I finally escaped back to my bed to sleep off the remainder of my hangover.

I woke to the sweet aroma of bacon and coffee. In that semi-conscious haze of first waking up, I imagined Mother over the stove, preparing breakfast for me. It was a few moments before I snapped back and realized I'd slept through the night. Peeking through the door, I spotted Sarah in the kitchen, and eased back in to pull on my trousers.

"Good morning."

"Good mornin' Mista Crawford." She poured a cup of coffee and set it on the table in front of me. "I hope scrambled eggs is okay. I took the liberty of snatchin' a few from the barn."

"Great ... call me James."

I sat and sipped as she slid a plate in front of me, standing by to watch me taste the eggs.

"Um ... delicious. Please sit down."

"I couldn't."

"Well I don't want you to stand there and watch me eat."

She eased cautiously into the chair at the opposite end of the table.

"Aren't the others hungry?"

"They already ate. Dad's out with Mista Luke tendin' fence, and the kids are cleanin' the bunkhouse."

A pang of guilt washed over me. Everyone was up working while I was sleeping off a two-day hangover. I felt a sudden urgency to get to work, but it wasn't enough to interfere with my breakfast.

"So how old are the children?" I managed with a mouth half full.

"Dolly's eleven, Tom and Billy are nine. They're good younguns and will work hard."

It hadn't occurred to me that they would work at all. "What about their father?"

"He was shot dead." She was coldly unemotional.

When I pushed my chair away from the table, Sarah bounced up and began to clear the dishes. When I stepped out on the porch, Dolly was marching by with an armful of blankets, followed by her brothers, toting loads they couldn't see over.

"Where you kids headed?"

When Dolly stopped, her brothers ran into her. "Down to the creek to wash these blankets. A pig ought'n live in such filth."

The two boys nodded their agreement.

"Great, just be careful not to slip on the rocks."

She dismissed my warning and led her little troop down the trail.

The sound of chopping across the pasture drew me out to where Luke and Henry were hacking at a tree fallen across the fence. I could see, with his shirt off, Henry had a muscular build for a man in his fifties. He smiled at me and continued to drive powerful strokes into the trunk as Luke strolled over.

"This guy can outwork them two bums we just run out of here."

"Good."

I jumped in to help, and by mid-afternoon we had the tree removed and a new fence rail up. Still suffering the ill effects of the Joplin excursion, I called it a day. Henry looked as if he could have gone on for hours.

Dolly was sweeping the porch of the bunkhouse as we walked past, waving us over to inspect the job she and her brothers were doing, beaming with pride at my approval. Over at the house, Sarah had a pot of stew simmering on the stove, and she had also engaged in some extensive house cleaning. I didn't realize how messy the place was until I saw it clean.

"That sure smells good. When can I tell the others we'll eat?"

"I'll have you eatin' almost anytime now."

"I'll go down to the bunkhouse and get enough chairs."

"No need, Mista James. We'll take our dinner outside."

"Nonsense." I went to retrieve the chairs.

Not since I was a boy had children sat around the Crawford dinner table, nor had any group this large dined together in the house since Mother died. Sarah had seen to it that the boys washed up and tucked in their shirts, while Dolly's hair was brushed, and she had changed into a bright, yellow dress. Dinner began as a tentative, quiet gathering, with only the clanging of spoons against bowls, until Billy finally piped up. "We saw turkeys. They scared us when they flew up."

"We scared them too," Dolly added. "It was 'bout twenty, right close to the house. They better high-tail it out of here come Thanksgiving."

49

We all laughed, which made Dolly seem proud of herself.

"We've got a lot of turkeys on the ranch ... and deer," I said. "We hunt 'em in the spring."

"Don't look too hard to hunt," Billy mumbled.

"Eat your stew," Sarah said.

At the end of the meal, Henry pulled a cigar from his pocket and presented it to me as a token of his gratitude. I'd not previously been a smoker, but I dared not refuse the gift. After Henry and his clan retired to their respective quarters, Luke and I sat together on the porch while I smoked.

"What the hell is going on here?" I asked after a few minutes. "We've run off all our help and taken on a family. I figure you know what you are doing, like always, but ... it just seemed to be a quick decision."

Luke paused before going into his explanation. "They're usually the best kind, I've found. You, me and Henry can handle the ranch. I figure we build a coop and buy some chickens. Eggs are getting good money now. The kids and the mom ..."

"Sarah."

"Sarah ... could handle all that. We can put in a vegetable garden too. Eat decent around here for a change. Sarah and the kids could do the gardening. Them boys will grow up and be able to help out soon."

"That's looking mighty far ahead."

"That's what you pay me for ... I'm tired of dealin' with no-goods. I'd like for it to be a little civilized around here for a change."

"Sarah *is* a mighty fine cook. I can appreciate having *her* around."

"Good chow makes everybody better at their work."

"What'll we pay 'em?"

"I figure a full wage to Henry and another full wage for the rest of 'em."

That meant the same payout as before, and I knew Luke was right about those last boys.

"And what on God's green earth were you talking about building another house?"

He laughed, gathering a response. "James, this ranch is gonna grow and prosper. You'll be takin' a wife one day and then there'll be younguns. A place needs children. You see how these kids soften up the ranch. We need to build a fine house worthy of this place, where you can raise a family."

I was in awe that Luke harbored such notions. It was obvious he had given it much consideration, reminding me what a thoughtful man he was and how much he cared about the ranch, and me.

"Aren't you getting ahead of yourself?"

"You ain't a boy no more. I think it's high time you start thinking about that."

That rubbed me the wrong way, but I was too interested in his plans to worry much about it.

"How 'bout you? You figuring on marrying one day?" It dawned on me suddenly that I had no idea how old Luke was, perhaps five or six years my senior.

"I'd like that." He smiled. "I figured I'd move in here when the big house was done."

That made sense. Luke deserved better than the bunkhouse.

"We could buy that hundred acres on the east side," he took a business-like tone. "The bank has it in foreclosure. We could sell the timber and buy milled boards to build a proper house. We could sure use more pasture. There's a bluff over there that would be perfect for the house, right above the river where you can see forever to the south. A pretty little spring dumps out there, makes a little waterfall."

Expanding the ranch was something I was always contemplating, but my ideas involved more grazing and more head. The house Luke was picturing never dawned on me. But I realized, as we expanded, we would need more beds.

"Think about it," Luke stood to leave.

I stopped him after a few strides. "Why don't you move up here into the main house, and let the rest of them take over the bunkhouse." He smiled, nodded and strolled off into the night.

At breakfast, Henry and Sarah were overwhelmed by our offer. It hadn't occurred to them that we would ask them to stay on, and they were thrilled with the wages. Henry pledged that such kindness would be rewarded, turning to instruct his grandchildren: "Now hurry and eat up, there's work to do."

Dolly was the first to finish. With wrinkled brows, she stood slowly, and pivoted toward me with an unresolved expression. "Why don't you have a dog?"

Luke shrugged.

"That's a very good point," I nodded. "No self-respecting ranch should be without a dog. We'll have to see what we can do about that."

I headed into town after breakfast. The banker was anxious to make a loan for the property with terms that seemed too good to be true, and in the same day, I was able to negotiate an agreement with the sawmill for the timber. My inquiries about a dog led me to a small farm just outside of town where a guy was raising a breed called Labrador dogs. He assured me that they were good hunting dogs but also made loyal pets. His description of hard-working, friendly dogs bred to swim ropes from boats to docks for commercial fishermen seemed like a perfect fit for the developing personality of the ranch. It also caught my ear when he bragged on the money he planned to make breeding them. A new litter of puppies would be along in a few weeks, so I gave him a deposit and found myself surprisingly excited by the prospect of having a pet. Mother would turn over in her grave at the notion of paying for a dog.

Luke and Henry were hammering out the infancy of a chicken coop when I returned. They had chosen a place well behind the barn.

"You don't want chickens up near the house," Henry wiped sweat from his forehead with the back of his hand. "They're nasty ... you can get the tuberculosis from chickens ... sturdy coop will keep varmints out at night."

"Looks like we're planning to get a lot of chickens," I said.

Luke smiled and went back to hammering.

I spent the afternoon wandering around the property we were buying. Luke was right about the bluff; it was gorgeous, a perfect home site. The view of the river was magnificent. The streambed curved sharply at the bluff, allowing visibility for long distances in each direction. The opposite bank climbed gradually through a lush, hardwood valley before rising into steep hills in the distance. Movement caught my eye. A mother otter and two half-grown pups were patrolling the bank in their comical, accordion gait. When she slithered into the water, one of the pups plunged in without hesitation, but the smaller one hesitated. The mother poked her head above the surface, barked, and the little fellow grudgingly slid off the bank. In the water, the youngster looked as lithe and graceful as the rest of the family, gliding through the clear water as though it were flying.

The Ozarks in all of its glory lay at my feet. I decided right there that the rest of the ranch would remain where it is. The house would be out here away from all of that. Isolation would be part of its charm. I eased down a game trail to the water. From a wide gravel bar, I looked up and could almost see the house. I imagined a wife and child waving down at me. I probably would have been there until sundown if a distance rumble hadn't awakened me from my daydreaming. The sky had grown dark in the northwest. When lightning flickered against the blackening clouds, I started back. My pace quickened when I felt the first cool breeze, a deafening crack of lightning urging me into a trot. The first huge drops splattered on my shoulder just as I ducked onto the porch. Sarah was standing with her arms folded, leaning against one of the cedar columns staring out at the downpour and gazing up at the sky.

"Gonna be a gully washer."

"Looks like it."

The rain pounded the ground like it was poured from a bucket. Spray from stiff gusts forced us to the middle of the porch. Henry ran from the barn, drenched by the time he joined us.

"It's good us gettin' this rain!" he yelled.

The three of us watched the weather, not bothering to try and talk over it. When the rain slowed to a sprinkle, I could feel Henry studying me.

"You don't much care for foul weather, do ya Mista James?"

"Not really." I went inside.

The storm had moved on to the south by the time we sat down for supper. It was amazing to see how quickly Sarah and Henry had become comfortable in their new surroundings. They talked freely about their day and teased the boys, their responses drawing laughs all around. The highlight of the meal was when the frog Tom was keeping in his top pocket found its way onto the table. Glasses spilled and silverware clanged on the floor as everyone scrambled to catch the unexpected dinner guest, adult laughter drowning out Dolly's scolding words. When the frog hopped into my soup bowl, Sarah covered her mouth to smother her smile.

"Here ya go." I fished out the traumatized frog, picked a piece of onion from its head and handed it to Tom. "What ya say we let him go back to the river."

"Yes sir," he stuffed the frog back in his pocket.

"Now," Sarah pointed to the door. Tom pushed himself away from the table and skulked out. I never knew what happened to the frog. I suspect Tom kept it in some secret spot.

When crews began cutting timber from the new property, I supervised closely. To the foreman's aggravation, I insisted on leaving some trees on the slopes to prevent erosion. Summer was halfway over, and there would be little time for new growth to take hold. We could cut some of them in the future, I figured.

When the chicken coop was completed, Luke and Sarah decided to go over to a neighbor's farm to see about purchasing some birds. Henry worked with me that day over on the new property, and when we returned, Luke was walking out of the barn with a playful grin on his face.

"What's up?"

"Nothin'," he smirked.

"Get some chickens?"

"No, Sarah didn't much care for the stock Bobby had." His expression promised more to the story.

Sarah was sweeping the porch as we walked over.

"Didn't care for Bobby's birds?"

"That was a scraggly lot, dirty and running crazy all over the place. Chickens like that don't lay good. We need good brood ... raise our own, like a family. We don't need no crazy, wild-ass chickens runnin' round here."

I couldn't remember laughing so hard. Luke and Henry howled along with me, and even Sarah joined in.

Chapter Eight

While Henry and I sat and waited for the train to deliver our expensive chickens, I couldn't help imagining what Mother would think. Earlier that morning, we'd been out to pick out a puppy, settling on the smallest of the females, figuring that'd be best for the kids. It was disappointing she wasn't old enough; I could have taken an armload of them home with me.

That was the day I was introduced to the hateful stares. Henry was accustomed to the way white folks looked at him as he moved about their world, but I wasn't. Just as the train was coming to a stop, an old woman glowered at us, making sure we took note of her disgust. When I stepped toward her, Henry caught my shoulder: "Come on. Let's see if those birds made it." His touch drew a wicked snarl from the woman.

The train was late, as was its habit, but our chickens arrived safe and sound, as well as loud and rambunctious. The two roosters seemed especially indignant over their travels. Unlike the birds I'd been around before, these leghorns were huge, bright white, the roosters crowned with a comical, red headdress. We'd chosen the breed based on reports of dependable production and large eggs. Despite Sarah's warning that only one rooster would rule the hen house, I ordered two just in case. But our chickens were all perfectly fit. Their squawking at every bump caused me to question the chicken project, but Henry looked awfully pleased.

When we pulled up to the barn, everyone gathered around, prompting more flapping and squawking.

"So what do you think?" I climbed down and slapped Luke on the shoulder.

He bent over to peer into the cages. "Looks like a bunch of wild-ass chickens to me."

Loud laughter caused the chickens to go crazy.

"They're earning their label," Sarah said bending over to look.

More laughs made the birds even more frantic.

"Okay, okay, before we kill 'em, let's show 'em to their new quarters," Henry handed responsibility over to Sarah and the kids.

Pecked fingers caused dropped cages, which elevated the chicken chaos even further. We enjoyed quite a show, Luke, Henry and I, off to the side laughing at the transfer of wild-ass chickens. The only causality was the smaller of the two roosters, which managed to escape. The kids were dejected after establishing the futility of chasing it around, apologizing profusely.

"That's okay, we'll get him tomorrow."

My prediction drew a raised eyebrow from Sarah. She shared my suspicion that the runaway rooster would likely become a feast for some fox or coyote before the sun rose again.

After supper, Henry and I sat on the porch, watching fireflies dot the darkness, rising in mass toward a million stars in a moonless sky. A family of coyotes greeted each other, yapping joyously just across the river, but then the night went silent. It seemed a shame to contaminate the tranquility with voices, but I felt compelled to explain my earlier behavior.

"About those storms ... you were right."

Henry continued to rock as if he hadn't heard.

"They do spook me. My folks were killed in storms. A tornado got my father and my mother drowned."

"Here?"

"Yeah. Dad was running with me in his arms when he was hit in the head. Mother drowned years later, saving a calf in a flood. "

"You were born here?"

"No. Adopted ... when I was ten. I was in an orphanage in New York. They brought a bunch of us out here on a train."

"I heard about that ... so you're one of them, huh?"

An owl broadcast its rhythmic hoots from a high limb over the house. It was his regular spot. He'd made a habit of hunting around the barn, and we appreciated his help with pest control. We even left the doors open for him on one occasion, but it spooked the horses.

"Go catch yourself a nice fat rat, Mr. Owl." Henry smiled.

We sat quietly, except for the creak of our rockers, until Henry stirred, ready to call it a night. "Seems about impossible that another storm would hit this place." He sounded like he was consoling one of his grandchildren. Easing out of his rocker, he stepped up to the edge of the porch and gazed into the darkness. "I believe you worry too much about things, James. You worry too much about how them folks looked at me." He glanced over his shoulder to gage my reaction. "That's just the way it is. I sure don't fret over it ... if it don't bother me, it shouldn't bother you neither."

"Well, it does bother me."

"Cain't nothn' good come of frettin' about such things. You need to put that out of your mind."

There was a ring of Mother's voice in his advice.

"Good night." He headed toward bed.

The next morning I was jolted awake by the shrill scream of the fugitive rooster. He had taken up residence on the arm of one of the porch rockers, and apparently softened his tolerance for people, studying us with curiosity as he held his ground. After breakfast, Sarah lured him to his new home with chicken feed.

It wasn't long before the chickens were running loose during the day and retreating to the coop to roost. Nightly updates provided entertainment at the dinner table. The big story involved a conflict between Billy and the smaller rooster. It had lost out dominance to the larger bird and was apparently taking it out on his handler, who proudly showed off his combat scar with each telling of the story. Despite Billy's harsh words for the bird, he argued successfully to keep it out of the boiling pot.

I went alone to pick up the puppy, not sharing where I was headed. Since the stares at the depot, I felt it best to limit Henry's exposure to townsfolk. When the fellow placed the furry ball of energy in my hands, it made me nervous. On the drive home, I held her on my thigh, where she would occasionally squirm into my shadow. When I realized the sun was bothering her, I shielded her with my hat.

Dolly had taken note of when the puppy was to come home and had not let my departure go unnoticed. She alerted the others, and when the car came to a stop, the whole clan descended on it like it was Santa's sleigh. Sarah nuzzled the puppy against her cheek, and then set it down. The children danced around the happy but confused newcomer, trying to draw a chase. The little gal waved her tail, pivoted her head in indecision and bounced over to Dolly. She cradled the puppy in her arms, suggesting "Susie." It was adopted unanimously.

An unexpected thing had happened to me on the drive from town. I'd become more attached to Susie than was logical in such a short time. The original idea was to get a dog because the kids wanted it, but after letting all of the children hold her, I took her into the house and prepared blankets next to my bed.

I hadn't shared my concerns with Luke about Henry and Sarah going to town and was over on the new property when he sent them to pick up chicken feed. They were gone when I made it back. Luke was sitting on the porch writing in a ledger, newly purchased spectacles on the end of his nose, the kids out front running in circles with Susie. Spotting me, she sprinted as fast as her stubby little legs would run. With her on my shoulder, I noticed Luke easing up ominously, setting his work to the side. I followed his glare. A wagon was coming in fast, a solitary figure diving, Sarah at the reins.

"What's wrong?" Dolly said as Luke and I hurried out to meet her.

Henry was curled up in the back, blood streaming from his mouth and nose, his left eye swollen grotesquely.

"Two men," Sarah managed through tears. "I wasn't out front when it happened ... he ain't said nothing."

Henry was barely conscious, groaning in agony as we carried him into the bunkhouse, and got him settled in his bed.

Luke and I jumped in the car, spraying gravel on the house as we took off. Normally, I was careful not to scare horses or throw dust all over the folks on the street, but I was in no mood to extend such courtesies, skidding the car to a stop a few feet from the sheriff's door. I threw it open, startling him from his chair. Richard Carpenter was a poor portrait of law enforcement, grossly overweight and his best years behind him. He pushed up the brim of his hat with a trembling finger.

"What are you doing about it!"

"About what?"

"You know damn well what!"

"Look James, them boys said your nigger was trying to rob 'em."

"You know that's bullshit!" I was so incensed that the sheriff's hand on his pistol caused me no alarm.

"James, I gotta live in this town ... and so do you."

"Who was it?"

"Them two you let go a while back."

He was mumbling an explanation when Luke and I stormed out, boots pounding the boardwalk, everyone stopping to stare. We knew where to find them.

They were slumped over the bar when I thundered through the batwing doors. I grabbed the closest and began to drag him out. Luke was right behind me, wrestling Pal into the street. Mike and I tripped over each other, shattering a table, bouncing beer mugs and poker chips across the floor. I landed on top and used the advantage to hammer the side of his face. Squirming out from under me, blood streaming from the corner of his mouth, he managed to get to his feet. I caught him a few steps beyond the boardwalk, tackling him into a cloud of dust. I was able to keep him down this time, pounding with everything I had. His face was smeared in blood, a cheek matted with dirt, but I continued to club him, oblivious to the pain of knuckles striking bone. When he went limp, I delivered another blow to his jaw and stood to finish him off with two kicks to the ribs. For the first time, a fellow acted like he wanted to separate us, but turned loose after my elbow caught his ribs. Luke was just getting to his feet, wiping blood from his nose with his sleeve. The men who beat Henry now lay prostrate and bleeding in the road a few feet from each other, the widening circle of onlookers suddenly silent. It didn't feel like enough.

The sheriff stepped out of the crowd, shaking his head. "Ya shouldn't oughta done that James."

"No, you should have taken care of it! Your time might be up if you can't handle the job any more."

The crowd gasped.

"I oughta throw you in."

Luke grabbed my arm when I stepped toward him. Wide-eyed spectators hopped aside as we left. It looked like everyone in town was standing in the street or lined up along the boardwalks, allowing me the evil pleasure of throwing up dust all over them.

We found Henry propped up with a stack of pillows, the children next to the bed with tear-reddened eyes. Sarah sat across from them, squinting, jaw clenched. I stepped up to the foot of the bed. "How ya doing, Henry?"

"I'm fine." He forced a weak smile. "No need to fret like this woman and these younguns ... that's a pretty nasty lookin' hand you got there."

It was swollen and bleeding. Sarah ordered me into her chair and sent Dolly to fetch water. The kids gathered behind her to watch as she cleaned my hand and then probed gently with her thumbs. "It's broke," she declared when I winced.

"It's okay," I shook my head and got to my feet. "What ya say we take a few days off around here." Henry and Sarah nodded.

"I'm a little sore myself." Luke rubbed his leg.

"Okay then ... good night." I left feeling as if I should have said something more.

Forgoing my normal porch sitting, I turned in early, but too restless to sleep. After considerable tossing and turning, Susie whimpered, and for the first time I reached down and lifted her into my bed. We curled together where we eventually drifted off to sleep, her muzzle resting on my arm. That's where she slept from then on.

Chapter Nine

Luke ended up with a bum knee, so none of us were able to work. Sarah kept the children busy and out of sight while we healed. It was eerily quiet around the place that week, which I found disconcerting, so I used the off days to amble around the new property, daydreaming, maintaining a snail's pace to accommodate Susie's short legs and need to sniff every clump of brush.

For three straight days, I sat for hours, legs hanging off the bluff, thinking, while Susie enjoyed a nap in the sun. Finally able to exhaust most of the anger over Henry's beating, my thoughts shifted in a direction they were increasingly turning, my growing need for female companionship. After Melissa spurned my proposal, I hadn't even spoken with another woman, other than Sarah, for months, except to do business in town.

Whenever I considered the possibilities, Annie Brice, over at the general store, always came to mind. She was pretty, and the way she smiled at me suggested she might find me acceptable. I'd known her since we were kids, but the thought of asking her out made me nervous. Despite my apprehensions, before the last embers of daylight were extinguished, I boldly decided on a trip to town the following day.

It was fully dark when I walked up to the bunkhouse, where Sarah leaned against a porch column.

"Sorry I'm so late."

"It's okay ... your dinner is on the stove. I'll warm it."

"I can do that."

"Daddy needs to talk to you."

I feared by her dire tone that Henry had taken a turn for the worse, but he was sitting up, telling the kids some yarn when I stepped inside.

"There he is. How was your day?"

"Nice. I guess I just need to roam around every once in a while ... does me good."

Susie's front feet were propped up on the sideboard, with Henry's arm draped over scratching between her ears. "I think you got a good one here."

"A friendly one, anyway."

His expression stiffened as he pulled his arm up across his chest.

"James, you're a good man, takin' us in like you did. God'll bless you for it. But we're too much trouble for you. We already got everybody in town against you."

Sarah sniffled behind me.

"I 'spect it's best we move on."

"What? ... No!"

Henry waved his hand. "I knew what you'd say, but my mind's made up."

"You can't come in here, get me depending on you and then just up and leave. It's not right."

I turned to Sarah. "Is leaving what's best for the kids?"

She shrugged.

I turned back. "You can run from these thugs, but there'll just be more of 'em in Texas, or wherever you go. I didn't have you figured as a man who'd run from trouble."

"You know it ain't like that James."

"And everybody in town ain't against us. It's just a few old timers who hate everything. Weren't you the one that lectured me about that? I don't have nothing to do with those people anyway, so it don't matter ... just today, I was thinking we needed to start teaching the kids to read and write."

He stared back stubbornly, undecided.

I turned back to Sarah. "What do *you* say?"

She shrugged.

"Look here, you just worry about getting well Henry." I pulled my hand back when I realized I was pointing. "We got lots of work to do around here, and I expect you up out of that bed doin' it soon ... I thought you were going to build that house."

He couldn't fight back a thin smile.

"Well then. I guess I'll see you tomorrow. Get some good sleep."

Sarah, tears in her eyes, reached out and brushed my arm as I passed.

I stopped by the jail first, feeling bad about how I talked to Richard in front of everybody. He was at his desk doing paperwork.

"Hello, Richard."

"Hi there James, how are you?" His tone was surprisingly friendly.

"I just wanted to come by ... didn't mean to be so ugly out there ..."

He shook his head and motioned for me to sit.

"Don't worry about it. You did us all a big favor by runnin' them boys off ... they rode out the next day. That wasn't the first trouble they caused around here."

"Well ..."

"Times is changin' slow," the sheriff spoke in a serious voice. "But you're a respected man in these parts. Don't worry about folks who ain't got nothin' to do but worry about what another man is doing." He snickered. "After the other day, I figure folks'll leave you be."

60

I managed only a nod and handshake before leaving.

At the Brice General Store, Annie was alone tending the counter. It was a relief to see her grumpy father wasn't around. I knew her well. When we were young, she was my favorite dance partner at the various social functions. We'd even kissed once, but really just a peck on the lips. She was a cute girl and had grown up an attractive woman, big, brown eyes and a perpetual smile that showcased darling dimples. Her thick, dark hair was bundled to perfection, drawing my gaze to her bare neck. She was petite, but shapely, always dressed to accent her figure. I have to admit though, I was a little intimidated by the force of her personality.

The door clanged behind me. "Well come in here, James Crawford! What in the world can I help you with?"

"I need a box of cigars."

"Why James, you're not taking up that nasty habit," she searched under the counter. "You fellows, I do declare."

"I guess I *am* taking it up. There's worse things, I s'pose."

"Well at least you're not chewing and spitting ... I don't have a whole box right now. I could order more."

"Okay, order me a box ... no, make that two."

She wrapped the half dozen cigars neatly up in a piece of paper, and laid them on the counter. "I hope you don't mind me keeping the box. They come in so handy."

"Not at all ... uh, by the way, I was thinking, maybe ... you and your dad should come out sometime. We don't have much company ... maybe lunch on a Sunday afternoon ... before the weather gets cold."

She kept her head down, adding up my purchases, a subtle smile forming on her lips. "It's awfully hard to get Daddy out."

"Oh sure, I understand." I fumbled with the payment. "Okay then," I turned to leave.

"But maybe, we could have a picnic. The weather has been so lovely."

I turned back to face her. "Sure, okay. That'd be nice. Sarah could prepare a lunch. The kids will love it."

"Oh," she frowned. "I thought maybe just us would be better. It'd give us a chance to catch up. It's been a coon's age."

"Of course, what was I thinking?"

"How about Sunday?"

"Oh, okay ... that'd be great. Should I pick you up here?"

"After church. In the automobile?"

I nodded. "If that's okay."

"Of course. I've never ridden in an automobile."

"Okay then, see you Sunday." Turning to leave, I tripped on a slightly raised board, and barely regained my balance before poking my head through the glass in the door.

"I'm sorry. I need to get Daddy to fix that ... See you Sunday, James."

Henry was sitting on the porch with Luke, Susie snoozing in between them, when I climbed out of the car. "Now this is a sorry lot. I guess I'm just paying you to sit around all day?"

They grinned. "Let me get these ribs healed, and I'll work your skinny behind under the table," Henry said.

Welcomed words.

Inside, a pot simmered on the stove while Sarah sat at the table thumbing through one of my books.

"I didn't know you read." I sat across from her.

She pushed it away with a sigh. "I don't ... did you mean that about the children learnin' to read?"

"Of course."

"Who'd teach'em?"

That raised a tough question. "I would." I shrugged, without much thought.

"Oh, I wouldn't expect a big landowner to take time to teach a bunch of servant kids."

"Big landowner?" I shook my head. "And you aren't servants. You're employees ... friends, more like family."

Sarah had a way of smiling with her eyes.

"Oh yeah," I suddenly remembered, but hesitated a second. "Would you mind preparing a picnic lunch for Sunday?"

"How nice. Who's going on a picnic? ... I'm sorry, I don't mean to be a nosey body. Of course, I'd be happy to make you a fine picnic basket. For how many?"

"Two."

"Now, do I understand properly from that blush on those cheeks that this is a courtin' type of picnic?"

"I thought you weren't going to be a nosey body."

Sarah belted out a deep, throaty laugh. "I'm sorry, but you know full well a woman cain't help askin' about a thing like that."

"She's just an old friend. Don't go making any more of it than that ... just being polite, really."

She flashed her biggest grin. "It's important to be polite...okay then, I'll fix a scrumptious picnic lunch for your lady friend."

As I went back out, I heard her say under her breath: "It's about time."

Outside, I settled into my rocker to read a letter I'd picked up in town.

Dear Mr. Crawford,

My name is Thomas Grey. I own quite a large spread northwest of Fort Scott, Kansas. I have become aware of the reputation of your fine stock and would be interested if you had any bulls or bred heifers currently available for purchase. If it be your pleasure, I would like to visit your ranch to inspect any stock you may have for sale. It would be an honor to meet you. Thank you.

Thomas Grey

I went inside to draft a response.

After dinner, during which Billy listed off a litany of misbehaviors by the rooster he was now calling Satan, I invited Luke and Henry out on the porch for a smoke.

"Got a letter from a fellow today." I puffed deeply to light the cigar. "Wants to come in from Kansas. Mentioned wanting a bull."

"That newest one is real good." Luke shook his head thoughtfully. "Don't know if I'd let it go. We might wanta keep him here."

"He mentioned bred heifers too."

"We're in good shape there ... when's he coming?"

"Don't know. I'll send a reply tomorrow."

"Speaking of heifers," Luke grinned, "I understand we're having a picnic."

I shook my head in playful disgust, turning to Henry. "Your daughter is quite a gossip."

They laughed.

"That she is," Henry nodded deeply. "She's a woman. Cain't expect no different ... who's the lucky young lady?"

"Annie Brice."

Luke bobbed his head. "She's a pretty one all right. But her old man's about as friendly as a rattler."

"Yeah, well, I didn't invite him."

In town the next day, after mailing the letter, and fending off the postmaster's inquiries about it, I went next door to pick up some stationery. Annie was standing behind the counter next to her father. He scowled as I walked up. She was sporting a particularly attractive smile, half of her hair wrapped in a loose bundle, the rest flowing in loose curls over her shoulders.

"Good morning James," she bid in a syrupy tone, prompting her father to shake his head in disgust.

"Hello Annie ... hello Mr. Brice."

The old man grunted and wandered into the back room.

"Never mind him," Annie reached across and patted my hand. "I'm glad you came in."

"I was thinking I need some better stationery than I've been using."

Annie hurried down an aisle and collected a box from a top shelf. I guess it's all she had, cause she didn't wait for me to say I wanted it. Always in a hurry, she was already scribbling numbers on a bill of sale when I stepped back up to the counter. She ripped a sheet off the pad and handed it to me. "I'm *so* looking forward to Sunday."

"Me too. I thought we'd picnic on this bluff over the river. It's really nice. We just bought the place."

"Oh, it sounds so charming."

"Okay then, I'll see you Sunday."

"I'm looking forward to it."

This time I remembered to step over the raised board.

Chapter Ten

My hand wasn't broken. Luke and I were out cutting fence posts after a week, but Henry reluctantly stayed behind to continue healing. Susie followed us out each day, exercising her considerable talent for mischief. Disaster was averted when Luke spotted a skunk before she did, and grabbed her right as she was catching the scent. She was left back at the house the next day, but managed to escape and joined us after a couple of hours.

Henry was able to join us at the dinner table, and we sat out front afterward. The first cool spell had pulled temperatures down to near perfection. There was something extraordinary about those first chilly nights. Perhaps it was anticipation of hunting season. That I had never grown fond of the sultry Ozark summers was likely a big part of it.

Luke broke a long silence. "We ought to put up some beef for the winter."

"Let's get a couple of those yearlings on corn."

He nodded. "I hope Dolly hasn't named the damn things."

We all chuckled.

"It lives on the ranch, I 'spect it's got a name," Henry chimed in. "That child has just got to put a label on everything. But I imagine when she tastes beefsteak she won't be much worried about it ... maybe we should be naming one of 'em sirloin."

We laughed again.

"We better start on firewood too."

"There's plenty down already over on the other place." Luke stood, ambled down the steps, and crushed his cigar butt beneath his heel. Looking skyward briefly, he turned and put one foot back up on the bottom step. "So tomorrow your lady friend comes to call, huh?"

A sudden pang of nerves washed over me. "Yep ... I think I'll turn in too," I flicked my cigar stub where Luke could crush it out for me. "Night."

When I pulled up to the general store, the door was ajar despite the "Closed" sign in the window. I found Annie behind the counter, writing something. She looked up. "Come in!"

Her smile reminded me again that she was one of the prettiest women in town. She grabbed a small handbag and stepped around the counter in a shin-length, blue skirt, quite a contrast to the long dresses she usually donned in the store. She wore a short matching jacket over a fluffy, white blouse. After a few steps toward me, she pivoted and retrieved a wide-brimmed hat from the counter that matched her outfit. The manners Mother drilled into me kicked in instinctively, and I opened both the door to the store and the passenger-side car door for Annie. I admonished myself for not being more talkative and tried desperately to come up with something engaging to say, but thankfully, Annie relieved me of that responsibility.

Well versed in the art of feminine charm, she listened with apparent interest as I answered her many questions about the ranch. As we pulled up to the house, the wagon was waiting out front with Nelly, the mare, hitched and ready, a box in the back covered by a red-checkered cloth. Sarah stepped out of the house as I climbed out of the car. "I figured the wagon was more appropriate for a picnic," she called from the porch. "Your lunch is in the back."

Annie gazed curiously at Sarah as I scrambled around the hood to open the door. I made the introductions as Annie stepped out. "Annie, this is Sarah ... Sarah, Annie."

Sarah curtsied. "It's an honor ma'am."

"It's very nice to make your acquaintance," a trace of caution in her tone.

We had just pulled away from the porch when Annie's curiosity got the best of her. "She's quite a beautiful woman ... light-skinned for a Negro."

"I suppose ... never really noticed."

Annie flashed a skeptical grin. "Does she stay in the house?"

"Henry, she and the kids live in the bunkhouse. Luke is staying with me until we build another house."

"Henry is her husband?"

"No, her father. Her husband was killed some time back."

"How sad ... so you're building another house?"

"Yeah, looks like it ... over on the new property."

"Oh yes, Daddy said you added some acres and were selling off timber."

"It's a beautiful spot. We could take a walk over there after we eat."

"Oh, let's do! That would be wonderful."

Feeling more at ease as we pulled up near the edge of the bluff, I spread the blanket on a grassy patch overlooking the river. The basket was stocked with freshly baked bread, a corn dish I was unfamiliar with, a raspberry pie and fried chicken. I suspected Satan had finally succumbed to the frying pan.

"What a wonderful spread," Annie gushed a couple of times as we ate. She had a pretty healthy appetite for such a small woman.

We ate and reminisced. She took great joy in bringing up the kiss we shared as children. After she finished eating, Annie reached out for my hand, and scooted closer, looking out over the river.

"The water is so beautiful ... so clear."

"That pool was where I used to go swimming as a kid."

"Is that where ... " she stopped herself.

"What?"

"Oh I shouldn't."

"No, what?"

"Is that where you and Melissa ..." her voice tailed off.

I was appalled. "What do you mean?" I stuttered.

"James dear, she was as loose with her mouth as she was with her virtue."

It took a few clumsy seconds to spit out an answer. "I was so young then."

She squeezed my hand. "Oh my. I didn't mean to embarrass you. I shouldn't pry so. I hope you don't think I am the worst gossip."

I was well aware, as was everybody else in that part of the country, that Annie Brice was a world-class gossip.

"There's no reason you should feel bad. It's different with boys. You acted as any boy would. Nobody blames the boy ... James please say something so I know you aren't angry with me."

"My Mom sure blamed the boy."

Annie gasped. "She found out?"

"She caught us."

Annie threw a hand over her mouth, her eyes swollen in devilish delight.

A distant voice stole our attention. "I am *so* sorry Mista James!" It was Dolly, standing near a clump of bushes, one of her brothers' shirt collars in each hand.

"They'll be whupped. I can promise ya that!"

"Come here." I waved them over. Dolly pushed the twins ahead as she approached.

"So what are y'all doin'?"

"They was spying on you and your lady friend. Don't you worry though, Mama'll whup 'em good for it. They'll get a blistering all right."

"Nobody needs a whipping. There's no harm done."

"They won't learn no manners if they ain't punished."

"It's okay Dolly, we weren't trying to hide or anything. Now y'all get on back up to the house."

Dolly released the boys, and they took off running.

"We're very sorry to interrupt your courtin' ma'am," Dolly curtsied.

"They're just precious," Annie drawled, as Dolly trotted away.

"Yeah," I stood to escape embarrassment. "Let me show you where we plan to build the house."

As I took Annie's hand to help her up, I caught a movement out of the corner of my eye. Susie was in a full sprint with Dolly in futile pursuit. When I motioned Dolly back, she stopped and held out her arms in an apologetic shrug.

"Hey girl," I bent down to scratch behind her ears. "You don't mind if she goes with us do you?"

"No, of course not," but she looked uncomfortable reaching down to pet Susie.

By the time we reached the bluff, Susie was already down splashing through the water chasing crawfish. As I described the home I wanted to build, Annie listened, saying only, "It's going to be so wonderful," half a dozen times.

As we began the walk back, I called down to Susie. She sprinted up the trail, stopped at Annie's feet and shook a cloud of spray all over her. Annie shrieked and jumped back.

"Susie! ... I'm *so* sorry."

"It's okay." She brushed water from her skirt. "It just surprised me, that's all. She's such a darling."

"That dress is so pretty. I hope she hasn't ruined it."

"Of course not. It's only water." Her tone didn't sound as forgiving as her words.

"I don't know why she does that. It seems she always has to get close to someone before she shakes off. I think that means she likes you."

"How nice."

On the ride back, I summoned the courage to reach for Annie's hand, and she smiled her approval, patting our clinched hands.

"Oh James, your place is so beautiful."

"I'm certainly lucky, and grateful."

"What a wonderful place to raise children."

I fidgeted involuntarily.

"Oh just relax." She giggled. "Men, I swear ... I'm just saying a bachelor like you is likely to marry at some point. Heaven knows *who* it might be ... now really James, that's not too unusual to assume is it?"

"I suppose not." I kept my eyes straight ahead, but could feel her studying me. I was relieved when we pulled up to the house.

The whole clan was waiting on the porch. Introductions were mandatory, but I didn't waste any words. Annie was gracious, saying to Sarah, "Lunch was just marvelous, dear. Thank you so much."

"You're quite welcome. Perhaps you'll come again."

"I'd like that ... if I didn't bore poor James to death."

"I don't 'spect you did."

On the drive to town, Annie scooted close, held my arm and laid her head over on my shoulder. I apologized for the kids and the dog again.

"Don't be silly, I thought the whole day was charming. I so hope we will do it again ... soon."

"Of course."

Annie spent the rest of the drive interrogating me on my plans for the house and the future of the ranch. She seemed especially interested in the guy coming from Kansas. I walked her to the door, where she took my hands and turned a cheek, allowing only a peck. "Thank you so much for a wonderful time. I do hope you don't forget to have me out again." She jiggled the key in the lock. "I suppose Liz Porter will be pestering you to have a picnic now that she's heard ... bless her heart ... there." She pushed the door open with her hip, and waved through the window as she locked up.

As I left town, I pondered Annie as a wife. I wasn't fond of all the gossip, and she could be a little pushy, likely to progress up to bossy once the vows are sealed. Still, I craved a kiss at the door. She was awfully good looking, but then so was Liz Porter.

Chapter Eleven

Henry insisted on going back to work earlier than he should have, heading right back in after just a few axe strokes. At dinner, I suggested a walk for the two of us the next day over to the new property.

"That'd be just fine. I 'spect Miss Susie would appreciate a walk too." At the sound of her name, she trotted over for some attention.

Like everyone else, Henry instantly fell in love with the spot, knowing exactly what kind of house he wanted to build, where it should sit and how to get started. He mumbled to himself as he stepped off dimensions and shoved makeshift stakes in the ground. On the walk back, he spoke more words than I'd heard from him since we'd met.

Henry also had substantial artistic talent. He sketched out a house similar to one he worked on in Springfield, intending to use it as a model for my house. It was far more elaborate than anything I could have imagined, two stories with a deep porch across the front supported by ornate columns.

Luke punched the paper with his finger. "Perfect."

"Let's not get carried away here." I took it back from him. "We don't need this much house ... it looks mighty expensive."

"It's perfect. A top-notch ranch needs a top-notch ranch house."

"It hardly looks like a ranch house ... more like some government building."

"It's just one idea. We can build any house you want."

"You could build this house?" I pointed to the drawing.

"Yes sir, I've been in on the building of many such homes. It'd be a great honor to build this house for you. Wouldn't have to be as expensive as you think neither."

"Well, okay then. We'll start to lay out the ground in the spring."

"Why wait? We've got a couple good months of weather. If we got it roughed in we could work during the cold months. Don't bother me none to work in the cold. I prefer it to the hot summertime."

Sarah and the kids gathered around the table, anxiously awaiting a verdict.

"Best get going," Dolly couldn't help weighing in. "You marry Miss Annie, you'll need a proper home, and I don't 'spect she'll want to wait too long."

Henry and Luke got a huge laugh out of that.

Sarah swatted her. "Hush!"

"I'm not going to marry Miss Annie." I stood and went outside to think. Luke and Henry followed me, continuing to make a case for starting right away.

I wasn't at first convinced, but in the end, I trusted Luke's instincts more than my own.

"Okay," I finally said. "What you say Henry and I work on the house, and Luke ... can we hire a hand or two?"

"Sure, there's a couple of good boys in town right now. We need more help around here anyway."

"We haven't got bunks for 'em."

"We can make room. They're livin' in town anyways."

I rose from my rocker. "Well boys, we've planned ourselves quite a bit of work. I better get my rest."

The next morning, Henry was at the table drafting detailed plans as Sarah prepared breakfast. To the side he was jotting down a list of materials and tools, which prompted me to worry again about the cost of such an undertaking. I didn't want to spend the entire proceeds of the timber sale on a house. That money was slated to pay as much of the note on the new property as possible.

I'd planned on getting in another day on the fences before shifting gears, but Henry and Luke insisted we all head straight over to the bluff, and the whole gang decided to come along. Sarah put aside her household duties and allowed the children time off to make the walk with us. It was quite a procession: Henry with the funny straw hat he had recently started wearing; Dolly talking non-stop about how things would be when the house was finished; Sarah yelling at the boys for the projectiles whizzing overhead; and Susie bouncing along, chasing sticks and snapping at grasshoppers.

"What a beautiful spot," Sarah said in a near whisper as she strolled up to the edge of the bluff. "My goodness ... God's hand for certain."

"It's the most beautiful place I've ever seen in my whole life," Dolly declared dramatically. "It should be called River View."

"That's awfully plain."

"How about Crawford's Corner?" Henry said.

Dolly sneered up at him. "It isn't any sort of a corner, Grandpa."

He shrugged.

"A proper name needs to be thought out careful," Luke said.

I shook my head. This is no way to run a ranch, I thought, the entire work force standing around debating a name for the future site of my home.

"Annie's Bluff," Dolly said.

"No!" I objected more vigorously than I had intended, prompting laughs from the adults.

"Look!" Billy pointed.

A thick bodied buck with tall antlers stood staring at us from just inside the trees. Put off by our presence, it turned and stepped back into the shadows, where it stopped to examine us, licking its nostrils and stomping a leg, before sneaking off.

"Correction, Buck Bluff," Dolly said.

"I like it."

Sarah and Luke's expressions suggested disapproval, but Dolly smiled proudly at retaining her status as the ranch's official name-giver. Henry missed it all. He was out of earshot, stepping off more dimensions for the house.

The next day I headed to town for a measuring tape that Henry needed to get started. Annie was attending to two women when I stepped into the store.

"I'll be with you in a minute, Mr. Crawford," she said, winking past her customers as they examined fabric. I stood by as they paid, responding to their suspicious glares with a nod and smile as they left.

"How can I help you …" the bell clanged behind the women. "Oh, James, it's so good to see you. I've been anxious to thank you again for such a lovely picnic."

"I had a nice time too ... I was wondering if you had a measuring tape."

"What type?"

"Henry is beginning to lay out the property of the new house."

Annie's face lighted up. "How wonderful! You're starting already ... hum ... I only have a three-footer, for sewing."

"I'll take that I suppose, until I can find another one."

"I can order whatever you need." She reached under the counter and produced a thick catalog. Guiding me to the proper section, she helped identify the tape appropriate for Henry's needs and earmarked the page.

Seeing her smile again made me yearn for that kiss. "Would you want to have some lunch?"

"That would be wonderful. Just let me fetch Daddy to mind the store."

Annie disappeared into a back room for an unusually longtime, returning in a different, fancier dress with a matching hat.

"Please forgive me," she said as she rounded the counter. "It takes us womenfolk a little while."

There was still no sight of her father. She turned the window sign around to "Closed" before locking up. "I hope your father's not ill," I offered.

"No," she frowned and shook her head. "Just being father. I suppose stubbornness comes with age, though I can't remember when he wasn't stubborn. ... I can't imagine you ever being stubborn, James."

That struck me as a peculiar comment. How could she venture a guess on how stubborn I might become?

As I began to drift off into the street toward the hotel, where meals were served in a lobby that doubled as a saloon, Annie gently steered me down toward Mollie's Café, a new place in town.

"It's okay isn't it?"

"Sure."

"I so enjoyed our picnic James," Annie said again as we strolled down the boardwalk. "Your ranch is the most beautiful place."

"Yeah, it was nice."

"I suppose we should have you over for dinner, but father is such an old sour puss. I'd be scared of what he'd say. He still thinks we're fighting the Civil War ... I'm quite a good cook you know. Your girl is also a good cook."

"Sarah. Yeah. You should join us for a family dinner."

"Family? How charming. You eat together, then?"

"Of course. The children are a joy."

"Of course they are."

Lunch consisted of a thin soup, tiny sandwiches and weak tea served in delicate cups. Annie took dainty sips as she chattered on about various people who had recently been into the store. She refused the apple pie, but I had to have it. But it was such a thin sliver that it did little more than whet my appetite.

On the stroll back, Annie waved to everybody whose attention she could attract, apparently no qualms about being seen with the guy who lives with blacks, molested the preacher's daughter and brawls in the street. Actually, she was aware of something I wasn't. With the resurrection of the ranch, a renewed appreciation for the Crawford name had been forming. People respect the affluent, their lesser sins easily forgiven. My banker possessed a rare discretion among our neighbors, so predictably, the scuttlebutt was vastly exaggerating my wealth.

The two ladies from before were marching across the street toward us. With one eye on them, Annie offered only a smile and a squeeze of the hands. "Please remember to have me to dinner, or perhaps Sunday lunch. I am so looking forward to more of ..." she paused. "Sarah's cooking."

Henry was ingenious with the tape measure. He cut a long, straight willow sapling and notched measurements in it using the sewing tape. As Luke and I headed out the next morning to continue building fence, Henry took his improvised measuring device to Buck Bluff.

An hour's work was enough to take my mind off Annie and get back to thinking about the ranch. It dawned on me as we were sinking fence posts that we should build a better corral to handle cattle when folks like the Kansas rancher came to call. That night, after I mentioned it, Luke and Henry started laying out a plan for a more elaborate network of corrals than I felt necessary, but I went along.

Henry was out first thing measuring the grounds while Luke and I cut posts and rails. It began to take shape after a few days and struck me as overkill. It had three separate holding pens with chutes between each. There was also a ramp for loading cattle on and off wagons, and a spot to isolate animals for individual care. The kids were diligent spectators, the boys asking continually why we were doing much of what we were doing while Dolly lent suggestions and looked hurt when they weren't acted upon. She of course named the corral before it had taken much form. Crawford Corral, it would be known by anyone she could convince to refer to it that way. She was disappointed that I didn't want to post a sign with the name displayed.

When word came that a large shipment of building supplies had arrived, Luke, Henry and I headed in with the wagon and Oldsmobile. It took three trips to ferry the first shipment back to the ranch. The bill was staggering. We needed to sell some cattle.

I found it curious that Sarah walked up as Henry and I were loading the wagon to head out for work that first morning. She had her hair tied back, wearing a plain, brown dress that had seen its better days.

"Daddy's little girl," Henry smiled proudly. "There were plenty of times Sarah helped me. I was paid by the job, and could get twice the work done with her. She's as good a carpenter as most men."

"Well, okay, great."

"Dolly'll see to all the cooking and other housework." There was a hint of hesitation in Sarah's voice. "She'll make sure the boys do their share too. I'd hate to be them boys."

Sarah's building skills were far better than mine. It probably made more sense for me to work on the ranch and hire Henry another helper, but I really did want to have a hand in building my own home. I was happy to let Sarah instruct me on how to measure and saw studs for the walls, and proud of the pile of boards that accumulated by day's end. Henry and Sarah rested on the stack before we headed in for the day. Henry talked about what we would do next, but my attention was focused on Sarah. Her face gleamed with per-spiration. She leaned back on her hands, damp dress stretching tight across her chest, hem sagging between slightly parted knees.

"What's wrong?" Sarah frowned, looking suspicious.

I swatted at the air. "Bug."

The Barry brothers were sitting on the porch with Luke as we came over from the barn. I would have thought that they would have called it a day by now and scooted on back to town.

"James, you remember Mark and Timmy," Luke said.

I'd seen them, but we'd never met. "Of course."

They shook hands firmly, both the kind of fellows who put off a positive first impression.

Dolly popped out onto the porch in an apron several sizes too large tied up under her arms. "Y'all get washed up. I don't want it gettin' cold ... go on now!" she shooed with the back of her hand.

Luke sauntered over to the watering trough as we scrubbed a day's work from our hands, a huge smile on his face. "The new lady of the house insisted the boys stay for dinner. Figured they'd just go to drinkin' whisky and not eat a healthy meal, not be fit for a full day's work tomorrow."

"Oh my," Sarah said shaking her head and grinning. "I'll have to douse a little water on that fire."

I laughed. "Let her be. We could use the discipline around here."

Dolly stuck her head out the door. "Well come on!"

Chapter Twelve

A week into the house building project, we got an unusually early frost. I appreciated the cool weather, but Sarah insisted the kids bundle up. It was the first I'd seen of their coats, and I wasn't satisfied.

The next morning, we found Annie alone in the store. "James, do come in!"

"Hello Annie. You remember Sarah."

"Of course. How are you, dear?"

"Fine, thank you. It's nice to see you again."

"What can I help you with today?"

"We need coats for the children."

"Hum ... I don't have much." She led us toward the corner of the store where she kept the hanging clothes.

Her only coats for children were style-less, canvas-looking garments, but with a flannel lining, they appeared plenty warm. Sarah assured me they were perfect. As we picked out the proper sizes, Annie caught Sarah gazing at a stylish woman's coat at the end of the rack.

"Isn't it lovely?" Annie pulled it out. "It just came in."

Sarah shook her head as Annie held it open. "I couldn't."

"Go ahead."

There was no mistaking the delight in Sarah's eye as she modeled the coat in the mirror.

"It's a perfect fit," Annie said. "And it looks just stunning on you ... you're so pretty anyway."

"No, I can't." Sarah smiled bashfully.

"Okay then, we'll take the four coats."

"We can't afford this, Mista James!"

"Mister James can certainly afford this," Annie assured in a condescending tone as she carried the merchandise to the counter.

Annie looked up as she tallied the goods, flashing a smile at Sarah, who was stroking her new coat in admiration.

"Miss Annie, we'd be so pleased to have you join us out at the ranch for Sunday dinner," Sarah said, not asking me first.

"That'd be just wonderful. That's so sweet of you. Are we talking about this coming Sunday?"

Sarah looked over to me.

"Sure." I shrugged.

Annie glanced at me with playful displeasure. "Don't get too excited James ... that would be very nice. Thank you, Sarah. Hopefully the weather will cooperate."

On the drive back, Sarah could tell something was on my mind. She waited until we turned into the ranch to ask. "You been awfully quiet. I hope the coats wasn't too much, I'll be able to pay you back just as soon ..."

"No, don't worry about that ... it's just ..."

"What?"

"Well, I hadn't quite made up my mind whether to invite Annie back out again."

Her eyes bulged. "Oh my Lord! My big mouth. I'm so sorry."

I felt bad I'd even mentioned it. "It's okay ... it's just lunch."

"Lord have mercy ... I hope you can forgive me ..."

"It's okay!" Sarah went silent at my abrupt tone. We remained quiet until I pulled up to the house, and she reached for the door handle.

"Sarah."

She turned, looking sad.

"It's okay. It'll be nice to have Annie out. I'm glad you invited her. It was the proper thing."

She forced a smile, but still looked ashamed.

We had quite a fashion show when the coats were distributed. The kids were thrilled with their new duds. When I apologized to Dolly because the more stylish coat we bought for her mother wasn't available in her size, she pragmatically declared: "Coats are meant to keep folks warm, not for show."

Annie greeted me at the door, dressed in yet another stylish outfit, brown skirt with a beige design embroidered on the hem, smartly matched blouse and slim cut jacket. Her hat had a sort of cowboy-style shape. With no one in the store, she took my hands, came up on her toes and pecked me on the lips, followed by a girlish grin as she straightened her hat.

On the way out of town, she waved at everyone like we were in a parade, scooting closer after we were beyond the last buildings and clutching my arm with both hands.

"Oh James, the weather is so perfect. I fear I won't need this jacket."

"But it is so pretty."

"Why thank you. I'd hoped you'd notice my new outfit. Tell me really, is it not kind of silly? They never quite look the same in the catalog."

"It's a shame your father couldn't join us."

Her grip tightened. "No it's not. He's a mean old man ... he wouldn't come anyway."

"Oh?"

"Forget about him. The day he's got nothing to complain about is the day he stops breathing."

"So I suppose he complained about you coming out here?"

"He complains about everything. He thinks I need to stay there to cook and wait on him like he was my husband or something."

"I don't suppose he much cares for you seeing me."

"His father was killed at Pea Ridge. People like that just can't accept living with black people ... but I don't feel that way at all, I really like Sarah and the kids. She's such a darling, and so pretty. I declare James, I get a little jealous."

"Your dad isn't the only one in town who thinks like that."

"I don't worry about what that crazy lot thinks. They're all just jealous of you."

"Jealous of *me*?"

"The ranch and all. Buying land, selling timber, building a big house ... and at such a young age ... and to be so wealthy."

"I'm not wealthy. Building that house may drive me plum broke."

"Oh come now." She swatted my shoulder. "Don't be silly."

When I pulled up to the house, Sarah and the kids were just coming out front where Henry and Luke were rocking. Susie leaped and tugged at the leash Dolly was struggling to hold on to.

"It's so good to see you all." Annie stepped from the car. "Thank you so much for having me out."

"It's a pleasure to have you." Sarah nodded graciously. "Your outfit is lovely."

"Oh, do you think so? I don't look silly? I wanted something proper to wear on a ranch."

"It looks just fine Miss Brice," Dolly said.

Annie grinned with a suspicious squint. "Please, call me Annie, dear."

Conversation around the dinner table was strained at first, awkward silences that would normally have been filled by the children, but they had been instructed by their mother not to talk too much. That didn't last long. Annie was much more formal around the others, which had an interesting appeal, like there was a part of her that only I was privy to. She seemed to be trying her best to ingratiate herself with everyone, dutifully answering questions.

"Miss Annie can't eat her lunch if we don't let her be," Sarah said, rescuing her from Dolly's inquiry about other suitors. "Girl, you're gonna be a nosey one."

Dolly frowned, but the boys enjoyed a good snicker. They straightened up when she shot a threatening glare across the table. Poor Annie, after that, it was like eating on stage. Sarah broke the uneasy quiet with reports on the progress of the house, which prompted Henry to retrieve his sketches. Annie's eyes lit up. "Oh my goodness, it's just magnificent ... what a wonderful drawing."

"Do you think you would like living in such a house?" Dolly said.

Gazes darted nervously around the table.

"Well of course, darling. I suspect anyone would, it's so beautiful."

Sarah rose to collect the dishes. "Why don't you take Miss Annie out and show her the progress."

"That would be wonderful," she said.

Annie removed her jacket, and laid it in the front seat of the car. She was striking in her form-fitted blouse. She reached out a hand for me to lead her. "Dinner was so delicious. I must be sure to tell Sarah again how much I enjoyed it. It's so nice to have such a good cook."

"Actually, Dolly does most of the cooking around here now. Sarah is helping on the house. She learned carpentry from her father as a child."

"My, she's really a find. I wish there were more black men around. She'd make such a good wife. Don't you think she's pretty?"

"I guess."

"Don't play coy with me James Crawford. How could a man not say she was pretty? She's gorgeous."

Annie went for an unprecedented time without talking, until the construction came into sight. The stone and beam foundation had just been completed, but Annie gazed up like Henry always did, admiring walls yet to be raised.

We strolled back along the high ground above the river, stopping a few times for small talk. The sun hung just above the hills when we reached the wagon. Turning to me, her smile faded as she reached around my neck and pulled me down. All my apprehensions about Annie vanished in that kiss. When I pulled her closer, her breasts tight against my chest, she suddenly pushed me away, as if she had a change of heart.

"Oh, my ... look at us," she straightened her hair. "I certainly don't want you to get the wrong idea."

I felt guilty, but she patted my forearm to let me know it was all right. "We just have to behave ourselves ... for a little while anyway." Her impish grin rendered me speechless. My eyes drifted down to her blouse, a perfect picture in my imagination of what lay beneath.

She caught me. "James! You men can be incorrigible ... but I guess you can't help it." She took a step toward me and looked up with a child's concern. "Do you think I'm pretty?"

"You're the most beautiful woman I've ever seen."

She sighed. "Oh James ..." Staring into my eyes for a second, she lunged, kissing vigorously, this time pulling me to her, tight enough to feel the bulge in my trousers.

"Oh my goodness," she stepped back without making eye contact. "I'm sorry ... I didn't mean to ... I don't know what came over me ..."

I watched in helpless silence.

"You're not angry are you? I just can't James ... not yet ... please understand."

"I do ... I wasn't really trying to ..."

"It's okay," She glanced back down at the river, her gaze lingering for a second. "We better go."

I nodded "Where's your hat?"

Annie checked her head, and turned to look. "Oh no." It was lying in a stretch of mud along a backwater pool. I climbed down to retrieve it, trying to wipe off some of the mud, but all I managed to do was smear it.

The whole gang came outside to bid Annie farewell. Sarah had a pie wrapped for her to take home to her father.

"Oh no, your hat," Sarah said.

"It blew off and James was kind enough to fetch it from down in the river."

"Weren't a breath of breeze," Dolly said.

"Well then." Annie started for the car. "It was so good to see all of you again." She waited for me to open the car door.

"That little Dolly says some funny things," she said on the way to town.

"That's just her way. I wouldn't pay any attention to it. She's really a very smart little girl."

"Of course, she's a doll."

Chapter Thirteen

A couple of days later, I headed in for lunch with Annie, stopping first at the post office. An answer had already arrived from Kansas. Thomas Grey wanted to visit as soon as possible, along with his daughter, Venice, and would appreciate advice on hotel accommodations. I hurried a response, insisting that I wouldn't hear of him staying anywhere but the ranch. I agonized briefly over the wording, but suddenly realized I was late for lunch, so I sent it and hurried over to the store.

My tardiness drew out a mood in Annie I was unprepared for. "I don't know," she whined. "I had planned to go earlier."

"What difference does it make?"

"I think another time would be better."

Her attitude dumbfounded me. "I'm sorry. I had a letter and had to get a telegraph out right away. It was important business."

"What sort of business?"

"A buyer coming from Kansas. Next week. I had to get confirmation out right away."

"Hum ... well, since you have such an interesting story to tell me, I suppose I will let you take me to lunch after all."

At lunch, Annie probed into every detail of the upcoming visit from the Kansas folks.

"Venice ... that's a funny name," she said over dessert. "I expect she's a little girl."

"I guess so."

The ranch was abuzz as the visit approached. In the midst of a modest drought, the activity produced a perpetual dust cloud, which had a bewitching ability to seep into the house despite Dolly's aggressive door monitoring. Sarah had been in town with Luke to pick out a few things to spruce up the house, apologizing profusely about the tab at the store, but I assured her it was what I expected. Luke added only a thin smile and shrug.

Annie let Sarah know she was unhappy I hadn't come to town. I figured as much, but I just didn't feel like being interrogated. I also wanted to dodge her earlier hint to be part of it in some way. Actually, I'd cooled on Annie a slight bit. After recovering from the last kiss, it began to eat at me how she was so darn interested in ranch affairs. I understood and could tolerate a reasonable amount of common, female busy-bodying, but Annie took it too far. She had an opinion about my affairs as if she had a stake in it.

But then I couldn't think about her long without recalling how she felt against me when we kissed.

Luke and I waited out front. Everyone was spruced up, the twins sporting fresh, short-crop haircuts, Dolly's hair brushed back and tied with a ribbon matching a newly purchased light-blue dress. Sarah was particularly fetching in a cream-colored, shin-length frock. Bellringer watched curiously from the nearest pen.

A distant dust cloud announced our guests' arrival. We watched the automobile slowly get larger. I recognized it as the four-seater Cadillac I'd seen in Joplin. Even at such a slow speed, the driver managed to skid to a stop, a wall of dust smothering him and his passenger. The short, corpulent driver waved his hat in front of his face and coughed. He rolled from his seat, landed awkwardly and sprung forward to shake my hand. He had a neatly trimmed white beard, his bald dome glistening with perspiration.

"Sorry about the dust," I said. "It's been so dry ... "

"Not to worry, my boy!" He bellowed in a kind of Santa Claus voice. "A ranch has dust ... Tom Grey!"

"James Crawford." We shook. "Welcome to our place. I hope you had a nice trip."

"Outstanding! ... your directions were perfect, the weather most cooperative and the company charming."

Luke opened the door for Venice. She stepped out, as tall as he was, in finely tailored slacks tucked into high boots and a delicate blouse that accentuated her eye-catching curves. Shining blue eyes smiled as she stepped forward with her hand out, hair flowing like red silk over her shoulders. The slightest trace of dimples framed a disarming smile, her dainty nose so very slightly turned up.

"Venice Grey," she said.

"James Crawford," I sort of grunted, embarrassed when I pulled my hand back after a lingering handshake. I turned to introduce the others, all lined up on the porch.

"Greetings to you all!" Santa roared after I listed everybody off. "Just call me Grey! And this beautiful angel is my darling Venice." She offered a friendly wave. "Hello."

Dolly started down the steps, and when the boys caught on, they hurried to catch up.

"I can get those darling," Venice offered as Dolly reached for a red travel case. Dolly looked back at her mother, knowing what to expect.

"Let them get your bags. It'll be the only chore they've done all day."

Dolly scowled and jerked at the bag, struggling with its weight.

"Those are awfully heavy boys," Grey warned as the twins stared at two large suitcases propped up in the backseat.

Luke and I rescued them, retrieving the bags as Sarah herded everybody inside.

"Give us a minute to freshen up, and I'll be happy to take a look at that big fellow I saw coming in here," Grey hollered from the porch.

I wandered out to the corral, leaning into the fence scratching Bellringer's forehead when Venice strolled up. She put a foot up on the bottom rail and reached out to pet him.

"He's a sweetie pie."

"Yeah, he's one of my best friends ... what this place is all about."

Venice pulled back and eased down to look at Bellringer's impressive son.

"And I take it this fellow's for sale?"

"I guess they're all for sale."

"But not that big guy."

"Bellringer."

"I know." She glanced at me with a condescending smile.

"I guess for the right price, even old Bellringer would have to go."

"That would be a mistake." Venice leaned back with her elbows on the rail. "When you have something truly special, you should never let go of it."

"Trying to run off without me!" Grey yelled as he hurried toward us dressed in more workman-type attire, including a big wide-brimmed hat. "There's always some young fella trying to run off with this one!" he roared laughing.

Venice grinned, apparently unfazed by her father's comment.

Grey examined Bellringer, and then his attention drifted out to the pasture. It was comical watching him dart around, strides too long for his short legs, almost tripping every few steps. Venice and I stayed back with the bulls.

"So, what *about* this one?"

"Gus ... that's Bellringer's successor."

"And everything is for sale?"

We exchanged smirks. "Well, I guess I see now what you meant about some things being too special to let go."

"Beautiful animals!" Grey bounced past us on his way to the house. "I'm famished."

We followed at a leisurely pace. "This is really beautiful country," Venice gazed out across the landscape. "I love your place. I hadn't been down in these parts before."

"Thanks, we sure like it here." From the looks of the clothes, baggage and car, I suspected the ranch was modest by the standard to which Venice was accustomed. "I imagine y'all have a nice ranch."

"It's big. Daddy has significant mining interests, and likes to spend his money on land. Now he's decided he wants to be a top breeder. Your Angus is just part of it. We're going down to Texas soon to look at some new breed."

"Sounds fascinating. Have you been to Texas?"

"Yes ... I wasn't very taken with it. I hoped to see Galveston, but the hurricane had just devastated it. Much of Texas is like Kansas, flat and dry. I really like it here in your hills."

We sauntered up behind the others, gathered around the fire in Luke's new cooking grill, which looked a bit like a little stone house. He'd been working diligently to have it ready for our visitors. I'd been entertained all week watching Henry come in from work, tell Luke what he should have done, and have Luke snap back: "It's just fine the way it is," only to tear it down and rebuild it Henry's way by the next afternoon. Sarah was about to put on rib steaks, and had potatoes and corn already baking around the edges of the grate.

"What a nice cooker." Venice rested her hand on her father's shoulder. "We should build one like this."

"Consider it done, dear! Our mesquite'll be perfect." He inexplicably wheeled and scurried inside.

"What would be perfect?" I asked.

"Mesquite. We discovered it in Texas. It's a scrubby little tree with terrible thorns, but the wood is excellent for cooking. It gives a wonderful taste to the meat. Daddy has a man from Oklahoma bring it up by the wagonload. He's threatened to go into the restaurant business selling mesquite-grilled steaks up in Kansas City ... not a bad idea. It'd be a good market for our beef, but he couldn't possibly do all the things he wants to."

Grey was loud and boisterous at the head of the dinner table, thrilled to have an eager audience. "These steaks are magnificent, dear!" he bellowed after every few bites.

"Thank you Mista Grey," Sarah said. "Only the finest beef at the Crawford Ranch."

He roared laughing. "This one's a jewel! Don't let *her* get away ... yes sir, you know how to do it up right, James boy. That's some fine animals out there too. They'll look good grazing the Bar G."

Venice placed her hand gently on her father's forearm. "Daddy, let's not be rude and talk business during Sarah's wonderful dinner. We don't even know if we can afford these fine animals, anyway."

"Yes, of course dear. Forgive me. Beautiful *and* smart! ... Now tell me James, how did such a young man as yourself come about such a fine ranch."

"Daddy, prying is no less rude."

"Of course. Excuse an old man!"

"No, I don't mind at all ... my father was killed in a tornado when I was younger. It was my mother who built the place up, made it what it is now."

"And James," Luke insisted.

"Mom was drowned saving a calf in a flood. I inherited the place and was lucky to hire Luke, who really runs things around here."

"Well, you've both done a fine job, a fine job! Sarah darling," Grey turned abruptly. "I've been smelling that dessert all evening, and really must have some."

"I almost forgot." She jumped up and began dishing up cobbler as Dolly served.

Afterward, I invited Grey out front for a smoke. Henry and Luke joined us, and a few moments later, Venice came out and held out her hand for a cigar. When I put a flame to it, she inhaled like an expert.

"Watch out for her!" Grey said. "Smoking cigars and such ... she'll be doing business soon. She runs the Bar G ... keeps my paws off the purse." His laughter disintegrated into a deep cough.

Prompted by Grey's inquiries, Luke ventured off on a long story about his younger days, growing up a short distance to the west in Oklahoma, making friends with a little Indian boy behind his parents' back. Grey followed with tales of his first journey out west from Cincinnati. His cigar flared and Luke ducked as he swept his arm in a wide arc describing the great bison herds blanketing the prairies. He'd known people killed by Indians and witnessed gunfighters dueling in the street.

Venice finally broke it up. "Daddy, a good night's sleep would do you well."

"You're right dear ... Thanks all of you for the most splendid hospitality. I've had a night I'll not soon forget! You really must come to visit us in Kansas ... join me in some bird hunting."

"I'd like that." I patted his back.

"Excellent. We'll see to it! ... Well good night then. I suspect my dear daughter will be taking her nightly stroll, just like clockwork. James boy, I trust you'll be kind enough to escort her ... Pleasant dreams all!" He waved grandly at the door.

Sarah and the kids emerged tired from cleaning up, prompting Luke to dismiss himself to the barn, where he and I were sleeping. Henry fell in behind them.

"It's probably been a long day for you too." Venice stepped off the porch. "I'll be all right walking on my own ... forgive Daddy ..."

"Of course not, it's a beautiful night."

She took in a deep breath of the crisp night air and started walking. "I'm so glad we came. The hills have much more charm than our endless prairies. I love our home and the sense of freedom out there, but I *really* like it here."

"I'm glad. We're all enjoying your visit. Your father's a great guy."

"Yes, Daddy is a darling ... life of the party ... he wasn't like that until after Mama died. He used to be so serious about everything ... I had to take over the business affairs. He's certainly happy, as you can see, but just not able to function like he once did. I think her death pushed him over the edge, but somehow, to a good place. Maybe it was the Good Lord's way of helping him bear life without her ... now days, he's always off on some new project, like exotic cattle from Texas."

The river grew suddenly louder as we passed an opening in the trees.

"I love the sound of running water." She looked over. "None of that at home."

"Many a night, back when I was younger, I'd camp down on the river. I never slept better than with the sound of running water."

"That sounds so nice. Growing up here must have been such a joy."

"It was. My mother taught me to hunt and fish early on, and I didn't need much else out of life."

"Your mother?"

"Yeah, dad was older, only really interested in the farm."

"You really should take Daddy up on his invitation. The bird hunting is spectacular, and we have some of the biggest bucks you'll find anywhere."

"Blacktails?"

"Whitetails mostly. We call them mule deer. They're a little farther west usually, but we see one every once in a while."

"So you hunt?"

"I killed a buck like *this* last year." Obviously proud, she held her hands apart. She must have realized I thought such a trophy seemed preposterous. "You'll just have to come and see for yourself," challenging my doubt.

We stopped on a high bluff with the current babbling beneath us, moonlight dancing on the riffles. Venice was stunning in profile, staring out into the bright night. When a breeze brushed the hair from her cheeks, I saw she was smiling.

"This is really a beautiful spot in the daylight." I took a step closer to her.

"It could hardly be more beautiful than it is right now."

"You've been here less than a day. There's much more to see."

"I can't wait."

"So do you ride?"

"Oh yes, I love to ...   Daddy used to buy me horses." She laughed at my expression. "Yes, there was a time when my birthday pretty much meant a new pony. I'm afraid I was a bit spoiled"

On the walk back, I coaxed her into stories of Paris and New York, and she seemed to enjoy reliving her travels, but emphasized that her parents insisted on them; she would have rather gone out west. At the house, I stayed at the base of the steps.

"I've enjoyed myself so much here. Thank you all."

"Oh, it's nothing. We've enjoyed having you ... we'll go riding tomorrow. I have a couple of mares of questionable lineage, but they're sweethearts and know the trails."

"That's the best kind. I look forward to it. Goodnight."

Chapter Fourteen

At breakfast, Dolly took it upon herself to show Grey her grandfather's sketches. He held them at arms length and squinted. "What a spectacular home! Is it far along? I'd love to see it."

"It's only at the floor right now." Henry shook his head. "Not much to see."

"But it's on the most beautiful spot in these Ozark hills," Dolly said with a deep head bob.

"Well I certainly don't want to come all the way from Kansas and miss the most beautiful spot in the Ozarks!"

Dolly giggled, and he laughed along. "It's called Buck Bluff," she explained. "I named it."

"A magnificent name! Whatever gave you the inspiration?"

"Well," she leaned forward. "We were all down there one day, and there was this big ol' buck deer." She reached up and spread her fingers over her head. "He was just a standing there looking, probably wondered why we was on his bluff. It was named after him."

"Well it's a wonderful and proper name!"

Dolly nodded proudly.

"Daddy, James was kind enough to offer to take me riding," Venice said. "Maybe we'll be heading over to this bluff."

I nodded.

"Fine then," Grey held up a finger. "Me and these younguns will take the Cadillac."

"I 'spect the wagon would be better," Luke said. "It's still a little rough."

"Excellent! ... where are my two little friends, anyway?"

Dolly halted in mid-step, scowling with a dirty plate in each hand. "They always disappear when there's work to do."

Everyone laughed.

"It won't be so funny when I get hold of 'em."

"You're a hard-working young lady," Grey said. "I should hire you to come run my household."

"I 'spect I'd do a good job. I do most of the work around *here*."

Sarah glanced over with playful disapproval, and Dolly burst out in a childish laugh none of us could resist.

Venice was already dressed to ride, and caught on that I was hurrying to get out in front of the rest of the crowd. We rode side-by-side, close enough to talk.

The morning chill sharpened the brilliance of the autumn colors. A fog bank rose from the river, the faintest trace of burning oak wafting on the breeze.

"So I guess you'll be hunting soon?" Venice asked.

"Absolutely. The rut will kick in here shortly."

"Yes, we'll start hunting when we get back."

"I haven't known many women who hunt, except my mother."

"When you grow up on a ranch, it's not like there's much else to do ... Because I drew cute little animals when I was little, Mama thought I should be an artist, bought me easels, brushes, you name it. She took me to Paris, thought I'd be inspired by the masters. She even had a teacher come out to live with us. I tried, I wanted to please her, but the whole time I just wanted to go out and shoot jackrabbits ... but in the end, she understood ... best she could ... I actually had a few, landscapes of the ranch, that weren't bad, but I don't put them out because I don't want people telling me I should keep painting." She looked over with an adorable grin. "I'd rather shoot jackrabbits."

She reached up to rub her horse's neck. The mare cocked its head in appreciation. "What a sweetie."

"That's Maybelle. Dolly does all the naming around here. This is Becky."

"Becky?"

"Don't ask me where she gets the names."

Venice spotted the foundation up ahead and urged Maybelle into a canter. She was looking out over the edge of the bluff when I rode up beside her.

"I think little Dolly was right," she said. "This may be the prettiest spot I've ever seen ... that was such a cute story about her naming it."

Venice swung the reins, steering Maybelle toward the tarp-covered foundation. She gazed up at imaginary walls like others had. "Perfect place for a home," she said softly. We tethered the horses, and took the trail down to the river. Venice picked up a flat rock and skipped it across the surface.

I tossed one that bounced a dozen times. She just had to match me, her rock skipping a dozen times before sliding into the far bank. I anticipated a gloating smile, but her expression turned serious. "Look, James, we want to buy Gus. I know you don't want to part with him, but that's the animal we want."

I was involuntarily shaking my head when she gave me the jolt of my young life.

"We'll pay two thousand dollars." She grinned at my wide eyes. "We can go into the bank today."

"You drive a hard bargain."

She smiled, going back to her softer voice. "Can we ride into town? I get tired of that noisy contraption."

"Sure. It's a nice ride."

We met the wagon coming up the trail. Sarah was driving with Henry next to her, Grey hanging his feet off the back with the boys yelling "Whoa!" at each bump. Dolly stood behind the seat exercising her grandfather's ears while Susie bounced behind.

We stopped to wait, Venice folding her hands contently on the saddle horn. "Daddy is having so much fun. I love to see him like this. The young ones are good for him."

"They're having fun too."

Sarah stopped beside us.

"I didn't think you were going to make it," I teased.

"They had to wait on an old man!" Grey bellowed from the back.

Sarah's smile confirmed Grey's tardiness. "We'll be back up at the house for lunch."

"Don't worry about us; we're riding into town."

"The two of you are riding to town?" She dropped her chin, wrinkling her forehead suspiciously.

"Something wrong?"

"Only that I ain't gonna be there to see it."

I'd yet to get use to the stares, not yet coming to grips with the reality that folks in town simply gawked at everyone. The old men who loitered on the boardwalk benches got an eye full that day. Seldom was a woman of Venice's beauty and style seen in those parts. There was going to be word of a scandal when one of the women from church saw the top buttons open on her blouse, revealing the slightest suggestion of cleavage. As we secured the horses, she acknowledged the men's interest with a wave. They returned the gesture as if she was some sort of celebrity.

Carl, the banker, instantly recognized the Grey name and fawned over Venice like she was royalty. He turned beet red, and I feared he'd be unable to complete the transaction, when Venice lowered her head to draw his attention from her blouse. "I'm up here, dear."

Venice was obviously used to financial dealings, so I mostly listened and grunted pithy replies. Our business was completed quickly.

"Are you hungry?" I said as we stepped outside.

"I'm starved."

"There's the cafe, and the hotel."

Down the boardwalk, a door swung open, a broom sweeping a fine cloud from inside. I froze, having neglected to consider what was about to happen. Annie stepped out, sweeping dirt into the street, and with a last glance before going back inside, she locked onto me.

"James darling!" she leaned the broom aside, dusted off her skirt and hurried to meet us.

She took my hands and pecked me on the cheek, never taking her eyes off Venice.

"Annie, this is Venice,"

"Why, you're not a little girl at all."

"Excuse me?"

"We were just guessing ... the day your message came."

"Oh," Venice smiled graciously.

"Annie owns the general store with her dad."

She glared her displeasure.

"Oh good," Venice said, "I'm so glad we ran into you. I'd like to buy gifts for the children."

"My, how sweet."

"That's not necessary," I said.

"They're just darling, and they've made such an effort to make us comfortable. Please indulge me."

"Well, James, I don't know how you could resist such a charming request."

They flashed fake smiles at each other.

"Then you're staying out *at* the ranch?" Annie said.

"Yes, we're having the best time."

Annie shot me a dirty look as she led us into the store, explaining that she didn't carry many toys.

"What about that?" Venice pointed.

"It's a baseball bat."

"I thought it might be."

They exchanged those strained smiles again.

"I ordered it for last Christmas, but nobody bought it."

"Do you have the balls?"

"I believe so," Annie searched a lower shelf. "Here."

After picking out a necklace for Dolly, Venice reached for a bottle of perfume on the end of the counter.

"It's the most expensive I've ever carried. Just plain silly, if you ask me. A lady wanted me to carry it, and then she never bought any."

Venice sniffed the bottle and slid it over next to the baseballs. Reaching for a rack of pipes, she held one like she was smoking it. "How do I look?" she said to me.

"Stick to cigars."

"Now James," Annie said with sugary sarcasm, "that's not a nice thing to say to a *lady*."

"Venice joined us fellows for a cigar last night on the porch, that's all."

"Oh my goodness, how interesting."

Those smiles again.

"We're having such a nice time. James was even kind enough to join me on a walk last night. What a beautiful bluff he showed me. The full moon was gorgeous ... very romantic."

"My, what a perfect host." Annie's civility was wearing thin. "Yes, I know exactly where you mean. It is a beautiful spot."

"Then you've been there?

"Yes dear, I've been there."

Venice picked out pipes for Henry and Luke, and produced a bill that Annie had to walk down to the bank to change.

After she'd returned, Venice put her change away in a small purse. "Annie, we would so love it if you would join us for a bite to eat."

That monumentally misguided notion stunned me.

"I really should stay open."

"What a shame," Venice turned and tapped my arm softly. "I guess it's just me and you."

"Where are my manners! How rude of me ... I expect you're leaving first thing in the morning."

Venice looked at me and shrugged, "We haven't decided. I wouldn't want to wear out my welcome."

"Of course, we would all be delighted if you could stay longer. But our little town must be a terrible bore for you."

"Oh not at all. I don't know when I've had a better time. We hope James will allow us to return the favor. Daddy made him promise to come out bird hunting with us in Kansas."

"My, how persuasive he must be. Let me just freshen up ... Venice, do you need ... " She patted her cheeks.

"I'm fine dear, thank you."

Annie took a ridiculous amount of time changing into a dress that was way too formal for lunch. Hurrying around the counter, she latched onto my arm like she was scared I'd escape, inexplicably offering no protest when we headed across the street for the hotel.

Venice ordered a beer, and I joined her. It dawned on me when Annie ordered a glass of wine that we had never had drinks together. Venice downed her beer quickly and ordered us another. "Me too," Annie held up her glass, gulping its contents. A third round came with dinner. As the ladies on either side of me cut into their steaks, there was no mistaking who was accustomed to drinking and who wasn't.

"Good steak," Annie said with her mouth full, wiping wine from her chin with her sleeve.

"But not near as good as those steaks we had on James' new grill." Venice gracefully took a tiny bite.

"New grill?" Annie glared at me.

"Well yeah. Luke built it out of rock." She stared incredulously. "Him and ol' Henry, fussin' about it, it was funny watching 'em ... it cooks really good."

"Well how nice ... how very *damn* nice."

Though I wasn't thrilled with Annie's behavior, I felt sorry for her. Venice was intimidating. I felt ashamed, not managing the awkward lunch better, but deep down there was a part of me that relished Annie's jealousy. I was unable to come up with anything helpful to say as I helped her back across the street, catching her once before she fell.

"Come in a second?" Annie said softly. She took my hand and dragged me inside. Squeezing my neck just shy of a choke, she kissed violently, squirming tightly against me. The wine was bitter on her breath.

"Oh, James," tears forming as she caught her breath. "If I have to come over tomorrow and make love in that river of yours, I swear I will!"

"Whoa Annie," I put my hands up. "It's not like that at all. It's just business. Anyway, a woman like that isn't interested in an old farm boy like me."

"That's probably true, but I don't want her around you." She stomped a foot. "She's a goddess!"

"She's not as pretty as you, Annie."

"Liar! What a mess. Today was a disaster. You probably don't even like me anymore. Don't be too disappointed in me, James. The wine made it all so horrible. Please forget all of this so we can go back like it was."

"It's okay," I wiped a tear away with my thumb. "Everything's fine. How 'bout I come in for lunch the day they head back."

She managed a childish smile. "And I suppose now, you'll hold me to my promise."

"What promise?"

"Never mind."

Venice was scratching beneath Maybelle's bridle when I walked up. We rode silently out of town.

"Don't feel so bad," Venice finally said in a consoling tone.

"About what?"

We rode several hundred yards without speaking.

"I've been an ungracious guest."

"How do you mean?"

"Poor, Annie ... please forgive me for all that."

"She's fine."

"No, I was ugly. I'm ashamed of myself. Believe me, I'm usually a very nice person."

"It's okay. She just gets real jealous. We've only seen each other a few times. I don't know why she acted like that."

"You should take care of that soon, you know." She kept her gaze locked straight ahead.

"Take care of what?"

"It's obvious you don't care for her the way she does for you."

"I do care."

"Of course, but Annie is in love with you. She's a darling little thing, and one day she'll find her a husband and live happily ever after. You don't want to get in the way of that."

"Well, thank goodness you're here to explain all this to us simple folks."

"I've offended you. I'm sorry. I meant no harm...I guess I just got defensive when she threw up her guard ... I admired the way she fought for you. She's really sweet, and pretty. You'd probably be better off if you did love Annie, but anyone can see that you don't ... except Annie."

At breakfast, Grey was in his same boisterous mood, waving his arms as he insisted I come hunting the following month. Otherwise, there was a melancholy around the table, but vows from Grey to visit again soon and an invitation to his ranch took some of the sting out of it. Dolly made sure by asking directly if the invitations were for all of them.

"Well, absolutely!" Grey's voice filled the room. "Wouldn't have it any other way!"

Venice's goodbyes were gracious but restrained. "We'll send for the bull," she shook my hand. I followed her to the side of the car, where she placed her hand gently on my arm, her eyes glossing over. "Please forgive me. I hope I didn't cause too much trouble."

"There's nothing to forgive ... have a pleasant trip."

As the Cadillac disappeared into the dust, Sarah watched from the porch as I settled into my rocker and the others dispersed in various directions.

"What sort of trouble?" Sarah asked without looking back at me.

I wasn't about to answer.

"I'm guessing Annie trouble." She glanced over her shoulder at me. "Hum, thought so."

"So *you* knew what was coming?"

"I didn't want to be nosey."

"Since when?"

She pretended to take offense, turning away to hide her smile. "Poor little Annie ... no way she can compete with the likes of Miss Venice."

"There's no competition."

"We'll see."

"Venice will end up marrying some tycoon or prince, not some farm boy. It's silly for Annie to be jealous."

"She couldn't help it even if she wanted. That Miss Venice is really something ... you might be right; she might end up with some fancy husband, but if I was to have to make my guess right here, I'd say she'll end up with a skinny Ozark boy."

"That's ridiculous ... skinny?"

"I'm going to put some weight on you this winter."

"You're as crazy as Annie."

"Maybe."

Chapter Fifteen

Sarah and the kids acted like I betrayed the ranch by letting Gus go, until they heard what I was paid for him. Barraged with suggestions on how to improve the ranch, I decided to just hang on to the money. It eased my anxieties over the price of the house.

About a week after the Grey's visit, two teamsters showed up in a heavy, mule-drawn wagon to pick up Gus, delivering a message from Grey. He wasn't taking no for an answer. They were expecting me to come up the following month. My only hesitation was Annie. Things were good between us again, and I hated to mess that up. After Venice left, Annie had done a magnificent job of pretending like nothing ever happened, being particularly affectionate. I was enjoying it. The comment about making love in my river hadn't escaped me, and I held out hopes that her jealousy might prompt her to make good on her promise, but unfortunately, that offer had fallen victim to sobriety.

To my surprise, Annie didn't pause when I mentioned Kansas. "That would be wonderful. A man needs time away for himself." I was careful not to talk about it too much after that, but she kept throwing in things like: "You'll have so much fun hunting with Mr. Grey."

The Kansas that Grey described sounded exotic and far away, but the ranch wasn't all that much farther north of Joplin than ours was south. The land opened up as I came down out of the Ozarks onto shallow, rolling hills, the leafless gray of winter trees lining the drainages separating them. I imagined enormous herds of bison grazing on the endless grass, stampeding as men chased them on horses, flinging arrows.

When I came over the crest of a hill, I knew immediately what I was seeing. Cattle dotted the landscape as far as I could see. Even from two miles out, you got a sense of how enormous the house was. Surrounded by a complex of other structures, it stood like a grand courthouse in the middle of a small community.

I turned into an ostentatious iron gate with a large, metal "Bar G" overhead. The road stretched a couple of hundred yards, lined with naked walnut trees. A curious trio of beautiful horses stared over a white fence as I drove past. The circular drive wound in front of white columns framing a huge two-story house, where Grey stood with Venice at the bottom of wide steps, his arms spread to embrace my arrival.

"Welcome my boy!"

"Thank you." I climbed out. "This is a nice place you have here."

"It'll do for now!" He laughed. "Help our friend with his things," he ordered a couple of teenage boys.

Venice stepped forward to greet me with a formal peck on the cheek. "We're so glad that you could come see us."

"It's nice of you to have me."

"Well come in!" Grey waved from the top of the stairs.

We turned into a study where he was pouring from a glass decanter behind a massive desk. Beautifully polished shelves full of expensively bound books surrounded us. He distributed drinks and held his glass up. "To friends!"

I almost choked. It was my first experience with Scotch.

"Over here, over here my boy!" Grey waved me across the room to the gun case built into the wall. "I insist that you use one of my guns. I love them, but I can't hunt with all of them."

Two guns with tubes attached grabbed my attention. I picked one out, raised it to my shoulder to look through the magnified scope and was startled by a huge buck, one of many trophies hanging between bookcases.

"Ha!" Grey clapped his hands. "You know your guns all right. You've gone and chosen daughter's favorite."

"It doesn't matter …"

"It's okay lad! There's another with a scope. I can't stand the damn things myself, makes me bug-eyed."

"I don't have a favorite," Venice said.

"Right!" Grey pointed skyward when a young Mexican woman at the door got his attention. "Let's eat!"

Beneath enormous chandeliers, we sat at the end of a long table, Venice and I on each side of Grey. He popped back up for another toast, red wine this time, holding his glass out in dramatic fashion like all the empty seats held important guests.

"To the hunt!"

Grey went on and on throughout dinner about the great hunting on the Bar G. His beloved quail hunting got the lion's share of the accolades, but he knew I was interested in deer.

"We've got a dandy buck picked out for you my lad."

"Picked out?"

"There's a really good buck hanging around, and we've made sure he hasn't been disturbed," Venice said. "He's big. You should have a good crack at him. How long can you stay?"

"I really shouldn't be gone long."

"Nonsense!" Grey threw up his hands. "We'll not have you running off. We need that silly deer-hunting nonsense out of the way so you can join me in some quail hunting."

"Well, I sure would like to do some bird hunting."

"Of course, excellent then! ... I wish you'd marry this one so I'd have a permanent bird-hunting partner!" His laughter echoed off the high ceilings.

"Daddy, we'll all be getting up early," Venice said, apparently not bothered in the least by her father's proposal.

"Ah yes! And your walk, of course, well." He stood. Venice rose to kiss him on the cheek. "Goodnight then ... maybe you'll propose on that walk!" His laughter turned to coughs halfway up the stairs.

I followed her out the door. She told me more about the ranch as we meandered around the driveway and down the road.

"I hope my father's eccentricities aren't uncomfortable for you. He's so sweet and means well."

"No, of course not. I love being around him."

"Well he sure likes you."

"I like him too ... I never had a buck picked out for me."

"It's not in a cage or anything. He's scraping along a certain fencerow. You wait him out a few days and you'll get him."

At the gate, we turned back.

"So tell me all about how Sarah and the others are doing."

"They're great. Got mad at me for selling Gus, 'til they heard how much I got for him."

She laughed.

"They'll probably have the house halfway up by the time I get back. I felt bad about leaving. Of course, Dolly's always grumbling about having to do the housework, and not pleased with how her brothers are taking care of the chickens. By the way, they have a spot next to the barn where they're throwing and hitting with the bat and balls you gave them. Dolly plays and even Sarah gets out and plays."

"Good. I'm so glad they're enjoying it. I miss them. Even though our visit was short, I grew to care for them all. I hope to return one day."

"Of course, any time."

We were almost back at the house when Venice finally asked about Annie.

"She's fine ... we're fine."

"I'm so happy to hear that. I think the two of you are precious together ... I still feel bad about all that."

"Yeah, me too, I didn't mean that stuff I said."

"Don't be silly. You were a gentleman ... I swear James, you're about the first one who has ever put me in my place." She looked over sheepishly. "I guess I need that sometimes."

When the bang on the door came, I wasn't entirely sure I had slept. A huge breakfast weighed heavy on my stomach as I followed my guide, John, out the door. He was full-blooded Cherokee, having kidded at breakfast that I could call him "Man with short pay," causing Grey to slap his leg, choke and spit coffee.

We turned out of the gate on foot, and eventually off the main road through three smaller ones. The morning was growing into a dull gray as we sat along a tree-lined fence next to a fallow field. A couple of hundred yards out, a small island of trees stood alone in the open country, barely visible through a low-hanging fog. As a light breeze blew into our face, an owl hooted one last time before surrendering the night. I'd hardly had time to digest much of it when John poked me, and pointed. A doe was trotting out of the fog right at us, the body of a much larger deer taking form behind her. The giant buck stopped suddenly, as if being pulled back by the safety of the trees. I figured it was a little over two hundred yards. John recognized my apprehension. "Aim at the top of the shoulder," he whispered as he placed a forked stick under the barrel to steady the shot. The colorless landscape danced wildly in the scope until John put his hand on the barrel to lower and steady it. There he was, standing like a sculpture, neck stretched, searching the air with his nostrils. Lowering the crosshairs, I squeezed as soon as they touched the top of his shoulder. I only knew I connected when John patted me on the back. "Good shot!"

The enormous buck had a body and antlers like no deer I'd ever seen. John insisted we go back for the wagon before field dressing the deer. It was a cool morning, so I held my opinion that it should always be done immediately.

We were in the barn when Grey bounced around the corner. "I knew it! ... Is it the one?"

John nodded. "It's him."

"Good show, James boy!"

Grey hurried back into the house to retrieve his Brownie, struggling with John's help to climb up onto the wagon. I sat on a box in the back. "I knew it!" Grey slapped his leg as we pulled out into the sunlight. "I just knew it!"

His celebration was something to behold, a much-exaggerated version of his normally delirious behavior. I imagined creatures of all shapes and sizes, for miles around, cocking an ear at his outbursts. He had me pose in all sorts of ways before handing John the camera. Grey and I struck several poses, and then he directed pictures of John and me. When the film was exhausted, John dragged the deer behind the wagon, and between us, we strained to load it.

My anxious host insisted we head straight back out for some bird hunting. I was tired, but not about to say no. I had never hunted with dogs. They were an unanticipated joy, two brown-and-white pointers bouncing through prairie grass in search of scent, while a brown version of my own Susie remained obediently at Grey's side.

"Point!" John called a short distance into our hike. Both pointers were locked in statuesque poses, tails high, staring into a bush that hardly seemed capable of hiding a single bird. Grey eased in close, motioning me up beside him. I couldn't make out anything in the scant cover. When Cocoa, the Labrador, was sent in to flush the birds, they erupted in every direction. The Browning Auto-5 shotgun ripped off five shots as fast as I could pull the trigger, hitting nothing but sky.

"Bird!" John called to the dogs.

The Labrador was the first to return one of Grey's quail, while one of the pointers, chased closely by the other, brought in another bird.

"Pick out just one bird," John tutored me as we continued down a long gentle slope toward a tree-lined drainage that split the rising prairie on either side. "Don't just shoot into the group."

The next covey flushed near the trees, most heading through a gap to the other side. I picked out a bird, pulled the trigger and it fell from a cloud of feathers. I turned to Grey as if I'd atoned for an earlier misdeed, but his gun was still on his shoulder. It popped again. A pair of quail flushed a few feet to my right, as if they were deaf and didn't hear the earlier barrage. I was too startled to get off a shot.

John handed me my first quail with a growing grin on his face. "Okay ... Pick out one bird, and after you shoot it, pick out another and shoot it."

We both had a good chuckle, and it wouldn't be John's last laugh of the day at my expense. On the next point, as we approached, the dogs began scooting along. Something was different this time. It was as if the birds wouldn't stay still for them.

"Coming your way, my boy!"

A large bird jumped, cackling wildly, just feet in front of me. My first impression was that it was some sort of giant parrot.

I couldn't process it before the strange bird glided over a distant hill. It was distressing to learn my parrot was a pheasant. It was several minutes before the laughter subsided.

Grey and I lingered at the dinner table drinking long after the dinner dishes were washed and put away. The whiskey felt warm and friendly this time, ideal for celebrating a perfect day and perhaps the best meal I had ever enjoyed, mesquite-grilled quail, pinto beans baked all day with bacon and onion, and cornbread dripping in butter. Uncharacteristically loud, my voice ricocheted off the high ceiling along with Grey's, who screamed laughter and pounded the table as I told stories about the twins, Satan the rooster and the wild-ass chickens, stories unlikely humorous except to Scotch-soaked ears.

"Ah!" Grey threw a finger into the air. An automobile was pulling up out front. "Daughter's home!"

We were toasting Venice's return when she came through the door. The click of boot heals on marble echoed in the foyer.

"Join us my precious!" Grey held up his empty glass.

"My, my," she shook her head. "It's a good thing I got back when I did."

Venice sat across from me and a young woman slid an empty glass in front her.

"Hey!" Grey shouted and threw up his hands. "Your lad here got his buck!"

"Hey, congratulations ... already, huh?"

"It wasn't but a few minutes," I began a boastful monologue with far more details than Venice or anybody else cared about.

An alarming warmth washed over my face, followed by an urgently queasy stomach.

"Excuse me." I got tangled in the chair as I struggled to my feet. The room spun as I hurried to the front door. Closing it as nonchalantly as I could manage, I ran down the long steps, barely making it to the garden before vomiting up my meal. I paced around until comfortable another such episode wasn't eminent before sheepishly slipping back inside.

Venice was standing over Grey, coaxing him to his feet.

"Ah, there you are!" Grey plopped back down. "A toast!"

Venice took the decanter from her father. "James doesn't want another drink Daddy."

"Well, okay then, it's off to bed!" Grey wobbled back to his feet. "She'll be joining us tomorrow!"

"I can't. I've got work."

"I'll not have it! ... That's always her excuse! Talk some sense into her James!"

"Okay, okay." Venice steadied her father. "We'll see. Let's just get you to bed."

Grey looked like he had no chance of making it up the stairs without her help. She glanced back after a few steps, "Do you need me to help you to bed too?"

A stupid smile leaked out.

"I was just kidding." She shook her head in playful disgust. "Go sleep it off."

Chapter Sixteen

Struggling to remember much about the night before, I was unfortunately able to recall too clearly my exchange with Venice and vomiting. I forced myself up and took my time dressing. Grey and Venice were sipping coffee, breakfast plates already cleared away, when I wandered into the dining room.

"There he is!" Grey howled. His pronouncement pierced my skull with a sharp pain.

Venice was dressed for the hunt in a tweed jacket like her father's. "How are you this morning?"

"I've been better." I sat at the remaining place setting. "I sure hope I didn't offend anybody last night. I'm afraid I drank one too many."

"Nonsense! It was a splendid hunt and libations were in order!"

"When are libations *not* in order?" Venice shook her head. She turned her attention to me. "Perhaps even more than one drink too many ... but of course you didn't offend anyone. You were charming." There was a hint of condescension in her voice.

John led the way in the Cadillac, bouncing down a dusty, tooth-jarring road that amounted to little more than wagon ruts. Venice and I followed their chalky silhouette, a merry band of hunters, Grey's arms flailing as he talked. The two pointers sat politely on either side in the back while Cocoa stood lookout, his front paws on the back of Grey's seat. He was a dutiful sentry, his head darting diligently in search of movement. He delivered a harsh scolding to a group of deer that had the temerity to feed next to the road, and paid his respects to countless rabbits that darted across. His two companions flicked violently at intervals, tossing Cocoa's slobber from their muzzles.

It was just over three hours before we pulled up in front of a rustic cabin perched on the highest point for miles. The rolling prairies stretched to the horizon in every direction, dots of stunted junipers defining the drainages between the hills. The wind blew ripples across the prairie grass like waves on an ocher ocean. An old barn sat near the house. Except for the car tracks leading inside, there were no other indications it was in use.

Venice was still pulling on her gloves when John called out a point. I was convinced the dogs had it wrong this time; surely there were no birds so close to automobiles that just pulled up.

"Go ahead," Venice said, pointing and smiling.

Grey waddled urgently around the Cadillac as John handed me my shotgun. Again, the birds startled me, not because I wasn't expecting them to jump, but I wasn't prepared for their size. I hadn't a clue what they were, but I wasn't about to make the same mistake I'd made with the pheasant. I dropped two.

"Good show!"

"Prairie chickens," John said.

We were just a couple of dozen strides down the hill when the dogs came to another point. This time I stood back as Venice stepped in behind them. She threw her gun up and dispatched a pair of quail with two shots like she had done it a thousand times.

By the time we reached the bottom, John was burdened with a sack filled with birds. He dropped them beneath a lone cottonwood and began the long climb back to the automobile. As we rested, one of the pointers caught a whiff of something and headed off down a brushy ravine, so I decided to follow. Suddenly, he slammed on the brakes, and locked onto a small clump of high grass. I knocked down two quail to the sound of Grey's hollering approval in the distance. Continuing on, I discovered the joy of working one-on-one with a good dog. He found two coveys in just a few minutes. With each returned bird, I petted my partner, thinking more about Susie each time. It reminded me of home. I would need to leave early the following morning, I decided.

I'd been about ready to wander over and check on the others, thinking surely we would need to head home soon, when I spotted the car coming down the hill, heading for Grey and Venice, mere specks in the distance. I began to hike that way, but as soon as John picked them up, he started in my direction. The dogs ran alongside the car as we drove up to the cabin.

I was surprised to find chairs circling a fire pit, a flame beginning to grow through a pile of branches. It challenged my imagination to account for the impressive stack of wood in this treeless landscape. My Oldsmobile had been pulled into the barn.

"We're staying the night?" I said.

"Of course! You'll thank me."

The fire was the perfect antidote for the late afternoon chill. John sliced bird breasts and ran them onto skewers with onion pieces. Sitting in a tight circle roasting our dinner, we ate as our individual skewers became done to our liking, washing it down with cool beer. By the time we finished eating, a glorious rose-color sun had descended below a slate cloudbank just above the horizon, the mottled sky above singed pink.

"Not a sunset like it," Grey said in an understated tone for him. He began to push himself up. "I think I'll feel best in the morning if I retire early ... good night children." He looked leg weary climbing the porch steps. As John called the dogs to follow him to the barn, Venice threw more wood on the fire. A three-quarter moon hovered low in the east, the chilled breeze drawing us closer to the flames.

"Too cold for a walk?" she posed after the fire had burned down some.

"Not at all."

We started down a long slope. "I hope you're enjoying yourself. Daddy just loves this place ... I do too."

"It's remarkable. I've never had such a good time."

"Well, I appreciate how kind you are to Daddy. He's having so much fun."

"He was quiet at dinner. He's okay isn't he?"

"Oh yes, campfires are one of the few things that quiet him at all. I've grown to love campfires." She laughed. "That was quite a lot of walking for him today. He's exhausted. But I encourage him to get as much exercise as possible. He'll be ready to go again in the morning, I'll assure you ... I hope all of this will keep him alive longer."

The wind died, the night suddenly quiet and still except for bats flitting about in the moonlight. The silence was interrupted by the chorus of a coyote family on the next hill over.

"They sound happy," Venice said softly.

"I don't know, they always sound sad to me."

"Well ... they're all together. It's a beautiful night, and you saw how many rabbits they have to eat. I suspect they're quite content."

"I can't argue with that."

We strolled up a long incline to the edge of a mound, the far side dropping more steeply than any of the hills surrounding it. Even in the darkness, the view was spectacular. Arms folded, Venice gazed into the night.

"What are you thinking about?" I said.

She smiled over at me. "Nothing really ... oh Daddy I suppose. It seems I'll be here forever to take care of him, which I adore, but I don't want to grow old without seeing more of the world."

"You have an awful long time before you have to worry about that."

"It's a terrible thing to say, I know."

"No, I understand."

"You do? ... You're lucky, or smart I should say, having Luke manage your affairs so you can travel."

"I don't really travel ... *you* could hire someone."

"I know, but Daddy wouldn't let me go, emotionally I mean. I'm as much a mother to him as a daughter. He needs me."

"Are you sure? It seems like what he wants most is to make you happy."

She shrugged. "I suppose. Maybe it's just me."

A stringy network of lightning illuminated storm clouds building to the northwest, a ghost image of endless hills lingering in the dark.

"Don't you want to go places, see different things?" Venice said.

"Sure, I guess, but I've been pretty happy there around the Ozarks."

"I want to go to Africa one day ... see the animals."

I'd certainly never given that any thought, and I liked the idea, but it sounded about as likely as me traveling to the moon.

The first rumblings of thunder interrupted a long silence.

"It's coming in pretty fast."

She nodded. "Have you been many places?"

"Just New York."

"New York? And you let me go on so before."

"It wasn't like that, I wasn't on a vacation or anything. I was in an orphanage ... they brought a bunch of us out here on trains. I was about ten."

"Really?" She sounded astonished, as if perhaps she didn't believe me.

"I was lucky. I think most of the kids were adopted simply as farm hands. Sure, I did plenty of that, but my mother really loved me. I was never sure about my dad though. He just wasn't a very friendly guy."

She stared without a word.

"It wasn't like I was the poor orphan kid. I wasn't particularly unhappy at the orphanage. I enjoyed reading my books and dreaming of the day I would head out west. I thought it was all a dream come true to get on that train, but most of the other kids were terrified."

A bolt of lightning reached down and pricked the prairie, closer and yellowish this time. A cool puff of breeze washed over us. Venice's silence was unsettling. She hadn't moved a muscle. The moon was at her back, her expression invisible in the shadow, but I felt that she was studying me.

I forced a laugh. "I thought, or hoped really, that we were going to Montana."

After a lengthy pause, she finally said something. "Yes ... I think I've heard you talk about it ... Jimmy?"

To say I was stunned would be to falsely claim any feeling at all. I was numb in disbelief, paralyzed and speechless. Lightning flashed nearby, allowing me to see the tear running down her cheek. In that snapshot that lingers, she appeared ready to reach out for me.

"Oh my God!" It took all of my breath to utter those few words.

"I knew one day ..." she wrapped her arms around me. I was shocked when her lips touched mine, but I didn't resist. She kissed with a passion that only alcohol could draw out of Annie. I didn't try to understand, I just pulled Venice tight to me.

A crack of lightning exploded overhead, startling us to jump apart. "Oh my gosh! Look at me, acting like such a school girl."

"It's okay."

"You don't understand ..."

A few huge drops began to fall. "Come on!" Venice took off running. We were thoroughly soaked and gasping for air by the time we made it back up to the porch. The cold wind on our wet clothes was tolerable only because we had just sprinted up the long hill. We sat close on a bench, our shoulders pressed together.

"My God, Jimmy, this is amazing ... Is it okay to call you that?"

"Sure."

"I can't believe this. When I was a little girl, I always dreamed I'd see you again one day ... but now it's really happened ... when you're a kid ... it was just so hard to adjust to my new life when I got here. Mama pampered me, but I didn't have any children to grow up with. I even longed for the girls at the orphanage, though I never really fit in. I was always daydreaming about how you would show up in the nick of time to rescue me from Indians or some gang of outlaws, and we would be married, like in some fairy tale." She giggled. "That's so silly, I know, just foolish kid stuff, but I held on to that hope for a long time. I've relived the kiss a thousand times ... so what does this make us, Jimmy?"

"I don't know."

"I guess we are sort of like brother and sister."

That wasn't a sisterly kiss.

"What's wrong?" Worry clouded her face.

"Nothing ... it's just a lot to take in."

"Yes, but wonderful."

"Of course. Should we tell anybody?"

"Why wouldn't we?"

"I don't know ... maybe we should wait. We can always tell everybody later, but we can't take it back once it's out."

"Why does it matter?"

I hesitated.

"Oh ... Annie? This doesn't affect the two of you. She'll love the story. We can be like sisters."

That struck me as highly unlikely. "There doesn't have to necessarily be anything wrong for Annie to drive herself crazy."

Even in the dark, and drenched, she was precious. The way her hair hung straight and heavy past her shoulders, and how perfectly the blouse clung to her as she heaved to catch her breath, was bewitching. Still burning from our interrupted kiss, I turned and leaned in, but she stopped me with a hand to the chest. "I better get out of these wet clothes or I'll catch pneumonia." She stood. "Oh Jimmy, I'm so happy about this," bending over to peck me on the forehead. She paused at the door, "Good night Jimmy ... I ... good night."

I stayed on the porch, trying to digest it all, until a stiff north breeze drove me inside. Grey and John were snoring obnoxiously from cots on either side of the room, the door to the one separate room pulled closed. In the dim flicker of lightning through a window, I spotted a ladder leading to the loft like the one I had slept in as a child. At the top, I found a mattress, perfect relief for my tired back. But sleep was elusive. I lay awake, the snoring more offensive each hour, trying to fully take in what had happened that night. Sometime in the early morning hours, the ticking of sleet on the roof finally saw me to sleep.

Chapter Seventeen

A rattling door slam ripped me from a deep slumber.

"Let's go sleepy heads! Don't want to get snowed in!"

"It's okay, Daddy," Venice said sounding sleepy. "It's not that bad."

"Nonsense my precious! Never take a chance. Wake your beau. Hurry now!" He pulled the front door closed like he was trying to rip the knob off.

The others were waiting by the cars when I stepped out into a landscape transformed, flakes floating gently earthward, the snow-dusted prairie fading into a distant winter fog.

Venice met me halfway. "Good morning, *James*," she winked and pecked me on the cheek.

"I knew it!" Grey bellowed.

Venice rolled her eyes as she climbed into the Oldsmobile.

The snowfall was getting thicker as we turned through the gate, but there was barely an inch on the road. "It's not that bad," I said. "We'll be fine."

"I know. Daddy just wants to feel like it's some great adventure. He'll talk later about how we barely survived the blizzard."

"I might be able to get ahead of the weather and make it all the way home tonight."

"Oh no, please don't. We have so much to talk about."

"I guess I could head back tomorrow. It *would* be a long day."

She turned to face me with a satisfied grin. "Good."

"By the way, where did *Venice* come from?"

She enjoyed a laugh before explaining. "It's silly. I'm almost embarrassed to say ... when I was a child, I always dreamed about exotic destinations. I loved geography and enjoyed reading about far away places. Daddy's library was one of my favorite places. Well, I got it in my head that I wanted to pick out a new name for myself, after some romantic place. Mother thought Paris was a bit tawdry, so I named myself Venice."

"You picked yourself a new name?"

"Isn't that awful ... I was so spoiled."

"You say that a lot."

"What?"

"About being spoiled."

"I'm sorry. It's just ... I think I could have been a better person had I not been pampered so."

"I don't believe that."

"You're sweet."

"At your age, running a ranch that big, taking care of your dad like you do ... I don't know how you could have turned out any better."

"Well ... thank you."

We rode with our thoughts for many miles. Finally, the snow played out into a chilly drizzle. Venice curled up in the corner of the seat.

"Scoot over here."

She did, and I wrapped my arm around her.

The house was a welcome sight, smoke billowing from the chimney, a steaming soup waiting inside. Just as Venice predicted, Grey went on about "beating the blizzard" during lunch as she and I exchanged grinning glances across the table.

It was welcome news that they had afternoon naps planned. I fell asleep in an instant, waking in a brief state of confusion about where I was, but when it came to me, it was all newly incredulous. I sat on the edge of the bed, pondering my incredible discovery, until voices drew me downstairs.

Venice was dressed to tend her horses.

"I'll join you." I darted back upstairs for a coat.

Four inches of snow had collected as we'd slept, and it was still coming down steadily. "Looks like Daddy is going to get his blizzard after all," I said as we stepped inside the barn.

Venice laughed. "Do you think it's childish, calling him Daddy? I always have. If I changed now, he might ... "

"No, I think it's charming."

Her smile was more beautiful each time I saw it. She snatched two brushes from a shelf, tossed me one and pointed to a stall. I stroked a grateful mare, the most beautiful horse I had ever touched.

"What's her name?" I scratched behind her ear.

Venice laughed like I'd delivered the punch line to a joke. "Paris."

"Ah, a tawdry horse."

She cackled childishly. "They're both so sweet. I don't take near enough care of them ... do I?" She patted the mare's neck.

"You're hard on yourself."

I didn't know if she was offended or just didn't have an answer.

Suddenly, she popped up, elbows over the top rail, excitement on her face. "Come for Christmas! All of you: Sarah, the kids, Henry, Annie. We'll buy them all wonderful gifts. Daddy will be thrilled."

"Annie?"

"Well of course you'd bring your fiancé."

"We're not engaged."

"I'm sorry, I didn't mean to …" She shook her head. "But wouldn't it just be a perfect Christmas!"

"That'd be too much trouble."

"Don't be silly. Come early so the children can help decorate. I can take Sarah and Annie into Kansas City for some shopping."

"No, I don't think that's such a great idea."

"Of course it is … I'll make things right with Annie, I promise. I know you're worried that this will upset her, but I think you're wrong. Annie and I will grow to love each other."

"It'd be easier if y'all came there."

"Oh, that's an even better idea!"

A pang of regret hit me in the midsection.

"I can't wait to tell Daddy."

As we continued brushing, Venice went on about Christmas while I countered with potential problems. She wasn't hearing any of it. As we headed back into the house, it was set in stone; Venice and Grey were coming to the Ozarks for what sounded like an extended Christmas visit.

Inside, we were instructed by the cook to join Grey in the study, where Venice's plans were met with thundering approval. "Splendid! Couldn't be a better Christmas ... we'll go shopping in Kansas City before, my dear."

After a drink, we sat down to steaks as big as the plates. While we ate, the boys were out back building a fire.

"It's going good," one of them stuck his head in the door.

"Come out for just a few minutes," Grey pushed himself away from the table.

The shoulder-high flames reached from a rock-lined pit in the center of a stone patio. The fire cast its silent spell, crackling loudly against the still night.

"That's enough for me," Grey said after a few minutes. He kissed his daughter, offered me a warm good night and retired.

Venice made eye contact across the fire. "I still can't believe it," she smiled and shook her head. "It's like a dream ... what have you been thinking about most?"

That uncompleted kiss and wet blouse had been dominating my thoughts. "I don't know. I guess I'm just trying to digest it. It still doesn't seem real. What about you?"

"Lots really ... do you believe in fate?"

I shrugged.

"I think we were meant to meet these two times, don't you?"

"Yeah."

She giggled at my lack of conviction. "I've always been such a hopeless romantic. I hope you don't think I'm not a lady, kissing you like that. I don't know what came over me." She sounded like she wanted to take the kiss back, which hurt my feelings a little. "Annie must never know about that."

"I'm sure she'd understand," I replied, knowing without even the slightest doubt that she would not.

"No!"

I nodded.

Our thoughts lured back into the fire, we stared, mesmerized, until Venice began conjuring up more Christmas plans. I just listened, recalling the chatty girl on the train.

It was disappointing when she came around, pecked my cheek and went to bed. I stayed behind, gazing into the coals, trying to picture the reactions when I told the others about our holiday visitors. They'd be thrilled, except for Annie. There was just no telling how bad that was going be.

There was well over a foot of snow on the ground the next morning. I wasn't going anywhere. Grey was bubbling at breakfast, re-energized by a long sleep and a new project to embrace. He quizzed me about Christmas gift ideas as I pleaded with him that they wouldn't be necessary.

"Don't be a Scrooge! Children must have Christmas gifts!"

After breakfast, Venice dismissed herself to her office where she had planned to spend the day catching up with bookkeeping and correspondence. It hurt my feelings a bit when she told me. "And I need you this morning," she directed at her father. "James, as much as you like to read, you must spend some time in Daddy's library."

Strolling along, scanning the endless titles on the high shelves, I glanced down on a table next to a reading chair. With renderings of sled dogs against red skies, the title grabbed me, *The Call of the Wild.* I sat near a window and read, losing track of time as I followed Buck on his journey. There were less than a third of the pages left when I stood to stretch. A young woman stuck her head in the door. "Dinner will be served soon, sir."

"My lands!" Grey bellowed as we sat. "I can't believe we didn't feed you lunch."

"No, it's quite all right. I had a nice day of reading."

"I'm sorry, James," Venice said. "I'm afraid we got busy and didn't even stop ourselves. It was a productive day though."

"I'm glad to hear that. Please, I had a wonderful time. I read most of *The Call of The Wild.*"

"Outstanding! Just read it myself. Wonderful book."

Venice put a nix on booze at dinner, deciding we'd had enough, but when Grey retired, she retrieved a bottle of wine and a pair of glasses, and waved me into the vast sitting room. We settled on the couch, facing the flames in an enormous fireplace. I coaxed Venice into a lengthy recall of her earliest days in Kansas, which eventually led back to when she and I crossed paths.

"I remember you, up on your knees, hanging out the window as if you were terrified to miss something. What do you remember about me?"

"That you talked a lot."

"What?" She swatted my shoulder. "I guess I still do."

"I thought you we were *so* pretty. I'd never been around any girls ... it broke my heart to see you pull out."

"Ahh, that's so sweet ... I cried."

"I remember."

She grinned over and looked back into the fire, turning back suddenly as if she had just remembered something. "I'm keeping you up." She stood and reached down for my hand.

"Not at all."

"Well, I'm a little bushed."

She hugged me, in a polite, cursory manner, but never had any woman's touch stirred me like the feel of Venice in my arms.

I had plenty to occupy my thoughts on the drive home. Travel on the wet roads was excruciatingly slow. Fortunately, the one time I got stuck, it was within sight of a farmhouse. A grumpy farmer reprimanded me for the use of such a contraption while his mules pulled the car out of a ditch. By the time I reached Joplin, it was late, and I was exhausted, so I took a room for the night. It was as if I was too tired to sleep. I lay awake thinking of all sorts of things. It crossed my mind that Darcy might be working.

The ranch looked deserted when I pulled in, but as I stepped out of the car, distant hammering explained. I threw my stuff inside and started toward the construction. Susie spotted me first and took off in a sprint.

That was a special moment. They welcomed me like some long, lost family member with hugs and backslaps. Everyone gathered around for my initial report on the buck before Dolly pushed me into the house to show off the work begun inside. The upstairs was framed, with the roof about half finished. The light leaking down the stairwell through a sawdust haze gave the room an otherworld feeling. I was amazed at the progress.

There had been a sort of challenge, initiated by Dolly, to see how much work could be completed while I was gone, prompting Luke and the Barry brothers to work exclusively on the house in my absence. They turned out to be a fine group of carpenters, according to Henry. He also bragged about the kids' contribution. Finally, Sarah broke up the celebration by announcing that she had beefsteaks set aside for the occasion of my return.

I walked with Luke on the way back. "So what's the big hurry?"

He shrugged. "We've started, so why not get it done ... we're all just anxious I guess. We worked after dark every day. Dolly's ready to marry you off."

"I'm afraid she's going to be disappointed."

"She's switched from Annie, deciding Miss Venice'd make a better wife."

"Well, that's not going to happen."

He laughed and slapped me on the back. "We'll see."

Dinner was a grand event with non-stop storytelling. After Tom and Billy filled me in on the latest chicken news, Henry got uncharacteristically wordy, bringing me up to date on the house. Sarah mentioned that she had been to town and visited with Annie, with an expression that promised more to come.

"Tell us *all* about Kansas," Dolly urged.

As I described the wide-open spaces, the magnificent ranch and hunting with Grey and the dogs, I found myself nostalgic already, wondering how it all would play out, whether I would be able to return to the Bar G.

"How's Miss Venice?" Sarah said.

Dolly leaned in to not miss a word.

"Doing well. She runs the ranch, so she was busy with business most of the time. She did manage to pull away and go bird hunting with us once ... handles a shotgun better than any of the men."

Dolly frowned, disappointed at the quality of information.

"Oh yes, I can't believe I forgot to mention it. Grey and Venice are coming for Christmas.

Everyone was delighted, except Sarah, who grimaced slightly.

"It's okay, isn't it?"

"Oh sure," Sarah snapped back from some thought. "There'll be a lot to do."

"We can have the new house ready by then," Luke declared. "Or at least far along enough so some of us can stay out there."

That seemed impossible at first thought, but then I considered what had been accomplished in my absence.

Sharing an after-dinner smoke with Luke on the porch, I felt firmly planted back at home. He caught me up on his plans. "The boys would like to stay on the ranch. When you move out there, I could stay in the bunkhouse with them, and Henry's clan can take this place."

"I'm not staying in that big house alone. How about Henry and them staying out there with me? They could have the bottom floor. You could have this place to yourself."

"That'd suit me. And I could sleep in the bunkhouse whenever company comes ... they'll be real excited about staying in the new house."

"They deserve it; they're building the damn thing."

Luke stared out into the darkness, searching for the right words. "It's a special thing ... the way they've all been about that place ... takin' to it like they were doing something really important. It seems bigger than just a house."

At breakfast, Dolly broke some news. "Miss Annie came out."

Sarah's head whipped around. "When?"

"I was up cookin' supper. The rest of you was down workin' ... says she came out on account of it was a nice day for a ride, but it was awfully cold and windy. Her cheeks were red as apples." Dolly scanned the table; puzzled that everyone was hanging on her words. "But I could tell from all the questions that she was only worried about Mista James, with the foul weather and all." She held her chin up proudly. "But I told her, 'Miss Annie, don't you worry one little bit. I'll guarantee you Miss Venice is takin' *fine* care of Mista James.' "

Sarah spit into her hand trying to bury a laugh. Luke and Henry didn't bother to hide their amusement. Dolly gazed around, bewildered. "What, Mama?"

"Nothin' baby."

Dolly scanned the room cautiously before continuing. "She seemed a little put out when she left, but I imagine that was just cause it was so cold."

114

Chapter Eighteen

Braced for trouble, I was stunned when Annie hurried across the empty store and greeted me with a long kiss. "It's so good to have you back darling. I was so worried." With an arm around my waist, she rubbed my chest. "Even though I knew you'd take perfectly good care of yourself for me ... Take me to lunch! Tell me all about it."

To my surprise, she led us over to the hotel, and acted genuinely interested in the hunting stories and my descriptions of the prairie sunsets. Her only inquiry was, "How is everyone?"

I felt like, "Just great" would suffice.

Annie steered the conversation over to the obligatory gossip update, but it went in one ear and out the other as I ate. There was no hint of a problem until dessert.

"So how's Venice? I hope she's well."

"Good, I suppose."

"You suppose? She was there wasn't she?"

"Yeah ... she manages the ranch and was pretty busy. She only went out hunting once with us. She was in Joplin a lot of the time."

"I'm sorry you didn't get to spend more time with her. She's such a dear."

"Maybe next time," I carelessly let slip.

Annie's eyes narrowed slightly. "Next time?"

"Well, you know ... if ..." She had this sort of dumbfounded stare that had a way of drawing things out of me I hadn't intended to cover. "I'm sure her father ... Grey," I corrected clumsily. "We'll have more cattle dealings ... I really enjoyed bird hunting with him. We ... me and him get along really well." I couldn't have sounded guiltier, and I hadn't done a dang thing wrong. That was when I finally admitted to myself that I was just a little scared of Annie.

"Hmm," was all she said.

I expected her to tear into me, but instead she seemed distracted by some thought. Forcing a smile, she reached across and took my hands. "Oh, James, I wish we could get away to ourselves, spend some time alone ... just the two of us."

"It might not be too late for another picnic. There's a nice place up on the other end of the river from the house."

"That sounds wonderful, if it's not too cold. I want us to be alone though. I worry about the children, although they're just sweet as they can be."

"I could have Sarah see to it that they leave us be."

"I'm sorry. I guess I just want you all to myself."

It was an unusually warm and still evening, a gibbous moon casting long shadows as I sat out front waiting for Sarah. Susie's head was up, alert, scanning for some critter she'd heard rustling in the brush. Finally, that familiar sigh from inside signaled another day's work done. Sarah came out, sat and stared off quietly.

"Nice night," she finally observed.

"Yep."

"I'm tuckered out."

"You're working too hard. You should slow down."

She waved me off.

A possum ambled into the moonlight. "No," I growled when Susie spotted the prowler. She lay back down, probably more bored than obedient. Such encounters were nightly events. The possum wandered on with no apparent destination in mind.

"Annie's coming out for a picnic on Sunday."

"I'll put together a nice lunch ... hope it ain't too cold."

"Thanks. ... Annie's peculiar about some things as you know ... she's worried about the boys spying on us again."

Sarah glanced over suspiciously.

"Just wants us to spend a day alone."

When she turned back, I saw in the moonlight that she found my request entertaining. "Keepin' younguns under hand like that can be a tall order."

"I know ..."

"What is it Miss Annie don't want them to see? ... you better be careful, James."

"What do you mean?"

"If I was as crazy stuck on you like Miss Annie, and I see Miss Venice coming into the picture, I might do whatever it takes to make sure you was mine for good."

"And what exactly would that be?"

"Get pregnant."

"That's insane! ... she wouldn't do that ... she couldn't even be sure I'd marry her."

"Oh James, honey, everybody who knows you knows full well you'd do exactly that. Annie sure as fire knows it."

"What even makes you think I'd do that, even if *she* wanted to?"

Sarah's smile grew. "Then you'd be different than any other man I ever knew. Turnin' away a woman sounds a lot easier here talkin' about it on the

116

porch ... Annie looks to me like she could be quite the little seductress if she took a mind to."

"That's ridiculous. I'm surprised at you."

"I could be wrong." Sarah stood. "I better turn in." She strolled off through the moonlight.

Annie had on yet another new outfit, dark slacks with a white blouse much like the outfit Venice had worn, and she was bubbling over the glorious, Indian summer day. When we arrived back at the ranch, the picnic basket was in the wagon, distant hammers explaining why no one was around. We headed the other direction, and well beyond the sounds of construction, we stopped on a high grassy mound beneath a single giant oak. The river shimmered through a break in the trees at the bottom of the hill, its distant hum the only sound in the sleepy afternoon.

"Oh, James, it's just a perfect day, and what a perfect spot." She unloaded the basket. "I think it will be a very special day."

Sarah packed beef sandwiches with delicious bread she had somehow found time to bake. There was also an apple pie. I found myself strangely attracted to the way Annie devoured her food. She was cutting herself a second piece of pie when she caught me looking.

"What is it, darling? ... Oh, I must seem such a pig. But I just love Sarah's cooking. Please have another piece so I won't feel like such a glutton."

"Sure."

After lunch was packed away, Annie laid back, hands cupped behind her head.

"Lay down next to me." She patted the blanket. "Look up through this tree."

There was something oddly beautiful about the symmetry of bare branches against the deep blue.

"Oh James, I don't know when I have ever felt more alive ... come here."

When I rolled up close to her, she pulled me down for a kiss, holding tightly to my neck with one arm, while taking my hand and placing it on her ribs, inches from her breast. She was holding desperately to the kiss when she began to use her free hand to unbutton her blouse. My body was responding properly, but panic overwhelmed my libido, and I pulled away.

Annie frowned. "What is it?"

"Nothing."

"Oh, James, I don't want to wait now that we know we love each other. I know we shouldn't, but I just can't help myself."

When I sat up, she eased deliberately up onto her elbows, squinting her displeasure. "What on earth is wrong? You look like you've been stung by a bee."

I groped desperately for the right words. "I guess I'm just a little nervous." It seemed plausible, but I didn't much care for the unmanly sound of it. Annie interpreted my hesitation as bashfulness, which she apparently found attractive. She came up on her knees, put her arms around my neck and kissed me, and then sat back on her heels and continued to unbutton her blouse. I involuntarily reached out to stop her.

"Ahh, how cute," Annie purred. "Come on now James, I've never even done it, and *I'm* not too bashful. I mean I am, but I want to be with you so much and show you how much I love you."

"It's not that I'm bashful, it's only ... it's just that I respect you so much."

Annie pulled her blouse closed, glowering suspiciously.

"You're just too important to me. I want to do the proper thing by you."

She didn't look the least bit satisfied with my explanation.

"We should wait until after we're married." The minute it left my mouth, I knew I'd made a terrible mistake.

Her eyes lit up and her mouth gaped open. "James, are you asking me to marry you!"

"No!" I was a little too emphatic.

Her smile melted into a frown.

"I mean, not just yet."

She glared through narrowed eyes.

"Please Annie, you just surprised me a little bit, that's all. You know I love you."

"I love you too, darling. I want us to always be together, but when you are ready to officially ask," she winked, "the answer is yes." She fastened buttons slowly with a naughty grin. "But don't wait too long, there are other suitors who just won't leave me alone, bless their hearts. I can't hold them off forever, and I don't want to be an old lady when I begin to have children."

We kissed again, but she plopped back suddenly, looking sadly down at the ground. "I am so ashamed." A tear dripped from her chin. "Please don't stop loving me. I was just so tempted because I love you so much. Please don't leave me because you think I'm not a lady."

"Of course not. Nothing has ever been harder to resist." I finally said something truthful.

We kissed again. I allowed my hand to come around from her back to touch the side of her breast. She pulled back after a few seconds, grabbing for my hand.

"Now, now. You're the one who wants to wait."

We hiked down the hill, and strolled hand-in-hand along the river, startling an otter from a nap on a sunny boulder. We talked, laughed and tossed rocks into the river. When she bent over to pick up a flat stone to skip, her slacks drew tight against her behind, and it struck me that I may have been a little too hasty earlier. It was a significant challenge knowing I could take her in my arms and make love to her, but Sarah's warnings kept ringing in my ears. Annie didn't make it any easier on the ride back.

"I'm so scared you don't respect me now."

"Of course not. Actually, I was thinkin' a minute ago that I might have changed my mind."

"Well," she grinned, "it's not too late."

When I hesitated, she swatted my shoulder. "I'm just teasing ... you were *so* right." She took my arm in both hands. "I guess since we're going to be husband and wife, we're supposed to tell all our secrets." This didn't at first get my attention, Annie being a master of revealing secrets. "I swear, as much as I try to keep pure thoughts, I think about us making love all the time. It's going to be so wonderful." She patted my arm. "You'll probably want to everyday ... Oh James, please hurry."

Henry and Luke were on the porch as we pulled up to the house. Sarah stuck her head through the door. "I've got supper almost on. Y'all come on in here."

Annie was the first to sit. The others settled in as Dolly served soup.

"So how was your day?" Henry asked politely. "It was sure nice weather for this time of year."

"It was wonderful," Annie gushed. "We took a walk down by the river ... it was just wonderful."

When Dolly came back around to pick up empty soup bowls, she grimaced at Annie's back. "What a shame Miss Annie. You stained your blouse."

"Oh my, I must have leaned against the tree."

"Looks like grass stains to me."

Annie's face blushed as the room went quiet. "Oh my goodness, I can't imagine how that happened."

"It coulda been ..."

Sarah swatted Dolly quiet.

A blanket waited for us in the car seat, so we draped it across our laps. We rode a couple of miles in silence before she whined: "I know you must think so badly of me, but I can't help how much I love you ... I just thought cause of last time, how excited you got ... Oh James, I still wish we had done it. I'll be dreaming about it all week."

I pulled her closer. "I probably won't be able to sleep tonight thinking about it."

She giggled and placed her hand on my thigh, tempting me to pull the car over immediately.

After a while, she sat up suddenly. "I meant to warn you. Those two no-goods came through. Came in to buy tobacco, and I could smell the liquor on their breaths. Please be careful. I don't trust them."

"I don't think they'll be making any more noise."

It was unsettling to hear that Tom and Pal were back in town, but by the time we reached town we'd both forgotten about it, and Annie dragged me into the store for a lengthy kiss, causing me to again question having rejected her affections. On the ride home, I found myself thoroughly confused, and more than a little frustrated.

Chapter Nineteen

Work on the house continued at an exhausting pace. The goal was to get the exterior done before the worst of the winter set in, the fireplace a top priority. Much of my effort was spent hauling supplies from town, which always meant lunch with Annie. She was doting over me so that I began to feel a daily need for it. And each day, she slipped something suggestive into the conversation that would drive me a little bit crazy, conjuring up the image of her beneath me, wanting me, flesh leaking from her blouse. Annie was as sure we were getting married as a person could be, chattering non-stop about it. She'd even picked out children's names. I felt a little guilty not sharing her enthusiasm, but just figured women got more charged up about that sort of thing. I got nervous when she expressed her belief that I was waiting for the house to be completed to propose. That sounded too much like a deadline.

Riding in for supplies as the year's first snow dusted the hills, I found Annie's mood as chilly as the weather. She maintained a polite sulk through our walk to Mollie's and remained uncharacteristically quiet until after our food was served.

"I understand you're having company for Christmas," she said without looking up from her plate.

"Well yeah. I thought I'd mentioned it."

"No dear, you didn't mention it. I had to hear it from someone else."

"How'd you hear?"

"Never mind, I just thought you might have mentioned it."

"Well, like I said, I thought I had. It's just a business thing. I didn't think you'd be interested."

"Oh, I'm interested all right!" She slammed her fork down. "I'm interested in why you kept it from me."

I held up my hands. "Shh," worried about the trio of old ladies staring at us.

"Don't shush me! ... you deliberately kept it a secret, and I think I have a right to know why."

The old ladies nodded.

She stared out onto the street, moisture forming in her eyes. "James, we really have to be able to trust each other."

"Trust!" Annie and the old ladies flinched. "This has nothing to do with *trust*. This has to do with how I run my ranch. I really don't think that should concern you."

She threw her napkin down and stormed out, leaving me to venomous glares from the three ladies.

It was a week before I ran into Annie again. I was in picking up a delivery at the depot, and as I rode by, she was sweeping the walk in front of the store. She eagerly waved me over.

"Weren't you going to drop by to see me, silly?"

"Sure I was. I just had a load of lumber to pick up."

"How *is* it coming along? I didn't get out there on my last visit."

"The outside is mostly done."

"I can't wait." She put her hands together like an anxious little girl.

She motioned me into the store, chattering on as if I'd never raised my voice to her. I listened patiently, relieved, as I watched her glide about the store tending to her business. Then, without even looking over at me, she delivered a jolt.

"I telegraphed Venice and told her how excited we are about their visit." She explained how she had asked Venice if she could order anything special for the occasion, and that Venice had responded with a request for candies and wrapping paper. Annie put a special emphasis on how "thrilled" Venice was to hear about "us." At lunch, she went on about how wonderful Christmas would be, allowing no doubt that she intended to be right in the middle of it all. Back in the store, she demanded a long kiss.

When I arrived back at the ranch, Henry was coming out of the barn. "Did you have a nice day in town?" he said with a hint of sarcasm as he glanced into the wagon.

"It was okay."

"Where's that shelving?"

I could only shake my head.

"That woman's got a hex on you boy." Henry chuckled.

Everyone on the ranch threw themselves into the Christmas preparations. Luke cut a shapely juniper that filled half the room, while Sarah and the kids found all manner of odds and ends to garnish it, including strings of popcorn, pine cones and pieces of ribbon tied in bows. Sarah and Luke went into town to purchase decorations, and of course, Annie inserted herself into the middle of that. I was soon fetching Annie from town to help Sarah with decorating, which turned out to be more supervision on Annie's part than actual participation in the work. Sarah wasn't bashful about pulling me to the side and complaining about Annie's "interference," but I fended off her objections, citing Christmas Spirit. Annie had stocked some "proper" tree ornaments in the store, and the kids were disappointed, mostly at me, when she insisted they replace their improvised adornments. Despite these minor points of contention, Christmas was shaping into a joyous celebration. One morning when Luke and I came in after killing a couple of turkeys for the holidays, they were all singing carols, decorating the room to the aroma of baking cookies.

But while everybody else was well immersed in the spirit of the season, Sarah sensed that something was pestering me. She asked about it later.

"Oh, it's nothing"

"Annie kind of nothing?"

"Well...I guess she's just getting ahead of me, and I don't think I can slow her down."

"No, I don't 'spect you can." She grinned. "She was telling the younguns today about how it was going to be when you two were married, already lining up Dolly to babysit."

"Damn." I buried my face in my hands.

"Dolly said to me after, 'Don't she know Mama?' My daughter's done made up her mind now that you're gonna marry Miss Venice instead of Annie."

"Well, she's getting way ahead of herself too, acting like the rest of you women, deciding on what us men ought to be doing."

"A lot of women would say a man might never decide nothin' if it was left to him alone."

"A lot of women have a lot to say."

Sarah laughed.

"So that's what you think? I need to decide something?"

"I don't go thinkin' about other folk's affairs."

"Oh really?"

"I'll just say one thing; the longer it goes on with Miss Annie thinkin' she's gonna be Mrs. Crawford, the harder it's gonna be for her to find out she ain't."

"And you're just so sure she's not."

"Cain't be sure about anything."

"At least you're not being nosey about it."

She stood to leave. "It's gonna be a mighty interestin' Christmas around here."

Chapter Twenty

It was a dreary afternoon on which Venice and Grey were to arrive, dark and colorless beneath a dense layer of low clouds. Luke and I sat on the porch smoking, bundled in our heavy coats, when a car appeared in the distance. Only Henry, who was out at the new house building shelves, was not standing out front when they pulled up.

"Greetings all!" Grey bellowed like ol' St. Nick himself. "Merry Christmas!"

The kids descended on a car bulging with cargo, covered by a canvas tarp, remnants of Kansas snow clinging to the edges. Grey rolled out of the driver's seat and greeted me with a bear hug. "My boy, how wonderful it is to see you, and how kind of you to allow us to share Christmas with you. We'll have a splendid holiday!" He always sounded like a politician addressing a crowd.

A few large snowflakes began to fall as the small mob mingled. I was the last in line to greet Venice. She took my hands and kissed me on the cheek, and then as if she'd changed her mind, she hugged me.

"Come on in outta this cold," Sarah said, her interest lingering on Venice's hug.

Luke and I stacked luggage and gifts on the porch, and the kids shuttled the presents inside where Venice directed their placement under the tree. When Grey stepped into the house, he shouted his deafening approval of the decorations: pine wreaths tied with red ribbon, popcorn strings hung on the walls like bunting; a red tablecloth with a decorative centerpiece made from ribbons and pinecones; and the ornament-laden tree in the corner. Holiday desserts baking in the stove lent a delicious aroma and made the place so warm it felt nice to have the door open. Sarah, Venice and Dolly huddled around the table making plans while the men migrated out to the porch.

"We were lucky to get in before the blizzard." Grey looked skyward into the large flakes. The thick shower was beginning to blot out hills and distant tree lines. "We caught the first of it coming in. Made it just in the nick of time ... a white Christmas! Just as it should be!"

We all seemed to notice Henry at the same time, coming out of the snowy haze. He donned no protection other than the hat and light jacket he always wore, but strolled along at a leisurely pace as if he was enjoying the weather.

"Greetings!" Henry called out in a good imitation of Grey.

Grey waddled down into the snow to shake hands. "I see somebody has to work around here!" he said and scrambled back up on the porch.

"Looks like a good snow." Henry brushed the powder from his shoulders.

"It'll be wonderful to see the place with a white coat. It's perfect!"

We were soon called in to dinner. The house seemed a little crowded, but comfortably so. It took but a simple question from Billy to launch Grey into an energetic oratory. He shared tales from his younger, pioneering days with a storyteller's animation, skillful at making just the right pause to inject drama. Venice continued to look over to me and smile warmly as her father held the other's spellbound.

When Sarah stood to collect plates, Venice and Dolly joined her, while we men rose to step out front. There was over four inches of snow on the ground and a half inch on the rockers, so we decided it wasn't such a good night for a smoke. We went in and sat around the table, the twins scurrying to seats on either side of Grey. Luke was up after a short time, ready to retire.

"Stay," Venice said to me as I started to join him.

Henry decided to take Luke's lead and herded the children out into the night. After an announcement of exhaustion, Grey hit the sack. As the women cleaned the kitchen, I listened to Sarah reminisce about the twins when they were younger. Venice laughed and encouraged her with questions. Finally, they finished, so Sarah bundled up, bid us good night and hurried out into the cold.

"Feel like a walk?" Venice said.

"Sure. I love the snow."

The clouds had vanished. A gibbous moon hung just above the hills, sketching long shadows on the snow. We trudged off down the road, following Luke's footprints.

"Remember when you asked me and Daddy to come for Christmas, how I said it would be nice if it snowed?"

"I remember. You know, we arranged this just for you."

"Well I sure appreciate that."

"It's the least we could do, you coming all this way."

I led us off toward the river, the crunch of footsteps strangely loud against the winter silence. When Venice recognized the bluff where we'd stood that first night, she smiled and reached over to touch my arm before gazing out into the bright night. Ice reaching out from its banks reduced the river to a peaceful trickle and an appropriately gentle gurgle.

"It's still *so* beautiful," she whispered.

"Like you," slipped out of me.

She turned and smiled. "You're so sweet ... oh James, I just love it here."

"I do too. I guess I forget how lucky I am sometimes."

"Will Annie be coming out tomorrow?"

"If I can make it through the storm."

We stared quietly out in the night. The silence felt inexplicably awkward. When I sensed Venice studying me, I glanced over and grinned, but she managed only a thin imitation of a smile. A mallard squawked from down on the river. When I looked over to gauge her reaction, she was still staring at me, with what appeared to be concern, as if she hadn't even heard the duck. Catching me off guard, I redirected my attention back down to the water.

"Jimmy?" She reached out to turn me toward her. Taking my cheeks in her hands, she stared into my eyes for a second before kissing me softly, briefly, stepping back to judge my expression. I threw my arms around her and kissed with a pent passion I hadn't been entirely aware of until then.

"Oh, Jimmy," she whimpered over my shoulder as we held tight. "I tried not to love you. I swear I did. But I can't help it. I love you ... Oh God, I can't help myself." She buried her face and wept.

I rubbed her back, trying to take it in and formulate a response.

"I know it's so wrong, with you and Annie engaged. But I just couldn't let you marry without telling you. I'd regret it the rest of my life. I hope you can forgive me one day ... I know you think I've had everything in the world I ever wanted, but I'll just die when you marry Annie."

"I love you too."

She held up her hand. "No ..."

"I always have."

"Please don't ... I can't take it."

"I'm not in love with Annie!"

She wiped her eyes. "But in her telegraphs ... she's expecting a wedding ring for Christmas."

"Well, she didn't get that from me."

"But she'll be here tomorrow?"

"It would've been hard to stop her."

"But ... I suppose, you could have stopped her. I mean, if you've always loved *me*."

I was shocked at what sounded like jealousy. Taking her hands, I pushed them together, held them to my chest and looked into her eyes, as I never had with anyone, sensing an unfamiliar loss of control, like some inner force taking over, not sure what I was going to say until the words came out of my mouth.

"I love you, Venice Grey. I have from that first night we stood here. I want to spend the rest of my life with you. I want you to marry me."

We shared a gentle kiss, and held each other. "Really?"

"Yes."

"You sure you are not just getting caught up in the moment ... it would just kill me ..."

"I love you, Venice. Please say you'll marry me?"

"I love you too, Jimmy. Of course I'll marry you!" We hugged and held on desperately before sharing a frantic kiss.

"I've made a real mess here. I hope the others won't hate me."

"They'll be happy ... they seemed to understand all of this before we did."

"What do you mean?"

"Dolly decided a long time ago that I was going to marry *you*."

"I knew there was something very special about that little girl ... I'm afraid I'll wake up and find out this was all a dream."

We kissed like it would be our last.

Slogging along arm-in-arm, we occasionally glanced over for confirmation that it was not all a dream. About halfway back, she tripped over a rock buried in the snow and pulled me down with her. As she lay laughing, I rolled over and kissed her. After I helped her back up, she giggled like a child, continuing to brush the seat of my pants well after the snow was gone. I turned her around to return the favor. She bent halfway over, and looked over her shoulder in delight, biting her lip in pouty objection when I quit.

"I'm not ready to go to bed yet," she whispered as we approached the house. "Is there a place where we can talk?"

"The barn."

We snuggled together on a hay-padded spot against the wall, kissing again before speaking.

"So how will you handle it with Annie?"

"I'll just tell her."

"Just like that? ... Tell her what?"

"That you and I are getting married."

"God, I like the sound of that. I can't believe this is happening ... I suppose you really should break off one engagement before you announce another one." She grinned. "How does if feel to be loved by so many women?"

The chilly breeze leaking through cracks prompted me to take Venice's hand and guide her over to a shallow stack of hay near the middle of the barn. I ran my hand over her as we kissed, the perfect curve in her waist stirring something primal inside of me. When I slid my hand beneath her blouse onto her tummy, she sighed approval, but pushed it away as I attempted to undo the top button. "Give me a little time," she sat up, incredibly cute with hay tangled in her chaotic hair. "We better turn in."

I kissed her a final time on the porch.

The moon had completed half its journey across the sky as I strolled along in no particular hurry, numb to the cold, toward the nearly finished new house. I tried to flush my guilt over Annie with thoughts of Venice, her lips against mine, the softness of skin under her blouse, but I couldn't avoid flashes of anxiety over the unpleasant task ahead of me the next day. I began to ponder what I would say to Annie, but nothing sounded right.

It was cold and dark when I came in, so I threw a couple of pieces of wood on the fire.

"Geez, what time is it?" Luke squinted at the growing flame.

"Late."

"Business meeting?"

"Something like that."

He chuckled softly and rolled over.

Chapter Twenty-One

Annie was elated that I had made it through the snow. We loaded packages into the car as she chattered on and on about how "wonderful" our Christmas was going to be, pretending to be relieved that Venice and her father arrived safely. Before we left, she went back in for a last check on her father. I had invited him one day in the store, but he told me he wouldn't eat at the same table with "niggers."

Scooting over immediately, Annie spread a blanket over us and snuggled close. "I'm looking *so* forward to our first Christmas together. Just think of how wonderful it will be when we have children. I can buy you a Santa Claus suit. There's one in the catalog that's just precious."

I'd been relatively calm on the ride in, concentrating on the snow-covered roads while remaining resolute in what lay ahead, but now that I was actually with Annie, I found myself petrified speechless.

"I've never cooked for you, but I am quite handy in the kitchen. I'll make pies and cookies for the holidays, and our daughters can help as I teach them. But I suppose Sarah will stay on. We'll need the help. She's such a wonderful cook. Still, I want to cook a lot."

I couldn't manage a thing to say.

"What's wrong, darling?"

"Nothing."

She looked puzzled. "Please tell me you aren't worried how I'll behave. I promise I'll be a perfect hostess. I'm not jealous any more ... now that I know I'll have you to myself."

I unintentionally let out a long sigh.

"What? What's wrong?"

I could only manage a headshake.

"Tell me!"

"Annie, I'm sorry ..." I couldn't get it out.

"Sorry for what? ... Oh my God!"

She shot across the seat and jabbed her elbow violently into the door, wincing in pain and grabbing it with the other hand.

"Are you okay?"

"What do you care! ... One night! She was here only one *damn* night!" She dropped her face into her hands, leaned forward on her elbows and wept.

"Turn this damn thing around!"

Annie wailed louder, as if reversing course made it worse. I backed into what looked to be solid ground, but when the rear tire dropped, my heart did the same. The tires spun when I tried to pull forward.

All she could manage between the sobs was, "Oh my God!"

As I collected rocks to put beneath the tires, Annie's heartbreak morphed into to anger.

"This is just great!"

"I didn't get stuck on purpose."

"Of course not. You're in such a hurry to get back out to your little tramp." She was up on her knees in the seat, leaning forward like she wanted to pounce. "You made love to her didn't you? Just like a man. That's all it takes. It's disgusting! ... a lady like me doesn't stand a chance."

"Of course we didn't do that." I was so out of breath from trying to free the car, I was almost gasping.

"Well I hope you're not fool enough to want to marry a woman like that. She'll never be faithful."

That made me mad, and I wanted to lash back, but it was pointless to argue.

"God knows what went on in Kansas!"

"That's ridiculous."

"God, all of our plans!" She began to sob again.

Mercifully, I got traction on my first attempt. Annie tore right back into me.

"So in just one night, huh? You were swept off of your feet? You loved me until last night? She was *that* good at it. God knows she's probably had enough practice."

I then proceeded to try to explain, trying to shed an innocent light on what had transpired the night before. When I finally said, "I only then realized that I had loved her all along," she stomped the floorboard with both feet. "Shut up!" After a few moments of glaring forward, she turned and slapped me hard on the shoulder. "You bastard!"

I knew she meant to hurt me with that particular name. "Wait a minute."

"Don't you *dare* say a word!" She seemed to be about talked out, so I kept quiet. There was nothing else to say.

At the store, I reminded her of the packages as she stormed onto the boardwalk, but she just slammed the door so hard all the glass in the front of the store rattled.

That Annie had "been unable to make it after all" was accepted with surprising disinterest, though Venice and Sarah exchanged ominous glances at the explanation.

Lunch was another loud celebration. Grey had given each of the children a riddle to challenge the group, and they laughed joyously at our silly responses, taking great pride in revealing the answers. The meal culminated in a demand by Grey to ride out and see the progress on the house.

The temperature was well below freezing, the snow powder dry, as Luke hitched the wagon. Venice and I set out to walk. She waited until out of earshot of the others. "So how was Annie?"

"Not good."

"How did you tell her?"

"She could just tell something was wrong. I was going to wait, but …"

"It's probably best. How did she take it?"

"I think she hurt her elbow slamming it into the door."

"Oh my." Venice took my arm and patted me on the shoulder. "Poor thing."

"I know. I hope she's okay."

"Me too, but I meant you."

Behind us, Grey's laughter disintegrated into an uncontrollable cough. We turned to wait, standing aside as the wagon passed. They were a couple of verses into Jingle Bells, the kids yelling the words as if trying to be heard all the way in town.

When we caught up, everyone was milling around inside, Grey's approval echoing off the unfinished walls. The twins ran upstairs ahead of everyone else. The master bedroom had a smaller version of the downstairs fireplace and a balcony with glass doors. Henry explained that it was designed to watch the morning sun through the trees. It also offered a magnificent view of the river and the hills to the south. As all the others drifted into the next room, Venice lingered over the rail.

"I just love it, Jimmy ... and I love you. I feel like I'm in Heaven."

We couldn't resist sneaking a kiss despite the others being in the next room.

"Let's get married next month," she said.

"The house won't be finished."

"Who cares? All that matters is that we're together. We can sleep in the barn," she said with a puckish grin. "You're comfortable out there." She pulled me against her and whispered, "We should start working right away on a family."

"How about getting married in a week?"

"You're so bad." She pushed at my shoulder. "I better stay out of that barn with you."

As we kissed, my hand drifted down onto her behind and she purred imperceptibly.

The steps alerted us, but not in time; Dolly stood in the door, staring, easing down the hall only after we'd made eye contact.

"Uh oh."

"What?"

"Dolly."

Venice glanced back over her shoulder. "She saw us kissing?"

"Yep ... they'll all know by the time we get back to the house. Little Dolly couldn't keep that to herself if her life depended on it."

"She didn't see your hand did she?"

"I don't think so."

As the rest of them climbed onto the wagon for the ride back, Dolly directed a cool stare at me, studying us as they rode off. Venice reached over and pulled my arm around her shoulder. "They have to find out soon enough anyway ... It's your fault, you know."

"Just mine?"

"You are fully aware, Mr. Crawford, that no woman could resist your kiss."

"Really?" I teased. "I *wasn't* fully aware that it applied to *any* woman."

She swatted me on the chest playfully. "Don't get any ideas mister, you're engaged now."

There were no immediate signs that we had been compromised, only uncomfortable stares from Dolly, who was uncharacteristically quiet during dinner.

Venice and I were huddled on the front porch when Sarah finally came out. Pulling her coat tight around her neck, she gazed out from the edge of the porch. "I had one of those talks with my daughter today that a mother don't much look forward to," she said with mock severity. "Started off with me explaining why Mr. James was rubbing Miss Venice's behind."

"Oh no!" Venice gasped. "I'm *so* sorry."

Sarah looked back over her shoulder. "I take it Miss Annie's been told?"

We nodded.

"You two oughta just go ahead and get married."

There was a pause before Venice said softly, "We are."

As they embraced, I noticed the beginnings of a tear in Sarah's eye. When she hugged me long and hard, it was obvious she was truly happy. "So when is the happy day?"

"Soon," Venice said. "Next month, maybe."

"Lord, y'all ain't give me much time to put on the wedding."

"The bride's father hosts that. We'll be married in Kansas."

I hadn't thought about it, but it made sense. The Grey's marvelous home would be perfect for a wedding. Sarah looked relieved.

"Sarah, I'm really sorry about Dolly seeing us. I'm so ashamed."

"You'll have younguns of your own ... takes some gettin' use to havin' 'em around. Don't worry about Dolly ... she's growing up." She laughed out loud. "It made that child's whole year, gettin' to spread it all around. I'm sure I'll be explaining it to the boys tomorrow."

132

Venice closed her eyes, shaking her head in embarrassment.

Sarah descended the steps. "My, my, it's gonna be somethin' around here. Ol' Grey's gonna holler like a moose."

We laughed. "How's a moose holler?"

She smirked at my playful challenge. "I expect you'll find out when you tell Grey."

We were still chuckling when she disappeared into the dark.

Venice and I snuck out to the barn. She pulled me down on top of her, and we kissed gently and thoroughly. I pushed against her so she could feel my arousal, and she pushed back, but suddenly catching herself, she put her hand on my chest.

"Not 'til our wedding night. I'm sorry. Please understand. I want to be with you so badly. Please don't tempt me."

"Sure, I understand,"

"Do you really? You are so sweet ... it won't be long darling." She stroked my cheek softly.

She pulled me back down next to her, squirming close in a manner that contradicted her desire to wait.

I refused to allow Henry to go to work the next morning. It was Christmas Eve, a time to be with family. And with no one working out at the new house, it made a perfect place for Venice and I to sneak away. It was there we began planning our life together.

Her tendency in business was the direct and simple approach, and she was taking a similar tact toward our wedding, describing the modest ceremony she wanted. It surprised me and hardly seemed possible at the Grey's place, but I certainly liked the idea of not making a big spectacle out of it. Plans to invite only those closest to us made sense. Her biggest concern was her father. She'd already decided Grey would have to come live with us in the Ozarks, despite knowing he wouldn't be inclined to leave his beloved ranch. I doubted he would, and didn't think he needed to.

Venice's attitude about the Bar G had always been that it couldn't possibly function without her, but with our marriage pending, she was anxious to relinquish the duties to a professional manager. "What about Luke?"

"Luke? What would *we* do?"

"Oh quit it," she slapped my shoulder. "He'd live in a magnificent home and manage one of the largest ranches in Kansas. We'd be very generous with the salary."

"I can't see him leaving. He's been here all along. He loves the place."

"*You* love him being here. I bet he'd jump at the opportunity."

As the day cooled and the fire burned down, we sat arm-in-arm, backs to the coals, daydreaming between kisses. The sun was below the hills when we started back. From the dull gray of twilight, we stepped into a bright and boisterous room where the twins were quibbling with Dolly over who was going to get the turkey legs.

"But what if I want a leg!" Grey said.

"You're all gonna get a turkey leg across the behind if you don't hush about it," Sarah said with a playful lack of force.

"Then I'll do without!" Everyone laughed.

As Sarah put the final touches on dinner, Luke and Henry sat at the end of the table going over a sketch while Grey listened attentively to another of the twins' stories.

"Okay!" Dolly got everyone's attention. "Looks who's under the mistletoe."

Venice and I looked up together and traded grins.

"You have to kiss her!" Dolly looked back at her mother, betraying Sarah's complicity in Dolly's little trap.

"Come on boy!" Grey said. "You can't go against tradition!"

In the past, I would have been embarrassed by such carryings on, but we agreed with our eyes and embraced in an at-the-altar kiss. The room went silent, everyone gawking when Venice turned to announce softly: "It's okay, we're getting married."

The room ignited in cheers and applause.

"I knew it!" Grey yelled.

"I knew it!" Dolly said.

We sat down to a feast with two turkeys and all the trimmings, with a half dozen baked desserts waiting to the side. Grey broke out his store of spirits and offered loud toasts to our future. Sarah and Henry even joined in the drinking while the kids watched in fascination as the evening grew louder.

Christmas Day was almost anti-climactic, except to the kids, whose gifts were more than they could have imagined. Grey raised eyebrows all around by giving each of the twins a single-shot .410 shotgun.

"Oh no!" Dolly turned to her mother. "They're too irresponsible for guns."

"Well, *she's* too young to wear jewelry," Billy shot back.

"Hush all of you," Sarah said. "Mr. Grey and Miss Venice don't want to hear you bicker over the beautiful gifts they gave you."

"But Mama, somebody's gonna get their head blown off."

"Hush, I said."

Dolly glared through angry slits as the twins snickered.

Venice waited until later, out in the barn away from the others, to give me a gold pocket watch with a beautiful buck etched on it. The engraving inside said:

"To Jimmy, Merry Christmas (1906) Love Venice." I had been suffering ever since the gift giving had begun inside. I hadn't purchased a gift for Venice. But she seemed to take a strange joy in it.

"I got what I wanted for Christmas." We kissed. "I guess we'll leave tomorrow."

I frowned.

"But it won't be for long," she said in a sweet drawl.

"I'll still miss you."

"I'll miss you too darling ... Come to Kansas soon! Next week even. You can bring back some of my things ... we have a barn." She smiled seductively.

"And you could come back here too."

"Jimmy dear, I have a wedding to plan. There's so much to do ... it's not very long, you know."

When it was time for them to leave, boisterous goodbyes subsided for everyone to watch Venice and I kiss at the side of the car as if it were the end of some romantic movie. Tears rolled down her cheeks as she climbed into her seat.

"I love you, Jimmy!" she waved and blew a kiss as they pulled away.

"Jimmy?" Sarah asked when we were back inside.

"Oh yeah, there's a good bit more to the story."

Chapter Twenty-Two

Venice was right. Luke jumped at the opportunity to run the Bar G. I was a little disappointed he embraced it so immediately, without even a suggestion of sentimental hesitation, but it was a joy to see him so excited. We decided to head to Kansas right away. He could size up his new home, and I would have some time with Venice. It caught me a bit off guard when he packed his things to stay on there. I surprised myself by feeling so melancholy about his leaving, and it made me nervous to think about running the ranch without him.

"You're going to love it," I promised as we pulled out of the gate. "The place goes on forever and the house is a castle. You'll spend a lot more time on horseback out there. It's a great country to ride in ... so open."

Luke smiled. "I know it's just perfect for me. I sure appreciate you and Venice trusting me with the job."

"We wouldn't have considered anyone else. We're lucky to have you. I just want you to know how much you've meant to this ranch. I couldn't have done it without you."

"Yeah you would have."

"Anyway, I'll miss you."

"So what's ol' Grey going to do?"

"I imagine we'll find out on this trip. Venice just decided right off that he'd come live with us, but that's before *he* had any say in it. I'm afraid it'd kill him to leave that place, and give up his precious bird hunting ... you're really going to enjoy that."

"Yeah, I've been giving *that* some thought."

It was almost dark when we came over a hill and Luke got his first look at the sprawling ranch. He stood to take it in. When we hit a big bump, he plopped back down. "I hope I'm up to it," he seemed genuinely concerned.

"Of course you are. It's just cows and numbers ... hell, I'm more worried about runnin' our place without you."

"You'll have Venice." He laughed. "You can go hunting."

"Well, I may have to come over and check on you a lot."

Venice and her father were waiting as the base of the stairs. She ran around to my side of the car before we came to a complete stop.

"Get that nonsense over with children!" Grey bellowed as we kissed, "So I can talk to my son-in-law about important things."

"Bird hunting, I'm sure," she turned to give Luke a polite hug. "Welcome to the Bar G. We're thrilled you're here."

"Come along now!" Grey waved impatiently. "We *must* toast this important occasion."

"Now this is what I'm worried about," Venice complained as we followed him into the house.

"What?"

"Him drinking more when I'm gone ... he shouldn't drink at all at his age."

"Oh, loosen up. He's just having fun ... so he's not coming to live with us?"

"I guess I should have known. It's the only real argument we've had since Mama passed. He can be a stubborn old mule when he wants."

I couldn't help but grin at her uncharacteristic display of frustration.

"He loves the Bar G," I put my arm around her. "It'd put him in an early grave to take him away. He'll be *fine*. Luke will take good care of him. Besides, you can come check on him any time you want."

"I know."

We had a couple of drinks in the study, each with a thundering toast. After introducing Luke to the gun case, we sat down to a steak dinner. Luke's eyes roamed his surroundings, in awe, as I had been on my first visit. It was decided over dessert that he and Venice would spend the next day in her office while Grey and I went hunting, which suited me just fine.

After dinner, we went out to "brush the horses." Venice had prepared a place with fresh hay and thick blankets. We lay between them, kissing, her catching my hand when it ventured too far.

"I'm sorry I'm so shy. It's not at all like me ... I'm nervous about ..."

"What?"

She blushed, not able to look me in the eyes. "Our first time. I'm scared I'll disappoint you."

"That's impossible ... but it wouldn't hurt to practice."

"Quit that." She poked me.

To see Venice, so composed in every other situation, and now acting like a bashful schoolgirl, was wildly exciting. We kissed again, and then she laid her head on my chest as I propped against a hay bale.

"Jimmy?"

"Yes?"

"Annie said something to me, once when you had excused yourself from the dinner table, she said you were quite a rascal with the ladies, said she'd have to settle you down."

"She's always got something bizarre to say. I wouldn't pay it any mind."

I bent down for another kiss, but she sat up, wanting an answer.

"I'm not at all a prude. I expect most men your age have had some experience." She smiled wickedly, enjoying the intimacy of the conversation. "I realize that you have probably been to a brothel like most men."

I took a moment to compose a response.

"You have!" Tell me about it, please ... Oh, I know I'm so bad, but you *must* tell me."

"There's not much to tell. Luke and I drank too much one night in Joplin and followed some guys over there."

"Was she pretty?"

"I guess, sort of. I was real young and she was kind of new at it."

"New at it?"

"About my age at the time."

"What was her name?"

"I don't remember."

"So it was your first time."

I hesitated.

"Jimmy!" I was amazed she actually seemed excited. "Please tell me."

"Well, it's kind of crazy really. I was just a kid. This girl in town, we were really just friends. We used to steal watermelons, smoke cigars. It wasn't like any kind of romantic relationship at all. Well, she and her friends heard somewhere that you couldn't get pregnant if you did it in the water."

Venice's mouth gaped and her eyes bulged.

"Well you know that pool below the bluff?

"Yeah?" she pressed anxiously.

"Well Melissa …"

"Melissa?"

"Yeah. Well, she just had to test the theory."

"And she must have had an awful time trying to persuade you."

I shrugged. "She was the preacher's daughter."

"Jimmy!"

"Well there we were, testing away, when something caught my eye and I looked up. There was my mother, up on the bluff."

Venice gasped. "She saw you?"

"Oh yeah. It was the only time she ever slapped me, hollering about how I'd have to marry her if she was pregnant, how she was the preacher's daughter and how irresponsible I was. At least I was smart enough not to tell her why Melissa couldn't be pregnant."

Venice laughed as if she'd never heard anything funnier. I was astonished that she so enjoyed such a conversation.

"So she didn't get pregnant, I assume."

"No. I was so naïve, she had to explain to me how she knew she wasn't pregnant."

"No!" she said in a loud whisper, devilish delight in her eyes.

"So, you *were* a rascal. My goodness, I don't know if it's safe for me out here with you ... were there any other times?"

"No."

"You and Annie didn't ever ..."

"No."

Venice looked away with a little frown.

"What's wrong?"

"Nothing." Her nervous smile seemed forced. "Oh, I guess ... I'm so afraid I'll disappoint you. You'll be patient with me won't you?"

"I'm as nervous about it as you are."

"You don't act too nervous out here in the barn."

We kissed and came perilously close to making love before Venice suddenly forced herself up, combing the straw from her hair with her fingers. "I'm sorry. Please understand."

"Of course. I didn't mean ..."

She put a finger across my lips to stop me, and then stood to go take care of the horses.

"So, is Melissa still around?" Venice asked from the next stall over.

"She married a lawyer and they moved off somewhere. Louisiana I think."

Venice grinned through the slats. "Good."

Grey and I started out after breakfast with our eager canine posse while Luke stayed behind with Venice. There was a gentle snow and a couple of inches of new powder on the ground, so Grey insisted we hunt close to the house. At dinner, Luke and Venice spoke as if the rest of us weren't at the table, a continuation of their day's work. Grey finally banged a spoon on his glass.

"Enough of that business chatter! We must discuss a proper honeymoon. Nothing but the best! It's my gift, anywhere in the world! Now, where will it be?"

Venice and I looked at each other, not knowing how to respond.

"Daddy, that's too much. We mustn't spend so much money."

"Nonsense! I won't take no for an answer! So, how about it? Paris? Rome? Ah, of course, Venice! Tour them all!"

Venice and I looked at each other, knowing what the other was thinking.

"Well, then," she said softly. "I think maybe Jimmy and I would like to visit Montana." I smiled my approval.

"Bravo!" Grey began to pour again. Venice was too caught up in the moment to worry about her father's drinking.

139

"To Montana!"

"Montana!"

After dinner, Venice and I sat in front of the roaring fire and discussed our honeymoon. We wanted to get into the backcountry and see the wildest places.

"We shouldn't forget the horses. They're probably lonely out there."

"They'll be fine. They've had plenty of brushing.

"I'll behave."

"It's not *you* I don't trust," she said with a naughty grin.

It was bitterly cold as we loaded up early. Venice wanted me to take considerably more than my car would hold, so we went through a prolonged process of switching things out, changing our minds several times about what should and shouldn't go, which made no sense to me since it all had to go eventually. Neither Luke nor Venice shared my melancholy, too excited about the new lives ahead of them. I just hated leaving Venice.

It was lonely on the road, and I tried comforting myself with daydreams of her and me together in the barn, which only made it worse. I attempted picturing myself fishing in Montana, but my thoughts kept coming back to the barn. I made it back in time for a late dinner, and my spirits rebounded when the kids began quizzing me about my trip. Henry reported on the progress he'd made, assuring me the bedroom would be completed before the wedding.

"That'll be the only room they need for a long while," Sarah quipped.

Henry chuckled and the kids looked puzzled.

The telegraph office reaped a windfall from the many dispatches going back and forth to Kansas. Much of it was correspondence between Sarah and Venice regarding the wedding, while Venice and I had plenty of messages for each other. Sarah was picking up the mail and telegraphs, and handling the shopping, so that I might avoid an awkward run-in with Annie. She reported back to me that Annie was acting as if nothing at all had happened, and had even faked enthusiasm when helping Sarah buy things for the trip to Kansas.

After a few weeks, Sarah declared she just couldn't go into town with all the work to do, and I reluctantly drove into the telegraph office myself. Annie came in as I was jotting down a message.

"Well, look who's here. James, how are you dear?"

I glanced at the operator before turning around. He stared over his glasses, eyebrows raised in anticipation.

"Oh, hello Annie. How are you?"

"I'm fine James, or I understand it's Jimmy now."

I glared my displeasure at the telegraph operator for sharing my messages. He looked down and started writing like he hadn't noticed.

140

"I understand congratulations are in order," Annie said with sugary politeness. "Of course, I do wish you both the most happiness."

Annie was always a mystery to me, but this was especially eerie.

"Well, thank you Annie. That's mighty kind of you."

"I understand you put your Montana trip off until summer. I think that is such a good idea. The little darling would just freeze. She'll have to come in and let me order some nice things for the trip."

It hadn't even occurred to me. Venice would have to shop at Annie's store. As fraught with disaster as that was, there was no way around it. Brice's was the only establishment in the area where certain items could be purchased, and Annie wasn't the type to let bygones get in the way of the new money coming to town.

"I am *so* looking forward to making the trip to Kansas for the wedding," she shocked me. "I understand they have a marvelous mansion ... my, don't look so distressed. Surely, you've heard the news ... it seems that Luke has become smitten with me. He's invited me as his guest."

"Well, no, I hadn't heard ... we'll appreciate you being there."

"Oh my," she wheeled around. "I've forgotten my list. It was nice to see you James."

"You too."

"She already ordered today," the operator grumbled after the door closed behind her.

Back at the house, I admonished Sarah for not sharing the news about Luke and Annie. Her grin confirmed she knew all about it. "I thought you wasn't interested in gossip." She poured sugar into some concoction she was mixing.

"Well, *that* gossip I am ... her and Luke, huh?"

"Oh, I could always see he took a shine to her. I think they would be good together."

"I guess. It's just a surprise."

"That don't bother you none?"

"Naw ... I guess Venice knows too."

"I s'pect ... wouldn't be too surprised if Miss Venice bumped that along her own self."

"Why would she do that?"

Sarah just shook her head.

Chapter Twenty-Three

Luke drove down in the Cadillac, loaded with more of Venice's things, to help transport everyone back to Kansas for the wedding. As we unpacked the car, I inquired nonchalantly: "So you and Annie, huh?"

"Yeah. Well, I just thought it'd be nice to have somebody at the wedding ... what do you think?"

"It's great. I just hadn't heard until I ran into her at the telegraph office last week."

"I'm sorry, I figured Venice told you. Yeah, I guess everybody can tell now that I always kinda liked her. Venice advised me not to hesitate this time. I admit I'm a might nervous about it."

"There's nothing to be nervous about. Annie's a wonderful girl."

Henry climbed into the Cadillac with Luke. They were swinging by to pick up Annie. Sarah and the kids went with me. Dolly began immediately yelling at the boys for hanging their hands over the side to brush the tall grass along the side of the road.

"You're sure in a mighty big hurry to get there," Sarah said after the tires slid around a second curve. I slowed down a bit.

Joplin was its usual beehive of activity as we drove up Main Street, slowed by more automobiles than I'd seen there before. Drunken laughter and ragtime piano wafted through open saloon doors while primly dressed couples strolled along the storefronts.

Dolly tapped her mother on the shoulder urgently. "Mama, there's a drunk man!"

"Don't point."

"What a disgrace. I bet his wife don't know he's carrying on like that."

Sarah and I kept our attention forward, concealing smiles from the children.

A few blocks later, Dolly spotted another impropriety. "Look there! That woman is standing on the porch in her night clothes for the whole world to see."

"Dolly, you'll enjoy the ride better if you just relax and not talk so much about it."

The boys couldn't contain their giggling.

"I'm enjoying it just fine. I've just never seen the like. Satan his own self probably lives in this town."

Sarah and I couldn't help but laugh.

We stopped for lunch a few miles north of town in the shade of a hackberry and enjoyed the sandwiches Sarah had prepared. The kids slept after that as we rode without conversation. The sun was hanging just above the horizon when we came over the hill and the Grey's spread came into view. "There it is," I said.

The kids stood and Sarah shook her head in amazement. "Lord have mercy. If that ain't something."

Sarah turned to repeat her lecture on how the children were to behave during the visit.

"I'll keep an eye on 'em, Mama," Dolly said.

"You just keep an eye on yourself."

"Yeah!" in unison.

"I mean it!" Sarah said. "I don't intend puttin' up with one bit of trouble from any of the three of you."

The usual reception committee was waiting out front. Grey waved his hands and bellowed greetings while I kissed Venice. The kids were strangely quiet, awestruck by the mansion and the surrounding grounds. After everything was unloaded and everyone shown to their rooms, Grey led Sarah and the kids out to visit the dogs while Venice and I settled onto the couch in front of the fire, where we shared a long kiss.

"Oh, Jimmy, I am so excited. I never thought I could be this happy."

"Me too baby."

"Baby? Is that me now? I like it."

We kissed again.

"I was thinking, if you agree ... of course I'd never decide anything without my husband."

"Of course."

She poked me. "Maybe we could drive up to the hunting cabin after the wedding. It's not fancy, but we would be alone. I'd feel funny staying here in the house on our wedding night."

"The cabin would be very romantic."

"Really?"

"Absolutely. I think that's a great idea."

"I want us to make love on the hill where we realized we had found each other again."

Her words sent a tingle through me. We kissed, straightening up quickly when the front door swung open.

"No, they have to stay outside," Grey was telling the kids. "They'll only misbehave inside."

"Then they wouldn't be no different than these younguns," Sarah quipped.

"Mama!" Dolly whined.

The boys laughed.

"Well, she ain't talkin' about me," she said to her brothers.

When the others arrived, Grey gave them the same grandiose welcome, referring to Luke as "Boss." Along with Annie's grand entrance, gushing ridiculously over everyone and everything, it was like watching a stage production.

The children gazed with astonished eyes at the beautifully set table with a ham, turkey and half a dozen vegetable dishes in the flickering light of candles in silver holders. Venice had laid down an edict that no alcohol was to be served with the children at the table, so Grey was forced to toast with tea in his wine glass. The children held up their glasses, proud to be included.

"To the newlyweds, may all their troubles be little ones!"

"Here, here!" echoed off the high ceiling to the crash of broken crystal. The twins stared at each other as if they wanted to cry, little more than the glass stems in their hands.

"Them glasses probably cost a half dollar apiece!" Dolly said.

"No they didn't," Venice said. "Don't worry about it at all. They break way too easy anyway. I've broken them the same way myself." Dolly narrowed her eyes suspiciously at Venice.

A young Mexican woman hurried out with more tea for the boys. "We're awfully sorry ma'am," Tom said as she wiped up the tea from the floor.

He smiled when she wiped his shirt. "No problem."

"There's an awful lot of food on this table." Dolly shook her head. "But I don't think I need so many forks."

We all laughed, and Dolly scowled at the twins for joining in.

"At fancy dinners, there are different forks for different purposes," Sarah explained. "There's a salad fork, a dessert fork …"

"But there ain't no salad."

"Dolly, just pick up a fork and eat," Sarah said in a frustrated tone.

The boys grinned and bobbed their heads in agreement.

"Least I didn't break nothing."

"Hush, all of you." Sarah looked over at Venice. "I'm sorry."

"No, they're precious. This is the most wonderful meal we've ever had around this table."

"Here! Here!" Grey bellowed and held up his drink.

This time the twins gently tapped their glasses as if they were made of eggshell, drawing smiles from everyone, including Dolly.

When dinner was finished, Dolly jumped up to start clearing off plates.

"No child, Maria will take care of it," Grey said.

"Well it ain't fair to make her do it all alone."

"I think she's right," Sarah winked at Grey. "It wouldn't be fair."

Annie joined Sarah and Venice in shuttling dishes to the kitchen, Maria visibly perplexed by such a strange turn of events. The heavy front door slammed shut.

"I don't even try no more," Dolly explained to Maria. "Even if you could make them lazy boys help out, they'd just probably break your pretty plates anyway."

The women headed upstairs to examine Venice's wedding dress as Grey ushered Luke and me into the study. We sipped Scotch while Grey listed off who would be at the wedding, adding animated antidotes about most of them. His sister had come in from Tulsa, and was staying at a hotel in Ft. Scott. There would also be a few folks from neighboring ranches, but the ceremony would be lightly attended. "That's the way your bride wanted it! I would have been happy to transport us all to Kansas City for a cathedral and ballroom wedding, but my darling wants it here."

I couldn't imagine what was taking the women so long. Grey had just about talked himself out by the time they came back down.

Venice and I sat in front of the fire after everyone else retired.

"You sure stayed up looking at that dress a long time," I said.

Venice grinned bashfully.

"What?"

"Girl talk."

"About what?"

"It's not important."

"What you say we go brush the horses?"

"No, we better not. I just don't think I could behave myself. I'm sure *you* couldn't."

"What's just one more night matter anyway?" I was only half teasing.

"I don't want our first time to be in a barn."

We kissed briefly before she pulled away.

"Come on, I think we should go to bed."

"Okay, I'm for that."

"To sleep! In our separate bedrooms. You *are* a rascal just like Annie said."

"I think I'll take a walk around before I turn in. Too excited to sleep."

"Well, don't stay up too late. I don't want you looking tired tomorrow."

Venice broke our kiss off short and started upstairs, stopping midway to look back down and smile.

A tap on the door woke me. The harsh sunlight leaking through the curtains told me it was later than I usually slept. One of the teenagers brought in a tray with a breakfast of steak, eggs, potatoes, muffins and steaming coffee. I was sitting up stuffing myself when someone else knocked.

"Come in!"

It made me a little nervous to see Luke already dressed in his suit. "Boy, breakfast in bed, you're really livin' the high life."

"What time is it?"

"Take your time. Annie insisted I get ready so dang early. It's our first date together, and she's bossing me around *already*."

"Get use to it."

He sat with me while I finished eating, and we talked about Annie and him. Despite the newness of their relationship, he was already talking about proposing, but terrified at the prospect of actually asking. I suggested a wedding might be just the thing to put him in the mood.

To the sounds of the first guests, I struggled with my tie. Luke insisted we stay in the room as he had been instructed. I began to feel the slightest flutter of butterflies as the buzz of voices grew. Finally, there was a tap at the door and Luke led me down to where I was to wait at the bottom of the stairs.

I'd not felt overly anxious up to that point, but my hands began to tremble so much I folded them in front of me to disguise my nerves. When a violin player began "The Wedding March," Venice and Grey stepped out and stood at the top of the steps. The first glimpse of her in shining satin sent a chill through me. I strained desperately to make out her face through the veil. As they began a deliberate descent, my tremors grew more violent. When I was able to make out her smile, I was consumed with a desire to leap forward to embrace her, but my legs would have been unable to carry me up to her.

Grey raised the veil and kissed her on the cheek. "Here my boy, take care of my precious daughter."

I took her arm and followed Luke's prompt into the sitting room, struggling with uncooperative legs not to step on the gorgeous gown. Venice was trembling as much as I was. The wide smiles of guests waiting in the sitting room turned my remaining nerves into mush.

As we stepped up to the minister, Luke and Sarah joined us on either side and handed us the rings when it was time. The ceremony drifted by, the minister's voice off in the distance somewhere, as if it were all a dream. It felt real finally when I lifted the veil and kissed my bride. The guests applauded wildly as we held on to the kiss, Grey's howling distinguishable over the others.

The violinist played soft music as guests filed by to wish us well. Grey offered a grand, champagne toast, and then we cut the cake as John snapped photos. Venice startled me by purposely making a mess of my face with the cake, but I found it adorable and smeared her face with cake also, her squeal a precious delight, a cake kiss even more so.

Luke made an emotional toast that caused Venice to blot tears from the corner of her eyes, and then we were called upon to dance.

"My, you're a good dancer," Venice whispered.

"My mother saw to it that I didn't injure the feet of our neighbor's daughters."

Her childish giggle gave me goose bumps.

Grey cut in and danced with his daughter as everyone watched. Soon, others came out onto the dance floor. Annie declared she must dance with the groom, and babbled on about what a gentleman Luke had been, and what a big position he had now. She sounded like she was ready to make the Grey mansion home.

Finally, Sarah took over the reception. "Okay now, these lovebirds have a good piece to drive. We better let 'em get going."

Venice hurried upstairs, where she changed into a more casual shin-length dress. Out front, with the help of the teenage boys who worked on the ranch, Dolly and her brothers decorated the Oldsmobile with ribbons and cowbells tied to the bumper. Our bags had already been loaded, so we climbed aboard in a shower of rice. Billy misunderstood the rice-throwing tradition, stinging my face with a tight pattern at close range.

As we headed down the drive, Tom, Billy and their new friends chased behind us. Venice took my arm and laid her head on my shoulder.

"Boy, little Tom was right," I said as I rubbed my cheek. "Billy can throw good."

"Poor baby," Venice said and kissed the cheek. She snuggled closer. "I never thought I could be so happy. You're really happy aren't you?"

"Of course …"

"I know. Forgive me darling … I know why you were quiet. I think you were overwhelmed."

"I guess I was. You were nervous too. I felt you shaking."

"That was excitement and happiness."

Venice eased her dress up, took my hand and placed it on her thigh just above her knee. "I don't feel bashful anymore," she whispered softly.

Despite keeping the accelerator to the floor, the drive seemed much farther than it had in the past, a tangerine afterglow defining the horizon as we pulled up. As I carried my bride inside, I could barely see the surprise she had prepared. Candlelight revealed that the cabin had been decorated with flowers and wide, white ribbon draped along the walls, the table crowded with food baskets and wine bottles. The bedroom door was framed in ribbon, and inside there was a newly purchased oak bed with a thick comforter and silk sheets, where I laid my wife down and made love to her.

Chapter Twenty-Four

When we finally got up, Venice packed a lunch basket, and we hiked out to the hill where we had rediscovered each other, spreading out a blanket beneath an early spring sun. With not a breath of breeze, it felt warm after a long winter. Venice enjoyed watching me eat, and I was surprisingly comfortable with it. She poured more wine when I finished and then scooted closer to me. After kissing, we laid our glasses down, kicking them over as we made love.

We lay together afterward, staring at the cloud-spattered sky.

"I wonder if I have a baby growing in me already. I hope I get pregnant here. I hope it happens out here."

"Well we won't know where it happened."

"Of course not. I'm just dreaming ... you will be such a wonderful father. You're so good with Sarah's children. They adore you."

"I don't know about that."

"Oh they do. Sarah even said it."

"Is that what you girls talked about up there in your room together?"

"Never mind about that ... I hope I haven't disappointed you, Jimmy?"

"What on earth do you mean?"

"I'm sure I'll get better with more practice."

"Don't be silly. You were absolutely perfect. I was scared I wasn't the prince charming you always dreamed of."

"Oh, Jimmy" she rolled on her side, propped up on an elbow. "I adore the way you make love to me." Venice eased on top of me. "Now, I want to make love to *you*."

"Is this the kind of thing you girls talked about?"

"Maybe."

We stayed at the cabin for three days, leaving only when our supplies ran thin. Our appetites for food and wine were almost as hearty as our hunger for each other. On the drive back to the Bar G, Venice chattered non-stop about how she was going to love living in the Ozarks, and that she and Sarah were going to be such friends, and how wonderful it would be when the baby came. I just listened, recalling that chatty little girl on the train. She was still talking when we pulled into the Bar G.

When we sat down to dinner with Grey and Luke, Venice just couldn't help herself. "Have you spoken with Annie since you took them back?"

"I'd not let that one get away!" Grey said.

"No," Luke said softly. "I figure I might come to Missouri soon,"

"Well Daddy can come with you. He can't be left here …"

"Blah!" Grey waved his hand. "Don't go telling either of us how to manage our affairs missy. You've got your own family to worry about now down in Missouri."

She relented with an obedient nod and smile, something we were all surprised to see.

We left early the next morning without waiting for breakfast. Venice was bursting at the seams to get started with her new life. She had Maria pack us a basket so we wouldn't waste time stopping at a restaurant. This time she snuggled against me, drifting off into pleasant thoughts, with little to say. Worried that she was tired, I suggested staying over in Joplin, but she was adamant about getting home.

It was late afternoon when we arrived. The place seemed deserted, until we heard Sarah and the kids playing out behind the barn. She was pitching a baseball to Dolly, the twins in the field shagging balls, when we came around the corner.

"Well, well," Sarah noticed us. "I was thinkin' y'all might never come back."

The kids ran to hug Venice, and Sarah stepped up afterward to embrace her. "It's goin' to be so nice havin' you here Miss Venice."

"Grandpa's got the bedroom *all* finished," Dolly blurted anxiously. "He's out there right now working on downstairs. Won't let nobody help cause it has to be *just* right. Mama made them Barry boys smooth out that road down there."

"Oh, I can't wait," Venice took a mini hop. "Come on Jimmy, let's hurry ... Well come on." She waved to the others.

"Mama said we cain't be nosey and interfering," Dolly said.

"Nonsense, this is for the whole family."

"I'm not nosey by nature anyway." She frowned when we laughed.

Sarah and Dolly climbed into the car as the boys ran ahead.

Henry was waiting for us out on the porch. "It'll be awhile 'til I'm all the way finished," he called out. "But it's livable."

I was shocked to see the oak floors polished, like the ornate banister on the stairway. Venice held her hand to her chest as she whirled around, appearing in awe of the place, which struck me as unlikely considering how she was raised.

"Come on!" Dolly hurried up the stairs.

The bedroom was a showplace. A plush, white bedspread draped over a new walnut bed with matching side tables. Our clothes had already been put away in the huge matching chest of drawers. The bedroom suit also included an armoire and a vanity with an intricately carved mirror and a chair with a red velvet seat. Matching drapes were tied open with ornate sashes, washing the room in the warm afternoon light of two big windows. A tear dripped from Venice's cheek. "It's just perfect. Bless you all."

"Ol' Mr. Grey helped us manage credit …"

"Hush," Sarah swatted Dolly.

"You all bought this?"

"Well, we wouldn't consider not having a proper wedding gift," Henry grinned.

Venice hugged each of them, and I thought I detected a faint blush on Henry's dark skin when she kissed him on the cheek.

"Now come on," Sarah said. "Let's get those things out of that car and carried up here so they can get settled in."

The twins raced Dolly down the stairs.

"Careful!" Sarah shook her head in disgust. "Get a good look at that before you go makin' yourself up a family."

I still hadn't gotten past my childish tendency of being easily embarrassed. Sarah found an evil pleasure in it, seizing on any opportunity to tease me. My mother had also been like that, and there were signs my wife might enjoy the same pastime. She reached around my waist and patted my chest. "Well, it's *too* late for that."

"I 'spect it is," Sarah smirked and followed the kids downstairs.

I would have expected Venice to settle in first, but she insisted on seeing everything else right away. Each stop was lengthened by Dolly sharing the names of chickens, horses and all the rest of the ranch's residents, including a few cow names I'm pretty sure she made up on the spot. Susie bounced along with us from station to station, showing a preference for Venice as if doing her share of welcoming.

As her first official act, Venice put her foot down, despite Sarah's plans to give us privacy; we would all continue to dine together. She prodded Henry to put the dining room at the top of his priorities.

At first, Venice was determined to do her share of the work in the kitchen, despite Sarah's objections. As a cook, she was a novice, and was able to persuade Sarah that she wanted to learn. Venice came as close to scolding Dolly as she ever would when Dolly suggested the lady of the ranch shouldn't do such menial work.

"There are three ladies of this ranch," Venice insisted.

But it became quickly obvious that Venice's talents and interests lie outside the kitchen. She became immediately obsessed with growing the herd and expanding the property, mounting her mare early each morning to check fences and cattle. Two weeks into our new life together, she organized a trip into town to adopt a lawyer for handling our will and other necessary documents, and then we stopped into the bank where she transferred an incredible amount from Kansas into our own new joint account.

"I didn't work for free," she said when the banker left us alone for a moment. And then she led me over to the store.

"Come in!" Annie waved.

"How are you darling?" Venice said. They traded polite cheek kisses.

Annie soon had catalogues spread across the counter, offering expensive suggestions about how to decorate our house, making a special point to draw Venice's attention to a newly acquired furniture catalog. But Venice knew what she wanted and said she intended to furnish the house mostly with things from the Bar G, though she did order new mattresses for the cabin and bunkhouse.

"Have you heard from Luke?" Venice asked as Annie wrote up the lengthy order.

Annie glanced up with a scowl.

"What's wrong dear?"

"No, I haven't heard anything. I thought he would ... he surely knows there's others ... I'll not be an old maid."

"Ah honey, he's probably just waiting for the right moment. You know how these men are; they're not in a hurry over anything ... and how could someone as precious as you ever be an old maid?"

Annie smiled. "Did he say anything?"

"Well, I know he cares about you a great deal."

I found myself inexplicably joining the conversation. "He told me he wanted to propose. He's just nervous, that's all."

Annie's eyes bulged. "Don't you tease me James Crawford."

"See," Venice said.

"I know I'm being silly. I'm sure he just wants it to be the right moment."

I ended up going across the street for a beer while they sorted out their business. I was surprised a few folks had heard about my marriage. A guy I didn't know bought me a beer.

Venice playfully chided me as we left town. "I hope Luke hasn't changed his mind, since you've announced his intentions for him."

I shook my head in regret.

"Don't worry, dear. They'll sort all that out. We have our own lives."

Luke showed up a couple of weeks later, and delivered a romantic proposal over a candlelight dinner, presenting Annie with a gaudy ring, no doubt financed by a Grey loan that would be forgiven with a toast at a later date. Venice insisted we throw an engagement party, and we did our first entertaining before Henry had put the final touches on the house.

The way Venice threw herself so completely into the ranch made me feel a little neglected. I wanted to spend every minute alone with my new bride. But when we made love in the evenings, she made up for it, as starved for my affection as I was for hers. We established the habit of walking afterward, sort of the married version of the late-night walk we use to take. This is when we talked about other things than ranching. Her favorite subject was children. She loved to suggest names, and I would recommend the silliest ones I could think of just to hear her laugh. On the first really warm night, she insisted we hike down and make love in the water where Melissa and I had. A nightly "swim" became a favorite activity on summer evenings.

We stayed so busy, with Venice's determination to build the ranch just as she had the Bar G, that I'd let our honeymoon slip my mind completely until Venice suggested we go in and order clothes for the trip. Annie tried to talk us into all kinds of things, including fishing equipment. She pulled out a brand new catalog with sporting goods that I was sure she obtained in anticipation of our trip.

"We're not really going up there to go fishing are we?" Venice said as I thumbed through the pages.

Annie flipped through a catalog to women's sleepwear, and Venice ordered me across the store. Annie was able to talk us into a pair of German-made binoculars that cost a ridiculous amount of money, along with jeans, boots and flannel shirts. As she wrote up the order, she informed us she'd be selling the store so she could move to Kansas when she married Luke, mumbling something angry about her father that I didn't quite understand. I was perplexed when on the drive home Venice raised the silly idea of us buying the store, but I steered her interest back to our honeymoon.

Chapter Twenty-Five

We set out on a sultry, late-June morning, our honeymoon itinerary including a stop by the Bar G. On the drive, Venice fretted over her fear that she'd find her father lonely and not taking care of himself, but he was waiting at the bottom of the steps, his usual loud and energetic self. We were a little disappointed when he told us Luke was in Oklahoma on business.

"Never you mind!" Grey ordered when Venice inquired. "The boy has it all well in hand. Your business is in Missouri now, and your thoughts should be on Montana."

John drove us up to Kansas City the next morning. It was getting dark when we checked into the magnificent Coates House Hotel. Venice made me dress up for dinner in new clothes I never would have chosen myself, including a tie, waistcoat and a checkered coat to which I took particular offense. But it was our honeymoon, and I wasn't about to disappoint her. We took a walk through the busy streets afterward and ordered champagne on the way up to our room.

On the train, we deposited our things in our compartment and made our way down to the dining car for a late breakfast. We were served just as it pulled out, and lingered over coffee until well out onto the open plains, staring like tourists at the landscape. After the waiter poured a third cup, Venice reached across the table.

"Isn't it hard to imagine. We met on a train heading west ... Even as children I think we fell in love, as much as a child can."

"Well, you were advanced for your age."

"You remember that?" she smiled.

"How could I not?"

"And remember how we talked about going to Montana. I was horrified at the thought of living in such a wild country, but then you talked about it in such romantic terms. I wanted to go so badly after that, but only if I had you to protect me."

"I wouldn't have been much protection as a skinny, ten-year-old kid."

"Oh, but you seemed so grown-up to me back then ... I cried for two hours after you got off. Sister Mary tried to console me as much as she could, but she didn't have much patience for such a small child so smitten with a boy."

We laughed.

"Come over here," she patted the seat next to her. I came around the table and sat close, my arm around her, leaning in as we watched the prairie scroll by.

After a minute, she turned to me. "Don't you think this is a perfect moment ... just the two of us, on our honeymoon, reminiscing about how we met ... our baby on the way."

It didn't register at first.

"I've only known a short time. I wouldn't have kept it from you for very long, but I thought this would be perfect ... Jimmy?" She looked worried at my lack of response.

"I'm sorry, I'm just surprised. I'm so happy ... I can't hardly speak."

Up to that point, having children was merely an abstract concept to me, but to actually hear that I was going to be a parent overwhelmed me with an instant joy I hadn't anticipated. My tears allayed Venice's concern over the dumbfounded reaction. She took great delight in explaining our kiss to an older couple seated across the aisle. We went back to our room and remained there until it was time to come out for supper.

When we stepped off the train in Livingston, Montana, the mid-afternoon air was brisk with a scent like fresh dew. The land was flatter than I would have imagined, but snow-capped mountains blended with the clouds in the distance. A trio of boys looked like they might wrestle over our luggage, but Venice hired them all, and they followed us down the boardwalk to our hotel, the smallest little fellow lagging behind with the heaviest of Venice's bags.

As we were checking in, a little man who had been standing in the lobby with his wife walked over to the desk to complain. "How is it they get a room when for us it was all filled up?"

"They was reserved," the desk clerk said. "More's coming every year to see the park. We're full up, like I told you before."

After following the clerk up to our cramped room, Venice proposed we head right back out and buy proper clothes like the locals wore, apologizing for the formal attire she had me wear before. The owner of the general store almost tripped over his feet scrambling around to wait on Venice, who seemed willing to add anything to the bill that he recommended.

"It's all very expensive up here," I pointed out as a pile of merchandise collected on the counter.

Venice poked me softly. "Don't go spoiling my fun ... oh yes, and we must buy gifts for everyone, but we'll wait until later." She giggled at my rolling eyes.

The storeowner promised to have our purchases delivered to the hotel, so we strolled arm-in-arm back down the boardwalk. Traffic on the dusty street was a mix of horseback riders, buggies and a few automobiles. It appeared that all the men in town wore the same round, wide-brim hat. Masculine revelry and the sour notes from an out-of-tune piano drifted across the street from a saloon, where a man with a long, black braid down his back waited outside the batwing doors. When a stagecoach came roaring down the street, Venice smiled and wiped the dust from her dress as if she enjoyed the experience.

Back at the hotel, she asked the desk clerk if we could have dinner brought up to our room.

"Ah, no ma'am," he stuttered, but his chubby wife came tearing out of a back room. "Well of course! We'll be up to take you order directly. Can we get you some drinks in the meantime."

"Can we have a bottle of champagne sent up?"

"Uh, sorry ma'am ... I have some white wine."

"That will be fine ... Oh yes, perhaps you can help us with something else. We would like to go into the mountains and see some wild country, maybe do some fishing. Do you have any suggestions on who we should talk to?"

It was clear by now that my wife intended to do most of the talking for us, but it seemed appropriate since she possessed such a natural talent for it.

"I think I know just the fellow," the woman answered. "Do the two of you ride?"

"Absolutely."

"Let me see if he's around."

"Thank you so much, and of course we want to make it worth your troubles."

"Oh no ma'am, it's just wonderful to have a lady of such grace staying with us."

"Aren't you sweet."

To the scowls of other patrons, the chubby woman led us over to the table by the window, picking up a reserved card as we sat. We were taking the first sips of coffee when a wild-looking fellow in dirty buckskin clothes, dark-stained moccasins, unkempt beard and long, gray hair tied in a bushy ponytail inquired at the front desk. He was pointed in our direction.

"So you the ones wants to go to the backcountry?" he scowled as he shuffled up.

"Oh yes," Venice pointed excitedly. "Please sit down and have breakfast with us."

He sat and gazed at us like we were from another planet.

"I understand you can arrange for a horseback trip into the mountains. We're told you're just the fellow to guide us."

"Maybe. I 'magine I'm closest thing to a mountain man left in these parts. Man cain't make a livin' on furs no more. But they's always some tenderfoots wantin' to go adventurerin'. Most give out pretty quick."

"Well ... I'm sorry, what's your name?"

"Jack."

"Well, Jack, I can assure you we'll hold up just fine. We're ranchers and both good riders."

"Don't matter to me."

"What kind of adventure can you provide?"

"I 'spect any you want."

"Okay, what would you recommend?"

"I 'spect if 'is me, I pack up in the Beartooths. Yellowstone country's getting all ate up with yahoos ... wanta get away from all that ... it'd take a couple a weeks. No hotel bed out *there*."

Venice gulped a deep breath of excitement. "That's perfect!"

"Is there fishing?"

"Fishin's good down low. We can hit the Yellowstone on the way in."

"It sounds like just what we are looking for. What is your fee?"

"I don't know; what ya payin'?"

"Oh my, Jack, you must determine that."

"We'll figure it later."

"When can we start?"

"Don't matter to me ... it ain't your time is it?"

"Excuse me?"

"Is it your bleedin' period?"

"Well, I never! ... I'm certainty not going to answer *that*."

"It ain't good. Grizzlies'll pester ya to death ... litterly."

I shrugged at Venice. It seemed a sensible consideration, despite Jack's lack of grace in expressing it.

"Well sir, I'll assure you that won't be a problem," she said as I struggled to suppress a grin.

"Don't matter to me ... I 'spect we could leave day after tomorrow if you'd be ready. You'd need to put up a account at the store."

"Of course." I relieved Venice of having to continue the conversation. "How about we meet in the morning here, and we'll go down together."

"Don't matter to me."

"It's settled then, this time tomorrow?"

Jack shrugged.

The chubby woman came up to the table.

"You eatin' Jack?"

"Already had a fish." He stood.

"See you in the morning." He looked like he didn't understand what I was talking about.

We watched him cross the street. "Are you going to be okay with him?" I asked.

"Oh yes, he's just what you'd expect, though I don't care to discuss my menstrual cycle with him. And you, grinning like a possum. Shame on you." She let a smile leak out. "Maybe we can talk him into a bath. I would think the bears would be *more* attracted to that odor he carries around with him."

By mid-morning we were on our way, a group of children running beside our horses. Our mounts were sturdy, built for climbing, four mules loaded with gear tethered in a train behind Jack's horse. We left town on a road south that ran parallel to the river, well worn from traffic to Yellowstone Park.

"Bastards!" Jack fired an obscene gesture to a passing stagecoach that threw dust all over us.

The flat valley floor narrowed between rocky slopes as we rode toward a powder-blue wall of snow-topped mountains. Scattered groups of antelope stared as we passed, the river's constant hum in the background.

"Will we see any deer or elk around here?" I said, my attention on a herd of antelope mothers, several youngsters nursing but others kicking up their heels playing with each other.

"They're in the high country. We'll see 'em later."

"Bison?"

"Ain't hardly none left ... might see one or two if we're lucky."

We made camp on a high spot over the river. Jack started handing gear to us as he unloaded the mules, making it clear that he expected help. After the tents were up, he built a fire, and I began to piece together my fly rod.

"Rainbow trout in the river?" I said

"Cutthroat ... fancy rig ya got there."

"My mother bought it for me when I was just a kid."

"Hum."

Annie's sporting goods catalog had come in handy after all. I'd ordered trout flies, leaders and a fishing hat that looked a lot better in the catalog than in person. Though it was a short, downhill jaunt to the river, I was out of breath when I made my first cast. On my third drift, a fish boiled just beneath the surface. The line tightened, heavy against the current, but went limp after a few seconds. I was able to land the next cutthroat. As I removed the hook, a pair of coyotes stopped on the far bank to make a quick inspection of me before trotting off on their rounds. I caught three of the golden trout by the time the chill of mountain shadows prompted me back up the hill, only then noticing Venice. From her perch, bathed in the last of the sunlight, she raised her hands and clapped as I trudged up the slope.

Jack roasted the trout on a grate of green willow branches. They were tastier than any fish I'd ever eaten. After our simple meal, Jack pulled out a label-less bottle of whiskey, sipped it and handed it to me. When I handed it over to

Venice, she took a healthy draw. Jack grinned his approval. We stared into the fire until the spirits loosened Jack's tongue.

"I 'spose I said an improper thing in town." He glanced at Venice. "Didn't mean no harm. We don't get many city ladies through these parts. Them around here wouldn't think nothin' about it."

Venice rolled her eyes. "Well, Jack, since you seem obsessed with it, I'm pregnant, so we won't have to worry about that."

"Oh ... I thought y'all was just now a honeymoonin'. Musta jump the gun, I 'spect." He chuckled.

"No!" Venice objected. "We were married in March, but put the trip off until now ... what do you find so damn funny."

"In town you said, 'I never'..." he waved a hand drunkenly.

"Well you *were* rude."

"Expectin' and all like you are, I figure you had to at least once."

I lost my grip on the laugh I'd been suppressing and rolled over on my side. Venice had just enough of the whiskey to finally acknowledge Jack's bizarre sense of humor, smiling as she kicked at me in feigned disapproval.

As the fire died, Jack stood and slipped his rifle into his tent, then retrieved a pistol from a pack and handed it to me. "Don't shoot no griz with that. I ain't filed down the sight yet."

"Why would you file the sight?"

"So's when a bear sticks it up your ass, you can pull it back out."

I rolled again in laughter, sitting up to gather myself as soon as I noticed how terrified Venice looked.

"It's to scare 'em," Jack explained. "They's hunted round these parts, and knows ain't no good comes from gunfire. If one starts nosin' around your tent, just pop it off, somewheres besides at me. Don't worry about it lady. We ain't likely to see no griz 'til we in higher country anyways."

We crawled into our tent as Jack strung the food bags in a tree a short distance from camp.

"Jimmy?" Venice said softly in the dark after we had settled into out sleeping bags. "Don't you suppose he's exaggerating about bears?"

"Probably just adding flavor to the trip."

"You think that's it?"

"Ol' Jack wouldn't have made it so many years if bears were so dangerous."

"Of course. I don't mean to sound so frail. I'm fine now. Good night my darling."

"Good night baby." I rolled over, wondering about the grizzlies in the high country.

The next day, we turned east, away from the river, following a small stream into a steep-sided canyon. We saw our first mule deer, three does staring at us, listening with big ears as we rode past.

"Critters ain't sacred of a man on a horse," Jack said.

It was cold that night at the higher elevation, where we camped in a small grove of aspens. Pulling ourselves away from the fire and the whiskey was difficult. Venice crawled into my sleeping bag after a short time, and we shivered together through a sleepless night. I felt like a little love-making would be just the thing to take our mind off of the cold, but Jack warned us that the scent of romance, "tended to make ol' griz curious."

"He was just kidding," I said.

"I don't care. You can ask him tomorrow for sure, but we're not taking any chances."

I had a sneaking suspicion that Ol' Jack was having a bit of fun with me with that "scent of romance" comment, but I'd ask.

Around the morning's first flames, we watched a dozen mother elk with their half-grown calves grazing in a meadow across a deep valley. Sitting with our backs to the fire, we sipped coffee and took turns with the binoculars.

"Ah," Venice said as she looked through the glasses. "The little ones are so cute. They seem so ... oh my God!"

An enormous bear sprinted out of the trees toward the elk, closing the distance with frightening speed, the smallest calf his target.

"Oh no!" Venice cried. She dropped the binoculars and covered her eyes.

The unexpected blast of a rifle startled us breathless. The bear skidded to a halt, and bounded up the slope away from the elk.

"Thank God," Venice gasped. "Thank you Jack."

"Griz gotta eat too." He thumbed a fresh shell into his rifle.

That night around the campfire, Venice went a little overboard, defending her behavior, insisting she wasn't a city girl, that the bear had only startled her, arguments animated by several pulls from the whiskey bottle. It was the first time I had ever really seen her visibly intoxicated. Before we turned in, she was whimpering about the poor, hungry bear.

"Gonna be tough ridin' tomorra," Jack said, warning her off of the booze. "But it don't matter to me."

I was delighted to discover in the tent that the whiskey had eliminated my wife's inhibitions about curious bears. That was also the first night I ever heard her snore.

We broke camp every morning and rode into new country, awarded on each day's ride with some new treasure: lynx kittens venturing from their hiding place while their mother was away hunting; little red foxes as fascinated with us

159

as we were about them; and the bison bull we startled into a grunting gallop. On the afternoon of the third day, after climbing all morning, we stopped and looked out over a vast mountain landscape from what seemed the highest point on earth.

"Ol' John Colter his own self broke this country."

"Who?"

"He's parta Lewis and Clark. Couldn't stand to leave it behind. Cain't say I blame him."

We followed Jack's lead and dismounted.

"We're going to camp here?" Venice said.

"I figured you romantics'd wanta view that sunrise from here. It'll come up right over there. Gotta stack lots a wood though. It'll be mighty chilly up here."

Jack assigned us to collecting firewood while he went out to kill squirrels for supper. We heard him shoot half a dozen times as we gathered fallen spruce and aspen branches, panting in the thin air after just one load. I was amazed Jack could consistently hit the squirrels in the head with the large-caliber rifle. He explained that to do otherwise would have destroyed the meat. It was apparent that he used the term "squirrel" loosely, since all of his kills were obviously not of the same species

As we picked the roasted meat from its bones to the light of a blazing fire, we watched a half-moon climb above the peaks. A distant wail was joined by a chorus of sad voices.

"Coyotes?"

"Wolves."

"They wouldn't bother us would they?" Venice said.

"Wolves don't bother folks. It's folks bother wolves. Best critter out here. When they's all kilt, won't be no use bein' out here no more."

"Why would they be killed?"

Jack shrugged and shook his head. "People kill wolves. Wolves kill coyotes. Coyotes kill foxes ... same thing, I 'spose ... just instinct probably."

The next day, we stopped high above a vast plain with a ribbon of water snaking down its center. In both directions, thin tendrils of smoke rose from the valley.

"Now you can tell your city folks back home that you seen the park," Jack said like the words tasted sour in his mouth.

"This is part of Yellowstone?"

"Yep ... shame ... don't take long."

"For what?"

"Took the good Lord a awful long time to build up a country like this," Jack glared down at the smoke. "Won't take much for folks to tear it back down." He swung the reins of his horse around, and we followed.

At our request, we began to set camp earlier each day so we could hike alone, explore the country in more detail and discover soft meadows where we'd make love. We became acclimated to the thin air enough that we could spend a good portion of the afternoon climbing and exploring. Jack wouldn't allow us to leave camp without a rifle, requiring me to demonstrate that I could shoot before allowing us to venture out on our own. Not to be outdone, Venice took the rifle from me and demonstrated her shooting prowess.

"Either of ya," Jack said. "Don't matter to me."

Each night, we drank from Jack's seemingly endless supply of whiskey, and he became more talkative, keeping us spellbound with stories of his earliest days, when bison herds stretched on forever. He showed us a scar on his back from a cougar and talked about the Nez Perce people, who he called: "as fine a folk as God ever put on earth." Prompted by distant howling, he explained how a wolf society was like ours, how aunts and uncles helped with pups and how the whole pack works together on the hunt. On our last night in the high country, Jack told us, eyes glistening in the firelight, about the native woman he had married, when he was still a pup, who died of measles while she was pregnant with his child.

Before returning to town, we set one more camp above the Yellowstone, vowing to return as we passed the whiskey in the flickering firelight.

"Best hurry," Jack warned. "Folks'll be out here soon cuttin' the trees, diggin up the earth and killin' all the critters ... I'm thinkin' a headin' on up north to Canada myself. Yukon territory. Maybe Alaska."

When Venice invited him to the Ozarks, he said, "Nah, I don't go that way."

As much as we hated for our adventure to come to an end, a hot bath felt like heaven, and the clean sheets and soft bed were an unimaginable treat. After two nights rest in Livingston, we took the train to Missoula, where I hired a native guide to take me fishing while Venice shopped for gifts. She chose sapphire jewelry for Sarah, Dolly and Annie, and the men each got a hat like the locals wore, garnished with a strip of Indian beads. After a couple of days in Missoula, we took the northern rail lines east and stopped overnight to take in the Great Falls. We shared a hike on our final afternoon, settling on a prairie ridge, arm-in-arm, watching a magnificent sunset. When a large moon drew our attention east, toward home, we strolled back to our hotel to pack.

Chapter Twenty-Six

Grey was waiting at the depot. He had reserved us the magnificent honeymoon suite at the Coates, and we dined at a renowned steakhouse, ordering a third bottle of wine to fuel the storytelling. The next evening at the Bar G, we picked up at dinner where we left off the night before. Before Venice called a halt to the celebration, Grey was making plans to look up this Jack fellow for an adventure of his own.

We skipped breakfast, the sun just breaking the horizon when we hit the road. We stopped in Joplin for sandwiches to eat as we drove. Afterward, Venice leaned over on my shoulder and dozed.

As we pulled up, Sarah eased out on the porch. We could see something was terribly wrong. She remained quiet as we walked up to greet her.

"What's wrong?" Venice said.

"Horrible news." Tears flooded her eyes. "I hate to tell it."

"What is it!" I said.

"They burnt down your beautiful home," Sarah's voice broke. "All your beautiful things ..."

We froze in numb disbelief.

"Daddy and the younguns is out there right now sorting through it, but it don't look like nothin's saved."

Jumping in the car, we sped down the trail. At the first sight of charred remnants, Venice broke into pitiful sobs. It didn't seem real, this "most beautiful place in the Ozarks" now a smoldering scar. We remained in the car, paralyzed, Venice crying into my shoulder. Henry walked up and the kids stopped a cautious distance behind. I finally climbed out on legs that didn't feel ready to support me.

"I'm so sorry Mista James, but I don't see a thing that survived."

"What happened?"

"Looks like somebody come and lit it on fire for meanness. You can see where they tied up below. Weren't no lightnin' storm, nor hadn't been a fire in the fireplace since you was gone ... happened night before last. It was a heartbreaking thing to witness."

"What'd the sheriff say about it?"

"We ain't been in. Them two that you and Mista Luke beat up are in town again. I thought it best to stay put 'til you got back."

I wheeled angrily toward the car.

"Jimmy!" Venice caught up and grabbed me. "Wait ... "

I jerked my arm back and cranked the engine.

"No!" I yelled when she started to get in and didn't look back as I sped off.

The sheriff was sitting out front as I slid to a stop. He rose to his feet slowly. "My home's been burned to the ground!"

He nodded. "I know, James, word's around. ... but they done left town. Nobody even saw which way they headed."

"My folks ain't been in, how do you know anything about it?"

"James, the damn fools was braggin' about it. I didn't hear of it 'til the next morning or I'd a locked 'em up already, but they was gone by the time I heard about it. I telegraphed in every direction to watch for them. Maybe we can catch 'em. They aren't a smart pair, them two."

As furious as I was, there seemed to be nothing to be mad at the sheriff about.

"I'm real sorry, James. We'll do our best to catch 'em. They'll come to justice if I can do anything about it."

"Yeah, I know ... thanks."

"James."

"Yeah?"

"Just so you'll know, there's folks in town that egged 'em on. Some bought 'em drinks after ... it's cause you got those negro folks living out there. That's not my say, mind you, I'm just warning you that there's folks thinkin' that way."

"Like who?"

"James, wouldn't do no good ..."

"Well, you just remember it's your job to keep the law."

"I remember full well what my job is, and I been doin' a proper job of it, and I ain't got no hard feelin' about you, your folks or anybody else, but I can't go arresting folks for crazy talk and buyin' whiskey for arsonists."

"I know ... I didn't mean ..."

"You got a right to be mad. Go home and take care of things and let me hunt those scoundrels down. Them others ain't got gumption enough to cause no trouble, and I'm keepin' a close eye out."

When I shut the engine off, Venice led the others off the porch. It was a tremendous relief when she hugged me and told me it would all be all right, and that we'd just rebuild. Leaning over the hood of the car, we began to plot the future.

"I figured you'd both move back up here," Sarah said. "Daddy's done put up a temporary wall in the bunkhouse. The boys said they can stay in town, but we'll all be fine in the bunkhouse. They oughta just stay."

Venice nodded to me.

"That's sounds good. I'd rather have them out here right now anyway." I paused; they all seemed to know what I was going to say. "It was them same two that attacked Henry."

"I figured," he said.

"Sheriff says there were others in town prodding them on, congratulating them and buying drinks."

"You all go tend the chickens," Sarah told the children.

"They already been tended," Dolly said.

"Now!"

"Mama we already know white people don't like ..."

"I swear I'll cut a switch!"

The three sulked off.

"I guess they done skipped town?" Henry said.

"Yeah."

"Do you expect trouble from the others?" Venice looked worried.

"No, they're all a bunch of cowards. Nobody even spoke up when Luke and I took care of those two last time."

"When was that?"

It dawned on me suddenly that perhaps it would have been proper to tell Venice about that piece of history before now, considering she was coming here to live.

"They beat up Daddy," Sarah explained. "Real bad. They was fired by James cause they said they wouldn't stay in the bunkhouse with black folks."

Venice gasped.

"James and Luke went in and roughed them boys up pretty bad, and they left after that, but now they've come back."

"Maybe we should just move on," Henry said. "Won't ever simmer down with us out here."

"No!" Venice and I refused to hear of it. "*Nobody's* going to be run off of the Crawford Ranch."

"We'll fight." Venice gritted her teeth. "And we'll rebuild the house better than it was before. We're all staying right here, and live wonderful lives together, and we'll kill anyone who tries to interfere."

Sarah, Henry and I traded astonished expressions.

"Do you know how to shoot?" she asked Sarah.

"No."

She looked over at Henry. He shook his head.

"Well, you're all learning, starting tomorrow. We're going into town to buy shotguns enough for everybody and plenty of ammunition. And we'll leave word that we mean to kill anybody that steps on Crawford land."

164

The next day, Venice insisted that Henry and Sarah accompany us to town. They didn't want to, but put up no real resistance. I saw her slip a little derringer into her purse that I didn't even know she owned, and it worried me a little.

As the four of us stepped up onto the boardwalk, we were faced with a couple of older men seated on a bench, glaring contempt.

They flinched when Venice took a quick step toward them. "You really should experiment with some manners. Staring like a couple of ignorant hound dogs is a sign of poor upbringing. You're embarrassing your mothers."

Sarah stepped up next to her and glared down in a way I knew infuriated them. I wasn't comfortable picking a fight, but I found myself proud of our women and ready to pounce on the first one who made an insulting comment. The two men cowered, staring down between their feet as we moved on.

Annie had only two 12-gauge shotguns and a .30-.30 rifle in the store, and we purchased all the ammunition she had on hand for each. She was nervous during our visit, not her usual chatty self.

"Annie dear," Venice said crisply as she wrote out a bank draft. "As you visit with your patrons, we'd appreciate you passing along that anyone stepping on Crawford property that hasn't been invited will need to hire the services of an undertaker."

"Well, I wouldn't want to gossip …"

Venice's icy glare stopped her.

Outside, Venice decided we'd have lunch at the saloon.

"They won't serve us in there," Henry said.

"Yes they will," Venice said with a clinched jaw.

"I don't know," I said. "They can refuse if they want, and I think they would. I don't know if we should go *looking* for a fight."

She stomped across the street like she hadn't heard me, throwing the doors open with a bang and glaring down each staring face as we sat. The bartender took our sandwich order, serving us without objection.

It was a quiet ride home, and Venice said she was going for a walk when we arrived.

"I'll join you."

"If you want," she said with a lack of enthusiasm.

We went the opposite direction from the burned-down house, walking several hundred yards before I voiced what was on my mind.

"Venice sweetie, I'm worried about you. I've never seen you in such a state."

She tried forcing a smile. "I know. I hope you can forgive me. I'll admit that I don't handle my emotions very well."

"I certainly understand."

She shook her head. "I've gone off and made it worse, roaring into town like some wild-west gunfighter."

"Don't for a minute think we don't all agree with fighting back."

"I shouldn't have …"

"No, I think it was the right thing." I managed a smile. "I thought Sarah was going to jump on those two bums on the boardwalk."

Venice managed a grin. "Lord help them if she does."

"That whole town's going to be scared to death of you two women by sundown."

"Oh, and poor Annie," Venice sighed. "I was so abrupt … it's like she'll be family. I must apologize."

"I wouldn't worry about it"

"But it's not her fault. I'll apologize tomorrow."

"Tomorrow?"

"I want to order lumber right away. I want to get that house back up as fast as we can, show everybody how Crawfords do things. Henry's working on a list."

Venice held my arm and leaned over on my shoulder as we stopped above the river. "I just have to keep telling myself that the only thing that matters is right here in my arms … and in my tummy."

Then I remembered. "Hey, we haven't passed out gifts yet, and they don't know about the baby."

Venice pulled at my hand and led me at a quick pace back toward the house.

"I'm really excited about helping with the house this time," she said with a fresh energy in her voice. "It will be so rewarding to build our own home."

"You can't work with the baby coming."

"Don't be silly … Oh Jimmy, I feel so much better now. I feel bad I got so upset when I am so lucky. I hope God can forgive me."

"I think God will forgive you just fine. I just hope he has mercy on the next old codger that stares at you like a ignorant hound dog."

Venice shook her head in embarrassment. "Jimmy darling, as my husband, it's up to you to control me in public."

"I don't think anyone can control you, baby."

At dinner, trying our best to shut out the tragedy, we told stories about Montana, the high-country, the wolves, bears and many of the tales Jack had shared with us. The kids were uncharacteristically quiet in wide-eyed fascination.

"I'd give about anything I had to see a world like that." Dolly stood to pick up plates.

"That can wait, dear." Venice motioned her back into her chair. She retrieved the boxes stacked in the corner and started handing out gifts. She was disappointed that the twins' hats were too big, but the ill fit didn't diminish their excitement at receiving them. "They'll grow into them," Henry said, his hat perched comically on his head.

Dolly was especially excited to receive the same piece of jewelry as her mother. "It's the single most beautiful necklace I've ever seen."

As everyone admired their gifts, Venice made an official sounding announcement: "Okay now, listen up, James has something else important he needs to tell all of you."

I hadn't up to that point understood that I would be making the announcement. Venice poked me when I hesitated.

They all whooped at news of Venice's pregnancy, and took turns hugging us.

"I'll help care for it, Miss Venice," Dolly promised eagerly. "I would love to care for a little baby."

Sarah looked at us with a reassuring wink, and we men retired to the porch for a smoke. For having suffered such a terrible setback, the mood at the ranch that night couldn't have been more upbeat.

The grim reality sunk in over the next few days as we cleared the rubble. The first order of business was to burn off what little hadn't been reduced to ashes. Everyone on the ranch participated. Even the twins chipped in with an energetic effort that not even Dolly could criticize. It was a messy chore. There was something especially cute about Venice, her hair tied back, face smudged with soot.

As had become our habit in recent days, we all headed down to the creek to wash off after calling it a day. As Sarah bent down to cup water onto her forearm, she slipped on a wet, moss-covered rock and took an arm-flailing crash into deeper water. Dolly ducked behind her grandfather to shield her laugh. The rest of us held it in as she rose slowly, her expression humorless.

"It ain't funny, Daddy," Sarah feigned anger as she wiped her face. The twins giggled. "I coulda been hurt."

"Were you hurt?" Henry acted concerned.

"No."

He burst out laughing, and the rest of us let loose, coaxing even a thin smile from Sarah. They teased and laughed some more, but my attention had been averted. Sarah was thoroughly soaked, her dress clinging skin tight, nipples pressing through her dress. Venice noticed too.

"I worry about poor Sarah," she said that night in bed. "She's still so young and pretty ... I wish we could find a husband for her."

"We?"

"Well, you know what I mean. How's she ever going to meet a man out here on the ranch?"

"How do you know she wants to meet a man?"

"Don't be silly ... she has a wonderful figure. We need to buy her more flattering dresses ... I saw that you noticed."

"I did not!"

"Quit that lying." She nudged me with her shoulder. "Don't worry, you're not in trouble. Any man would look. I couldn't help looking myself ... I just don't want her to be lonely."

"I know, but I just don't see how she'd meet a black man. There just aren't many around."

"I don't know why it would have to be a black man."

"Venice!" I scolded.

"I know. I just don't know why that has to be."

"You talk about causing trouble ... I think Sarah's life is best left up to her, anyway."

"I know, but I can't help but worry."

Lord help the next black man Sarah's age who comes through town, I thought as I turned off the lamp.

Chapter Twenty-Seven

Just when we finished clearing off the last of the charred remains, as if on some divine schedule, a tropical storm blew in with soaking rains and washed away most of the fine ash. As soon as the first load of lumber was delivered, we began building at a feverish pace. Everyone participated. Dolly even hiked out each morning after cleaning up the breakfast table. She had a knack for building like her mother and grandfather.

"Mama says I can saw boards even straighter than Mista James," she said one day after Venice complimented her work.

"Child, I said no such thing."

"You did too, Mama. If I was to tell a lie like that you'd whup me."

"Now whenever have you been whupped."

"Well, I just ain't deserved it."

We all laughed. For the first time, I saw her in a slightly different light, more adult than the little girl I'd known up to that point.

When Luke received word of the fire, he rushed over to help. This of course was coupled with Annie's involvement, which was more hindrance than help, not only because she lacked any real work skills or physical stamina, but Luke's attention was constantly diverted to her numerous spells of exhaustion.

After a week, Venice expressed her concern that the Bar G was being neglected, but I persuaded her the ranch was fine. The staff could run the place as good as any of us, and Grey was probably reveling in his freedom.

"That's what I'm afraid of," she said.

"Besides, you can't stand in the way of love."

She smiled and raised a suspicious eyebrow. "Mr. Romantic all of a sudden."

"All of a sudden?"

She had a good laugh.

It was on the seventh night at dinner that Luke announced he and Annie would be married in a month. After congratulations all around, Annie chattered on about having the wedding at the Bar G, like ours, though, she explained, they would have to invite more guests.

I feared a wedding so soon might delay construction, but when I voiced concern to my wife later, she said simply: "You can't stand in the way of love."

Luke took it upon himself to return to the Bar G a couple of days later, and Annie made a dramatic, tearful scene at his departure. Venice lent comfort as she drove Annie back into town.

"I swear," Sarah shook her head as they drove off. "That woman acts like she's in some Shakespeare tragedy. I think she missed her calling."

With the experience of building a house together, we were an efficient unit. I'd honed my skills somewhat and Venice turned out to be a tireless and effective worker, but a little grumpy when you suggested she take it easy. Sarah helped me out by enforcing periodic rest periods for her. It was embarrassing to see little Dolly swing a hammer with better efficiency that I did.

The day we started setting the beams for the second story, Venice informed me that she would be driving to Kansas with Annie to begin wedding preparations.

"Two women can't travel alone."

"Don't be ridiculous. I can take perfectly good care of myself."

"What if you have a flat tire?"

"Hum, I suppose you should show me how to do that before I go."

"I'll go with you."

"No, you stay. I know you're already upset about the wedding slowing down the house, and we won't be gone but a few days ... we'll be just fine on our own. I wanted to take Sarah, but didn't even mention it because I knew you'd get cross about it."

"Since when have I gotten cross with you?"

"You're sounding a little grumpy right *now* ... it will all get back to normal soon."

As we went through the mechanics of tire changing, it was obvious Venice could handle it just fine. I'd send her with three spare tires. I knew she'd be carrying her derringer, which was some comfort, though I wondered if it could kill even a squirrel. I saw to it that they left early, having Annie spend the night on the ranch to avoid her habit of being late.

"Don't worry Mista James," Henry stood next to me, watching them drive off. "They'll be just fine. I 'spect Miss Venice could handle anything you or I could."

"I know."

While she was gone, I worked every day until it was too dark to see. Despite my urging for them to break off earlier, Sarah and Henry insisted on sticking with it as long as I did. We were greeted with Dolly's reprimands each evening for coming in late for supper. The week flew by.

I hadn't realized how much I missed Venice until I saw her waiting up on the porch. I'd knocked off early and been down to the creek to clean up since she was due home that afternoon. We embraced and kissed like it had been months.

"Let's take a walk," she whispered.

Dolly was inside preparing supper; it would have been impossible for Venice and me to be alone. Heading upstream from the house, we found a secluded patch of thick grass and made love.

The children were unusually quiet during the meal and seemed to be sulking about something. Venice and I were sitting on the porch after dinner when Dolly came out and said good night in an unusually somber tone.

"What's wrong, darling?" Venice said.

"I don't reckon I should say."

"I can tell something's wrong. What is it dear?"

"Well Miss Venice, there is, but I best not talk about it."

"Oh come on, I won't say anything."

I poked my wife for such questionable behavior.

Dolly leaned in as if she had a secret. "Them two ignert boys done got themself in trouble, and when Mama gets a temper, she spreads it all around to everybody. I knew she got mad about tattling, but I was just trying to do the right thing so them two boys'd be raised proper."

"So what did you tattle on dear?"

She looked back over her shoulder. "I don't know. I'm in enough trouble already."

Venice put her hands up. "I'm sorry. I shouldn't have asked."

"Well," Dolly stepped in closer. "Them two idiots think it's a fun game to sneak and follow folks and spy on 'em. Well, they saw that you was ... I'm almost too embarrassed to say."

Venice gasped.

"I explained to them that it was just a regular thing and that's how married people make babies. I told 'em it weren't nothin' unusual, but that they didn't tolerate peekin', and they were sinful to keep watching. Them two numbskulls made an excuse that they couldn't make out what was goin' on."

Venice listened in eye-bulging horror, both hands over her mouth.

"I do admit wonderin' why if you gonna already have a baby why you'd be tryin' to make up another one. If it was so you could have twins, I don't recommend it ... well, as I was sayin', them two ignert fools went askin' Mama if it was true what I told 'em, and then she got so mad I didn't have no choice but to tell about how they was spyin', and then I was accused of tattle telling. I swear, when Mama gets mad ..."

Venice sighed. "I can't believe ... we should have been more discreet."

"What's discreet?"

"More secret."

"Well, I 'spect so."

Sarah was moving around inside as if she was about to come out.

"Good night," Dolly whispered, and took off running for the bunkhouse.

Sarah came out after Dolly had escaped her notice.

"Oh, Sarah," Venice whined. "I'm ... we're *so* sorry."

She glared her displeasure. "Mista James, when you said we should educate these younguns, I didn't understand exactly what you had in mind."

"I feel so ashamed," Venice said. "I'm just mortified."

"Me too," I said.

Venice poked me in the ribs for my lack of sincerity.

"We're just so ... we just ... God this is embarrassing." Venice's voice was cracking as if she might cry.

"Don't fret it *too* much. There ain't nothin' wrong with wantin' some time alone with a husband, especially since you been gone. We're pretty tight here for the time being. It's just with these ill-behaved younguns, a person's gotta be awful careful. It's my fault. I should have 'em more under control."

"No," I said. "They're just being boys. It was our fault."

"And I s'pose my daughter just couldn't wait to tell you all about it?"

"No, not at all," Venice said. "I had to drag it out of her."

"That'd be a first." She started down the steps. "I better get out there, they're probably pestering dad about it right now."

Venice covered her face with her hands. "Oh my God ... those poor children."

"Oh, it was high excitement for them." I stood and reached down for her hand to take her inside. "I can only think of one thing to get our minds off such embarrassment, and we'll have a door closed behind us this time."

She pretended to resist.

The next evening she complained desperately: "The twins are staring at my breasts! I had to avoid them all afternoon." She slapped my shoulder when I laughed. "It's not funny! It's horribly embarrassing ... they should be talked to."

"They're just being boys ... try and understand darling, your *beautiful* breasts were the first ones they'd ever seen in person. How could they get that off their mind so soon."

She buried her face in her hands and fell back on the bed.

Chapter Twenty-Eight

We left the Barry boys well armed and camped out at the construction site while we were away at Annie and Luke's wedding. Venice also put the sheriff on alert and made sure it got around town that the place wasn't being left unattended. Such precautions were excessive, with the two troublemakers on the run, but we were in no mood to take risks. At the last minute, Henry decided to stay and work on the house, opening up the option of Sarah leaving the kids. Dolly was indignant, but not even a few tears could sway her mother.

Venice had seen to it that our wedding was modest and practical, but Annie veered off in another direction, with Grey providing whatever funds she cared to employ. The night before the wedding, there was an extravagant feast and a trio of musicians from Kansas City performed. There was an elaborate banquet and reception after the wedding, before the newlyweds departed for a lengthy honeymoon in New Orleans. Venice was miffed about the extravagance of the wedding, knowing her father bankrolled it all, but he was having such a good time entertaining that she tolerated it.

When the first cool breezes of September arrived, Venice was beginning to show. I put my foot down about her working, but it didn't prevent her from being out there everyday, lending advice and encouragement. Henry was incredibly patient with her. When the exterior of the house was completed, I started putting back firewood. The baby would be born in the coldest time of the year, and I wanted to be as prepared as possible.

Venice decided we needed to head up to the Bar G for a few days before it got too cold, and despite my assertion that we needed to let Luke and Annie have their space, she cleverly got her way with me, as usual. "I need you to take Daddy hunting. I want to know how he's doing. He's not going to be able to walk like that forever."

I didn't bother to suggest that it'd kill Grey for sure if you took away his beloved bird hunts, aware that she likely had other motives. I sensed it wasn't Luke or Grey she really worried about; she wanted to make sure Annie wasn't running rampant with Grey's bank account. I also think since she wasn't allowed to work, she was getting a little bored.

Not unexpectedly, Venice insisted on joining us on the hunt. I finally agreed to her walking behind, observing from a short distance, mainly because she looked so damn cute in that tweed coat, buttoned tight around her belly, accentuating the perfect curve in her lower back.

Venice was thrilled with what she found in Kansas. Grey out-walked all of us, killing twice as many birds as I did. Luke had a firm hold on the Bar G with big plans for the future; and Annie had seized control of the household, running it efficiently, and was becoming annoyingly overprotective with Grey. While we were out hunting, he groused about only being allowed to drink twice a week. That struck me as a little beyond Annie's prerogative, but Ol' Grey found no sympathy in his daughter.

A few days after we got back, Sarah returned from town in a tantrum. "Old man Brice says he don't sell to black folks, though that wasn't the terms he used."

"That son of a bitch! ... I should have figured."

"I s'pose you'll just have to buy supplies yourself now that Miss Annie's left."

Venice snorted. "Well we're not doing business with *that* man."

"But it's the only store in town."

"We'll go to Joplin or Neosho until he sells the store ... we might just open our own store."

I shook my head. "We'll just order whatever we need from catalogs. That's how it's all going these days anyway."

Not about to tolerate such bigotry, Venice was ready to cut ties with the church and any other whites-exclusive activity, which was everything in town. It sounded like she wanted us to remain more isolated than I thought was healthy. She made up her mind to teach the children to read, write and do arithmetic, vowing to do the same for our children.

She was determined to out-teach the whites-only school, laying out detailed study plans, ordering all kinds of books and supplies and blocking off different parts of the day for group and individual study. Teaching unearthed a new love for her, fueled by the kid's innate thirst for learning. In bed at night, I had to compete for her attention with whatever she was studying in preparation for the next day's lesson. I enjoyed peeking through the door at her when I came in from work, the perfect portrait of motherhood, preciously pregnant in her rocker, attentive children at her feet listening to her read.

Five days before Christmas, Dolly came running out to get me; the baby was coming early. The concern on Sarah's face and the urgency in her voice frightened me. I drove faster than I ever had, nearly flipping twice, the whole time praying a tire wouldn't give out. The two minutes it took for the doctor to collect his things were excruciating. We raced back to the cabin, arriving just minutes before the baby was born. I waited alone after he went in with her.

Not long after I heard the faint cry, the doctor slipped back out the door with a pained expression. "He's early James, he's awfully small."

"Is he going to make it?"

"First week'll tell a lot. You can go on in."

Sarah was just handing the baby to Venice after wrapping him in a blanket. I was stunned at how tiny his body was. Sitting close to her, I laid my head down on Venice's shoulder, too nervous to reach over and touch the baby.

"What'd he say?" Venice said.

"First week is probably going to tell."

"Best try and get him to eat," Sarah urged. He nursed eagerly. "He'll be fine if he eats like that."

Christmas passed with little notice as we held vigil. The doctor's tone hadn't offered much encouragement, but Venice and Sarah were determined to will the little fellow to live. Sarah slept in the room with Venice and the baby, holding him while Venice dozed. I slept on a makeshift bed just off the dining area, spending the days feeding the fireplace and waiting in helpless anxiety. Henry took time out of his work each day to sit with me, but it was Dolly who offered the most comforting words.

"Cain't a baby have no better care than Mama and Miss Venice," she voiced a reassuring confidence. "He just needs to grow a little, that's all. Mama said he was doin' just fine, eatin' like he oughta. Don't you fret Mista James; God'll look after a fine baby like that."

After a couple of weeks, our son had gained some strength and a little weight, his crying more vigorous. Only then did Venice and I have that moment we'd expected the day of our child's birth. She handed our son to me. I don't ever remember being so nervous, sitting for fear of my legs buckling. I wanted to talk to the little guy, but couldn't quite come up with anything.

"I figure it's about time to give that child a name," Sarah said.

Up to that point, we'd shared an unspoken fear that a name would make it more painful if the child didn't make it. But it suddenly seemed absurd that we hadn't named our son.

Venice smiled up at me. "So Mr. Crawford, what is your son going to be called?"

"Theodore."

She frowned.

"After Theodore Roosevelt. We'll call him Teddy."

"Teddy! ... I like it."

"That's a right friendly name," Sarah agreed.

"Theodore James Crawford," Venice declared.

"Perfect," Sarah nodded.

I went in the next day to send word for Grey to come meet his grandson, and he arrived the following afternoon with Luke and Annie. His whooping scared the little fellow at first, but once he got a handle on it, Teddy was content in his grandfather's arms. Annie, like all women, was anxious to help with the baby, a bit miffed when Sarah steered her out to the kitchen. Sarah had staked her claim on Teddy's care and wasn't going to be denied.

Grey looked weepy when they left, and even more disappointed when Venice told him how long it would be until she was comfortable traveling with Teddy. It was her asking him again if he wanted to come live with us that finally prompted him to climb into the car.

Teddy embraced life with a voracious appetite and powerful vocal chords. Henry claimed he cried so much because he was always in somebody's arms and didn't get enough rest. But Teddy had become accustomed to being held and vehemently voiced his displeasure over crib confinement when he was in the mood for attention, which was most of the time.

"That child's gonna be spoiled rotten," I overheard Dolly say one day.

"All baby's smell that way," Sarah teased.

"Mama!"

"Maybe he just needs his diaper changed."

Dolly laughed. "Mama, you been in a good mood ever since little Teddy came."

"Baby's make a house feel good."

"They *sure* do."

Henry was disappointed that Teddy arrived just days before he completed the bedroom and nursery. And then Sarah and Venice decided it best not to make the move till the house was finished. Sarah began to help Henry finish out the interior while Dolly handled domestic chores. The twins made themselves scarce, the distant popping of their shotguns prompting Dolly to grumble about their absence.

When the house was finished, Henry escorted us inside with pride. Venice declared the house "perfect," which wasn't far from the truth. Henry had seen to every detail, walnut shelves and cabinets, highly-polished oak floors, an enormous rock fireplace and intricate banisters framing a wide staircase in the middle of a high-ceiling room. There were more windows than I'd seen on any other structure, based on Henry's belief that the trees and hills made the best wallpaper.

Sarah was adamant that Venice, Teddy and I start having family meals to ourselves. She believed it important to developing a family unit, and we figured she probably felt the same about her own family. We hated watching her prepare our meal and then rush back to help Dolly cook, but she wouldn't have it any other way. When I shared with Venice how Mother had done things, she embraced the tradition of having everyone on the ranch join us for Sunday lunch. It was a great time to catch up, and Venice had each of her students recite something they had learned that week. Everybody at the table was taking great pride in the kids' progress.

On a late-summer afternoon, as Henry and I were building fence, enjoying a chuckle over something one of the kids had said, he put his hand to his chest, laboring to regain his breath.

"Sit down!"

"I'm fine." He waved me off as he leaned against a tree. "I just got a little winded."

I held the canteen up for him to drink. "It's awfully hot. We need to call it quits."

"I'm fine, James."

I fanned him with my hat.

"I'm okay. Don't bother with that."

That night I talked to Venice about it. "He's slowing down," she said. "We won't let him argue with us about it."

"Oh, he'll argue about it."

"But surely he knows he has to at some point."

"Venice, when he admits that, he admits he's getting old. No man is going to accept that too easily. ... maybe he *did* just get a little overheated. It was pretty hot."

"No, Jimmy, he needs to slow down ... maybe he should retire."

"I just don't want him to feel like he's not needed."

"Well, you're right about *that*. Sarah was worrying the other day that as her dad got older, they wouldn't be needed here any more."

"What? They're like family, it's not about how much they are needed ... of course we need 'em. This place doesn't run itself."

"I told her that, but it's bothering her, and I know Henry has got to be thinking about it too. You need to make sure they know they have to stay here permanently."

"You don't think they *want* to go do you?"

"They're scared to death of the thought. Poor things. You have to make sure they know."

"Hmm, maybe ... "

"What?"

"If they had their own place ... maybe we should build a house ... deed them the land."

"That's prefect! Let's tell them tomorrow."

"Whoa now. Let's be careful. Ol' Henry'll blow all up with pride. I think maybe I should talk to Sarah about it first."

177

It took a couple of days before I caught Sarah alone. "I want to talk to you about something."

"What's that, James?"

"Things are going real good now on the ranch." Concern flashed in her eyes. "Venice and I think it's time to pick out a place to build you a home." She looked puzzled. "Maybe carve out a spot on that new tract."

Sarah's incredulous expression caught me off guard. She raised her hand to her chest. "James, we couldn't never afford that."

"There wouldn't be any cost. It's our payment for everything you've done around here, and what you mean to the place ... me and Venice insist."

Shaking her head in slow motion. "Oh my Lord in Heaven," she sniffled. "I don't know ... Dad ain't gonna just accept charity like that ... I hadn't thought I'd ever have a house of my own ... God has blessed us too much already."

"We're blessed to have you here. We're doing this because we don't want you to ever leave."

She blotted tears from her cheeks. "If it weren't so improper, I swear I'd kiss you right on the lips."

"I think a hug'd be proper enough."

Sarah stepped back and wiped her eyes. "I'd like to plant my own garden."

"You'd make the kids do all the picking."

She smiled. "I mean a flower garden, right on the front of the house, so you could smell 'em when you sat on the porch ... it's gotta have a big porch."

"Sarah, there's one more thing I want to talk about."

She looked worried.

"Henry's getting along too much to keep pushing like he's been doing. It's time he took it a little easier."

"I know," Sarah shook her head. "But gettin' him to do somethin' he don't want to do is gonna be mighty difficult. A man as prideful as my father ain't gonna admit he's gettin' old without a tussle."

"Yeah ... I think building a new house would be easier on him than running fence. I figure he's got another house in him anyway."

"I reckon that."

Venice delighted in telling me a few days later how Sarah laid the law down to her father as she never had before, not allowing any argument about the house, the land or his slowing down. I would have loved to have listened in on that conversation, but I knew I'd be getting ample details from Dolly.

Dolly got her first opportunity to sit alone with Teddy as Venice and Sarah hiked out to the new property to scout potential home sites. They came back excited, and Venice insisted that everyone join us for dinner that evening so we could discuss it. Dolly was just as anxious to tell about her babysitting experience.

"He cried once, but I picked him up and he settled right down. I just think he wanted some attention. I was thinkin' he needed changin' but I checked his drawers, and they weren't dirty. Then I was scared that he was hungry, cause Miss Venice wasn't around for him to feed on her bosom."

The boys giggled, Venice cringed and Sarah shook her head in embarrassment.

"There ain't nothin' funny about that!" Dolly reprimanded the boys. "You ol' two dumb numbskulls."

"You're the numbskull!"

"Ain't nobody at this table too big to get a switching" Sarah said.

"I 'spect Grandpa is," Dolly said.

"Well I 'spect *you* ain't."

Dolly glared over at her snickering brothers.

Venice changed the subject. "Oh, we found the most wonderful spot. There's a little valley with lots of big trees and a spring branch that looks like it keeps a permanent flow. The spring is just a short distance up, coming out of a cave under a large rock wall ... the most gorgeous blue pool."

"It was awful nice," Sarah beamed. "'Bout as pretty a spot as I've ever seen."

"I know just where you're talkin' about," Henry said. "It *would* be about perfect. But I want to look for signs of flash floodin'."

"We thought we'd build up the slope a bit," Venice said.

"We?" I grinned over at Venice.

"Oh of course this is your place," she said to Henry. "The decisions are all yours, of course ... I'm sorry, I'm just excited about it."

"I think we should decide it all together," he said.

Smiles shone all around the table.

179

Chapter Twenty-Nine

Henry designed a far more modest cabin than we felt he should, but we left that up to him and Sarah. He agreed with the women about building up on the slope, pleased with their choice of sites among a half dozen towering white oaks. The porch would command the view of a pretty little valley spared completely from the scars of man. We learned early on that it was a favorite haunt for a variety of wildlife, including a bear and her two cubs. After coming across them one morning, we began to tie Susie up while we worked. She'd already suffered a lapse in behavior a few days before, running off after a bunch of turkeys.

Henry, Sarah and I built the cabin while the Barrys handled the ranch work. We maintained a modest pace, taking off the coldest days and keeping workdays short to ensure Henry didn't get too exhausted. He didn't put up too much of an argument. We all went back to dining together, Venice still honing her kitchen craft as Dolly served as willing instructor. As Easter drew near, we were nearing completion of Henry's cabin.

The sheriff showed up at the ranch on the first really warm afternoon to inform us that the men suspected of burning our place had been arrested in Arkansas and were being transferred to Missouri. I'd have preferred never hearing of them again. I certainly didn't care for the prospect of being involved in a trial. Venice took it in stride. She'd been preoccupied in previous days. I asked her about it one night in bed.

"It's nothing really ... I hoped to be expecting by now."

"Isn't it awfully soon?"

"I want a little girl so bad. And I want her to be close to Teddy's age."

I squirmed up against her. "We'll just have to work harder on that."

"I'm worried."

"I'm sure it'll be fine."

"You sure seem to be okay with everything ... I'm not keeping you up am I?"

"No ... baby, we just had Teddy. Maybe if you'd relax, you might get pregnant." Her frown turned halfway to a grin. "Your body might be like me; we don't work so well under pressure."

She laughed, but quickly pretended to be serious, placing her hand on her lower stomach. "You may be right. Maybe we've been trying too hard."

I tickled and she squealed. "I didn't mean *that.*"

The quiet and pleasant summer snuck past us. It didn't seem possible that the leaves were starting to change. An unusually early snow was falling the morning Teddy took his first steps, a milestone celebrated with much hoopla and a special dinner. Beautiful, like the season's first winter blanket always is, the storm was a portent of things to come. That was a bitter winter, with more snow than I had ever experienced. And the one spell of slightly warmer temperatures was punctuated by an ice storm that broke dozens of massive branches and destroyed fences all over the property. I worked out in the cold with the boys as much as I could, repairing fence, feeding cattle and busting ice so they could drink, but Venice was adamant that the boys were hired to do that work. My job was raising Teddy.

We spent the bulk of our time together in front of a blazing fireplace. I was assigned the task of tending to my increasingly mobile son while Venice worked with her students. I'd sit and listen when he napped, impressed with the children's knack for learning. Venice had a way of bringing out the best in them. When the weather warmed, she let them out early, allowing all of us to enjoy the spring.

We started taking Teddy down to the river that summer. We fished, swam and had cookouts. I even hosted a few camping trips for the kids. Venice joined us on the first one after I won an argument over whether Teddy was old enough. Even Henry spent a few nights on the gravel bar with us. Venice and I took advantage of the nicest days with horseback rides through the hills while Dolly sat with Teddy. She enjoyed playing mother to him, but Teddy was not happy being left behind. "He cried almost the whole time" was Dolly's normal report. We paid her a babysitting fee, agreeing that it was unnecessary to mention that to Sarah.

Almost every summer evening was spent on the porch. Teddy dozed off early, and Venice put him to sleep just inside an open window. We sat for a half hour at a time without saying a word, taking in the night sounds. Occasionally, a group of coyotes howled out in the distance, prompting Susie to raise her head and cock her ears, but she dropped her head in disinterest when they went silent.

The sheriff drove back out on an August evening to let us know the county attorney wasn't going to prosecute the arsonists after all, due to a rash of witness memory lapses. That was fine with me. I didn't want to dredge it all back up, but Venice was unnerved that they were still "out there."

The only other matters that threatened our tranquil summer were when the twins were caught spying on their sister as she bathed and Venice's announcement that she'd met a new friend in town.

She flashed a puckish grin at me as she brushed her hair. "I met the nicest lady today, and we began to visit. She talked about how she grew up here and mentioned that her father was a preacher, and then it hit me. She was *that* Melissa."

"What?"

"Oh relax. We're all grownups now. She's very nice … you'll be happy to know that she's still *very* pretty. I can see why you wanted to ... uh, go swimming." I adored a particular laugh Venice enjoyed so, throaty and deep from her chest like she'd lost control, and mischievous like she'd discovered something she shouldn't have, but on this occasion, I found no charm in it.

"You didn't let on that you knew anything about that?"

"I swear Jimmy, I think I'll be embarrassed to take my clothes off in front of you, knowing you've seen her. She has a beautiful figure." Venice cocked her head as she studied herself in the mirror. "Do you think I gained weight with Teddy?"

I rolled my head in frustration

"You were children. We had a good laugh out of it."

"What!"

"Don't be so sensitive."

"Please tell me you are just aggravating me."

"The poor dear's husband was killed, so she came back to be close to her parents. She has a little boy. I thought it would be nice for him to play with the children. He's just a little older than Teddy. They could be friends."

As my thoughts strayed, I found myself remembering Melissa fondly.

She wheeled around to challenge me. "And what is that wicked little grin! Oh my God, you're picturing it right now."

"Don't be ridiculous."

"I don't believe you mister. With that naughty smile on your face?"

"Quit it."

"Oh my, I've touched a nerve. Forgive me sweetie ... I hope I can behave myself whenever she comes to visit." Her cackling caused me to share that concern.

We went to Kansas for Thanksgiving. Annie had delivered a healthy baby girl, Elizabeth, a few weeks before our visit, and Venice fawned over the child as if it were her own. I noticed a frailty in Grey that I hadn't seen previously, but it didn't affect the volume of his voice or his determination to hunt birds. We had a wonderful time roaming the hills during the day and toasting our day in the field over dinner.

It had been a mild winter up to the point when the Bar G crowd arrived for Christmas. Venice and I were in our rockers watching Teddy play on the porch when they rolled in.

"Ho, ho, ho!" Grey bellowed from the car as he waved at the kids, running up from their cabin to greet him. Henry and Sarah arrived after a few minutes and provided more cooing over baby Elizabeth. Annie looked anxious as Dolly held her, though Dolly looked strikingly mature in the way she handled the infant. Venice remained quiet and her smiles looked forced. That night, as we turned in, I asked her about it.

She let out a sigh. "Oh, I've accepted it, Jimmy. I really have ... I just remember my mother combing my hair as we'd talk. I'd mostly talk. She'd just listen. It's when I would dream, and I'd share those dreams with her. It just seemed like everything was possible. I used to tell her that you would one day be my husband. How foolish that must have seemed to her then. And now look ... I'm ashamed of myself sometimes for wanting more when I have so much."

"You've got no reason to be ashamed. I know lots of families with children *years* apart."

"I know. Sarah says fretting over it is part of the problem. I don't really believe that, and I doubt that she does either."

"I was thinking, and I believe it's really too early to even discuss this yet, but maybe we should adopt a little girl. Look what a good thing adoption was for both of us."

"That's a marvelous idea, and I'd thought of it too, I just ... that would be like accepting, finally, for good, that we wouldn't have our own. I can't, not just yet."

"Even if we have many more of our own, maybe we should adopt anyway."

She hugged me and we tried again to conceive a daughter.

Venice had a craving for the company of others that I didn't share. Her earlier rantings about shunning anyone from town were merely a reaction to loosing the house. Though those experiences made her quite particular about her circle of friends, she was increasingly asking people out to the ranch. When she decided to host a Christmas party, I encouraged her, until I saw how crazy it made her. She handed out instructions as if failing in the tiniest detail would be a catastrophe. When the twins slipped out, I was tempted to join them, but decided to be a supporting husband and went about my assignments along with everyone else.

We were dressing, guest arrivals still more than an hour away, when I finally got around to asking who was attending her soiree.

"Oh let's see," she spoke to my reflection in the mirror as she put her hair up. "Jesse ... you haven't met him. His family bought the store from old man Brice. He has a new bride, Miriam. She's just precious. And they have family visiting. The doctor and his wife are coming, and oh! I forgot to tell you; Melissa's coming."

"What?"

"Relax, she's very nice. I saw her last week. Her little boy should be a perfect playmate for Teddy ... did you see what your son did to the decorations on the table?" She scowled and shook her head.

Venice's innate composure took over as her guests began to arrive, and she greeted each as if they were the guest of honor. The house was beautifully decorated with all manner of festive food and drink set out. Dolly was assigned coat duty, and the twins helped with horses and buggies. Annie served as a sort of co-host, and Venice made sure Sarah was recognized as a hostess also, rescuing her from those who might assume it was her role to fetch them drinks. Henry and Grey settled into the corner together, occasionally bursting out in laughter as they enjoyed watching the affair unfold.

Melissa was among the last to arrive, stunning, as she stepped in and embraced Venice and Annie. "Jimmy!" Venice waved me over.

"Melissa, you look beautiful as always," I gave a polite kiss on the cheek. Annie frowned at the comment.

"Oh dear, where is your little one?" Venice said.

"I left him with Mom and Dad. He's at that age he can be such a handful."

"Oh my. Teddy was so looking forward to meeting him."

"We'll arrange it soon."

The party came off without a hitch, the guests' reactions all Venice could have hoped for. The area had never experienced such an elaborate celebration. I knew, as the last of them left, Venice's Christmas party would become an annual event.

Chapter Thirty

Finally accepting that I didn't share her obsession with socializing, Venice sought avenues for interaction that didn't involve me. Her initial idea was a book club, but I reminded her that Sarah couldn't read, so she decided instead to form the "Ozarks Ladies Club." I thought it was a fine idea until Venice invited Dolly. This meant Teddy was mine during these activities. I certainly didn't mind the time with my son, but I had envisioned it an opportunity to slip out hunting or fishing. Teddy was still a little young for that.

It did seem appropriate for Dolly to be in the club. Approaching her mother's height, she was becoming an attractive young lady. She had mostly outgrown bickering with her brothers, though they weren't ready to turn loose. They made fun of the way she walked, swinging their hips in an exaggerated fashion while holding out their shirts to imitate her breasts. She would only respond with a dismissive, "grow up."

One day when Venice took Dolly in with her to run some errands, they stepped into the general store to find a young black man sweeping. He was tall and thin with bright eyes and a contagious smile. Venice told me about it that night like she'd memorized every word.

"'How can I help you ladies today? '" She imitated his formal politeness. "I waited for Dolly to say something but for once in her life ... I had to step in and do all the talking."

"Oh no, you hate that."

"Hush ... you should have seen them; they were so cute. It was *so* obvious that they liked each other. He's a handsome young fellow. Poor Dolly, she was so nervous. She asked me on the way home if he would think she was too young ... made me swear to not to breathe a word of it."

"It didn't take long for you to break that promise."

"Quit it. They're just children. I think we should invite him out for Sunday lunch, maybe have him out with Jesse and Miriam."

"Now don't get carried away. You better make sure all of this is okay with Sarah."

"Yes, you're right. I'd need to clear it with her."

"And you're not suppose to say anything about it, remember?"

"I'll talk to Dolly tomorrow."

Dolly was thrilled at the prospect of having Charles out, but Sarah was dead set against it. A protective instinct reared itself that none of us anticipated. She decreed that still a few weeks shy of sixteen, Dolly was too young. She seemed plenty old enough to me, but I dared not enter the fray. The morning after Sarah and Dolly argued about it, Sarah bluntly informed Venice that she had overstepped her bounds. Venice told Sarah that she intended to invite new folks to her home as a matter of common courtesy, and they didn't have to attend if they didn't care to. That was the only time I'd ever heard them have cross words with each other.

"I hadn't seen nothing like it from that daughter of mine," Henry told me the next day as we walked along the fence line. "I wouldn't expect her to be so protective. She even told me to mind my own knittin' when I tried to talk some sense to her ... I guess it might be because she was just a child herself when she met that no-good husband of hers."

"How's Dolly takin' it?"

"She's her Mama's daughter, madder'n a fox in a trap. They ain't been talkin' a lick." He laughed. "Them two boys are about to meet up with two sides of trouble. They don't realize every time they tease their sister about that boy, they're just makin' their Mama madder too."

I laughed knowing that the boys were simply incapable of avoiding that particular brand of mischief. "Well, I guess since Venice invited them, they're all coming out Sunday. She's not too happy herself. She thinks with y'all being the only black family around ... excuse me for sayin' it ..."

"Ain't no problem."

"Venice figures it would be proper for y'all to be there."

"Well, I'd come myself, but I figure it'd just make Sarah seem unsociable. I agree with Venice that it'd be proper for us to be there ... Lord, I don't want that woman after *me* too."

"Yeah, I guess you're right."

Henry laughed at a thought that crossed his mind. "Can you imagine how them boys'd act at the table. We'd have a war on our hands."

I laughed with him. "I think we're gonna have a war on our hands anyway."

Jesse and Miriam arrived with Charles and a big announcement. They were expecting a baby. Like mothers-to-be tend to do, Miriam took up with the baby of the house, Teddy, who wasn't really a baby anymore, while Jessie, Charles and I retired out to the porch.

"So where are you from originally?" I asked Charles.

"Ft. Smith."

"And you like the work you're doing now?"

"Oh, yes sir."

"Charles will have his own store to manage one day," Jesse said. "He's got a real knack for the business."

"Will Miss Dolly be joining us for lunch?" Charles asked.

"I'm afraid they can't make it today, Charles."

"That's a disappointment. She seemed nice."

Jesse grinned at me.

"She's a very nice young lady, smart as she can be and very sweet."

I didn't know what else to say. I was sure Charles knew Sarah and her family lived on the place. It was a relief when Venice called us in for lunch. Sarah had been over earlier to help with the meal as she always did for guests, but Dolly had been conspicuously absent. I stayed out of the kitchen. It was awfully quiet in there.

Charles sat down at the dining table, gazing around at the room. "You have a very beautiful home. Everybody says the Crawford house is the finest around, and I can see that for myself."

"Thank you, dear."

He placed his napkin in his lap, and gazed around the table. "This is a fine meal. I sure appreciate you inviting me."

"Well, we are so happy you came. You must come again ... actually, I must admit, our dear Sarah is responsible for this roast. She is such a good cook."

"It's a disappointment she couldn't join us."

"It certainly is." Venice's icy tone wasn't lost on anybody. Charles looked puzzled.

I pulled Jesse to the side after supper to explain that Sarah and Dolly's absence was a simple matter of an overprotective mother. "The two ladies of the ranch had words over it."

"Oh my goodness, you *do* have a situation on your hands," Jesse said.

Venice went back to her foul mood after they left. It was actually a relief when she opted not to take a walk with me. When I stepped out on the porch, I could hear arguing in the distance. The kids were out having some batting practice. I'd walked about halfway over to the field when I heard Sarah call out to me. I waited for her to catch up.

"I need to talk to you," she said in a panic-stricken tone.

"What's wrong?"

"Oh, James, I can't believe what I've done."

"It can't be all that bad. You look like you've seen a ghost."

She wiped her eyes and sniffled, looking down as if ashamed.

"Come on now. It can't be that bad."

"I'm so afraid you'll be angry, and you'd have every right."

"What is it, Sarah!"

"Well, you know how me and Miss Venice have ... didn't see eye-to-eye on Dolly. I know I've been an old bore about it, but ... I didn't even understand it myself. It seems just yesterday she was just a little girl, and now she's grown up so ... oh, and Dolly just hates me now too ..."

"So what's so terrible?" I begged impatiently.

Sarah looked down as if she couldn't say it. When she looked up, her eyes were clouded with tears. "We was cookin' you lunch and Miss Venice was trying to talk to me about lettin' Dolly come ... Oh James, it just slipped out ... I said when she had her own daughter she could worry about it then."

"Oh Sarah."

"I know. It musta sound like I was tryin' to say somethin' about her not havin' a daughter ... and how bad she wants one." Sarah put her hands over her face and wept.

She was right. Nothing could have cut Venice deeper. I couldn't muster a response at first, finding myself in awe that Sarah could have said something so insensitive. But hearing her cry, it was obvious that she had simply made a mistake.

"She knows you didn't mean it like that." I didn't manage much conviction.

"See, you know how awful it was ... I'm so sorry ... but I know sayin' I'm sorry ain't nothin'. You just cain't take back such horrible words ... she's sure to run us right off the place."

"That's just silly. It'll blow over. I'll fix it," I said, immediately wishing I hadn't.

"Oh please, James, please make her understand how I didn't mean it. I'll be praying for forgiveness every minute."

"Come on." I put my arm around her and turned us back toward the cabin. She only gathered her emotions as we arrived. Henry, seated up on the porch, nodded that he understood what was happening.

I found Venice upstairs on the balcony, leaning on the rail, Teddy napping in the next room. I eased the door shut behind me. "What you looking at?"

"You can see the babies now. Watch, they'll stick their little heads up."

A pair of red-shouldered hawks built their nest in the fork of a nearby black oak tree just above the level of the balcony. One of the parents glided in, and pointy little faces popped up.

"Looks like three."

"That's what I counted."

The adult bird dropped from the nest and glided off.

"I ran into Sarah on my walk." I paused, but Venice didn't offer a response. "She's pretty upset."

"The poor dear." She just stared as the other hawk parent glided in with more nourishment for the youngsters. I put my arms around her from behind, laying my chin on her shoulder. I could feel her convulse slightly, and then sniffle.

"It was an awful thing she said," I whispered.

"I suppose it was, but I'm not letting it concern me. She has a right to not want me to be a part of her daughter's life. I guess I was getting too close to Dolly."

"That's nonsense."

"No, she made it clear, and I respect that. It made her mad enough to hurt me, so it must be very important to her."

"I don't believe she was *trying* to hurt you. I think she just misspoke."

I leaned on the rail next to her. "Venice, Sarah is scared you're going to ask them to leave."

She whirled around with a stunned look on her face. "No! How could she think such a thing?"

I wiped a tear from her cheek.

"Oh Jimmy, what a mess. I didn't mean to upset everybody. I didn't think she would be so upset about inviting that young man out here. Dolly was so excited ... I should have waited to have them out when Sarah was over all of this. Whatever must poor Charles think?"

"I think Sarah is reconsidering."

"Well, I'm not even going to comment. It's none of my affair."

I couldn't help a little smile. She poked me with an elbow.

The hawk babies were climbing over each other to get to the food. "Hungry little guys."

Venice pushed herself up from the rail. "I have to speak with Sarah."

I reached out to stop her. "Give it a little time. I think this is a time when she needs to come talk to *you.*"

Chapter Thirty-One

We were on the porch the next afternoon when Dolly came bouncing up.

"It's a fine day for porch sitting," she said.

Venice nodded. "It sure is. Would you like to join us?"

Dolly hopped up the steps, grabbed Teddy and sat with him on her lap.

"Mama's done changed her mind about the whole thing ..."

"Mama has changed her mind," Venice, the teacher, corrected.

"She has changed her mind. She now thinks it would be correct manners to invite any new boy in town to dinner."

"Well, that's nice."

"Says we ought to have him out to *our* place ... *that'd* be proper. Says we ain't had ..."

"We haven't had."

"We haven't had y'all over either, and it was time we did."

I hoped Venice wasn't going to start making every conversation an English lesson, though I understood she was likely preparing Dolly for her next meeting with Charles, who had a very polished way of speaking for a fellow his age.

"Mama'll be over to make things right as soon as she can do it without blubbering. She's been a sobbin' like a baby, and about as mean as a copperhead. She ain't...she *hasn't* been ornery at me so much cause she figured she wronged me, but them two brothers of mine ..." she shook her head. "Even Grandpa got yelled at."

"Oh my ... it was just a simple misunderstanding. I hate that she is so upset ... I'm sorry I butted in. I shouldn't have."

"If I was to tell her you said that, would it be okay?"

"Certainly."

"Lord knows I don't wanta be nosey or nothing, but I think it'd help. ... I even hate to see them two stupid boys get in so much trouble. Them two just don't know when it's best to shut up."

We laughed together.

"So was your lunch nice? ... when Mister Jesse and Miss Miriam came out?"

"It was very pleasant. Sarah cooked a scrumptious roast ... they're going to have a baby."

"That's nice." Dolly nodded.

Venice glanced at me with her mischievous smirk. "And, oh yes, the young man ..."

"Charles."

"Yes Charles. He's a very impressive young fellow ... he asked about you."

"Miss Venice, don't you dare tease me."

"He asked if you'd be dining with us, and he seemed a little disappointed ... he said he thought you were nice."

Dolly cocked her head suspiciously. "I don't know, you got that look in your eye, like when you're teasing."

"That's what he said," I confirmed.

She put Teddy back down with his toys. "So what else did he have to say?"

When Venice leaned in and started to share the details, I excused myself and spent the rest of the afternoon down on the river.

Sarah came over the next day, and I fled the premises when the hugging and crying started, joining the Barrys, the twins and Dolly on the baseball field. When I came in for supper, Sarah and Venice were working together in the kitchen, jabbering and laughing like a couple of teen-age girls. It was like a homecoming when Henry and the kids arrived for dinner. As dessert was being served, Tom finally expressed what the rest of us were thinking. "Arguing ain't so bad if we have a makin'-up dinner like this." Even Dolly found humor in her brother's comment.

When it came time for Charles to visit, Venice sent me in to pick him up. The women advised Dolly not to go with me, "You don't want to look too anxious," Venice said. Charles was dressed in a sharply pressed suit, shiny leather shoes and carried a scraggly bouquet of flowers.

"Those are nice. Dolly will like those."

Charles looked puzzled. "Well, they were intended for Miss Sarah, for the kindness of inviting me out for lunch."

"Oh, of course."

"Mister James, does Miss Dolly consider that I'm comin' courting?"

I was caught off guard. "No ... I just think she's always anxious to meet other young people her age who come into the area."

"Maybe I should give these flowers to *her*."

"No, I think it's appropriate the way you planned it."

"I wouldn't mind so much mind if it was courting."

"You wouldn't want to look too anxious." I was especially proud of that advice.

"I guess I *am* a little anxious. But I know it's good advice not to *look* anxious."

"I'd just give the flowers to Sarah."

He nodded.

It had all been carefully choreographed, Dolly nowhere in sight when Charles stepped into the cabin and handed Sarah the flowers.

"Well, thank you. Come in and make yourself at home."

I felt for poor Charles, all eyes on him, the women studying him like a museum exhibit. But he seemed to take it in stride.

"It smells mighty scrumptious in here. Thank you very much for inviting me. I'm awfully hungry. I'm not yet very good at making my meals. I was mostly eating at my folks place back home. But Mister Jesse and Miss Miriam are real nice about inviting me over to eat. Miss Miriam is a fine cook. Might make the finest fried chicken I ever ate."

I wondered who would do the listening in a Charles-and-Dolly relationship.

Finally, Dolly glided out from the back room with a new, pale-blue dress, her hair braided with a matching ribbon. "Hello, Charles." She offered her hand. "It's good to see you again. Welcome to our home. We're all so glad you could make it." Venice and Sarah had been extensive in their preparation. "Have you met my brothers? ... Tom and Billy."

They all shook hands. The boys had also been coached, directives laced with threats, I was quite sure.

"Charles, please excuse me, I need to help Mama with lunch. Perhaps you fellas would wait on the porch until we call you."

The twins came out and joined the men, and were unusually chatty. Charles enjoyed their squirrel-hunting stories.

When we sat down to eat, Sarah emphasized Dolly's role in preparing the meal.

"This is delicious cookin' Miss Dolly." Charles' remark drew grins around the table.

"Do you like to play baseball?" Tom asked.

"I sure do. I used to play with my brothers all the time."

"Well we got a field, with a backstop, and a bat and two balls and everything. We buried flat rocks for bases and home plate is almost exactly the correct shape."

"How many brothers do you have?" Dolly asked.

"Four ... and two sisters. We were poor, so we just cut a sapling. Mama made us a ball out of yarn tied real tight."

"You can play with *us*," Billy said with enthusiasm. "I catch pitch good, and Dolly can hit it pretty far, if I ain't pitching."

"You play too?" Charles looked pleasantly surprised.

"Oh, more when I was little, just so I could look after the boys."

There was a quiet pause, everybody waiting for one of the twins to respond. "She still plays," Billy said, "and we never needed no lookin' after."

192

"Dolly, maybe you should take Charles over and show him the baseball field," Venice suggested.

"Yeah, we can hit some!" Tom said.

"I need you two to help me here," Sarah said. "Besides, Charles is dressed too nice to be playin' ball."

Charles looked disappointed.

Dolly led him down the road, not through the pasture, which was her usual path to the ball field. As we sat on the porch watching them disappear around some trees, I caught a glimpse of movement in the shadows. "I'll be right back."

The twins didn't hear me coming up until it was too late to flee. Sarah was standing on the edge of the porch, arms folded and shaking her head as we returned. "I should've known. Thank you James ... get inside and wash those dishes!"

After almost an hour, we spotted Dolly and Charles returning. They were holding hands, but when they noticed they were in our line of sight, they turned loose and added a little space between them.

"Well, I suppose I ought to head back to town," Charles said as they made it up onto the porch. "It was sure nice of you folks to invite me. Lunch was mighty delicious. And thank you Miss Dolly for the nice walk."

"I enjoyed it. Please come again. I think my brothers would love for you to come play baseball with them."

"I'll do that."

We were about halfway to town before Charles said anything. "It was Miss Dolly thought we should try holding hands ... to see if we liked it."

I nodded.

"I suppose we did, since we kept on ... did her Mama see?"

"I don't think so."

"You don't think it was improper, do you?"

"No, not at all."

As we came into town, Charles stressed how much he would like to come back out to "play baseball."

Chapter Thirty-Two

While I remained content with life on the ranch, Venice's interests were growing well beyond its borders. She was always coming up with projects for the Ladies Club, and the other members were happy to follow her lead. New families were constantly moving in, and the club established itself as the welcoming committee, with our dinner table hosting most of the newcomers. The ladies also decided it a good idea to sponsor a number of community functions, dances, holiday celebrations and such. I thought their mention of a parade was silly. But I was fine with all of it, happy to see my wife enjoying herself so much, until I learned it would involve me. Venice snuggled up to me on the porch one evening and explained how all the ladies thought it a shame the town didn't have a community center. Of course, I instantly identified "all the ladies" as Venice. Before the evening was over, she had me talked into donating funds for the construction.

I had escaped yet another of the club meetings with Teddy and Susie when Charles and the twins found us down on the river fishing. Charles needed a horse, and the twins assured him there were ample horses on the ranch and that I would be amenable to a purchase on credit. We hiked right over and picked him out a pretty mare, daughter to Venice's favorite. This precipitated regular trips out to the ranch. Charles was fond of baseball, but nobody misunderstood his reason for coming out to the ranch.

A boy about the twin's age named Michael started riding out with Charles to join in the baseball games. His mother, Vera, was a member of the Ladies Club and had become close to Venice and Sarah. One afternoon, I was strolling over to get in on a little batting practice when I ran into Dolly on her way back. She had a scowl on her face, so I figured she'd been into it with her brothers again.

"What's wrong?"

"It's not anything worth talking about."

"I hope Charles and you haven't had a disagreement."

"Oh no. He's a fine boy who wouldn't do anything to disagree about ... it's just those dumb brothers of mine."

"What did they say this time?"

"No, it wasn't like usual. Tom told Michael to tell all the kids in town to come out, and we could have a real baseball team. Michael didn't want to answer, and dumb ol' Billy kept on pressing him about it. It was Charles had to explain that the other white folks don't want their children out here. I hated to see the look on those boys' faces. They just been too sheltered to understand."

"Is there anything I can do?"

"There isn't anything *to* do, Mister James."

An awful sense of failure consumed me as Dolly walked away, but the more I thought about it, the more confused I was about what I might have said.

It took a little time for me to get comfortable with how close Venice and Melissa were becoming. Melissa was on the guest list of every one of our functions, and Venice spoke of her with an enthusiasm absent in conversations about her other friends. Melissa was one of the few women on Venice's intellectual level, and they often spoke of politics, especially women's absence in them. There was just the one small issue that bothered Venice about her friend.

"Why do you suppose we still haven't met her little boy?" she said once again as we prepared for bed one night.

I assumed Melissa simply enjoyed escaping her parental burden by leaving the boy with her folks. She never was as chatty about her child as other women, and I had never even seen them around town together. I didn't want to disappoint Venice, but I thought Melissa just wasn't very maternal by nature. My curiosity was piqued the day before when Venice mentioned the child, and Sarah shot an ominous glance in my direction.

I caught her alone in the kitchen after breakfast. "What was that look you gave me yesterday?"

"What look?"

Sarah didn't hide her feelings any better than I did; her 'what look' was more suspicious than the look itself.

"Come on, what is it?"

"No. I wasn't happy about when Venice was stickin' her nose in my business, and I'm not gonna stick mine in nobody else's."

"Now, you *have* to tell me ... what's the gossip?"

"You might not think it such idle gossip if you saw for yourself." She looked like she'd seen a ghost.

"I swear, it's so aggravating when you won't get to it."

"Okay, but I'm not ever going to admit sayin' it ... I can't believe you hadn't heard. Rumor's been around for a long time. I'm sure Annie ... Lord knows it's surprising she hadn't blabbed it to Miss Venice ... but it's not somethin' a person would wanta get caught spreading."

"What on earth are you jabbering about, Sarah?"

"I thought it was just ol' lying gossip, like it usually is, until I seen it myself."

"What!"

"I saw the preacher's wife in town a week or so back, and she was toting that youngun around ... Melissa's boy. I got a good look at him."

"Okay, so?"

"Lord help me, that child looks so much like you it gave me a shiver."

Nothing registered.

"Everybody knows she had that baby when she's married to that lawyer. And everybody knows the boy is too young for back when y'all ... well, you know. But still, some's insistin' it's your boy, with Melissa not being so firm with her virtues and all."

"You don't believe that, do you?"

"I sure don't, but James, wait 'til you see this child ... that boy is the spittin' image ... I worry a whole lot about when Miss Venice sees ... she's *gonna* find out."

As Sarah talked, it began to come back to me. "Oh shit."

"I know James, this is a bad situation."

"It can't be ..."

"Remember now James, I'm not the one spread this rumor to you, but I was just thinkin' you ought to know since Miss Venice is askin' so persistent about that boy, and folks around town accusing you of being with that woman when she was married."

"It was just before she got married."

Sarah gasped. "Oh no! ... I don't believe it. Oh James, I just wouldn't a thought it of you." She gazed at me with a dumbfounded scorn I'd never seen from her before.

"I was in a bad state just after my mother died. Melissa was just being a friend ... I was so lonely."

"Well, that's mighty friendly ... oh my Lord, what's Miss Venice gonna do?"

"She'll understand."

"I hope you're right, but I'm awful nervous about it ... what a scandal!"

"Just keep quiet about it. I'll take care of it."

"I wouldn't say a word. You know that. But I'll be praying for you ... and I suggest you be doin' the same. The good Lord can't be happy about a sin like *that.*"

Never before had I been so completely without a clue on how to handle a situation. I headed off, wandering parts of the property that I hadn't seen in years, trying to digest the shocking news and figure out how I was going to tell Venice. I'd let it slip to Sarah, so any form of denial was out of the question. I tried to persuade myself that Venice would understand, that it was simply a youthful mishap before I even met her, but no amount of wishful thinking made that seem even remotely possible. The very fact that I never told her about those few days with Melissa would attach meaning to it.

I lay sleepless that night, a feeling of impending doom growing by the minute. The only thing I had decided was I needed to tell her soon. But how and when escaped me. The next day, Sarah was cooking breakfast for us when Venice mentioned that I didn't sleep well. Sarah looked over her shoulder with an I-bet-he-didn't smirk.

"We may just have to take a nap this afternoon," Venice said.

Sarah shook her head down at the sausage spitting in the pan. I decided I would tell Venice that night.

Her particularly affectionate mood only complicated things. After she came down from putting Teddy to bed, she joined me on the big rocker on the porch, cuddling close. "I think a little exercise upstairs is what you need to help you sleep."

"Venice, there's another reason I couldn't sleep ... and I'm afraid you're not going to like it."

She sat up. "What is it?"

"Well, before you ... you remember when I told you about the other women I had been with before we were married?"

"Yes," she said with narrowing eyes.

"Well, I left one out. I forgot ... no, I didn't forget; I was ashamed."

"Okay ... and I suppose you want to tell me now?"

"When my mother died, I just went to pieces. I was left all alone with the farm. I was just a kid. I just sort of did nothing but lay around. I almost lost the farm. I was *so* devastated, so lonely."

"Okay."

"Anyway, Melissa came out and stayed with me a few days, just to help get me through it. She was just being a friend really."

"How sweet of her."

"We weren't even romantic before that, except ..."

"I remember."

"She was engaged ..."

"When she came and stayed with you?"

"Like I said, she was really just worried about me, and I was doing *so* bad."

"What a dear ... so it was really just medicinal."

"Well, don't make it sound so ..."

"Tell me, Jimmy, how many treatments did you require?"

"It was a long time ago, way before I met you."

"We met when we were children. How long was this before she married?"

"A couple of weeks."

"Oh my God!"

"I know." I shook my head.

"But she loved *you*, and had to be with *you* one last time, or a bunch more times it sounds like. Tell me Jimmy, did you love *her* too. Do you love her now?" Tears were streaming down her cheeks.

"Of course not!"

"You kept it a secret for a reason. Why is it? ... How foolish of me! ... I see you looking at each other ... Oh God!"

"We do not!"

"I'm not blind!" She pushed back angrily when I reached for her. "And so what made you decide to tell me now?" Now she sounded scared.

"Well, I just heard about a little complication in all this."

"Complication?"

I couldn't get it out.

"What complication, Jimmy!"

"Melissa's boy ... that we've never seen ..."

"Oh please, God, don't tell me ... "

"I guess he looks just like me."

"That doesn't mean anything. Have you seen him?"

"No, I only *just* heard. But I guess the rumor has been around a while."

"Who *has* seen him?"

"I don't really know ..."

"Who told you!"

"Sarah."

She stood, walked out to the edge of the steps and leaned on one of the columns. I stepped up behind her, but didn't dare touch her.

"She just saw him a day or two ago in town with his grandmother," I said in my most contrite voice.

"She hasn't been in town for at least a week."

"She only told me yesterday. She'd heard it before, but was sure it was just more gossip. But she said the boy looks just like me ... she's really getting on to me about it."

"She should ... does she know it might be true?"

"Well ... I sort of let it slip out."

"Just great! ... Well, it certainly explains the mystery behind why Melissa hasn't let us see him."

"I guess so."

She slapped my hand away. "Leave me alone."

As I set out into the darkness, I could hear Venice sobbing behind me. I wandered toward the river with Susie. She might have been the only friend I had left. We sat on the bluff trying to assess the damage. A fever of panic hit me when I considered the possibility that she would leave me. I thought about spending the night on that rock, scared to go back to the house where the most

198

terrible news of my life might be waiting. Susie lay next to me, feet kicking as she chased some dream rabbit. I hated to wake her, but the suspense was tormenting me.

There was to be no resolution that evening. Venice lay with her back to me, and didn't stir as I crawled into bed. I knew she was awake, but I dared not say anything, as I rolled over and braced for another sleepless night.

Chapter Thirty-Three

I woke alone in the bed, the house eerily quiet. When I strolled into the kitchen, Venice was feeding Teddy as Sarah prepared breakfast. I tested the waters. "Good morning."

"Good morning," Venice answered with icy formality.

"Morning." The dour tone in Sarah's greeting wasn't lost on Venice.

"That's right Sarah darling. My husband has finally shared with me the secret you, and it seems everyone else in the Ozarks, have been keeping from me."

"Oh no, I wasn't keepin' any secret. I was just tryin' to do the right thing."

"Of course you were. Please do me the honor though, of not discussing it any further with anyone until we can sort through some of the complications of my husband's promiscuity."

"Miss Venice, I didn't mean to …"

"Please, let's not discuss it."

After breakfast, Venice asked Sarah to take Teddy out to play. She snatched him up and hurried out like the place was on fire.

"Well now," Venice said with ice in her voice. "We have a lot to talk about."

"Yes, but I'd like to say something first."

"By all means"

"I'm so ashamed about all of this. I love you dearly, and you are the only one I have ever loved. Please don't let this come between us."

"Jimmy, dear, I believe those are things we should put off until later." She spoke in a crisp, businesslike manner. "We have more immediate concerns. Apparently, you have another son, and Teddy has a brother. We need to have a discussion with the child's mother."

"Well, I don't think …"

"I'll arrange that. Now, whether this boy is your son or not can't be verified, though it seems that's the case. There's no point being in denial about it. Sarah's description of the boy seems to remove any doubt. I'm sure you wouldn't want past moral lapses to mar your current behavior. You have responsibilities. The child's mother got a decent inheritance, but you can offer much more. That has to be considered carefully … I bet when you were wallowing around with her you didn't think about all this … And then there's the matter of how to handle this publicly. The child is threatened with a terrible stigma to carry through life. And I suppose the boy's mother has concerns about her own reputation, though perhaps not as much as one would hope. Now, we can't afford wasting any time concerning ourselves at all with the shame and embarrassment this brings upon me. I'll suffer that alone. That seems to be the least of *your* worries anyway."

"That's not true ... I did a stupid thing when I was a kid. I can't reverse it now."

"Well when you put it like that, I feel so much better. I can go on with my life as if nothing ever happened."

"I know you're going to make me suffer, and I deserve it, but if you are leaving me, just do it."

"Is that what you want?"

"Of course not. It'd destroy me. I'd rather die."

Venice's jaw began to quiver and her eyes glossed over with tears. "Your childhood pal could always come out and administer treatment ... save you again."

"That's ridiculous!"

"Tell me, Jimmy, when I was saving myself for our wedding night, did you require treatment then?"

"Of course not! You know that."

"And you hadn't seen her at all since siring her son? ... well of course you've seen her, but I mean ..."

"Only seen her in town."

"Do you love her?"

"That doesn't deserve an answer."

"Answer me or I'll leave for Kansas right now!" She stomped her foot on the floor.

"No, of course not. I don't, and I never did."

"Does she love you?"

"Of course not."

"How do you know that?"

"I think I could tell."

Venice broke down, elbows on the table, sobbing into her hands. I stood and came around to hold her but she swung an elbow to keep me away.

I spent the day roaming aimlessly around the ranch with Susie. The kids were playing ball and motioned me over when they spotted me in the distance, but I just waved and led Susie off in another direction, not wanting to answer questions about why there were no lessons that day.

Venice remained cool to me in the following days, immersing herself into teaching. The daily contact with the kids seemed to have a therapeutic effect on her that everyone benefited from, except me. She was trying to make amends with those who had unfairly suffered from the fallout, apologizing to Sarah in front of me at the breakfast table one morning.

"Oh that's not somethin' to apologize to me about." Sarah gave me a dirty look. "You got every right to be mad."

"But not at you. I was rude because I was so hurt that my husband has conducted himself like a rutting pig."

Sarah whipped around so we wouldn't see her laugh.

When it was time for the Ladies Club to meet, I thought perhaps Venice would cancel it, but instead she informed me that she would ask Melissa to stay afterward so we could discuss her son. Venice was still not using her name, referring to Melissa as, "Your son's mother." Just thinking about it made me queasy. Melissa was the one woman in the region I could picture standing up to Venice; there was no telling what kinds of fireworks might go off.

Sarah cleared the house, taking Teddy out to watch the kids have batting practice. Melissa sat with a friendly smile, expecting our visit to involve some pleasant topic.

"Melissa dear," Venice started. "I must insist we meet this young man of yours. I know he has to just be a darling."

"Oh I know. You must forgive me. His grandmother always begs to have him, and I just can't refuse her. You are right about him being a darling, though."

"Yes, I understand he is quite a handsome boy ... from some of those who *have* seen him."

Melissa's eyes narrowed. "Well, yes. I'm his mother, so I can't be objective, but I think he is a beautiful child."

"And it's such a shame he lost his father."

"Yes ... Venice, you seem to have something on your mind."

"No, not really ... well, I must admit a curiosity. I've heard he looks a great deal like someone I know well."

"Venice dear, surely you are not going to let rumormongers cloud your good judgment."

"Of course not, but I suppose I'm just the curious sort ... what's his name again."

"Robert ... after his father ... Venice, darling, if you have a specific inquiry, I would be happy to help you resolve any uncertainties you may be suffering."

"Well, I understand the two of you were intimate the weeks before your marriage, and of course I wouldn't pass judgment ..."

"Of course you wouldn't."

"It's just with word that your son is the mirror image of a man you slept with about nine months before he was born does give rise to certain questions, especially with me, since that man is now my husband."

"You seem to have already jumped to the conclusion that Robert is James' son, but he's not. Because the boy vaguely resembles your husband, and really, what child that age really looks like any adult anyway, you've let a town of busybodies plant some horrible thoughts in your head. I would think your husband would be quite unhappy with you."

"My husband has wisely held his temper ... really dear, don't you think I should have a right to at least see the boy."

"I don't know that you'd have any *rights* in regards to my son ... James dear, you haven't said a word."

"Well, if I have a son, I'd like to know it ... and I'd like for my dear wife to understand that whatever has happened, I have only loved her in my entire life."

Melissa's face softened as if she were surrendering. "Venice, whatever happened in the past, please take my word that we were just irresponsible adolescents. We never felt anything approaching the special love you two share. I look upon you both with such envy, not jealous of your husband, but that both of you found someone so perfect for each other and love each other in a way many of us will never know."

A tear ran down her cheek. "Robert was a fine man. And I tried my best to love him. My parents pressured me to marry because they knew I had a wild streak, and they wanted me to settle down." She took a handkerchief from her purse and blotted her eyes. "I came to James uninvited, I think as much to rebel against my parents as anything. I was such a child. And I truly did worry he wouldn't recover from his depression. I know how this all sounds, but it's the truth. Not *everything* about me is bad ... we will never know with certainty who the father is, and for that I am eternally shameful, but I do love Robert very much, and I would hate for him to suffer for something I did. If he *is* James' son, I would beg that he not grow up with the stigma of not having been my husband's child ... I'll bring him to see you. Tomorrow. It'll actually be a relief."

"Melissa, thank you for all you've said," Venice said softly. "I hope you understand my attitude."

"Of course I do."

"We all want what's best for the boy, and we all know the mother can be the only one to know that. We'll honor your wishes. Please consider though, we might fall in love with the boy, and he may after all be Teddy's brother."

"I want him to be around you all, and I hope, dear Venice, we can one day be friends again. I've so feared this day, most of all I was afraid I would lose your friendship."

They hugged and both gave me a look saying I wasn't welcome in the room.

Chapter Thirty-Four

"Oh my God," Venice gasped when Robert climbed from the buggy. Even from up on the porch, there was now no doubt in either of our minds. I followed her down the steps to greet them.

"Hello, Robert. I'm Mrs. Crawford, but you can call me Aunt Venice."

"Hello," he said sweetly.

"Robert, this is your ... this is Mister James."

"Hi there big fellow."

"Hello."

His eyes locked on to Teddy, standing next to his mother with a grip on her skirt.

"Come in." Venice led everybody into the house.

"Robert has never had a playmate," Melissa said. "I'm sure he doesn't know quite what to expect."

We sat in the living room, and Sarah served tea. "Oh my word, what a precious child," she squatted down to Robert's level. "Hello. My name is Sarah." Robert stared in confusion.

"I bet these younguns would like a cookie."

"I suspect they would." Melissa smiled.

"Well," Venice took a deep breath as the boys followed Sarah into the kitchen. "I must say ..."

"Yes, I don't think there's much doubt. He looks nothing like Robert, or me for that matter."

We shared polite conversation while Teddy introduced Robert to his favorite toys. The ladies chatted about their club as if the day before hadn't happened. Venice was still being cold to me in ways others wouldn't detect, like avoiding any eye contact. After a while, Dolly and the twins came in from the baseball field and Venice introduced them to Robert. The twins responded with their typical disinterest, but Dolly leaned over to greet him. When she got a good look at the boy, she glanced up at me with a puzzled expression.

Melissa and Robert joined us the next Sunday for lunch, part of an unspoken understanding that they were now an extension of the family. Charles was already a regular, always eager to join the twins in batting practice afterward. Dolly preferred taking walks with her boyfriend, on which, according to the latest reports from the twins, they had been spotted kissing. On one such Sunday after lunch, we all decided to walk out and let Teddy and Robert watch the others play. As we approached, Dolly was batting and Billy pitching.

"Strike!" Billy threw up his fist as Dolly swung and missed. She stood, the bat in one hand, her other hand on her hip, yelling something out at Billy we couldn't quite hear.

The next pitch hit her in the face. She went limp and fell to the ground. We rushed over.

"I'm sorry! It just slipped," Billy said to his mother.

"Let me see." Sarah pulled Dolly's hand away. Charles knelt beside her, racked with concern.

"It was a accident," Billy pleaded.

Dolly's eye was swelling. "You did that on purpose!"

"I promise I didn't."

"I don't think he would do that," Charles said.

Dolly scowled angrily at her boyfriend. "Everybody knows he could knock a fly off a fence post ... so you're defending *him* against *me?*"

"No, I just don't think he meant to. That's all."

Charles was demonstrating a shared trait with the twins of not knowing when to shut up. Dolly eased up into a sitting position with her mother's help.

"It'll be fine," Sarah said. "But you're gonna have some swelling."

Dolly pushed Charles away as he tried to help her to her feet. "No thank you."

"Don't be mad at *me.*"

"You should be punching him right now. You said I was your girl, and you're 'spose to protect me."

"Against your own brother?"

"Mama, it wasn't on purpose," Billy said. "I swear it wasn't. It just slipped."

Sarah nodded that it was okay, and led Dolly back toward the house.

"You can just stay out here," Dolly yelled at Charles when he stepped up to walk beside her. He retreated, and stood sadly with the twins as they watched the procession pull away.

"Here," I passed Teddy off to Venice, and went over to talk to the boys.

"It'll be okay," I said. "She's just hurting right now. She'll get over it."

"I sure hope so," Charles said.

"She probably won't be kissin' you no more," Tom warned. "She can be mighty begrudging."

"Oh, it'll work out fine." I patted Charles on the back. "Just give it some time."

"I'd really like for her not to be mad right *now.*"

"Maybe you could take her some flowers," Tom said.

"Yeah! I think that'd make it better." Billy added.

Charles thought for a minute. "But why do I have to go apologizing and bringing flowers when I didn't do anything wrong?"

"Well, that's just what you do when people are feeling bad," I said. "Wouldn't you take her flowers if she got sick."

"I sure would."

"I really didn't mean to," Billy said again. "I hate she wanted you to punch me. I hope you don't decide to."

"Naw, I wouldn't do that."

Tom threw in his two cents. "I think if you *was* to give flowers, then she'd forget any bad stuff."

"But what bad stuff?" Charles said.

"I think you was suppose to act sorry and not go talkin' about how I didn't mean it," Billy said.

"But I didn't think you did."

Tom said, "I didn't think so either, but I thought it was at least possible."

It took all my strength to not start laughing.

"Mama's got flowers in her garden right now," Billy said. "You could get those and give 'em to her. And then maybe say you want to walk out and do some kissin'."

"I wouldn't say it exactly like that," I said with a smile.

"How do you know anything about kissing?" Charles said.

"Oh, I don't think that's the important thing to think about now," Tom said. "Dolly's pretty mad."

Charles bobbed his head. "Let's get those flowers."

It occurred to me that harvesting flowers from Sarah's garden might cause the boys a different type of problem, but I decided to let that work itself out. I walked back to the house as they hurried toward the garden.

Dolly was lying on the sofa in the family room, a wet compress on her eye, Sarah seated at her side. Sarah smiled up at me when I asked about her, saying it was going to be fine. When the boys showed up, an odd collection of flowers in Charles' hand, he knocked tentatively.

"Charles is here to see you," Venice announced as the three boys peered anxiously through the screen door.

"I don't want nobody to see me lookin' like a hideous monster."

"But Charles wants to say he was sorry and go out for some kissin'!" Tom called out.

"Mama!"

"Good Lord." Sarah stood, a grin on her face. She ran the twins off and asked Charles inside. He stepped in carefully.

"Here, I'll take those," Venice offered after Dolly had seen the flowers. Charles sat next to Dolly as all the adults watched in fascination. I felt sorry for poor Charles.

"I'm sorry for whatever I did wrong," he said in a pitiful voice.

"I forgive you Charles. I know you're a good boy and just don't like slugging people, even if they did just harm your girl."

"I don't think Billy hit you on purpose," I couldn't help but interject.

"I know you're most likely right Mister James. I guess I was just mad cause it hurt so much."

"Well how come when *I* said it …"

"Charles," I stopped him, "maybe Miss Dolly would feel better sitting out on the porch."

Dolly exaggerated the struggle of sitting up. "I 'spect I could try." She turned back toward us from the door. "You can all just wipe those silly grins off your face. Charles and I don't care for any nosiness about our business."

The house quickly cleared after that. I felt a twinge of regret seeing Robert go, but made sure my hug wasn't overdone. When everyone had gone, except for Dolly and Charles, who were rocking together on the porch swing, Venice took Teddy up for his nap. After a few minutes, she got my attention from the top of the steps, waving me upstairs. I followed her into a guest bedroom. She put her finger to her lips for me to be quiet. I feigned disapproval when I realized she was inviting me to join her in eavesdropping on Charles and Dolly.

"I hate that it hurts so bad," Charles was saying. "I just wish I could do somethin' to make it not hurt so much."

"Oh Charles, I think I will be okay," Dolly said with a bit of suffering in her voice.

"Do you figure if I was to kiss it that it might not hurt as bad?"

"I suppose if you was to kiss it real soft, it would probably help a good deal."

Venice smiled devilishly, standing on her tiptoes to see. She lost her balance, catching the windowsill with a thud.

"Charles is gonna whip the fool out of you numbskulls if y'all don't leave us alone!" Dolly yelled up.

We tiptoed away, suppressing giggles. Venice took me by the hand, led me into our bedroom, lay back on the bed and reached for me. We made love for the first time since we'd fought, the breeze blowing gently through the balcony door, our son asleep in the next room and a young couple discovering their love for each other downstairs.

Chapter Thirty-Five

As the north winds began stripping leaves from the forest, the ranch was abuzz with activity. Along with our family's holiday planning, the Ladies Club was preparing for its first event at the newly completed community center. The Fall Social was to be a grand affair, unprecedented in the community. Venice hired a quartet from out of town, and the ladies prepared sandwiches and desserts. The hall was decorated in autumn colors to match the theme. The 25-cent admission was earmarked for a few folks around town whom the ladies identified as needing assistance.

I'd never seen Venice have as much fun, insisting on handling details so others could enjoy themselves. We shared a laugh watching Charles and Dolly's awkward dancing, quickly looking away at a threat of being detected. Venice and I enjoyed a few dances, and then she went around pairing up those who were watching from the side. She instructed me to dance with each of the ladies who were without escorts, including Melissa, and with no suitable dance partners for the twins, she pushed each out for a dance with their sister. The event was such a success the ladies immediately decided it should be duplicated in the spring.

At home, everyone's attention shifted to the upcoming holiday season. Annie proposed bringing Grey to the Ozarks for Thanksgiving, insisting it was better for him to travel before the bitter cold set in. He was a little more subdued than normal during the visit, but not enough that I thought anything was wrong.

When we arrived at the Bar G for Christmas, Luke and Annie greeted us out front.

"I didn't want him out in this cold," Annie said. "Hurry in where it's warm."

Venice, Teddy and I were the only ones from the ranch to make the trip. Sarah was worried about her father traveling in the cold weather, but claimed a desire to have a family Christmas of their own. Henry wasn't taken in by the guise, but didn't put up much resistance. The twins were disappointed, but Dolly was quite happy to be spending the holidays with Charles.

Inside, Grey sat, staring at the fire, not recognizing us as we hugged him. When he held out his hand to Teddy, asking, "And who is this little fellow?" Venice darted out of the room. Annie followed.

"This is your grandson, Teddy," I said.

"Good ... well, good then," Grey said softly and stared back into the fire.

In the kitchen, Annie was filling in Venice on Grey's dementia and how fast it had come on.

After a night to gather herself, Venice put on her most positive face and sat with Grey for hours, patiently answering the same questions again and again about who Teddy and I were. We left after a week, Venice with mixed feelings about whether she should stay on. I think in the end, it was too painful there. This spawned such guilt in her that she wept most of the way home. We vowed to return in a month, but we both sensed we'd never see Grey again.

Word came two weeks later. Annie's lengthy telegraph stressed that his death had been peaceful and painless, assuring us that either she or Luke had been there with him the whole time, and how everyone on the ranch was heartbroken.

Henry insisted on traveling to Kansas for the funeral, and Sarah couldn't bring herself to refuse him. Luke drove over to help transport everyone, and it began to snow as we pulled in beneath the gate at the Bar G.

On a frigid, gray morning, a gentle snow falling, we laid Thomas Grey to rest in the earth he so loved. Venice wept only a little. As the minister talked about what a fine man he was, I caught Venice gazing across the open landscape, the land she had helped tame with him. She received mourners afterward with a silent stoicism, remaining composed even as they wept in her arms.

She insisted on leaving first thing the following morning. We both wanted to escape the empty feeling in the house. Luke came along a little later in the day with the others. Neither Venice nor I rose to peer out the window at the sound of their approach, as we normally would have. Luke startled us by bursting through the door, breathless, announcing that Henry had developed a cough and fever on the ride back. I hurried into town to fetch the doctor, and wouldn't take no for an answer when he balked at coming out.

Henry had a nasty case of pneumonia. The doctor gave him an even chance of making it through. The skies were dark and the snow deepened as the waiting began. Venice spent the bulk of the daylight hours down at the cabin, having postponed any studies until Henry got better. For three days, Venice returned in the twilight discouraged that Henry had shown little progress. But on day four, her report was much better. All of his symptoms had improved, and he was eating heartily, even joking with the kids about Sarah being so overprotective. By the sixth day, there was no doubt Henry was going to be fine.

"I wouldn't have ol' Grey a lookin' down from Heaven and thinkin' his funeral killed me," he said.

Henry's recovery was a badly needed boost in an otherwise dreary winter. The weather remained dismal, snow piling up in huge drifts, driven by a persistent and brutal wind. Teddy developed a fever in February, which launched Venice into a panic. Despite the doctor's reassurance that he would recover, she hung by his bed day and night. Teddy's bug eventually spread to the rest of us, and for weeks, it seemed there was always someone on the ranch who was sick. Charles caught a particularly nasty version of the illness. I felt it might have been Dolly's insistence on bringing him out to the ranch for recovery during particularly lousy weather that may have contributed to the severity of his symptoms. Venice kidded one night that Charles wasn't getting better because he was enjoying the nursing so much.

When the first warm day broke through in April, everyone was finally healthy and spirits were improving. Venice continued to pester all of us about wearing coats, hats and gloves, scolding the twins once after finding their coats hanging in the branches of a tree. She finally eased off when I complained to her that I'd brown like a baked chicken if I wore my coat another day.

As the woods bloomed with spring color, Charles joined the twins for his first turkey hunt. I presented each of them with one of my father's turkey calls, and we had to endure their practice for a few days before the boys took to the woods. I opted to stay close to the house, not feeling the passion for the hunt I had in the past. It was more entertaining to hear stories about the kid's hunts. After the boys all killed a gobbler, the baseball games started again. It was only because Dolly continued to participate that the twins saw much of Charles after turkey season.

A minor stir rippled through the ranch when Dolly decided to pose a few awkward questions to Venice, instead of her mother, about marriage, sex and the propriety of certain types of touching before wedlock. Venice had the good sense to speak with Sarah about it, but Dolly felt betrayed, and for about a week the three of them were cold toward one another.

The Dolly-and-Charles issues became a little more serious after a Sunday lunch in June. They were out on the porch as usual, the rest of us in the sitting room, when suddenly we could hear Dolly crying. "Oh no! ... do you have to?" was all I could make out. Finally, Charles came back in to politely say goodbye, and as he rode away, Dolly came in with tear-swollen eyes and hurried over to cry into her mother's shoulder.

"Oh Mama, it's just terrible!"

"What is it baby?"

Dolly raised her head, her chest heaving as she forced it out. "Charles has a promotion to another store ... down in Arkansas. He's gonna be leavin' Mama!" She buried her face again and wept.

"Oh baby, it'll be all right. Arkansas's not that far …"

"It's all the way down to the Hot Springs!" Dolly wailed, and buried her face again.

"Well y'all can write, and maybe you could go to visit."

"Oh, Mama, a boy like Charles ... there's gonna be a lot of other girls that'll be seeing what a handsome boy he is ... and me up here in these damn ol' hills."

Venice was unsuccessful in fighting back tears, but Sarah was the perfect mother with her soothing tone. When Sarah and Dolly left for the cabin, Dolly was still sniffling. It looked like it was going to be a long night for both of them. I figured it would only get worse down there when the twins learned they were losing their best friend.

The next day, Charles rode out to talk to me, his visit timed so that Sarah would have her children busy, helping with dinner chores. He carefully stepped up onto the porch where Venice and I were seated in the swing. "Good afternoon," he said.

"Well hello, Charles," Venice said. "It's so good to see you. I understand congratulations are in order."

"Ma'am?"

"Your promotion."

"Oh, yes ma'am. Thank you." He just stood there awkwardly, looking down toward the cabin.

"Please sit down, and join us."

He eased into one of the rockers. "I hope y'all don't mind me coming out, it being near supper and all. I'm not staying or nothing. I guess I was just needing to talk."

"Sure darling, what is it?" Venice asked in a gentle voice.

"Well, Dolly wasn't too happy about me getting a promotion. Oh, she's proud I did good to get it, but she don't like the idea of me leaving ... truth is, I don't want to leave neither ... or not without *her* anyways."

Venice's abbreviated gasp was probably only perceptible to me.

"I was thinking about asking Miss Dolly to get married, but I know we're awful young, and to be honest, well, I'm a little scared of Miss Sarah. She's not going to want her little girl going all the way off to Arkansas ... I think Dolly would say yes, though."

"Oh, Charles, I think that's a wonderful—"

I stopped her. "Well, Charles, have you and Dolly talked about it yet?"

"No sir, and I think I should have, cause I'm scared she might be angry I didn't already talk about it."

"I think she'll understand," Venice said.

"It's kind of embarrassing to admit it, but I wouldn't quite know how to go about saying it to Dolly. You know how she is. She might not be pleased if I wasn't to do it in a proper way, and I don't quite know what that would be."

Our grins weren't making it any easier for him.

"And I was also wondering if I would ask Miss Sarah for her hand, since Dolly hasn't got a father, or ol' Henry ... or could I just ask *you* Mister James?"

"I think talking to Sarah would be more proper."

"But, I'd rather ask you."

"Nonetheless ... I think first you need to talk to Dolly."

"I know, but ..."

"Just ask her to marry you," Venice said.

"Charles, I think however you ask, she'll be very happy."

"I've never been so nervous in my whole life ... if she was to say no, I'd just be so sad."

"I'd be surprised if she said no." Venice fidgeted, beside herself with excitement.

"Do you think I should just go on over there right now and get it over with?"

I grabbed Venice's knee before she could comment.

"Well, I think if you feel that way, now's as good a time as any."

"Oh Lord," Charles said under his breath as he gazed down toward the cabin. He pushed himself slowly to his feet, nodded his appreciation and rode off at a snail's pace.

Chapter Thirty-Eight

Venice and I were cleaning up after dinner when we heard a knock at the door.

"The most wonderful news," Dolly said, with Charles behind her, "Charles and I are getting married!"

After hugs and handshakes, Venice invited them in to sit with us.

"Mama didn't *even* put up a fuss. I'll of course be goin' down to the Hot Springs with Charles. He's gonna make a high salary, and we'll have a house and cute little children. I can get a job until I start having babies, which I don't 'spect will take very long, but Charles has been too embarrassed to talk about *that* so far."

We listened, waiting for Dolly to run out of breath.

"Oh Miss Venice, would you help us plan a proper wedding. Now, I'm not askin' you to spend no money or nothin' like that, but you've got such good taste."

"Well of course I'll help. Your mother and I will work together."

I cleared my throat conspicuously.

"Yeah, Mama'll want her say for sure. Since there are only white churches in town, I was wonderin' if we could have a wedding here at your beautiful home."

"Of course you can."

Dolly smiled and leaned over to kiss Charles, but he pulled back. "We can kiss in front of folks now that we're engaged," she said, forcing a peck on the lips.

"Mama was crying, which I expected, but I promised her we'd be comin' back to visit often, we'd need her help when a baby was comin' ... Mister James, I 'spect Charles could use a man talk if you wouldn't mind." Poor Charles looked down and shook his head. Dolly patted him sympathetically on the back. "He's bashful about it."

She stood. "Well if you'll excuse us, me and my fiancé, we have a lot to discuss."

We followed them out the front door and sat, watching the happy youngsters stroll off hand-in-hand.

Venice sighed. "They are so sweet together."

"Yeah. I think their marriage will be a lot like ours."

"Oh I hope so ..." She caught me grinning. "How do you mean?"

"Poor ol' Charles won't get a word in edgewise."

"Quit that." She swatted at me, and laid her head on my shoulder.

It was just a few minutes before Sarah sauntered up. "Where are our lovebirds?"

"They went for a walk," Venice said. "They have much to discuss."

Sarah smiled. "Charles is a good boy. I couldn't have wanted no better, but I sure hate losing my little girl ... and they just seem so young. I wish they could stay around here."

"We'll have a wonderful wedding. Let's sit down and talk about it tomorrow."

"I don't want them children takin' advantage of you. They'd be just as married without one of your big parties."

"Nonsense. How often do I get to throw a wedding?" She turned quickly to me. "And they should have a nice honeymoon, that will be our gift."

"No, that'd be *way* too much," Sarah said. "I got a little money saved, but I want it to get 'em started ... Besides, they aren't even thinkin' about a honeymoon right now."

"I bet Charles is." Venice jabbed me as Sarah scowled.

"You're just going to have to indulge us on this," Venice said. "When are they talking about?"

"Charles needs to get down there to his new job. But his bosses said he could take a couple of weeks. That's some mighty nice folks he works for. I imagine a week or ten days."

"My, we need to get to work."

Venice insisted on a wedding that struck the rest of us as preposterous, and not possible on such short notice, but she was not to be denied. Sarah and Dolly drove with her to Joplin, staying three days to shop and make arrangements. Along with a wedding dress, they beefed up Dolly's wardrobe for her new life and used the opportunity to purchase the fast-growing twins new dress clothes. She also hired musicians and paid a printer double his fee to produce invitations overnight.

Enthusiasm for the wedding consumed the ranch. I had seldom seen Venice so happy, until she came in from town one afternoon and threw her purse angrily at the sofa.

"What's wrong?"

"I could just spit."

"Why?"

"I can't find a preacher. They're all too busy. Damn bigots!"

"I hadn't thought of that ... should have. It's not a big setback. We can get a preacher, or even a judge, from up at Monett or Joplin ... Don't let it mess up the time you're having."

Venice looked a little puzzled.

"I've never seen you enjoy something so much."

She sighed. "I have ... I'm not going to let that ruin it. It's just, how can it be that so many people feel that way. What are they scared of? ... Let's not let Sarah and Dolly know."

"Venice, I think they probably already knew."

After her experience with the town's preachers, Venice reduced her portion of the guest list considerably. There were about thirty attendees at Dolly and Charles' wedding. Venice and I stood in as best man and matron of honor, and Henry gave the bride away. A husband and wife team played their violins beautifully as the bride came down the stairs. Venice found a preacher in Monett willing to do the ceremony for a healthy fee. The highlight of the ceremony for me was seeing Dolly swat at Charles when he tried to put the ring on the wrong finger. Poor Charles looked terrified when told he could kiss the bride, but he handled it admirably. Dolly told Venice beforehand that they had been practicing. After the vows, there was cake, champagne and dancing. At the height of the revelry, I caught a glimpse of the twins sneaking out the kitchen door with a bottle of champagne, and figured I'd be hearing more about that later.

After awhile, I slipped out for a smoke with Luke. We walked a short distance from the house, music and laughter floating on the warm, night air. It was the kind of night you wanted to just listen. As we were stomping out our cigars, the bride and groom stepped out into a shower of rice. I'd taught Charles to drive the Oldsmobile enough so that they could make it down to the original family cabin, which had been temporarily vacated and decorated for the newlyweds. They waved like they were setting out on a long journey. The boys were nowhere in sight.

I found them seated against tree trunks in the woods, a couple of empty champagne bottles between them. They were too sick to do any spying, so I left them to their suffering.

Another women's organization formed in town, spearheaded by the preacher's wife and members of the congregation. It was obviously a pushback to Venice's club and its racial makeup. She had an idea of which of her members would bolt, but a few disappointed her. Trying her best to take it in stride, she couldn't help lashing out every once in a while. When I caught wind that they were going to hold a social at the community center as Venice's group had earlier, I worried about how she would respond. She decided to fight back with graceful disinterest, friendly with all of the women in town as if nothing had happened, but I was scared she'd grind her teeth down to nubs.

A week before the social, I ran into the sheriff. After a handshake and polite greeting, he shifted nervously. "James ... about this social comin' up. Well, them old betties come in here ... I just wanted to let you know so you wouldn't get in an awkward situation. They want me to be there so not to allow no black folks inside."

"What? So they're now going to try to keep us out of the community center we paid for?"

"Oh you and your wife could come …"

"We wouldn't be caught dead there, and you can tell that gaggle of bitches to go straight to hell, and this town can damn well know they'll never get another dime of Crawford money."

"Now don't think I'm a part of all that. I was just warning ya like I figured you'd want me to."

"Of course not. You wouldn't pander to constituents ... have your damn social. Venice was right, I'm getting sick of this town too."

I threw as much dust up as I could on the way out.

"What's wrong?" Venice said when I came storming back into the house.

I explained. "Maybe we should just sell this place and move to the Bar G," I said in frustration.

"Calm down, Jimmy. This isn't about place; it's about time. It takes a long time to civilize people. Things will change one day ... besides, I'm not letting anyone run me out of my home."

It always seemed that whichever of us had our dander up, the other took a calmer approach. I suddenly felt ashamed. "You're right ... let's not tell Sarah."

"She told me about this a couple of days ago." Her smile had a taming effect.

"Holding it at the community center *we* built galls me the most."

Her smiled melted. "Yes, well we won't have to concern ourselves with helping that town anymore ... I would love to know who attends that social."

A fellow in town named Clyde Loggins had just launched what he called a newspaper, but it was little more than a gossip sheet. One of the first things he covered was the social, and Venice got her wish. He listed most of the attendees in his write-up. Some of the names were quite a disappointment to us. They'd sat at our dinner table and been part of the Ladies Club with Sarah. I mentioned the possibility that some may have not known that black people weren't allowed, but Venice would hear nothing of it. Nobody listed in that article would ever set foot in her home again, she vowed.

Against my urging, the Saturday after the social, Venice invited the new editor out to a gathering at our place, lavishing guests with drinks, hors d'oeuvres and an enormous meal. She got what she wanted. The article made Venice sound like royalty, holding court over a list of invitees conspicuously absent of those who had attended the social. An undeclared war was being waged, and the first salvos seemed to favor Venice.

Her next line of attack reversed an earlier vow. By offering to pledge money for upgrades to the community center and purchasing a piece of property for a city park, she was able to bully the town council into naming the facility The Crawford Community Center. She also demanded the park allow all races and creeds. It wasn't like her to want something named after us, but her intent was to provide a constant reminder of who paid for the community center, especially when whites-only events were held there.

Chapter Thirty-Seven

When Dolly and Charles returned to the ranch for their first Christmas together, Dolly was beginning to look pregnant, the father-to-be doting over her like she'd break if allowed to do anything for herself. Annie and Luke were enjoying a similar bliss, proud to show off a precious, new daughter, Deborah. Venice's Christmas party was another big success. The guest list was smaller but the attendees were treated like royals, including a gift for each of them. She made sure the editor was on hand to collect the names of her guests for publication, more for the benefit of those not invited.

Venice always got a little depressed when the house went quiet, and it was time to take down the decorations. That year she was particularly somber. As I expected, being around a baby girl set her yearnings in motion.

"Little Deborah is just an angel. Oh, Jimmy, I want a girl so bad."

"They still run the orphan trains."

"I thought of that, but I want a baby ... maybe I could go to St. Louis, and check into adopting ... I wouldn't mind doing some shopping. We all need clothes. Sarah could go with me." She grinned when I shook my head. "I bet Sarah would love to go."

"For how long?"

"Oh quit it ... just a few days. We'll take Teddy."

When they left, I took the opportunity to sneak off to Kansas for some hunting, but a blizzard blew for two days, and I stayed in and read. Luke was out working with the entire crew, hustling to get cattle fed in the storm, and Annie stayed busy with a baby and a toddler. I headed back home before I should have to escape the loneliness of being in that house without Venice or Grey.

Venice was exposed to the newest automobiles in St. Louis and started right in on me about buying a new one. It struck me as an unnecessary extravagance, but she had her heart set on it. I was able to put her off until spring, but as the weather warmed, we were on the train to St. Louis. It was amazing to see how many automobiles were on the road. There were so many new choices. We decided on a Packard Model 30 that could seat five easily, with a windshield and a covering. As silly as it was to buy a new car, I did like the idea of having protection from foul weather.

It was a glorious morning for the drive home. There wasn't a cloud in the sky, and the sun felt good in the crisp air. "We need to take more driving trips," Venice said as we drove. "Maybe we could go to Montana."

"That's a long drive ... remember, on the train we had something to keep us occupied."

Venice laughed. "Well, I suppose we could just pull over if need be."

"But wouldn't we have Teddy?"

"Spoil all the fun ... of course we'd have Teddy ... hey, let's stop and pick up some sandwiches, and then find a place for a picnic."

We parked next to a bridge over a swift stream slicing through a high-walled canyon. After making our way carefully down an incline, we hiked a short distance up a mushy gravel bar and sat in the shade of an enormous sycamore. The woods were alive, the hum of water tumbling through the rocks blending with the ruffling of new leaves in a brisk breeze. As a cacophony of small birds harmonized, a lovesick turkey gobbled a short distance away.

That night we stayed in an Inn, and arrived back at the ranch before lunch. Tom had killed a turkey and was plucking feathers when we drove up. Susie had been monitoring the bird's undressing, but pulled away to dutifully bark at the shiny new contraption.

"Lord have mercy," Sarah drawled as she came out of the cabin shaking her head, Teddy close behind.

"It rides so smooth," Venice picked up her anxious son and hugged him.

Sarah climbed into the car at Venice's prompting. "My, my, this is more comfortable than the best house chair."

"We thought you would like to have the Oldsmobile," Venice said.

"What? I cain't drive one of these things."

"I could drive it," Billy offered with as much enthusiasm as I'd ever heard from him about anything.

"Or me!"

"Now there's a couple of good ideas," Sarah said.

"We're plenty old enough."

"Seems to me somebody mature enough to drive an automobile would be mature enough to clean up after themselves." The twins' shoulders drooped in unison. "Maybe I *should* learn to drive."

It turned out Sarah needed little training. She'd ridden enough to have a feel for it, and took quite naturally to driving. Acting like a child with a new toy, it was a side of Sarah I hadn't seen. And with the new car came heightened interest in driving by Venice. The two of them were always looking for excuses to drive, using their automobiles to get around the ranch to places they would have walked before. They both had a talent for flattening tires, and it was often me out fixing them and going into town to order more. And neither seemed especially attentive to their fuel level. After a while, they started calling on the Barrys for help to avoid my grousing. It was nice to see them enjoying themselves, but I still seriously questioned the wisdom of buying the Packard.

My doubt turned to dismay when the only two vehicles on a 1,400-acre ranch ran into each other. I would have been angry if it hadn't been so funny. It would be years until the two of them lived that down.

Sarah's driving about town didn't set well with the old codgers who loafed along the boardwalk. There were still few autos in the area, and for one to belong to a black woman was unbearable for many townsfolk. And Venice driving her new automobile into town didn't help. People were as jealous of us as they were hateful of Sarah and her family, but they all seemed harmless. I should have known better.

A couple of months after Sarah had taken possession of the Oldsmobile, I was reading on the porch when Jesse pulled up in his new automobile. Sarah was with him. As I stepped up to the edge of the porch, I could tell something was wrong besides another flat.

"So what's up?"

"They punctured all her tires." Jesse came around the hood as Sarah slowly climbed out. "Right in front of the store, but of course, nobody saw a thing."

"You tell the sheriff?"

"Oh yeah," Sarah said. "But he didn't look much like he wanted to be bothered."

I was glad Venice had driven to Joplin for the day. She'd want to go right back into town and pick a fight. "Okay, I'll go in tomorrow ... Jessie, can you ask around about how many tires are in town?"

"Sure."

As he drove off, Sarah sat with me. "I should've known. I shouldn't have been flauntin' it."

"Nonsense ... we're going to get to the bottom of this."

"It'd just be more trouble if you did. If somebody *was* to get in trouble over it, they'd just hate us more, and then what would they do? Burn our cabin down?"

A sudden chill came over me.

"Miss Venice is gonna make herself crazy over this."

"She sure is."

"I have a feeling there's worse evil in that town than we might know about. I don't want nobody gettin' hurt ... you have to keep Miss Venice controlled."

"And what do you think the chances of that are?"

Sarah grinned. "My, my, she's gonna be mad as a hornet."

She was right, and may have been able to hear Venice from down at the cabin. Listening as long as I could, inciting her further by trying to calm her down, I tried to escape by going to bed, but she was right on my heels. By the time I dozed off, she'd committed herself to getting rid of the sheriff.

My vehement objections weren't nearly sufficient to keep Venice from going into town with me. As I began the work of replacing the tires, she stormed down to the sheriff's office, not noticing, scratched into the paint on the door: "Nigger stay home." As I worked, three old men sat on a bench and watched.

"That's why I wouldn't have one of them damn things," one of them called out.

"I wouldn't expect you to have one," I said without looking up from the tire. "They don't hand them out for loitering."

They spit and shut up.

Venice slammed the sheriff's door loud enough for everybody in town to hear, and they probably did since most were gathered along the street watching.

"That man is incompetent! I'll see that he doesn't get elected again," Venice said loud enough to solidly plant the rumor.

When she saw what was carved in the door, she glared at the gawkers as if each had written the profanity themselves. Most turned away and moved on, but a couple of men just stared back hatefully. I called her over for help to keep her from inciting an incident. Following her back in the Oldsmobile, I pondered whether or not to mention her dangerously fast driving, but after watching her slam the car door with all the anger she could muster, I decided to let it go.

Sarah was preparing a nice dinner for us. Venice insisted she stay, and despite Sarah's resistance, Venice, as she always did, got her way.

"We can sand it down and re-paint it," I told Sarah as we ate.

"No need to bother. I don't imagine I'll be drivin' in much anyway."

"You can't let those low-life scoundrels intimidate you," Venice said.

"Oh, I know how you'd want me to stand up to 'em, and I'd like to, but there's just nothing to gain." Sarah gazed off through a window. "Just like up in Springfield. People are prejudice about blacks or Jews or something else, but it's jealousy drives 'em to evil. It wasn't so much that there was black folks around; they were mad a bunch of 'em did well for themselves. Largest grocery store in town belonged to a black man." Sarah turned back to Venice. "Used to be folks'd look down on us as unpleasant curiosities, but when I drove an automobile in town, it was just too much."

She took another couple of bites as if contemplating something important.

"I got a letter from Dolly. Things is workin' out real nice down there. There's a fair-size black community, and they found a church and they have friends over to dinner and such ... folks seem to like her cookin'."

Venice looked sadly at me, and then at Sarah. "You'd never think of leaving here would you? You should never let anyone force you out of your home."

"Ah, Daddy'd never leave that cabin. He loves it too much." She changed the subject. "I got a bear's been nosin' around the place down there."

"I can come shoot it."

"Naw, it's just a youngun. If we keep it clean enough, he'll move on. It'd be a shame to shoot anything that wasn't old enough to know any better."

Sarah's bear became one of the Crawford Ranch's most enduring legends. Apparently, the young bruin hadn't read the same texts on bear behavior that Sarah had been citing and was not moving on. We got daily reports of its nocturnal snoopings from the twins, enjoying a laugh at their descriptions of their mother running it off. Sarah became especially outraged when it decided to dig in her gardens. Her crusade included stern words to the men of the house for careless misuse of food. Henry kidded that she was on "crumb patrol."

Venice and I were enjoying our coffee on the front porch one morning when the twins walked over to share the latest.

"Mama *whipped* that bear!" Tom said

"What?"

"She's been shooing that thing away every night," Billy explained. "It was coming up on the front porch, sniffing for something to eat. Last night, she yelled, 'git!' and then swatted it with a big stick she had ready for him."

They acted it out, imitating the bawl the bear let out at the sting of Sarah's stick on its hide. We doubled over laughing.

The bear apparently got the message and never showed up again.

Chapter Thirty-Eight

Dolly and Charles arrived early for Christmas ecstatic to show off their son, Christopher. Annie and Luke were along the next day with their third daughter, Mary. Teddy took center stage, visiting with anyone who would listen, but not necessarily stopping his chatter after he had exhausted his audience. We were relieved when Melissa came over with Robert. Teddy worshiped his older brother, and Robert always took a keen interest in Teddy. I would catch myself just gazing at Robert as if I had never seen him before, my reflection in his face stronger each time. It was a strain not to openly love him as my son, and sad that the boys didn't know they were brothers. Venice caught me staring a number of times, but we avoided talking about it.

A few days after all of the company was gone, Venice surprised me a little by announcing that she wanted to go to Kansas the following week. This was welcome news in a number of ways. It was the first time she'd expressed a desire to return to the Bar G since her father's death, and of course, I was always up for some bird hunting.

She reacted as I hoped, a fond smile accompanying her few nostalgic episodes. We had good hunts and great fun showing Teddy around the ranch. We returned to the Ozarks with a sense of renewal, as if some wound had been closed.

Once the weather turned nice, Venice and I spent hours at a time on the porch, reading. "There'll be a war in Europe," I broke a long silence late one early summer afternoon as I folded my paper and put it aside.

"Surely we wouldn't get mixed up in that." Venice didn't look up from her reading. "That madness doesn't concern us ... but I'm afraid we will." She closed the magazine and laid it in her lap. "Men feel a need to go to war like it's some great adventure, like a game. Our boys will feel left out if they don't get in on it. It's so foolish. If women ran the world we'd never have a war."

"Yes, I've seen first hand your talents for diplomacy."

She grinned. "We women would find other ways to settle our differences without cannons or bayonets ... we probably wouldn't have to be worried about *any* war if women could vote."

"I figured that's where you were headed."

"You think it's wrong for women not to vote too, so don't tease me about saying it ... Missouri is just a stick in the mud. We'll never get it until it goes national."

"I'm sorry my love. I do agree with you. It's a travesty. I'd certainly vote to change it."

"Oh, don't get overwhelmed with emotion. You're a man, so it doesn't concern you ... I think I would like to go to one of those rallies. We women need to be heard."

"Yes darling, you've always had *such* a problem being heard."

"You really are trying to get my dander up, aren't you?"

"I'm teasing. By all means, you should go to your rally. I'd go with you but I'd feel like I was in the enemy camp."

"And I suppose you would find a reason to go to the Bar G while I was gone ... thin out that awful overpopulation of birds."

"Wherever I'm needed."

We laughed, and then rocked with our thoughts, enjoying a colorful sunset. In the late-afternoon shadows, a mother deer with a pair of white-speckled fawns eased along the edge of the trees. One of the youngsters stared at us and then scurried along in a panic after discovering its mother and sibling had moved on.

Venice sighed. "I love it here. It's like a haven from all the craziness in the world ... a sort of Garden of Eden."

"I'll have to be careful not to be led astray, like Adam."

"Yes, I could tempt you with one of Sarah's apple pies."

"Maybe you should take a bunch of your pies when you go to your rallies. The men will listen then."

"Or maybe we ladies could wear our fig leaves."

"Now there's a rally I would attend."

Venice burst out in the laugh I adored.

Teddy was growing into a sweet but very inquisitive youngster, which resulted in the summer's only mishap. Reaching into some brush for a ball, a copperhead bit him on the hand. His mother went into a state of panic I hadn't witnessed from her before. He had a little swelling, but I it looked like a dry bite to me. He was ready to go out and play the next day, but Venice kept him inside. When he finally got his release, Venice made herself crazy trying to keep him away from snaky places, which is pretty much everywhere on an Ozark ranch. That lasted about a month. As his mother resigned herself to the inevitable, Teddy went back to sticking his hand in any hole that interested him.

Summer blended seamlessly into autumn, but as the leaves faded into winter brown, an ill wind blew across the ranch. Henry was in bed after a bout of strained breathing, which we feared was a heart attack, but he refused to let Sarah call the doctor out.

"What's he gonna do anyway?" Henry said. "There ain't no medicine for being old."

He was up again, out roaming the property with me, long before Sarah was satisfied with his health, but she remained mum about it. He wanted to do some landscaping around the spring up the valley from their cabin, including a rock bench where he could "think." The morning he decided to get started on it, he followed me down a game trail that paralleled the spring branch. Henry had a sketchpad to draw up his plans. It was a gorgeous fall morning, trees blazing against a deep blue sky, just cool enough to wear a flannel shirt. When the spring came into view, I turned to say something to Henry, but he wasn't there. I ran but a few strides before spotting him face down in the leaves. As I rolled him over, I realized instantly he was gone.

Even the twins, who were starting to look adult, cried as we buried Henry next to Father. I read the same Psalm that Mother had me read at my father's funeral. The boys stood on both sides of their mother as they escorted her back to the cabin. I stayed behind as the Barry boys began to fill in the grave. It startled me when a tiny hand touched mine. I hadn't heard Teddy walk up behind me. "Come with us, Daddy." We walked with his mother, hand-in-hand back to the house that Henry had built for us.

Sarah remained eerily to herself for weeks. We feared something beyond her father's death was weighing on her emotions. Venice was terrified that she was contemplating leaving, but I kept her from broaching the subject as long as I could. I think I was afraid of what she might say.

"What's wrong dear," Venice finally asked one evening. "You haven't been the same since your dear father left us. It's been some time now. I fear something else is bothering you."

"I s'pose a person's always got somethin' bothering 'em."

"Please, what is it?"

"I guess I took it harder than I figured I would, dad's death and all ... With Dolly gone and them boys growing up, I'll be by myself before too long. Billy's already spouting off about leavin' to play baseball ... now what kind of ambition is that?"

"You'll always have us dear," Venice said softly. "Teddy needs you ... we need you."

"I don't need to be bothering y'all with my moping. I'm fine."

"Maybe it would do you good to go down and visit with Dolly and Charles."

Sarah nodded. "I know you're right. Little Christopher'll be gettin' around pretty good by now. I 'spect Dolly could use a hand."

"There," Venice said. "We'll go in and make arrangements tomorrow."

"Maybe them hot springs'll do some good for this sore back."

We kept an eye on the twins as they fended for themselves for the first time. They were surprisingly adept at rustling up meals, though lagged considerably in the area of cleaning up afterward.

Sarah's trip had the desired effect; she came back her old self again. Venice went about as long without talking as I could remember as Sarah gushed about the kids, her grandson and what a nice life they had carved out for themselves. Perhaps for Venice's benefit, she added that she missed us, and the ranch, so much it made her realize she could never leave.

"Did you meet any particularly interesting people down there?" I sensed a more specific inquiry buried in Venice's question.

"There's all kinds of interesting people down there. The church is so nice, and all the people are so nice."

"Hum. All kinds of people?"

"None I'd care to mention," Sarah said.

Venice looked pleased with herself. It sounded to me like Sarah had merely directed her to mind her own business, but it turned out my wife's instincts were right on the money. She soon reported that Sarah was receiving mail, and being very closed-mouth about it. I got on to Venice one evening when she informed me the letters had been sent from "Daniel."

"Well how could I not look?"

"Leave her alone. She'd tell us if she thought it were any of our business."

"Well you're just going to take all the fun out of it."

"For *you* maybe. She has a right to her privacy."

"I know. I just want her to be happy."

"Me too, but I suspect she's the best judge of what makes her happy."

Venice pushed at my shoulder. "Oh, pooh on you ... okay, I won't say anything else. I promise."

Remarkably, she was able to maintain her silence, and even quit making her little comments to me about it. That lasted a few weeks, until Sarah announced another trip to Arkansas.

As we waited on the depot platform for Sarah's train, I'd made up my mind not to waste any effort of trying to thwart my wife's nosey inquiries, but Sarah immediately relieved Venice's curiosity by admitting Daniel was one of the reasons she had gone back right away. With dramatic effect, she waited until we were driving back to tell us he was coming to visit the ranch.

"That's wonderful!" Venice launched into a mild hysteria. "When? I knew you'd find somebody ..."

"Whoa! Just calm down Miss Venice. This is just a gentleman I met who mentioned he'd like to see the ranch. I *had* to invite him."

Venice beamed, but astonishingly, added nothing.

Chapter Thirty-Nine

Daniel stood well over six feet with the upper body of a man who made his living with his brawn. Imposing figure that he was, he had a bashful demeanor that at first made him seem dull, but on the drive home, he sounded sharp responding to Venice's interrogation.

"I'm a lumberman," he said.

"That explains the muscles," Venice said.

I glanced back and saw Sarah shaking her head.

"Is your family from the Hot Springs area?"

"No ma'am, most of my folk are down in Texas ... East Texas. I was born down around Crockett. I move around quite a bit for my work."

"Do you have children?"

"No ma'am, I've never been married."

"Daniel my friend," I said. "Don't feel obligated to share your entire personal history with my nosey wife."

"Oh, I'm sorry." She cocked an unappreciative eyebrow my direction. "Forgive me for being interested in people I meet."

"That's not a problem at all, Mrs. Crawford."

"Please call me Venice." She turned to me. "And thank *you*, Mr. Crawford, for being kind enough to point out my bad manners. I don't know what I'd do without you."

"Happy to help any time."

Sarah let a snicker escape, and Venice grinned over her shoulder. "Well, we're glad you're here Daniel. Please feel free to treat our ranch as your own."

"That's mighty gracious, Mrs. Crawford. Thank you for having me."

"It's Venice, now."

"Sorry ... Venice."

We put Daniel in an upstairs bedroom. He appeared a bit uncomfortable with his surroundings in the beginning, but smiled contentedly, nodding approval as we sat on the porch while the women prepared dinner. "This is a mighty special place you have here, Mr. Crawford."

"Call me James. Thanks. I've been blessed."

"So your folks passed?"

"Yeah. My father got killed in a tornado when I was young. Mother drowned in a flood saving a calf ... he would've been the sire here on the ranch, but

228

Venice offered too much to turn down. That's how we got together. They came over to buy cattle, Venice and her dad."

"Well I'll be ... met buyin' and sellin' cattle."

"Venice ran a huge ranch for her father out in Kansas. She knows as much about it as anybody ... actually we'd met earlier, but that's a long boring story ... Sarah's father built this house ... twice. The first one burned down."

He nodded. "Sari told me. I wished I could've met Henry."

"When Venice's father was alive, the two of them could be a lot of fun. We had some great holidays around here."

"I imagine you still do."

"Sure we do. I didn't mean to sound so gloomy ... we lost Henry, and then Dolly left. The boys are starting to get the itch ... we just worry about Sarah leaving."

"The way she talks about this place, and you all, and that youngun, don't sound like she'd ever leave on her own account ... it's a fine thing Sari has folks care for her so much."

We discovered over dinner that Daniel was quite a talkative fellow once he got to know you. He was smart and thoughtful, with interesting stories about his travels. "My goodness, that's about the best meal I've ever eaten," he laid his napkin on the table. "Y'all feed me like that again, you may not be able to run me off."

"Sarah's the cook," Venice said. "I just get in the way."

"Well, my compliments to both of you."

"You should take Daniel out on the porch," Venice said. "The night's too nice to sit inside. Jimmy and I will clean this up." Sarah nodded her appreciation.

As we washed dishes, Venice went on about how Daniel and Sarah were perfect together.

"He's so much darker than she is. I wonder if that matters to her."

"Why would it?"

"I don't know ... but don't they look so good together, him dark and handsome, her more feminine. She has beautiful skin ... and that figure at her age, with three children, I wish I looked like that."

"Now, now, everybody knows that Venice Crawford is the most voluptuous sight in the Ozarks."

She smirked. "Well, that's very kind, but silly ... I'm happy to be second." She laughed, and we kissed without touching with our wet hands.

Sarah interrupted. "My goodness, you two just can't be left alone for a second ... Teddy came out front with us ..."

"Oh my word, I'm sorry."

"We're glad to have him, it's just we're gonna take a stroll, so I'm puttin' him inside."

"Have fun."

Sarah shook her head in mock disgust at Venice's tone.

It got a little crazy after Daniel left. Sarah's writing was still rudimentary, so she solicited Venice's help in drafting responses to his letters. It was no surprise they squabbled. Venice couldn't have kept her suggestions to herself if it meant a genie would grant her three wishes, and Sarah didn't mince words defending her personal affairs. They sulked around each other until another letter arrived. When the boys asked Venice if their mother was getting married, she told them: "I'm sure it's just a matter of time." That made Sarah angry, left the boys confused and me ducking whenever I saw either of the women headed my way in a foul mood.

Sarah headed back down to Arkansas a few weeks after Daniel's visit, and he was back in the Ozarks two weeks later. I teased him that he might purchase a permanent seat on the train. He smiled. "I s'pose we look like a couple of school kids."

"I'm happy for y'all ... but I'm going have to get the doc out here to sedate my wife if you don't announce something soon. I don't know why she gets so worked up about stuff like this."

He just smiled.

At the breakfast table, before we took Daniel in to catch his train, Sarah was in an especially chipper mood considering he was leaving. It wasn't lost on Venice. She studied them suspiciously throughout the meal. When Sarah wiped her mouth and dropped the napkin on her plate, she said nonchalantly, "I have something to say, but I worry about how Miss Venice takes big news." Venice's eyes bulged in anticipation. "Gettin' too excited about things ain't healthy." When she reached for Daniel's hand, and they smiled at each other, Venice leapt to her feet, banging the table and startling Teddy into dropping his milk. The two women hurried around the table and hugged.

On the drive in to the depot, Venice couldn't contain her enthusiasm. When she brought up decorating the house for the wedding, Sarah cut her off. "I know you'd throw the most beautiful wedding possible, and I love you for it, but we're gettin' married down in Arkansas."

Venice gasped.

"Daniel has a church, and I *don't* have one, and that's where we ought to get married ... that's where we met." Even Venice had no argument. "But we wouldn't expect you to come down all that way though."

"We wouldn't miss it!" A sudden panic struck her. "So where will you live?"

"Well," Daniel said, "that's something I'd like to talk to you about. My whole life, there's nothing I've wanted more than to settle in a beautiful place like Sari's."

"That's wonderful!" Venice clapped her hands. "You can work for us." She turned to me. "We could use a man who knows timber."

"To tell you the truth," Daniel said. "I always wanted to be a farmer or a ranch man."

"Well, you've come to the right place. I look *so* forward to the wedding." Sarah looked concerned. "We've got so much to do. Hey, you two boys could go over and hunt birds for a few days while Sarah and I get things ready. Do you like to hunt, Daniel?"

"I used to love to hunt with my brothers, mostly squirrels and rabbits. We'd go all the time when we were little."

"What do we have to do?" Sarah said.

"It'd be hard to get any time off," Daniel said. "I want to put back as much money as I can."

"We can go hunting any time you want," I said. "You've got to take care of business first."

Right before they kissed goodbye at the depot, Sarah glared over at us, aggravated that Venice was staring, but it did nothing to redirect her attention. As they held a long kiss, Venice squeezed my arm so tight it hurt.

Chapter Forty

I peeked around the congregation as inconspicuously as I could manage. Ours were the only white faces in the church. A few of the looks felt unfriendly, and some people seemed to be going out of their way not to notice us, but several were especially gracious, having made a point to introduce themselves before the ceremony. Venice smiled and nodded as she made eye contact around the sanctuary, struggling to maintain her patience in spite of a restless Teddy.

Finally, Sarah appeared through the door in the back of the church dressed in the understated dress I'd heard her and Venice debating in recent weeks. As she started up the aisle, an elderly white-haired woman winced at hitting an out-of-tune piano key. Daniel and Sarah stood strong before the preacher, as if together they could move a mountain, but their answers to the vows were a bit delicate. The kiss was brief, but looked well rehearsed.

Teddy loved riding the train, and kept his eyes glued to the window on the trip home. It allowed Venice and I to relax, read and maintain an unspoken agreement to keep conversation sparse. I was taking less frequent advantage of the scenery than I would have normally, remaining captive to my newspapers. War was blazing in Europe, modern weapons yielding unthinkable casualties. Many journalists were expressing a sense of inevitability that the United States was going to get involved, despite many politicians' determination to stay out of it. I began to ponder how I should respond if we did become a combatant.

Venice's response to my mention of it was slightly hysterical. "Absolutely not! I'll not have you die for such a worthless purpose." I dropped it there, deciding to take it up later if the situation ever actually presented itself.

The twins were getting to the age that their futures were often a subject of conversation, but mostly between Venice and Sarah. Venice was determined they go to college, even hopping on the train to Pine Bluff to look into getting them admitted despite a lack of formal schooling. She returned ecstatic. The boys need only pass an exam and take a few courses designed for such students. Venice couldn't have been more confident that her pupils could pass any test.

She sent the boys right back down, with Sarah, to take the test. Sarah and Tom returned like conquering heroes, but you would never have known that Billy scored a few points higher than his brother. Tom came back excited with the idea of studying biology, but Billy usually ducked out of the room when the discussion arose.

Venice wasn't going to let such an occasion as the boys' acceptance into college slip by without a party. My suggestion to wait until just before their departure, almost six weeks away, was a waste of breath. She made the usual big deal out of it, even inviting the editor of the newspaper. Venice presented both of the boys with a Bible and a dictionary, a bank draft tucked in the pages of the dictionary. Sarah shook her head as the twins gaped at the checks.

Several days after the party, Jesse pulled me aside in the store.

"Did you see the article about the party for the boys?"

"No, I don't look at that stuff."

"A bunch of these local yahoos are stirred up about it."

"Stirred up about what?"

"About you giving the kids money, and the amount."

"They had no right to print that."

"Whether or not they do doesn't matter to them ... there's folks in town whose kids studied and went to school and did good enough, but the parents couldn't afford college. They can't stand them black kids going. These are people who don't believe there should even be such a thing as a negro college."

"Neither do I."

Jesse grinned. "That's a little different."

"It's none of their damn business anyway."

"I know. I was just giving you a heads up."

"Well thanks."

It turned out the newspaper had reported a much higher amount than we had actually given, a figure I had to admit would raise some eyebrows. Venice remained unusually quiet about the whole affair, likely feeling bad for having encouraged the writer in the first place. She put up no objections when I banned reporters from Crawford property, a prohibition that would be short lived.

A couple of weeks after all that nonsense, Billy sulked up and sat next to me on the porch, the check we had given him in his hand.

"I need to give this back."

"Why?"

"I ain't goin' to college, or least not right away."

"Baseball?"

He nodded. "Mama and Miss Venice are gonna be mighty disappointed. I'm scared to even tell 'em."

"So what are you planning to do?"

"I don't exactly know. I figured I'd head east and try to get tryouts for Negro League teams."

"Hum. Well, you'll still need some money." His eyes brightened. "Why don't you hang onto that for now."

"Mama'll have something to say about that ... if I don't make it, I'll go to college, but it don't matter how much a good job pays if the whole time you're doing it you just want to be playing baseball."

It turned out Sarah had been resigned to Billy's need to get baseball out of his system before he could move on with his life. Instead of fighting against his dream, she spent her energies coaxing promises from him that he would come back and go to school if he didn't make it. Sarah was conflicted on the issue of our financial support. We had helped Tom with college expenses, and it didn't seem right to deny Billy the same support, but she didn't want to encourage baseball as much as college. In the end, Sarah agreed to less than what we gave Tom, likely hoping for more help when Billy was back and in school. But Venice pulled Billy aside before he left and explained how wiring money worked.

He boarded the train with one suitcase, enough money to live on for three or four months and a little extra cash I slipped him to buy a proper glove and cleats. He hadn't a clue of where he was going to sleep that night and couldn't have been more thrilled about it. He seemed to have a fair understanding of what he was going up against, but had an unwavering confidence in his arm.

"He may just make it," Sarah said as his train pulled away.

It was a couple of months before we got word that he was doing well, living in Chicago. He was staying with a coach and his family, an arrangement based in part on Billy's ability to chip in on living expenses. It was money apparently well spent. His new mentor, Gus, had been one of the best hurlers in the league before blowing out his arm. He understood pitching and recognized Billy's talents. Gus not only worked with Billy on his pitching mechanics but also helped him get work at a grocery shop owned by an avid baseball fan. Gus introduced him to the manager of the American Giants. After a quick demonstration of his skills, Billy was invited to work out with the team before games, and began to throw batting practice. It was good to see the pride Sarah had at how adept he was at taking care of himself.

Chapter Forty-One

Tom left for school on an unseasonably cool August morning. Sarah stood at the edge of the platform, arm around her husband, staring through proud tears until the train was but a trail of smoke over a distant tree line. Even Daniel sniffled a little. Teddy made the mistake of showing a trace of emotion, prompting his mother to take out a handkerchief and thoroughly embarrass him with words meant to comfort.

Venice had been fretting over Teddy getting lonely when all the kids were gone, and her first remedy was to give him his own horse as a companion. We had a new foal from one of her favorites, and he named it Cherokee. She was soon regretting it though, especially after our surprisingly adept little horseman took it upon himself to ride into town to see Robert. Teddy's tendency toward mischief seemed perfectly natural to me, and I didn't get as upset with him as his mother, which made her unhappy with me.

"You're no help," she said, restarting a conversation we'd had many times before as she brushed her hair in the mirror. "Standing there like you want to laugh at the terrible things he's done."

I climbed into bed.

"It encourages him, I hope you know ... you could at least listen when I try to discuss raising our son."

She scowled at my lack of response.

"You spoil him so, and make me be the bad guy. He's going to grow up to hate me."

"Don't be ridiculous."

"He can get away with anything around you, and you don't support me ..."

"I do too."

"Like this silly gun business. We agreed that twelve was the proper age."

"*You* decided that."

She wheeled around angrily. "Jimmy Crawford, you know darn well that's what we agreed."

"It's just silly for him to have to wait for some arbitrary age. We both shot at that age."

"But ..."

"He's perfectly mature enough. I really must insist this time."

She squinted. "Insist, huh?" She turned back and continued brushing. "And I suppose you'll see that he knows it was you, that his Daddy had to save him from his mean old witch mother again."

I couldn't help but chuckle. I went over and hugged her from behind. "How about *you* tell him tomorrow."

She forced a half smile. "I suppose you might possibly be right this one time."

Venice embraced it with her usual enthusiasm, deciding that as teacher she would take the lead in the shooting lessons. Teddy saw his mother in a completely new light when she busted every stick I threw off the bluff.

Teddy's next conquest was the automobile. Venice laid down the law that he wouldn't drive until he was fifteen, and I knew that would be put to the test. I caught him breaking his mother's rule when she was off in St. Louis visiting her suffrage ladies, and he thought I'd be in town longer. He avoided her ranting, but my punishments held up longer. I didn't hear a word of complaint out of him for the entire two weeks of his punishment, though he sulked around so I was sure to notice.

"What is it between the two of you?" Venice queried on the porch one night after Teddy stomped back inside. "He acts as if he's mad at you."

"He is."

"Did you punish him for something?"

"Yes. It's not a big deal."

"What did he do?"

"Well dear, part of our agreement involved him not having to disappoint his mother."

"How disappointed would his mother be?"

"Not at all, really. Don't worry about it."

"He hasn't done something dangerous has he?"

I paused to consider the nominal danger of driving the car around the ranch. "No, I just caught him driving the Packard around in the pasture."

"What!"

"You can't say anything."

"We'll see about that. And what was your punishment?"

"Two weeks, no horses, no guns."

"That's just a slap on the wrist."

"Better than you saying a month and then giving in after a few days."

Venice grinned.

"I also said that if he whined it would become four weeks ... and any more driving would push it back to sixteen."

"My, you are the stern one aren't you? Well at least I'm not the mean ol' witch *this* time."

We were sitting on the porch one brisk morning when we heard the first turkey gobble of the spring, prompting me to dart inside and dig through my father's calls to find one for Teddy. He immediately made me regret it. His first attempt at using it sent a chill down my spine and his mother winced, but to our surprise, a turkey gobbled just up the river. Teddy's next attempt sounded no more like a turkey than his first, but the gobbler sounded off again.

"Hey," Venice whispered, he's getting closer."

"You don't think he'd come up to the yard, do you?" Teddy said.

"You never know, try again."

I frowned at Venice for encouraging the terrible racket.

The turkey sounded even closer the next time it gobbled, but then it clammed up.

"I think he's gone," I finally said when my ears had suffered enough turkey calling.

Teddy loved the fun, new game of talking to turkeys, the distant yelps of his call a constant. He was getting better, but I figured he's already scared most of birds off the place, so I decided to slip away to Kansas to hunt turkeys with Luke. I plotted with Venice, having her cite study as the reason Teddy couldn't go with me. He was grounded to a week inside the house for sass during their discussion of why he wasn't included in the Kansas turkey hunt, but Venice let him off the hook after a day.

I was quite surprised to discover on my return that Teddy had killed a turkey on his own.

"So you just let him hunt all by himself?" I questioned Venice.

"I did no such thing. I assumed you'd told him it was okay, I mean since he just went ... Oh my God, I did let him! That little scoundrel! He's in *big* trouble."

"Big trouble" didn't amount to much, and as usual, his punishment didn't last long. The issue of him hunting alone seemed to just fade away after that. We of course had a soft spot for hunting, and Teddy had demonstrated maturity while handling a gun.

Other than Teddy's escapades, it was a quiet summer. I worked around the place most mornings and spent the afternoons with my wife and son, fishing, riding and taking automobile rides through the country. Evenings were spent rocking out front, counting fireflies and wishing on shooting stars. You had to drag me off the ranch during that period, but Venice was traveling more with her various causes.

It was looking like U.S. involvement in the war was inevitable, but with me getting too old for the proposed draft, and Teddy many years away from fighting age, Venice's anti-war sentiments took a back seat to women's issues and a new cause she had embraced, criminalizing alcohol. She was increasingly involved in state and national efforts, traveling to meetings and disseminating information at gatherings in our home. After I sat in on one of these meeting for about ten minutes, I began referring to her ladies group as an angry women's club. Teddy and I pretty much disappeared during meetings after that.

Chapter Forty-Two

Venice's meetings grew in size and frequency. By purchasing a large advertisement for Crawford Angus in the newspaper, which made no sense for us financially, she was able to bully the editor into covering her club activities like they were big news stories. He hired his niece, Katherine, fresh out of school, and she got caught up in Venice's movements as much any of the ladies. Her reporting amounted to poorly disguised editorials, but papers were selling, so the editor didn't bother himself with his niece's bias.

The issue of a woman's suffrage turned out to be a lot bigger deal in the Ozarks than I would have ever expected, in large part due to my wife. I imagined that something like ninety-eight percent of local men were against giving women the vote, and at least half of the women agreed with their husbands. For the most part, women in the region had always seemed happy to leave government and politics to their men, but local women were now being more vocal publicly and at home. More than a couple of husbands were placing blame for their growing domestic discord on my wife. And Venice continued to fan the flames of conflict by feeding juicy quotes to Katherine. "Who cares, really, what he thinks," she responded to what some legislator had said about the women's vote. "I'm more interested in what his wife would say about it."

Sarah told me one day after she came from town how much people were talking about Venice. "She's got the whole town stirred up. Wives against husbands ... those ol' tobacco-spittin' fools offered up a mighty unfriendly gesture to Daniel and me today."

"Don't tell Venice."

"Oh, I don't tell her nothin' like that. She's makin' enough noise out there as it is."

"She means well."

"I know she does, but keepin' everybody stirred up makes it worse on those you're trying to help, sometimes. That old man Jackson damn near killed his wife beatin' her last week."

"Why don't you say something to her?"

"Oh no, that's your job ... I've hinted at it, but she can be stubborn as a mule. Only one that could get through to her is you ... James, she's even been talkin' about makin' liquor illegal. That'll make them men a lot madder than women voting."

Venice's crusades were a financial boon for the newspaper. Beside readers' thirst for what she was going to say next, many copies were purchased to keep up with the latest scathing letters to the editor about Venice and her supporters. When I went in to complain about the letters being published, the editor told me that he had not run several that were poorly veiled threats.

But Venice would hear none of my caution.

"So just because somebody wants women and black people as servants only, I'm suppose to tamp down my right to speak?" she said one night in our bedroom.

"No, of course not. I just wanted you to know ... and to be careful. I worry. You know, our house was burned down, and they almost killed Henry."

She looked startled. "Are you scared of that again?"

"No, but I wasn't scared of it back then either."

Venice stopped brushing her hair, and walked out to stare over the balcony rail. I followed, leaning next to her. "Sarah says folks have started makin' cracks to them."

"Like what?"

"Well, I'm sure you can imagine without me having to repeat it. I'm not saying give up your causes. I just want you to be careful."

She nodded.

She broke a short silence. "Sometimes I wonder about it myself. I just think how much happier I was just raising Teddy. I wonder if I shouldn't just adopt a child, or two, and not worry about anything else. But then I feel guilty. Because of my good fortune, I'm in a position to help every woman, and it would be selfish not to help."

"I understand, and I think you're right. I just wonder if quibbling locally doesn't do more harm than good. Your fight is national. Missouri will never pass it on their own ... Let's quit paying for that silly advertisement."

Venice grinned sheepishly. "You're right. I have perhaps gone about some of this wrong. It's all much bigger than this little clump of hills."

"Maybe you're right about adopting."

Venice surprised me by not answering right away. She stared quietly out into the canopy of trees. "I know I've been a little fickle on that. I can't quite understand it myself. I so love raising Teddy, and it was so nice when the kids were here ... Now, Teddy's grown up and he's only interested in you men."

"That's not true."

She sighed. "It's fine. That's how it should be. I just miss it though. And while I want to have more children, I feel there is so much I want to do first."

"Like change the world?"

She smiled. "That, but I'd like for us to travel a bit first."

"I'd gladly go back to Montana."

"I was thinking some place different, exotic, Alaska, or maybe Africa."

"Teddy's old enough to go now."

"It'd be so much fun. We need a trip, the three of us. Get away from all this."

"I tell you what, why don't you get on a train to St. Louis, spend some days shopping and make arrangements there for a trip. Wherever you choose. Surprise me when you come back."

"Jimmy, you don't mean it!"

"I do."

"What if you don't like my choice?"

"I'll love it, and so will Teddy."

"How exciting ... I think an African Safari would be *so* exciting. I've read about them."

"That sounds perfect."

"Oh, Jimmy, I do think this is what I need."

"Just don't spend too much time with the local activists in St. Louis." I grinned.

"No, not this time."

It was more than a week before Venice returned, ecstatic that she had booked us on a three-week African safari. She had also purchased what she deemed proper uniforms for such an expedition, mostly in drab greens and khaki, and picked up a copy of Theodore Roosevelt's *African Game Trails* for Teddy.

"Can we even sail?" I said. "It seems dangerous with German U-boats out there."

"The contract says we can go at any time of our choosing, as long as it's within a year of the end of the war. I'm not even sure there is any danger where we'd be going. Everybody says the fighting is about over anyway ... Oh you boys will just love it. We'll be in tents with guides and cooks, but it's very first-class camping. We can hunt anything we like, but I don't want Teddy around anything dangerous. He can hunt antelopes. There must be a dozen different kinds ... oh, you should see the photographs."

"What kind of guns will we need?"

"They have all of that. Just think of the pictures we can bring back. We'll buy one of those new cameras. It will be so educational for Teddy."

"I suspect that's the sort of studying he'd like."

Venice smiled. "It is going to be a wonderful experience for him."

"And for all of us ... I think I'd like to shoot a leopard."

"But they're so beautiful."

I shrugged. "They seem so mysterious."

"Well, you can shoot what you like, but only antelopes for Teddy."

I bowed with a smile.

Teddy was ecstatic, impressing us by reading Roosevelt's adventures all the way through in a week, and then immediately re-reading it in smaller pieces, educating us each evening about life on safari. He also began paying close attention to the war. We decided to wait until hostilities had ceased, but with the U.S. in the fighting, we expected it to be wrapped up soon. Then we'd be off for East Africa.

Chapter Forty-Three

One of Venice's quirks that bothered me at times was how she dismissed all my questions about our finances. I was happy she was willing to handle our books and banking, but she acted at times like she was keeping a secret. We'd been married several years before she filled me in on the extent of our interest in copper and gold mining. There was even a sapphire mine. She threw money around like it was confetti, so I figured there was no reason to worry about any of that. It was simple curiosity that prompted me to dig around in the desk drawer for safari paperwork. I just had to know the cost.

It was actually less than I had feared, but more interesting than the price was the address of the travel agency on the receipt. The trip had been purchased in New York. She hadn't said a word, taking advantage of my disinterest to say almost nothing about the trip other than to talk about the safari.

That evening in bed, I brought it up. "I think I'd like to go to New York soon."

She glanced at me. "That's surprising. I think you'd hate it there."

"Why would you say that?"

"I think you'd rather go for mountains or wilderness, some place where you could go fishing or hunting."

"Don't you like New York?"

"I can tolerate it."

"Maybe it's changed. When were you last there?"

Venice grinned. "So you just couldn't stand not knowing?"

"Why New York?"

"I just wasn't happy with what I was finding in St. Louis. It was a much better place to book the trip. I didn't bother to mention it because I was just so afraid you'd be angry how much I spent, with the travel costs, the safari and the shopping, and ..."

"What else?"

"Oh, Jimmy!" her sudden enthusiasm gushed out like air from a balloon. "I met with some amazing women. I met Lucy Burns. She was involved in the women's movement in England and now is one of the most important women leaders in this country ... she might come here to visit us! ... I wrote a small draft ..."

I put up my hand. "Don't even tell me how much 'small' is. We're not broke now are we?"

"Don't be silly. I'm sorry I didn't mention it. I know I should have. I didn't really think you'd be interested ... Let's not make too much of it. We won't keep any more secrets ... do you think there are any secrets that are okay to keep from a spouse?"

"Not many. I guess I wouldn't necessarily care to know about a blemish on your behind."

"Jimmy! That sounds just awful. Let's pretend the blemish is on *your* behind."

"Either way, I think there are certain things better kept to ourselves."

Venice laughed. "Okay then, agreed."

After she turned off the lamp, I said, "I hope I won't have to wait for a blemish to clear up to see your behind. I so enjoy looking at it."

She giggled and rolled over to kiss me.

"Now that you mentioned it, *Doctor Crawford,* I do think I have a little spot back there. Would you reach back to see what you think it might be? I hope it doesn't need treatment."

Since the cat was out of the bag, Venice didn't hesitate contacting Katherine for coverage of her trip to New York. Reports of her meeting with Alice Paul and Lucy Burns drew predictable results: angry letters to the editor and new, energized supporters at her meetings. But a couple of the regular attendees quit coming after that. For some of the area's women, the right to vote just wasn't worth what they were suffering at home. Others felt that it was unpatriotic to appear divisive while America was at war. But there were still those who were militant, unmoved by the criticisms and committed to any action that would forward the cause.

All the noise associated with Venice's politics quieted as the holiday season neared, primarily because she immersed herself in preparation for her favorite time of year. We went out to the Bar G to spend a family Thanksgiving, where Teddy, Venice and I had a wonderful time together, hunting and taking advantage of unseasonably warm weather for some long horseback rides.

The weather remained mild through Christmas, allowing the children to play outside. They had apparently stored a year's worth of energy for the holidays. The conversations between the youngsters became more interesting with age, and I found pleasure in just sitting on the porch listening.

"Hey," Charles said as he came out and sat next to me as the children played in the leaves.

"Hey ... just watching the kids ... I remember Ol' Grey, and Henry, they would just kind of sit off to the side and watch. I'm beginning to understand that now."

Charles looked puzzled. "They're growing up fast."

"They sure are. So what's going on inside? It sounded like an argument."

"Dolly and her Mama bickering about something or other. I swear, they both act like they can't stand to live away from each other, and then when they get together they squabble over every little thing. Do you understand that?"

"I don't think anybody understands that. It's why men go sit on the porch."

Charles laughed. "When are we going back out hunting, just us men?"

"I guess we should plan that while everybody's here. Next month would be good. Luke's started hunting ducks on a small lake, when it's not frozen. Quail hunting's always good in winter."

"Well, I been taking care of younguns plenty, while Dolly goes to her sewing club ... don't know if they actually do any real sewing. I hadn't seen any new shirts or dresses. I think they just gab and gossip."

"So you figure she owes you?"

"Well, I wouldn't dare say it that way, not so *she* could hear anyway. But I was sent to Fort Smith for a few days, and they had Dolly work in the store. They think she does real good. I could take off easy enough."

"Will Dolly work for you?"

"Oh she will. She acts all bossy, but she likes me having fun and thinks hunting is a healthy, sort of wholesome thing. Heck, after that last hunt she even said I should get a hunting coat."

"Great then. We'll get it planned while everyone is here."

Before long, all of the men had been driven to the porch by the din of female conversation. Daniel and I listened as the twins and Charles worked out the details of our hunt. Teddy monitored the planning with wide-eyed interest, bobbing his head in agreement with every decision. Charles turned to fill me in on the details after everything was set.

"Hey. Maybe you'll get that hunting coat for Christmas."

Charles' face lit up like he hadn't considered such a possibility.

He didn't get the coat, but when I told Venice the story, she purchased him one and presented it to him when he arrived on the train for the men's trip to Kansas. She decided not to join us, citing it inappropriate for a woman to be on this particular hunt. She was a little hurt that Teddy looked relieved. A better three days of hunting couldn't have been scripted, and Teddy went on non-stop to his mother about the trip when we got home. Venice acted excited for her son's sake, but I could tell she was feeling left out.

"I'm not," she said when I asked her about it. "I just feel sometimes like I'm loosing my little boy."

"It's natural for a mother to feel that way, but it's not true at all."

"It's fine. I don't want to be one of those mothers who coddle their son too much."

"You should really go on the hunts with us. This men's label is just something to keep the other women at home, but we want *you* there."

She cocked her head with a challenging smirk.

"And dearest, these are all men, so of course they enjoy being in the company of someone so beautiful."

She slapped my shoulder. "That's just silly. I mean, at Christmas with Sarah, Melissa and Annie ... she hasn't gained an ounce after those children ... I felt like an old hag around them."

I laughed, and hugged her, giving the attention such a comment was designed to solicit.

"And Dolly is just precious," Venice said. "She's going to be as pretty as her mother."

"Yes, I'll admit that ours is a particularly handsome group of women, but I am privileged to be married to the most beautiful angel in the Ozarks."

"Enough with all that ... I must admit though, I really do enjoy the hunts."

"Good. You'll go next time."

"We'll see ... I know the tobacco spitters ..." she laughed. "That's what Sarah calls them ... they would love this conversation. They think we women are all trying to be men just because we want equal treatment. For them to see me out hunting with you all ..."

"Why would you worry what they think? Besides, they'd see you belong because you are the best shooter among us."

"Women are the best at many things, they've just not had the opportunity to demonstrate it."

Per her instructions from the national movement, Venice began toning down her public rhetoric with the United States in the war. In England, women had been called on to work in the factories while their men fought in the trenches on the European mainland. Suffrage leaders there were waiting until after the conflict to resume their call for the vote when women's contributions to the war effort could be used to their advantage. American women were following the British lead now that their own countrymen were dying in battle.

Despite her lower profile, criticism of Venice didn't abate. Robert remained a steady conduit of the town's gossip to Teddy, who constantly asked us about it. It was also likely that Robert was the reason everyone in town knew we were waiting on the war to end to go on safari. Venice was being characterized as an elitist, selfishly waiting for the dying to stop so we could go on an opulent vacation.

It had an ugly ring to it that touched a nerve with even her milder critics.

I was also coming under fire. Though a little older than the men they were calling, many my age were volunteering. Each time I caught wind of another

246

criticism, I looked inward, questioning my behavior, but quickly came back to my honest belief that the war was insane, unworthy of my service, much less my life. I agreed with Venice about the useless waste of humanity and shared her feelings about my responsibilities to her and Teddy.

There were times when I felt guilty that whenever we discussed the war it was in the context of when we would be going to Africa, but Venice didn't hesitate. She felt the war was in no way her concern because she had not been able to participate in electing the men who made the decision to fight. We stayed mostly to ourselves on the ranch during that period, reading about the war and listening to Teddy educate us on Africa.

Chapter Forty-Four

An armistice was signed in the fall of 1918. Newspaper reports suggested a greater sense of relief than celebration. The estimates were more than 100,000 Americans killed, and that was but a fraction of the 20 million worldwide deaths some were calculating. We didn't attend the celebration in town. There was a local young man killed, which stirred resentment toward those who didn't serve. Venice also rejected the idea of celebrating after so many young lives were wasted.

She saw to it that everything about our African adventure was first class. For the cruise to England, Teddy had a room to himself with a view from a port window. Our cabin was magnificent. The meals were delicious, served in grand dining rooms on the finest China and linen beneath magnificent chandeliers. Musical entertainment with dancing was provided nightly, but Venice and I mostly huddled outside along the rail in the evenings, listening to the water wash along the hull. The moonless nights showcased the heavens in its greatest glory. It was never very long before a falling star streaked across the sky. We exhausted our wishes after a single evening.

Poor Teddy was often in his room studying. Venice was determined that he continue his lessons throughout our time at sea. She tempered this torture by purchasing books on Africa and the animals that lived there. It seemed funny to educate a young American boy in such detail about Africa, but Venice felt learning anything was worthwhile.

"Besides, no one can know everything," she said as she gazed out at the black ocean. "You never can tell when anything you read might come in handy."

"Yeah, he might become ambassador to South Africa one day."

"Don't say that."

"Speak of the devil."

Teddy was sauntering up the deck toward us, sliding his hand down the rail.

"You finished, sweetie?"

"Yeah."

"Well then, what are some animals you look forward to hunting?"

"*Panthera leo* and *Panthera pardus.*"

Venice thought it would be fun for Teddy to learn the genus and species names of the animals we might encounter. She got him to sign on by convincing him that to study biology like Tom, the Latin names were important to know.

"What is that?"

"Lion and leopard."

"Well you are certainly not hunting either of those!"

"You said what did I *want* to hunt."

"I said which did you look forward to hunting. You can't look forward to hunting something you are not going to hunt. We've been over this enough times."

"Can I take a walk?"

"Don't stay up too late."

He didn't acknowledge her last instruction as he ambled off.

"So help me Jimmy, you better not try and talk me into anything like that."

I smiled, holding my hands up in defense.

"I just hate being the one who gets blamed for being responsible," Venice said, not really sounding like she meant it. "You're not much help you know. I have to set the rules and you're just his buddy. You never speak up when he argues back to me."

"I figure you can take care of yourself ... okay, I'll see to it that he shuts up about it. And I'll even make him learn the Latin names of the stuff he *might* get to hunt if he keeps quiet about lions and leopards."

"Such a stern disciplinarian."

I put my arm around her. "Now if you don't start having an absolutely fabulous time, and quit worrying, I might have to discipline you with a spanking."

"I *am* having a wonderful time, but I understand you must do what you feel is necessary."

We laughed and went inside.

In Liverpool, we boarded a less luxurious but comfortable ship to South Africa, running into stormy weather around the Cape Verde Islands and then suffering several hot days and sultry nights through the tropics. It was a relief to finally sail into Cape Town harbor on a cool morning. We spent three nights there, waiting for our next ship, touring the city, shopping and enjoying a wonderful dinner each night. Teddy found a pith helmet like his namesake had worn, and Venice talked me into hats for us, wide-brimmed with a band of zebra hide. The shop owner assured us that all the white hunters were wearing them.

The smaller vessel we sailed up the eastern shore was a capable transport with more modest accommodations, but what it lacked in amenities was made up for with friendly service. I actually enjoyed the meals more than on the luxury ship, even though they were served in tight quarters with smelly dinner companions. Venice didn't share my and Teddy's fascination with that part of the journey. To Teddy, it was a perfect piece of his safari adventure.

Another component of Venice's educational approach to the trip was her insistence that Teddy keep a daily journal. He whined when he first heard about it, and then complained again when Venice informed him that he had to start when we left the states, but he took to it quickly, even mentioning later that he'd like to write a book one day. It was impressive to read the detail in the stories he'd heard over dinner from an old Afrikaner man about the Boer Wars. I had also listened intently as the weathered storyteller held Teddy spellbound, but I felt pretty sure most of it was lies. Venice couldn't get past her disgust that he always had bits of food in his unkempt beard.

As we sailed into the shining port of Mombassa, I thought Teddy was going to explode. After so many days at sea, there was something not quite real about the tropic glare on a hundred whitewashed buildings nestled in waxy greenery above a sapphire bay. A friendly young black man with a permanent smile met us on the dock and chattered the whole buggy ride to the hotel, but I never understood more than a few scattered words. Our waterfront hotel was draped in lush foliage alive with colorful birds, and our balcony had a wonderful view of white sands and palm trees. We had a delicious fish dinner and slept better than we had our entire time onboard ship.

The next morning at breakfast, Duke Bingham introduced himself with a thick British accent. He was an inch or two shorter than me, but his broad chest and thick biceps suggested he was up to most any physical task. His sun-baked hide spoke to his experience, though he appeared only slightly older than me.

"They call me Duke," he greeted us with a firm handshake. "The reason for that is, well, I was a Duke ... am one I suppose. So, it's Venice and Jimmy, is it?"

I smiled.

"That's not right?"

"Venice is the only one who calls me Jimmy. Everybody else calls me James."

"I rather like that better anyway ... James it is then."

"And I'm Teddy." He offered his hand.

"Ah of course. I'll be very anxious for us to hunt together Teddy ol' man. I do hope you're not offended if I call you Ted. I had a dear friend by that name, and I fear I may slip at some point."

"That's okay. I like it."

"Good then." Duke explained that our luggage was being packed for the drive into the bush and one of his men would take us to secure the proper permits while the automobiles were being prepared. We'd have the afternoon off to explore the town before leaving first thing the next morning, but we were exhausted by the time we got back to the hotel and napped, leaving the room only for a brief, early dinner.

We started off on a well-worn road paralleling the railroad tracks to Nairobi, passing through red-rock hills and then down onto a brushy plain. After a couple of hours, we veered west, away from the tracks, across vast acacia-speckled savannahs with mountains in the distance. We spotted our first wildlife near the base of one of the strange rock islands that dotted the flatland: a pair of giraffes that looked to be socializing with a small group of buffalo. After that, we were in constant view of some manner of animals, from the gray herds of wildebeests grazing in masse, to lone cheetahs skulking in the tall grass. By mid-afternoon, we were following barely discernable tire tracks from earlier safaris through scattered woodlands.

After a dusty, tooth-rattling seven hours, we arrived at camp, a half dozen tents beneath a giant baobob, an upside-down looking tree that appeared to have it roots growing into the sky. Beyond a massive carpet of grass, the dark, lower slopes of Mount Kilimanjaro grew from a distant thread of foliage, its flat, snow-packed crown glowing above a layer of clouds. One young man was hacking away at firewood with a machete while another pair was busy cooking. Duke told us the others were out scouting for game. As Venice and I settled into our tents, Teddy studied the herds with his binoculars.

"I saw giraffes, gerenuks and wildebeests ... and zebras, and a warthog," he told us later as we enjoyed drinks in camp chairs around a fire. "But I didn't see any elephants or lions."

"They've been hunted a bit now, tend to shy away from sound of an automobile or the smell of people," Duke said. "Last time I camped here, a pair of silly wildebeests looked so interested I thought they were going to wander into camp."

"It's just beautiful," Venice said as she took a sip of wine. "That tastes good. We'll be missing that if the law passes."

"Yes, your American prohibition. Rather foolish, if you ask me."

"My wife and her friends have been calling for the ban," I shared with mock disgust, "Even though she has always enjoyed her wine."

Venice looked a little embarrassed. "Well yes dear, I support what I think is best for everyone, not just myself. You can't argue that the world would be better off without alcohol."

"I could debate that with you, love. But we've no shortage of spirits for your time here, so you needn't worry about it until you return home."

"The animals don't look too hard to hunt," Teddy said.

"Don't be fooled by the abundance, lad. Everything out there is hunted daily by lions, leopards, cheetahs and hyenas, and you can see that they are making out rather well. Wait 'til we try to get close enough for a shot ... we'll be after the nicest trophies, which makes it considerably more difficult."

"What will I hunt first?"

"I thought we'd start you off with a fine impala buck."

Teddy beamed.

Duke turned to me. "I was hoping to get here earlier. The boys have baits in a couple of trees ... been hanging for a few days now. A big tomcat started coming right away to one of them, and we had another show up last night on the other bait."

"Leopards?"

"Oh, yes, sorry. Leopard can be the hardest to bag, but our new kitten was still in the tree when the sun came up this morning, so we'll start there. We'll hunt the big boy in the evening. If you kill in the morning, maybe your bride can take the other one."

"I don't want to hunt leopards."

Duke looked displeased.

"Anything else though."

"Then I can send you out to see if you could scare up a kudu, or even a sable. There's been a small bachelor herd in the area with some very nice heads."

"That would be fine, or I *would* like to see Teddy shoot his first trophy."

"Outstanding. I'll send you out with Tau. I have to be with James for leopard."

Tau looked to be a mere teenager, but exuded the maturity of middle age. Friendly and chatty, his English was impeccable. He shared his history on the drive out, describing the great swamp to the south where he was raised, how the water came from distant mountains and vanished into the Kalahari Desert. I began to doubt him when he described the enormous owls that lived there. Teddy was most impressed that his name meant lion.

After a dinner of impala steaks and an unfamiliar mix of vegetables, we sat around the campfire drinking beer cooled in a water bag. The camp staff sat in a semi-circle at the edge of the firelight and sang for us. One of the oldest bellowed a line, and the others responded in harmony, sounding like they had rehearsed it a hundred times. Despite being near the equator, the evenings were cool. With our jackets wrapped around us, we stayed out by the fire after our singers retired.

A series of powerful, cough-like grunts drowned out the other night sounds. "Oh my gosh. What was that?" Teddy whispered.

"Lion. Sounds like the old boy is hunting."

We remained quiet, listening to the ghoulish laughter of hyenas and the sawing noise of a distant leopard that Duke identified as our big tom. One particular zebra seemed determined to fill any void with silly barking.

"They've just killed," Duke explained a flurry of hyena cackling. "Or else they've stolen a nice piece."

"What would they steal?" Teddy said.

"Any sort of meat they can get. They'll take from leopards, cheetahs or lions. Cheetah hunts in the day. Leopard gets his kill in a tree as fast as he can so he's not bothered. Besides, we've laid out a nice buffet for him anyway. I'd say lion. There's a smaller pride about, might have trouble fending off a big group of hyenas."

Duke stood. "Ted old fellow, I've got you set up in my tent for tonight. We can get you your own digs if my snoring's too much."

"I don't mind snoring."

Duke turned to us, "I must insist you turn in now. And stay in your tent until we are up and about in the morning. I've not invited any night guests, but you never know."

As I stretched out beneath my mosquito net, listening to the sounds of some of the earth's great predators, I sort of envied Teddy being in the cot next to Duke.

After waking at an obscene hour and eating breakfast in the chilly darkness, we arrived at the blind well before sunrise to discover that our leopard had already left. A young guide who had been keeping a vigil whispered and waved his hands, miming how the cat leapt from the tree.

"Well, that's it then," Duke said. "I say we give those sables a go."

One of the gun-bearers was assigned the duty of running back to camp to fetch a different rifle and then catching up as we cut across country. When he arrived smiling proudly with the new weapon, he didn't appear to be winded in the least.

I thought we all looked a bit silly tramping along together. Besides Duke and myself, there was the tracker, and two gun-bearers. Walking up on a deer in the Ozarks with such an entourage would be impossible. The tracker worked well in front of us, eyes fixed to the ground in search of spoor. Duke walked ahead of me, the heavy double-barrel rifle ready at all times. The gun-bearers brought up the rear. The tracker kept looking back to make sure he remained within protective range of Duke's rifle.

We came to an abrupt halt fifty yards from a mother rhinoceros and her calf. If I'd seen nothing else in Africa, the trip would have been worth that one encounter. She stared stupidly in our general direction, the very essence of power and strength, an adorable pig-like youngster at her side. Muzzle held high, she searched the breeze for our scent. The boys scattered as Duke took my arm and escorted me quickly toward a group trees.

"She'll not want us around the tyke," Duke whispered as he watched through the low fork of a tree.

"Would she attack?"

"The damn things are so uneven in temper you never know. Our gal was looking a little put out with us. Never hurts to be cautious around rhino."

"She saw us?"

"No, they're blind as bats, but she heard us and likely smelled us. When they have a calf that new, she's not concerned with who or what has come too close, she's looking for where to attack ... very dangerous, that gal."

With a twitch of aggravation, the nervous mother ushered her little one off into some thick brush. We stayed put for several minutes before continuing our hunt in another direction.

After a couple of hours, the frustrated tracker turned back, shrugged and complained. Duke yelled something at him I couldn't understand, and shook his head in disgust. "They haven't all moved to Europe." We headed back to camp not long after that.

From a hundred yards out, we could hear the celebration, Tau's voice distinguishable among the others. Not only had Teddy shot his impala, but Venice killed a black sable antelope that Duke raved over. "That's as damn fine a head as I've ever seen," he repeated several times.

"Oh yeah," Venice snapped her fingers and darted quickly into her tent to retrieve her Kodak. We took shots from all sorts of angles, until Duke warned her not to use up her film.

Teddy and Venice stayed in camp that afternoon, reading after baths in canvas tubs filled with fire-heated water. The shadows were growing long when we set out. Bent low at the waist, we eased quietly through the trees to a blind built of dead branches with grass weaved in to fill the gaps. About forty yards in front of us, the thick limb of an acacia grew almost horizontally, fifteen feet off the ground, a warthog secured to it with wire. We were close enough that I could make out the blanket of metallic green-and-copper-colored flies and smell the putrid meat. There was a notch carved in a limb where the gun poked through the brush, allowing me to remain motionless when our quarry came to the bait. The intensity on Duke's face made me nervous.

As the sun slid into the canopy, we stared through an opening in the trees into a blinding brightness, our baited branch a mere silhouette. This didn't make sense to me; I couldn't possibly shoot into the glare. But I realized after sunset that we were cleverly positioned for a shot in the final minutes of twilight.

We were staring at a faint, rose-colored opening in the blackness when our tracker slowly held his hand out to make sure we didn't move. I heard it, the leopard's claws digging into the bark. And then suddenly, there it was, not in the sense that I could see a leopard in a tree, but the silhouette of the half-eaten bait had grown considerably, the tearing of flesh and crunching of bones eerily loud. When the cat ripped at the carcass in a way that I could see light under its belly, I had a sense of my target. Duke patted me gently on the back. I struggled at first to make out the sights, but when the unsuspecting cat rose in a feline stretch, I squeezed the trigger.

The muzzle flash blinded me, but Duke slapped my back, erasing an instant of doubt. "Good show!" His voice was strangely loud after a couple of hours of silence. He jabbered something at our tracker, who waved his hands indicating the leopard was down for good.

"He's done," Duke said. "Let's have a look!"

I felt a pang of sadness when I saw the beautiful creature lying in the grass, but my partners' excitement brought me around.

Duke warned, as we celebrated around the fire that night, that we had enjoyed exceptional fortune thus far, and not to assume that everyday would be so successful. "Though I must say, getting our leopard out of the way is quite a good start. We'll move on tomorrow. That's the only reason we stopped here."

"What about the lion?" Teddy said.

"Plenty more where we're going."

"What other animals will we be hunting?" Venice asked.

Duke looked puzzled. "Well, you purchased a trip to hunt all of the dangerous game. You've got your leopard, now we've got lion, elephant, buff and rhino."

Venice looked stunned. "Just how dangerous is it?"

"I'm right there as backup. Tau's a crack shot. It's as safe as it *can* be. But they do call it dangerous game for a reason ... If a lion charges, I'll allow one shot if there's time, but I can't wait for a second. If we wound a cat or a buff, it's up to you whether you go into the brush with us. They always head for the thick stuff. I wouldn't blame anyone for staying behind, but most want to see it through ... that's where I earn my quid. It's why there aren't a lot of white hunters with gray hair. I have nightmares about going after a buff."

"Well *you'll* certainly be doing no such thing," Venice said.

Duke grinned, watching for my response.

"I'll make a good shot to begin with."

He knew then that I was going in with him if necessary, as I'm sure Venice did.

"Which is the most dangerous?" Teddy said.

"Ah, the subject of much debate, and a popular topic of conversation. Depends on who you talk to. If a chap's been roughed up by one or the other, he's usually going to say that one. Going in after a wounded buffalo has created its share of widows. They've a mean streak about 'em when you've put a bullet in them. There's nothing deadlier than a rhino's horn, and nothing more unpredictable. A lion can kill you with a single swipe of the paw, and the charge is so fast it's stunning. Some hunters just freeze. A wounded leopard will hunt *you*, coming in behind you in the thick stuff. Very unhealthy if he gets to the back of your neck. But the elephant is my choice. They're mean, not at all like those fellows you see in the circus. They can pluck you right from that tree you climbed to escape the buff or rhino. It's tough to knock one down, and they usually have their mates around to take issue with shooting a member of the herd."

Venice stared at Duke, eyes bulging and mouth agape, and then looked over at me in terror. "I had no idea," she said softly. "Have you ever had a client injured while hunting?"

"I've tangled with buff and leopard myself." He rolled up his sleeve to show us a scar. "But never a client scratched by what we were hunting. My second season, a French chap got bit by an adder. I'm afraid that didn't end well."

"How so?"

"Unfortunately, that was it for him. A good example of why you listen to the guide. Poor bloke decided to go out in the middle of the night, after a healthy share of wine, to inspect a trophy he'd taken that day. Adders are night prowlers."

"Oh my God. Was that near here?"

"Right here actually. Not to worry though, we've been killing all we see for years. The boys collect a bounty if they kill one. We've not seen an adder around here for quite some time. But do watch where you step and don't wander from your tent at night. We'll be in new country next, so I can't really say what we'll find there."

"What other snakes?" Teddy said.

"The mamba's the worst. You're a goner if he gets you ... can crawl as fast as you can run and raise up and bite you in the arm. A rather unpleasant chap."

"Are we in danger of seeing one?" Venice said.

"I don't anticipate it ... boomslang's poison is as bad as any, but they hardly bite. And there are of course cobras, bad sorts if you come across 'em."

In our tent that night, I tried my best to calm Venice. The thought of her son strolling among a bevy of deadly snakes was unbearable, and the concept of dangerous game was not one she was handling well. What bothered her most was that neither Teddy nor I appeared near as concerned with the dangers as she felt we should be. She could see hunting the world's most dangerous game thrilled me, and Teddy was obsessed with all that was Africa.

Chapter Forty-Five

As we ate breakfast, some men led a string of six stout horses and a dozen mules into camp. It felt unnatural sitting with our coffee and looking out on the beautiful morning while the dismantling and packing of camp bustled all around us.

"I'd like to see the lad shoot a larger caliber to see if he can handle it," Duke said. "The same as memsahib shot at her sable."

"Mem ... what?" Venice said.

"Memsahib. I think it's actually Indian, but it's what they use here. It's a term of respect."

"I like it. Now you were saying about Teddy?"

"Let's see how he handles the rifle you used on your sable."

Venice rubbed her shoulder. "That kicked like a mule"

"It's nothing, my dear, compared to what we shoot at the big stuff."

"Well, I'm not interested in *that.*"

"I am!" Teddy said

Venice scowled at him.

"I was thinking kudu for the lad, but they are larger than your elk. You need a bit heavier caliber than that pop gun he used on impala."

"I can shoot it if Mom did."

"Very well." Duke stood. "Let's get our shooting over with here so we won't go making a lot of noise at the next camp."

Duke set up a target, and Teddy took quick, confident aim and fired.

"That wasn't bad, huh?"

"And a good shot it was!" Duke said as he stared through his binoculars out at the stump, a hole drilled in the center of the paper. "Try again."

Teddy shot, and then quickly pulled the bolt back, injected another shell and fired again. He turned with a proud smile. Duke nodded deeply in admiration. "So you do a bit of shooting at home, do you?"

"Sure, we hunt deer in Missouri and Kansas. Sometimes it's really long shots."

Duke shook his head as he walked back to where the mules were almost loaded. Venice lectured me as we followed. "This doesn't mean he can hunt something that will charge at him or that he'll have to climb a tree to escape ... I don't even believe I've seen him climb a tree. I don't even know if he can."

"If a rhino is chasing you, you can climb a tree."

"See, it's *that* attitude that scares me. This is real danger. He could be killed. *You* could be killed. I would have never have booked this trip if I had known we were all risking our lives."

"Well I'm glad you did. I love it here. Relax and enjoy yourself. Duke will take care of us. Teddy is having the adventure of a lifetime."

Duke rode in front, his big double-barrel across the saddle, as we headed into country thicker with trees and brush. We saw our first elephants after just a short ride. Duke pointed out the matriarch and explained how the others, sisters and aunts, helped raise the calf. The herd bunched tight around the little fellow as they watched us pass, reminding me of Teddy when he stepped out to inspect us, only to be shoved back beneath his mother with her trunk.

Teddy said, "They don't look like they'd charge."

"Those wouldn't. They're relaxed. You can tell if you've been around 'em enough. She just wants to be left alone ... she's not going to let us hang around too long, though."

We had lunch next to a pond in sight of an enormous crocodile sunning on the far bank. Duke stoked Venice's nerves when he warned Teddy away from the bank. "Ol' croc makes a living on things that get too close to the water."

We stopped for afternoon tea in the shade of a large acacia surrounded by a rolling landscape freckled with herds of game. About an hour before sunset, we arrived at our next camp among taller trees scattered enough to allow us to see hundreds of yards in every direction. Two of the tents were up before drinks were served. A large fire was soon crackling and supper served as the last light faded. I was surprised at the enormous pile of firewood. When I commented, Duke explained that a fire would burn all night to keep away "uninvited guests." He let me decide whether to pass that on to Venice, but Teddy brought it up before I could mention it to her.

"It's for the lions isn't it ... the big fire?" Teddy asked Duke.

Venice nodded that she had assumed as much.

"Just a precaution lad, nothing to be concerned with. I don't really know why we do it any more. It's only the horses I worry about. The lions are scared to death of us since they've been hunted. I've never had one come into camp. ... I guess Tsavo's still on everybody's mind around here."

He stared thoughtfully into the flame, the flickering light casting a ghostly glow on his face. "We drove through that country, that railroad. When it was being built, a couple of lions made a steady diet of the workers, coming into the camps at night and dragging some poor soul off to a terrifying death. I've heard the stories a couple of different ways, can't say exactly how many ... a hundred or more ... shut the work down until a fella named Patterson killed 'em."

"Have there been others like that?"

"No, no lad. That's one ol' tale that means nothing these days. This was a frontier back then. All this about lions should be put to rest anyway. I suppose there's really not a need to make these lads stay up all night and keep the fire burning."

"No, let's keep the fire," Venice said.

It takes only a few days to feel like you've been in a camp a long time. A routine is established: up before dark, hunt all day and dine by firelight. You could easily find your way around camp in the dark, though you dare not. With this familiarity comes a comfort that allows you to concentrate on the hunt.

After a week, I had shot as much big game as I cared to. Killing my lion was far less dramatic than any of Duke's stories. We spotted a beautiful black-mane fellow strolling along the edge of some trees before he saw us. He was quartering our direction, so we knelt and waited. When I shot, he folded and didn't move a muscle afterward. My buffalo took off after I fired, and Duke immediately dropped him with an impressive backup shot.

"Sorry, couldn't risk it," he explained as we stood over the trophy while a runner went back to camp for help. "Either shot would have killed him within a hundred yards, but I couldn't tell that then. Don't want to let him have a run at you in the bush."

"It's okay ... he's a good one then?"

"Bloody good. He's a grand head all right ... we've done quite well for ourselves so far, haven't we now?"

Duke and his crew took every bit as much pride in our successes as we did. I felt a little guilty telling him that after shooting the buffalo, I just didn't care to kill an elephant or a rhino. But it turned out to be just fine with him. He preferred going out with Teddy. He was fascinated with the shooting prowess of his young client, and was beginning to test him at some very long distances. I wasn't entirely pleased that Teddy was learning to take shots I felt were unsporting, but I just couldn't bring myself to object.

When Venice mentioned the abundance of birds and told Duke about hunting in Kansas, he got excited. The following morning we headed out of camp with Tau, a pair of gun bearers and three helpers to fetch and carry birds. We shot sand grouse, spur fowl and francolin to the constant cheers of our entourage. That evening, as the sun was setting, we blasted away at doves swarming into a waterhole. The numbers of birds was staggering. We had never enjoyed hunting more, and were adding tasty variety to the camp menu.

"A regular family of marksmen," Duke said one evening after one of the gun bearers excitedly pantomimed Venice's crack shot gunning. Teddy had a new story every night to tell about some long shot he'd made. "Bloody remarkable," Duke was always adding in disbelief.

"I've come to a decision that I think will surprise you," Venice said one evening with only a week left in our safari. "You might question it, but I'm quite sure ... I want to shoot an elephant."

I was shocked. "Really?"

"Yes, I know it seems odd after everything I've said, but I've come to Africa, and I want to hunt the greatest prize. I think it would be quite something for a woman to kill an elephant."

"Well love, we've some damn fine bulls close by. The boys spotted a fine group this morning ... We'll shoot the big rifle tomorrow to see if you're up to it."

"I'll be just fine, I can assure you."

"Right then, we'll have a go for ele! ... James, you'll hunt with us. We could use another gun."

"And me?" Teddy said.

"No!" Venice said.

He kicked at the ground, and was ordered to apologize to a couple fellows he threw dust on. He sat and sulked until Venice tired of his mumbling and sent him to bed.

"Don't be too hard on the lad," Duke said. "I can't say I blame him. When I was a boy—"

"Don't *you* start. I get enough of that with his father." She stood. "I'm going to bed."

"Quite something, that one," Duke said as Venice disappeared behind the tent flap. "I suspect she's like that mother elephant, protective of her calf but fearless on her own."

"That she is."

"Well, it's good to be on edge a little when you're hunting elephant."

Venice didn't flinch when she fired the heavy-caliber rifle for the first time, though I know it was shear determination and not a lack of punch. It sounded like dynamite going off. She hit the target dead center, so we didn't make any more noise with practice.

The camp was quieter that morning, a sober mood noticeable even among the cook staff. We set out before sunrise toward the peach blush defining the horizon, moving cautiously right out of camp. It was little more than an hour before we glimpsed three bulls at about 500 yards, strolling into a thick stand of trees. We stalked up to the edge of the forest and listened, fearing we'd been winded, but the sound of leaves being stripped from the branches told us they were feeding. Duke nodded confidently and led us in a giant semi-circle to get upwind, where we crept in close, halting every few feet to listen. Finally, I smelled them, cattle-like. The low rumbling of their stomachs betrayed where each was. Duke waved us into position, and we slipped quietly forward, stopping every few steps to listen. At one point he twirled a finger in the air, indicating the wind was swirling, alarm in his expression.

I'd just got my first glimpse of gray hide through the brush when a deafening trumpet startled me breathless. The bull took off in a trot, circling to the left, head cocked, keeping an angry eye on us. Branches snapped as he plowed through the brush with his brothers, the earth throbbing through my feet. Finally, the inflamed beast stepped out with a clear field of view. His tusks were enormous, long and curved, almost meeting in front of his trunk. With ears flared, he danced a quick, agitated jig, dipped its head and threw his trunk up with a terrifying scream. Duke and Tau had guns to their shoulder, so I threw up my rifle. "Take him," Duke whispered.

The bull laid its ears back and charged, managing only a few steps before Venice's rifle exploded. A cloud of dust blew up on his forehead, and the giant's legs folded beneath him as he skidded to a halt on his chin.

As the breeze carried away the dust, we recovered our collective breath. After a long few seconds of stunned silence, Duke erupted in a complete doubling of all the emotion he'd displayed on the trip thus far. "Bravo!" he bawled. "Absolutely marvelous! And he was coming for good, mind you. Damn fine shot!"

I continued to shudder uncontrollably. Venice hugged Duke as Tau hurried over pumping a fist over his head. Venice was still shaking when I hugged her. Duke began barking orders to the boys, and a line of helpers soon formed, like ants, between the camp and the kill. Duke's camera was the first item back, and we posed for a second round of the same photos we had just taken with Venice's Kodak. A group of tribesmen in skirts, leather sandals and shaved heads showed up with machetes to butcher the elephant.

"Hope you don't mind," Duke said. "We can't take all of this anyway. They'll make good use of it."

"No, of course," Venice said as she watched them begin to hack at the carcass. "What can they do with it all? It'll go bad in no time."

"They'll dry it on big fires," he pointed to the boys gathering firewood.

We followed the newly worn trail back to camp. A couple of times one of the young men passed and whooped congratulations with a pumping fist.

We had a wonderful night, drinking and sharing stories, the best of the trip. Venice and I slept late before eating breakfast and going on a bird hunt. Teddy was long gone before I peeked out the tent flaps. He and Duke had left at sunrise. Our son decided he wanted an eland, determining after a three-way negotiation with Duke and his mother that it was the biggest thing he would be allowed to hunt. Its horns were far less impressive than the kudu Duke urged him to go after, but he insisted on killing the biggest thing he could.

Teddy got his eland, and we celebrated around our second to last campfire dining on choice cuts of the day's kill. After another fabulous bird hunt the following morning, we ended our last day on safari in the company of a spectacular sunset reflected from the glass surface of a large waterhole as waves of doves flocked in to water before roosting.

That night we sat around the fire with competing emotions. Our trip had been everything we could have asked for, but I could have stayed in the bush a year. I believe Venice was starting to feel the same. Duke and the boys were in a highly celebratory spirit over the success of the safari. It was the first night Tau shared a drink with us. Duke had held back a special bottle of brandy, and even Teddy was allowed to imbibe a few sips. The more Duke drank, the more he boasted about our shooting prowess.

"Best family of shooters I've come across, no question about that. Bloody excellent! ... and the boy ... and that bull ..." Duke was sounding drunk for the first time since we'd met him. "And you've come right 'round haven't you, love?"

"How do you mean?"

"The way you faced that bull ... he meant to kill, mind you ... stood right in there and made a perfect shot. I can't tell you how many men have run and left me with a tricky chance ... and to think, you were scared of snakes when you got here." Duke cackled and threw back the remainder of his drink. "Now you look like you belong here ... we haven't burned a fire for a week, ya know." He poured and held up his glass. "To the flaming-hair Memsahib!"

She smiled coyly. "Well, Duke, I *do* believe you were trying to scare me in the beginning, but I appreciate your purpose. I've decided not to be angry with you and to recommend your services if I'm asked ... I've found that I quite love it here. I'm terribly sad to leave."

"You'll be back."

"I don't know," Venice said. "There's so much of the world to see and so little time."

"My bet is that Africa 'll pull ya back, all right. She's seductive, a regular siren, she is."

"I certainly wouldn't wager against it."

Chapter Forty-Six

Sleeping in our own beds after the long trip felt great, but a melancholy I'd felt on the ship followed me home. It was hard to reconcile the euphoria of a once-in-a-lifetime adventure with the disappointment that it was all behind us. A lukewarm greeting from Sarah and Daniel complicated those feelings. It worried us, making us feel strangely guilty, but after about a week, Daniel explained.

"I know it ain't a real thing. But it just felt that for a time there, while you was gone, that I owned my own big ranch. Things were so quiet, and me and Sari'd just walk, and sit, and just couldn't be any happier." He gripped the armrest nervously. "What would you think if I was to buy a little piece of my own? That little valley couldn't be no prettier; I see why Henry loved it so, but it ain't no count for cattle. Just up the river, there's a tract for sale; bank has it. It'd make good pasture. I'd like to get a few head of my own."

"Well sure, I'm always in favor of expanding. I understand you wanting your own place ... we'd be happy to make a loan."

"Wouldn't be no time 'til I could pay it back."

"Don't even mention it ... this doesn't mean you'd be moving over there does it?"

"Oh, no. We love our place too much. I'm just wantin' to get a place for some cattle."

"Well good then. It's done."

Venice was furious with the price the bank offered Daniel. It was as much as refusing to sell to them, she declared angrily, and tore off into town on her own. She returned surprisingly soon, with a price that stunned all of us. As a gift, we gave them a yearling bull from the Bellringer bloodline.

Daniel and Sarah became obsessed with their new project, and we discussed it in some manner each day. It didn't require a great deal of discussion, but when it's your first such purchase, there's much to talk about. Venice and I listened, reveling in their enthusiasm.

Katherine outdid herself on the story about Venice's elephant. It was more a manifesto on feminine courage than any kind of sound reporting, taking up half the front page with the eye-popping headline: "Face-to-face with death." The photograph of Venice standing next to her trophy ran next to the dramatic account of how she bravely held her ground as the murderous monster charged. It was a powerful symbol to her supporters and critics. Some argued that it was unpatriotic to take such an extravagant vacation so soon after so many died, especially considering we Crawfords hadn't made the sacrifice of serving. Others saw Venice as a woman who simply didn't know her place. But to the Ladies Club members, the image represented a woman's ability, and right, to do anything a man could do. She was quoted in the story as saying it shouldn't at all be unusual for a woman to hunt dangerous game. "Shooting a gun takes no particular male talent." When asked about her bravery, she commented that just being a woman took courage.

Billy showed up to spend the off-season on the ranch about the time that Daniel took possession of his forty acres, happy to help with clearing land and building fence. I was eager to chip in too. It felt good to build something again. Daniel was a man-possessed, working like he wanted to get it all done in a day so we could move on to adding a small hay barn. His pace was hard to match, but I dared not quit before him. It was usually dark by the time I made it back home.

I came in exhausted the day after we put the final touches on Daniel's barn, not pleased to see Venice donning her favorite dress. I was too tired to entertain. But it was a relief to see only a couple places set at the dinner table. "Only two?"

"Yes, Teddy, or Ted as he is now insisting," she rolled her eyes, "is eating down at Sarah's. She made a cherry pie, and you know how he loves it ... darling I know you're tired. We'll have a nice dinner and let you get your rest. Go take a quick bath."

Venice came in, lifted her dress so she could kneel beside the tub and pushed up her sleeves. Taking a sponge, she washed my back, shoulders and chest as she told me how nice it was of me to be helping Daniel, and how it was one of the millions of reasons she loved me. My wife was in a particular amorous mood, and I feared I was too exhausted to fully enjoy the evening ahead, but I got my second wind when she served a slow-cooked beef roast, well known as my favorite meal. Something was up, but the suspense didn't interfere with me gorging myself.

"I love it when you eat so," Venice said when I asked for more potatoes.

"I hope you still love me when I'm fat."

"I'm not worried about that after the way you worked today."

"I suppose ... um, very good. Thank you for such a fine dinner. I just wish I could be sharing in that cherry pie."

Venice stood. "As a matter of fact, Sarah also made you one for the occasion."

"Ah, so there's an occasion?"

She returned with a piece of pie and set it down in front of me.

"Yes dear, there's an occasion."

She won my complete attention with her sugary tone. I set my fork down, and she reached across the table for my hands.

"Oh, Jimmy," her eyes clouded up. "I'm pregnant."

"What! Really?"

Venice's tears let loose when I hugged her.

"Can you believe it? I'd like to say I hadn't given up, but ... I am so happy. I guess all we had to do was go to Africa."

"It happened there?"

"Or on the way. I just wasn't able to fend you away from my cot. Ravished out in the wilds where I was defenseless."

"I don't recall you trying to fend me off."

She giggled. "How could I resist such a handsome hunter?"

"Sarah knows?"

"I'm sorry darling, but I wanted to wait to tell you until I was sure."

"And you're sure?"

"I've already been sick in the morning."

"I didn't notice."

"I kept it from you so I could tell you properly."

"When will you tell Teddy?"

"Tomorrow, if that's fine with you."

"Of course."

Venice snickered. "He was so curious about why he's spending the night at Sarah's. He's scared to death he's going to miss something."

"Spending the night?"

"I thought it'd be nice ... just let me put aside these dishes, and we'll get you up to bed ... by the way, your curious son might be asking you about it. He asked Sarah a question about babies yesterday."

Robert's education of Teddy on the reproductive process yielded more misunderstandings than sound information. When we informed Teddy that he was to be a brother, he asked if that's why he had to spend the night at Sarah's, "so we could make the baby." Teddy frowned as we fought back the laughs.

"No darling," Venice said, "the baby comes nine months after."

"So when will *this* baby be born."

"Around April, we think."

"Didn't you keep count?"

"Well darling, you don't get pregnant every time, and it's not always exactly nine months."

"How do you know when you're going to have a baby, or when it will be?"

Venice looked at me. "I think it's time your father has little talk with you."

A sudden panic consumed me, but there was no getting around it. "Come on buddy. Let's go for a walk."

265

We strolled out to the bluff and sat. I explained sex, pregnancy, childbirth and a woman's menstrual cycle in the plainest language I could. Teddy listened in wide-eyed fascination, apparently thrilled to be let in on the secret. He offered some challenging questions, but I managed for the most part to answer to his satisfaction.

When the holidays rolled around, Venice was beginning to show. We had a wonderful trip to Kansas for Thanksgiving, where she insisted on joining us in the field, but didn't shoot because of concerns over the effects of noise on the baby.

I had never seen Venice as excited as when her Christmas party guests began to arrive, the glow of pregnancy appearing more than a cliché. Everyone understood how special it was for us and gushed enthusiasm. Even more than usual, she was the center of attention, reveling in talk of the baby, but she was coaxed, without a great deal of persuasion, into several tellings of the raging-elephant story. Everybody wanted some of Venice's time, but a few hours into the evening, Sarah decided that she looked fatigued and insisted she retire while the party was in full swing. She didn't look tired to me, and argued that she felt perfectly fine, but relented and retired before the party broke up, enjoying a grand exit up the stairs to the hardy well-wishes of her guests.

Though neither Venice nor I had been able to discern any reason for Sarah's concern, we had developed an almost parental trust in her instincts. She hadn't liked something she had seen at the party and was adamant Venice not engage in anything more strenuous than a short walk until after the baby came, pointing out to Venice's chagrin that she "wasn't a spring chicken anymore."

At a doctor's visit the next week, he found no particular reason to be concerned, but still, Venice acquiesced to Sarah's prodding, doing nothing in the way of work and trying her best not to concern herself with any of her political causes. We spent much of the time in front of a roaring fireplace, reading and discussing the future. Teddy was of an age that hanging out with his parents wasn't that much fun, and like his father, he couldn't take staying inside even in the most miserable weather. Venice and I got in the habit of going up for a long nap after lunch, usually not coming down until dinner. As anxious as I was for the baby to come, I would miss those long afternoons.

Chapter Forty-Seven

I went for the doctor in a driving rain. Venice was confident and calm this time, but I panicked, almost sliding the Packard off the muddy road a couple of times, only to discover the doctor was out delivering another baby. But it turned out his absence was of little consequence; my daughter had been born while I was away. Mother and baby were both doing quite well thanks to Sarah's capable assistance.

Propped up on several pillows, Venice cradled the tiny infant against her chest, lifting her gaze when I stepped into the room. "Hi there. Sorry we started without you."

Hurrying over to sit on the bed next to them, I pushed the perspiration-matted hair off her forehead. "Are you okay?"

"Of course," she said in a soothing voice. She looked down, and her smile grew. "I told you it was a girl."

"I had a feeling you'd get your way ... you usually do."

She smiled.

I stroked the baby's tiny cheek with the backs of my fingers. "She's beautiful ... like her mother." I was very careful of the baby when I leaned in and kissed my wife. "So what shall we name her? I know you've given it much thought."

She snickered under her breath. The name game had been an obsession of hers in recent weeks. "I thought Margaret. We'll call her Maggie. Isn't it cute?"

"I like it."

"Go check on Teddy." She let Sarah take the baby.

He had been inside the house the entire time, young ears traumatized by the sounds of his mother giving birth. My assurances did little to comfort him, and he demanded to see her. Venice's smile was instantly calming, and his concern turned to awe as Sarah returned Maggie to her mother for the baby's first nourishment.

Venice smiled. "She's hungry," she said to Teddy.

I had included breast-feeding in my facts-of-life talk with Teddy because he had specifically asked what babies ate since they had no teeth. He understood what he was witnessing and was mesmerized, reaching up and gently stroking Maggie on the back as she nursed. I was a little surprised Venice breast fed in front of him.

"She's so small." He sounded concerned. "Is that okay?"

"You were small like that too."

"Come on, let's give our girls a rest." I patted Teddy's shoulder.

We went into the kitchen to sample the cookies Sarah was baking when all the excitement started, and I answered Teddy's questions. He jerked his head nervously when he heard Maggie crying.

"It's okay buddy. Babies just cry, it doesn't mean anything. She probably just needs a diaper changed or something."

He winced.

Sarah was thrilled to have a baby on the ranch and would not be denied the role of primary caretaker. She insisted on taking a room in the house those first weeks, which I felt a little unnecessary, but it was a real treat that she was willing to get up during the night. Maggie was a fussy baby. Sarah credited a common stomach ailment babies suffered and assured us it was nothing to worry about. Venice had an unwavering faith in Sarah and took comfort in her diagnosis.

I was busy that first week of my daughter's life. A storm's high winds snapped a lot of big branches, and we had half a dozen breaches with cattle roaming the countryside. When I came in late, I pretended to be put out at never getting to hold my daughter. If she wasn't in Venice's arms, she was in Sarah's.

"I 'spect you'll get a few more chances than you want," Sarah said, standing to go change a diaper. "Would you like to hold her right now?"

"I'll wait my turn."

Teddy looked puzzled over the adult laughter. Then he got a whiff of what we were joking about. "Ooh, yuk!"

After a couple of weeks, Venice decided it would be a good idea if Teddy and I went camping down on the river, concerned that he was showing signs of feeling left out. Setting up on my favorite gravel bar, we fished a little before supper and then dined on cold, fried chicken beside a small fire. I told Teddy about the days when I camped at that spot as a child, and about the day I learned to fish. He giggled as I acted out the big crawfish clinging to my finger. It was a glorious night, moonless and dark, the Milky Way a cloudlike belt slicing the sky in half. I pointed out constellations my mother had shown me when I was about his age.

When Teddy started yawning, we turned in. I could tell by his breathing that he had fallen immediately to sleep, so I climbed out of my sleeping bag and put a few more limbs on the fire. Walking out to the water's edge, looking down into a black mirror, a falling star streaked overhead leaving a long green tail, the reflection at my feet making me feel closer to it. The dank air drew me back to the fire. I lay on my side, head propped up on my elbow, and drifted back into my boyhood. When the flame at last melted down into the coals, I crawled back into my bag and slept soundly.

Not long after Maggie was born, Venice was blessed with another cause for celebration. Congress passed the 19th amendment, giving women everywhere the right to vote. Missouri ratified it thirty days later. The Ladies Club immediately put together an event honoring the passage of the law and rented the community center. The celebration got a big play in the paper and women from neighboring communities even showed up.

I wasn't sure whether most men didn't feel welcome, were staging some sort of protest or just simply didn't care to attend, but their absence put a damper on dancing. As one of the few men there, Venice directed my dances until I was near exhaustion. Later, at home, she scoffed at my complaint of being forced to dance so much.

"Don't you dare pretend that you didn't enjoy yourself. You looked quite happy with all that attention from the ladies ... I saw you out there."

"That's nonsense."

"I thought I was going to have to come out there and cut in with Melissa."

"That's not true!"

"Calm down, I'm teasing you ... but tell me honestly, when you are dancing with her, and you have her in your arms, it has to cross your mind? ... do you remember it fondly?"

Her tone was innocent enough that she almost lured me into telling the truth.

"Of course not. We were children for goodness sake."

"I'm sorry dear. I didn't mean to upset you ... you *do* seem to hold her closer than the others."

"Maybe closer than ol' Mrs. Bailey ... she's so fat I couldn't get any farther and still reach."

Venice laughed. "That's a terrible thing to say!"

"Well this is all crazy talk, and I don't care for it. You're the one who made me dance with 'em."

"I'm sorry. I'll behave ... I like that the women think you're handsome."

"They do not. I thought you were going to behave."

"Poor baby. I'll stop."

We finished undressing and crawled into bed. Venice stared at the ceiling with her hands behind her head.

"I was standing over Maggie's crib today," she said softly into the darkness. "I was just thinking about how fortunate we are, and it makes me feel a little guilty, like I don't deserve all of this."

"Why would you say such a thing?"

"I always thought that not having a little girl was our bad thing ... everybody has bad things in their life. It scares me a little."

"Why would your good fortune scare you? That doesn't make any sense."

"Oh, I don't know ... sometimes it just seems too good to be true."

"We should just be happy for our blessings."

"I know you're right, but still, you can't help what your mind thinks."

"That's silly ... if you'll go to sleep you'll quit worrying about it."

"I'm sorry. I'm keeping you up. I know you are so worn out from all that dancing."

"I am."

"Don't you grow old on me Jimmy Crawford. I've still got a lot of use for you."

She kissed me and turned over to go to sleep.

The ladies' celebration and Katherine's story drew the expected nasty letters to the editor, with Venice the target of most of the venom. She wasn't mentioned by name, but references to "people so rich they have time to waste" were no mystery to anybody. When I stopped by to again voice my objections, the editor pulled out a few letters he hadn't run. "People like that should always be looking behind their backs," one of them read. The other said: "People with a lot of money should mind carefully to their own business. That much wealth is hard to hold onto." I thanked him for showing me the letters but was relentless in my displeasure at his role in keeping it stirred up. He was quick to remind me of my wife's hand in the stirring. My words were wasted; controversy sold papers. I considered mentioning the threatening letters to the sheriff, but quickly dismissed that idea as even more futile.

Of course, none of this, or anything I had to say, put a damper on Venice's activities. Armed with the vote, she dove straight into the day's political issues. She was preaching to her Ladies Club that it wasn't enough to have the vote. It must be used for positive change. She used the newspaper as a megaphone for her message, and it was reaching out farther all the time. Mainly due to Venice and the various controversies she drew attention to, the paper began delivering to neighboring communities. Katherine had begun to write a column, allowing her to shed the pretense of being an unbiased reporter. Many of her pieces about Venice fell just short of hero worship.

While Venice held meetings and organized letter-writing campaigns, I was delegated to caring for our children, which I enjoyed. I even tried my hand at teaching. Teddy was thrilled until Venice got wind of our meager pace and a few days of fishing instead of studying. She began leaving me with daily instructions, throwing a tantrum when she caught Teddy shooting me a glance she interpreted as collusion to defy her. We went through a period where Teddy and I landed in her bad graces at least once a week, and then at night, she revisited the old complaint that I let our son do anything while she had to be the mean old witch. It made her madder when I laughed.

"So help me, Jimmy," she stepped up to the edge of the bed where I was reading. "I better not ever hear of y'all talking behind my back about how mean I am."

There was little patience left in me for this particular argument. Without looking up from my book, I tossed a barb. "Then we'll make sure you don't hear about it.'

"Dammit!" She stomped her foot.

"This is a ridiculous argument." I folded my book. "If you have to dictate Teddy's every move, then put aside your politics and stay home. Maybe I'm not the best father, but maybe I'm better than you think. Maybe you just don't see it."

"You think I'm gone too much, neglecting my family?"

"No, I'm just tired of getting lectured about everything I'm doing wrong. You know, I *do* have a ranch to run." I opened my book again and started reading.

Venice stared over me for a few seconds, a hint of contrition in her expression, before going over to her vanity and brushing her hair.

The next morning she acted like we'd never argued and made a big deal out of spending the day with us while Sarah took care of the baby. "Whatever you want," she told Teddy.

"What about studying?" he said.

"Why don't we all play hooky for the day."

When she noticed Teddy glancing over to me for approval, she flashed her displeasure at me, but then let it go. We had a wonderful day on the river, fishing, skipping rocks and enjoying another of Sarah's picnic lunches.

When Maggie was six-months old, Venice traveled to Jefferson City to visit state legislators. In the write-up, Katherine asked her if she was considering running for office. She inflamed her detractors with, "I don't know. I haven't decided yet, but if I don't, other women should." Once planted, the seed grew. Those closest to Venice began to assume she would throw her hat into the ring at some point, and she did little to discourage them by continually pointing out that Montana voters had been sending a woman to Congress for some time. She was quoted as saying: "There's just no reason at all why our governing bodies shouldn't consist of equal numbers of men and women, and for that matter, proportional to our racial make-up." Though concerned as always about reaction to such comments, I couldn't bring myself to say anything. I'd never seen her happier. Besides, I was pretty sure that not even I could persuade her to tone down her rhetoric.

As busy as she stayed, Venice still reserved evenings for me and the kids, making every effort to return from trips in time for dinner together. We liked to sit and watch Maggie crawl around, oftentimes an adoring older brother down on the rug playing with her. But it was never long before Venice picked her up. Aware that her special affection for Maggie was obvious, she always made a point to force conversation with Teddy. He received further attention by reading to us. It was becoming a nightly activity, and on cold nights around the fireplace, he'd read *Treasure Island* or *Alice in Wonderland,* often in a childish voice intended for his sister. Maggie listened as if she understood. Those were some of the best evenings I ever remember.

Chapter Forty-Eight

With our blessings, Sarah was spending most of her time with her husband, working always on their new place. When Venice was at home, she usually had her daughter in her arms, but she was often traveling to Jefferson City or making day trips around the region where she was asked to speak to women's and other civic groups. It was left up to me to look after Maggie much of the time. She started walking in April and by summer; she was all over the place. Teddy was a big help, but at fourteen, he was beginning to work a few days a week out with the boys, especially when he could do it from horseback. The three of us took advantage of mother's absence to do some things she wouldn't approve of. It's a certainty she'd objected to how early I let Maggie play in the shallows of the river, but Teddy and I hovered protectively over her, and she never sat in more that a few inches of water. If Venice caught the three of us driving through the pastures, a heavy-footed Teddy at the wheel, Maggie standing in my lap squealing approval, I'd never hear the end of it.

Maggie loved to play in the leaves, but Venice banned the activity after discovering a tick on her. I'd let Maggie play in the yard when her mother was away, but was always careful to inspect her thoroughly before her mother returned. I was out front about to do such a check one evening when I noticed a pair of headlights coming.

"There's Mama," Teddy warned, hurrying over to help me do a quick tick inspection.

For once, Venice appeared to be driving at a reasonable speed. The car came to a stop before I was able to make out in the dim light that it was not my wife. A male figure stepped out, and after a second, I recognized the sheriff's profile.

"Here," I handed Maggie over to Teddy and started down the steps.

"Hi, sheriff, what brings you out this way?"

He hesitated. "James, I'm afraid I've got some bad news. Your Packard was found on the road. Mrs. Crawford was not with it ... I didn't know 'til right now that *you* wasn't with her."

"She broke down?"

He shook his head with foreboding certainty. "I'm afraid not, James, there was a struggle. The ground was roughed up, grass tromped down ... we found a spent shell casing, small caliber like a .25, and there was some blood on the grass."

I had no faith in his investigative competency and was sure he was mistaken.

"James, I'd say Mrs. Crawford's been kidnapped. If it was someone just wantin' to do her harm, they wouldn't have carried her off like that. I 'spect she ain't an easy one to kidnap. Kidnappings are becoming more common, and your money ain't no secret. There was enough dust on the road that you could tell they headed north in an automobile, but not much after that. Coulda turned off to Oklahoma ... anywhere really."

I was too stunned to speak. Teddy was behind me, up on the edge of the steps with Maggie in his arms, tears streaming down his cheeks.

"James, there wasn't much to go by, like I said. The normal thing is to get the federal boys in here. They deal with this kind of thing and have a lot more experience. I figure you'll be gettin' a ransom note ... is there anything you can think of that would help us figure out who this might be?"

Shaking my head slowly, my jaws quivered so badly that I struggled to get the words out. "You know we have enemies. Hell, they burned down our house ... do you think this is about money?"

"Cain't say. I imagine it usually is ... James, I hadn't never had a kidnapping. They might threaten to hurt her if we call in outsiders, so I'm leaving that to you. I told that bonehead deputy of mine to keep quiet about it, *and* that couple who found the car ... new folks in town. I think it'll be quiet for a little while anyway."

"Let me think about it."

"Okay, then," the sheriff put his hat back on. "I 'spose I better be gettin' back. I'm real sorry James. I'll do everything I can."

"Yeah, thanks."

Feet anchored to the ground, I watched tear-blurred taillights disappear into the darkness. Teddy eased down next to me.

"They wouldn't hurt her would they?"

"No, they want money." I took Maggie from him. "Go down and ask Sarah and Daniel if they could come up to the house."

He took off running.

The disbelief had yet to morph into grief as I stepped inside. I just stood there, paralyzed, not knowing what to do. Feeling lightheaded, I plopped down into a chair, startling Maggie into a whimper. "I'm sorry sweetie." I whispered and patted her.

Denial dug in its heels. It didn't seem remotely possible that our idiot sheriff could just drive up and say Venice was not coming home. I had zero confidence in his skills as an investigator. And kidnappings were something that happened in the big city, not the Ozarks. I even stood to look out the window, half expecting to see headlights, someone bringing her home.

But too quickly, my imagination began to form horrifying images of my precious wife in the possession of depraved men. Maggie cried when I

274

convulsed the first spasm of uncontrollable sobbing. We were both bawling when Sarah burst through the door. She took the baby without saying anything, her eyes already red and swollen. I wandered back out onto the porch. Teddy sat alone at the far end, bent over, face in his hands.

I strolled over but could only manage a pat on the shoulder. "I'm gonna kill 'em," he said without looking up.

"We'll get her back."

We both drifted into our own terrible thoughts. After a while, Sarah came out, rocking several minutes before saying anything. "Oh James," her voice trembled. "I can't believe it. Who could do such a thing?"

"I don't know."

She asked what I knew thus far, and I struggled to get the scant details out.

"You got the money to pay?"

"We don't know what they're asking, but we'll come up with whatever it takes."

Daniel strolled up tentatively, sat and listened as Sarah and I discussed the possibilities.

"You two need your rest."

"I can't sleep," Teddy said.

I shook my head.

"Well if you can't rest your mind, at least rest your body. Go up and lay down. We got a lot ahead of us."

I nodded and headed upstairs to be alone. Lying fully dressed on the bed, staring up into the darkness, I wondered what Venice was feeling at that very moment. I knew her thoughts were of the children and me, and I knew she was furiously plotting to get home to us. She was brave and a fighter, which brought me an instant of comfort, which turned quickly to fear. I worried about the resistance she would surely put up, and her inability to keep her mouth shut. Assuming the small caliber casing was from the derringer she carried and the blood from one of her abductors, she had already made one of them very angry. The possibility that I had been trying with great effort to expel from my mind persisted, growing like a cancer, thoughts of what evil men might do to my wife pushing me to the limit of sanity. At some point, exhaustion overwhelmed grief, and I drifted off into a merciful slumber.

The morning was already bleeding bright through the curtains when I opened my eyes. It was another half hour before I was able to roll out of bed. Sarah was banging around down in the kitchen, and though I dreaded conversation, it was torture to be alone with my thoughts.

She was feeding Maggie, who squealed, pushing the spoon aside and reached for me. "I'm done anyway." Sarah stood.

I picked up my daughter, who squirmed in my tight embrace.

"I'm gonna cook you a big breakfast." Sarah slid a frying pan onto the stove. "You need to keep your strength up."

"I will, but not this morning."

She shook her head, but didn't argue. Taking Maggie back, she sat at the table across from me. "What are we gonna do, James?"

"Just wait ... it's all we can do."

I drove the Oldsmobile in to see the sheriff. He was expecting me and handed over his report. "Cain't think of nothin' else."

I read.

"We'll go back out and take another look today." The sheriff pulled open a drawer and handed me a pair of small shell casings. "We ended up finding a second one in the car."

"From the little derringer she carried," I said.

"James, I been thinking. We need to get them federal boys here right away if that's what we're going to do. Time's critical ... we just ain't equipped to deal with somethin' this big here."

I had already decided; I wasn't going trust my wife's life to local incompetence.

"Okay ... let's keep it quiet."

His nod exuded little confidence.

"Your car is down at the livery. I'd like to let the investigators take a look before you move it if you can get along without it for a while."

"Yeah, I'll leave it."

Stepping back out on the boardwalk, I froze in indecision, wondering if I should go down and have a look, but I decided it would just feed my anxiety. After several minutes, I got in the car and went home to wait.

Chapter Forty-Nine

A pair of federal investigators arrived from Chicago in less than thirty-six hours. Agent Allenby appeared to be in his early forties. He asked the questions while his younger partner took notes and offered little in the way of comment. His demeanor was cold and detached as we sat around the dining room table, where he pressed me with his interrogation. The first questions were mostly no surprise. What enemies Venice and I might have, who would have known she'd be on that road at that time and why had she gone into town. But then he began to ask about our relationship, apparently exploring the possibility that I might somehow be involved, or that Venice had perhaps arranged her own disappearance. "I have to ask."

"Don't waste any time on any of that. We couldn't have loved each other any more."

Sarah chimed in. "It ain't nothin' like that, I'll guarantee. There wasn't a couple more in love."

Allenby looked a little aggravated at Sarah, but invited her input. "Well, okay. Ma'am, anything you can think of that we'd need to know?"

Sarah pulled out a chair, sat and commenced a long explanation of Venice's controversial public image, her political involvement, the letters to the editor and the history of animosity between the Crawfords and some of the townsfolk. The agent scribbled furiously as Sarah recalled how she and her family had come to live on the ranch, how people in town reacted to them, how her father had been beaten and that our house had been burned down. Allenby looked over at me, obviously astonished I hadn't mentioned these things. He encouraged Sarah to go on, and she spoke for ten minutes.

"Why haven't we heard anything," I said.

"That's not unusual. Mr. Crawford, you need to prepare yourself for the possibility of not receiving a ransom note. You and your wife apparently have enemies. We won't know for sure that it is a kidnapping until we hear from the kidnappers. Sometimes they get cold feet after they've taken their hostage ... and, you have to realize, even if you pay a ransom, there's no guarantee they'll hold up their end of the deal." Sarah and I shared desperate glances as he scribbled something on his pad. "We'd like to stay out here if that'd be all right. And we need to keep it quiet about us being called in on the case."

"Of course," Sarah answered for me. "I'll set up rooms downstairs. Please make yourselves at home."

"Thank you ma'am."

"How would they contact us?" I asked.

"Mail. Some have used the newspaper. One group last year took a child hostage and used his father as a go between."

"How did that turn out?"

The agent just shook his head ominously.

"We'd like for you to go into town and have the sheriff come out and visit us. Tell him to keep his mouth shut about it and not do any more investigating. Local law enforcement can be a real hindrance ... and a danger. We'll get out to the crime scene after that."

He paused. "Tell anyone who has to know that she sprained her ankle horseback riding ..."

"Everybody 'round here knows she wouldn't fall off of no horse," Sarah interrupted.

Allensby pondered.

"More likely she'd trip over a child's toy," she said.

"Good! ... sprained her ankle. Doctor would know if it was more serious ... say you're making her take it easy, no visitors, because you want her to take a break."

Sarah bobbed her head in agreement. It seemed to matter to the agent that she approved.

"Does she keep a calendar?"

Sarah rolled her eyes. "Oh Lord."

"Real busy?"

I nodded. "I'll contact everybody."

"No more than about a week ahead."

"That nosey Katherine will wanta get out here and write a big story about it," Sarah said.

Allensby looked to me for an explanation.

"Young reporter ... worships Venice. She'd see it as a big story if Venice stubbed her toe ... I'll take care of it."

Allenby shook his head as he stood. "Okay then. All of you get some rest. Just act as normal as you can around here *and* in town. Keep a keen eye on your children. This could take a while. And please tell us anything you remember, no matter how insignificant it may seem." He looked at Sarah as he closed his notepad. "You've been a big help, ma'am."

It was as if time ground to a halt. Minutes seemed like hours as the grief came in waves: images of what Venice was going through, thoughts of how impossible life would be without her and occasionally a fleeting optimism that only made things seem more hopeless once it was gone. Trying unsuccessfully to give my mind a respite, I forced myself to work, but I mostly just stared at fence posts or gazed out across pasture. Sleep was hard to come by. I mostly lay awake, suffering terrible thoughts through endless nights. Sarah and Daniel spent every waking hour in the house with us, but we talked very little because there just wasn't much anyone could say. Teddy's solitary brooding worried me, but I just didn't have the capacity to be of any help. I spent much of the time with Maggie, trying to escape into her carefree world, where none of the pain existed.

I drove into town every morning to check the mail, each time with a strange mix of anticipation and fear. It was a struggle to hide my feelings from a postmaster who found great sport in spreading other peoples' business, but I listened and did my best to act interested. It became harder each time to return home to Sarah and Teddy, seeing their faces as I shook my head.

It was on the eighth such trip into town that I was handed an envelope with a typewritten address.

"No return address," the postmaster said. "People ought to know letters can get lost. Mind you, we wouldn't lose it here, but still, it oughta have a return address."

I suppressed the urge to punch the man in the face. "Yes, it really should."

Pulling over just outside of town, I tore open the envelope.

Mr. Crawford

Your wife has been an ungrateful guest. But she is in good health and will remain that way for a payment of $75,000, half in ten-dollar bills, half in twenty-dollar bills. You have a week. We'll be in touch. Any attempt to involve the law or any other wrong moves on your part and you will never see her again. We'll be watching.

Allenby read the note without emotion.

"So?" I said.

"What I expected ... we've got time to consider our options."

"What options! We'll pay. There are no options."

Allenby nodded.

"Does the letter give any clues?"

"It was postmarked in Texas."

I was astonished that I hadn't noticed.

"But it may not mean anything. They could have easily jumped on a train just to mail it ... try and throw us off. Do you have business in Texas?"

"No ... well, we've sold cattle to Texans before like we have folks in about a dozen states ... but no, not really."

"These guys don't look stupid, probably not amateurs. We could tell they covered their tracks at the scene. There were two automobiles that left in opposite directions. They tried to make it look like they headed north, but the car that headed south probably had your wife in it. How many people in the area have automobiles?"

"Not that many ... but more in the last year or so."

"Could be some locals working *with* outside folks ... can you put that much money together?"

"Of course."

"We don't recommend you pay them, but we don't know how close they're watching. You need to be seen gathering the money. If they still don't know we're in town, they may be feeling pretty confident."

"How damn confident do they need to feel? They have my wife!"

"They could lose their nerve. I've seen it happen before. The more confident they are, the easier it will be to apprehend them."

"Apprehend them?"

"The drop is the best time ... maybe the only chance."

"But they said they'd kill her. I'll be alone when I meet with them ... Venice will have seen them. That will be the best clue of all."

"I don't mean to alarm you, Mr. Crawford, but I'm afraid we seldom get eye-witness testimony. Even if they return her, they probably aren't letting her get a look at them ... probably wore masks when they took her and kept her blindfolded after that ... you need to brace yourself for the worst."

The agents had me hide their automobile in the barn, and they refused to go outside, even staying away from the windows. Allenby assured us that it was just a precaution, but it was haunting to think that we could possibly be watched so closely. I was careful to follow my instructions.

The bank couldn't have been more difficult to deal with. Because I didn't care to explain why I needed to make such a large withdrawal, the banker suspected I was acting out of spite. His wife had quit the Ladies Club, and he knew we weren't happy with the way Daniel had been treated. I gave that up pretty quick, and took most of the cash from our Kansas bank and the Bar G vault. Annie insisted that she accompany Luke when he came down with the money. Her wailing just made things worse. It was a relief to see them leave the following morning.

You could see that Allenby expected a bad outcome, and I resented him for it. I understood that his feelings were based on his considerable experience, but it made me angry. There was no way I could survive if I wasn't absolutely positive this case was different. They wanted money, and that was no problem. I refused to give into his pessimism, continuing to remind myself that if there were one person who could survive, it would be Venice.

With the ransom together, and a firm understanding with Allenby that I wanted no interference with the delivery, we waited. He agreed too easily for my comfort. Sarah sensed it also and voiced her distrust to me. We were both scared they'd go behind my back and follow me, more interested in catching criminals than keeping Venice alive. Since they'd made assurances that I'd be allowed to handle it on my own, it begged the question of why they even stayed. When I asked, Allenby said they always saw it through as a matter of policy. "And you're free to change your mind at any time."

It was an excruciating six days before the letter came, this time postmarked from Arkansas.

Mr. Crawford

On July 1, at 8 a.m., you will leave your ranch, alone on horseback with the money. You will follow the river west for five miles until you get to a bridge. Beneath the bridge will be an envelope with further instructions. You will be watched the entire way. If anybody follows you, your wife will be killed immediately. If anyone leaves your ranch besides you, we will kill her. If you inform the cops of this letter, we will kill her. If you come armed, we will kill both of you. Any attempt to do anything other than exactly what we tell you, and your children will be next.

"Nothing," I announced somberly when I returned home. As he had for the few days prior, Allenby nodded skeptically.

Chapter Fifty

I left at precisely eight, as the ransom note instructed. I'd slipped the money into saddlebags a few days earlier as the agents gorged themselves on one of Sarah's huge meals. The canvas bag where I had been keeping the money was stuffed with rags to make it look like the money was still there. A downed fence and escaped cattle were my excuse for getting out before breakfast. Still, despite my best efforts, I feared that Allenby knew what I was up to.

Leaving the barn at an angle so I wouldn't be noticed from the house, I rode in a wide circle before joining the riverbank. The horse continually wanted to break into a canter, likely feeling my anxiousness, but I held it back, trying to look casual and inconspicuous in case I came up on anybody. I'd tell them I was out for a ride, trying to get away from it all, but the stuffed saddlebags might be hard to explain. I rode along in a dreamlike state, numb to the early heat or refreshing breeze in my face, nothing around me catching even my slightest attention.

I knew the bridge and understood why it was chosen. The crossing was in a steep canyon with high bluffs lining the river where a lookout could easily hide and watch in safety. As it came into sight, I was careful to not look up, or back. Earlier on the ride, I caught myself glancing behind me, instinctively worried that I was being followed by Allenby or kidnappers. At this point, such an innocent mistake could be fatal.

There was a canoe tucked beneath the bridge, out of sight of anyone crossing over, an envelope tied to the seat instructing me to paddle downstream until I was contacted. Tethering my horse in a stand of trees out of sight from the road, I started down the river in a scrambled state of fear and hope, clinging to the belief that I was going to see Venice soon.

After an hour, I began to panic. At the impatient pace I'd been paddling, I figured I'd traveled five miles. Allenby warned me that the kidnappers could have me show up at a false delivery just to see if I was followed. He didn't have to tell me that they could simply shoot me and take the money. I began to wonder if I'd done the right thing by going it alone. What would become of the children if I were murdered along with their mother?

"Jimmy!" Venice's voice rang from inside the trees on the left.

I almost tipped the canoe searching. I couldn't find her.

"Over here," a gruff male voice called from the opposite bank.

A tall, thin man with a bandana covering his face, wearing a long, black coat and a wide-brim hat, walked out onto a gravel bar and waved me over with his pistol. He held it on me as I stepped out and pulled the canoe up onto the gravel.

"Turn around."

He frisked me with one hand as he held the gun against my back.

"Okay," he pushed me, almost causing me to fall. "Let's see it," he pointed at the canoe.

I retrieved the saddlebags and laid them down where he indicated.

"Face down," he said.

Nose pressed to the gravel, I dared not look up as the man dug through the bags. Venice was alive, and as careful as the man was being to disguise his identity, my assumption was that they were going to leave us be when they had their money.

"Get up."

Despite the mask, I could tell by his eyes that the gunman was smiling. He whistled and waved across the river.

At first, it was just a movement in the shadows, but then Venice, flanked by two other masked men, materialized into the sunlight. I gulped a lung full of oxygen, realizing I had been holding my breath. She was blindfolded with her hands tied behind her back. The cream-colored dress she'd proudly modeled for me just weeks before was ripped off her shoulder, torn at the hem and filthy. I wanted to call to her but was too petrified to make a sound.

"Don't look back," the man said from behind me. "Keep your eyes across the river. You'll stay here one hour after you are called over. Understand?"

I nodded.

"One wrong move and you're both dead. Keep your eyes across the river, or you're dead."

The crunch of gravel told me a second person had come out of the woods to help with the bags, lighter steps like a woman or boy. As they hurried back into the trees, I kept my eyes locked on Venice, the sunlight glistening off her tear-stained cheeks. A pair of horses galloped off behind me. After several minutes, the two men across the river backed into the forest, leaving Venice standing alone.

"Stay there, Jimmy!" she called. "It has to be an hour. They've left somebody behind."

I watched on wobbly legs, time suspended, my thoughts ricocheting wildly from unbridled joy to abject terror. Venice stood statue still, fear-frozen, shining in the sunlight like an apparition, an angel I still feared I'd never touch. She looked in good health, but I knew the deepest scars wouldn't be visible.

Finally, we heard a pair of riders speed away. Venice looked back as if she could see. I waited several minutes, making certain I didn't go over before the hour was up. I slipped hurrying into the canoe, making a huge bang and splash.

"Jimmy!"

"It's okay!

I paddled franticly across, and almost fell again getting out.

"Oh, thank God," was all Venice could get out through her sobbing as I removed the blindfold and untied her hands. I held her tight, sharing her tears, until she got control of herself.

"Are you okay?" was all I could get out.

"I'm fine ... Oh God, I thought I'd never see you again."

A sudden urgency came over me, a fear that the men might return. "Come on, let's get out of here," I grabbed her hand, nervously pulling her toward the canoe.

We headed west, downstream. It would have been impossible to paddle back to the bridge against the current. Like a bashful schoolboy at his first dance, I couldn't form the words I wanted.

"How are the children?" Venice finally said.

"They're fine. They've missed you terribly."

"Oh God," she wept. "I just knew I'd never see any of you again ... I never knew there could be such horrible people."

"Did they hurt you?"

"I'm fine, Jimmy." Her tone was unsettling. "I'm back with you, and that's all that matters."

I was scared to press the issue.

"Who was it?" I said

"I don't know. I was always blindfolded. I have no idea Jimmy, but I don't care. I'm back with you, and I'll see my babies soon. I prayed so hard ..."

I paddled at an exhaustive pace, without an inkling of where we were headed. I knew very little about the river past the bridge and had no idea when we would find a road or house. The kidnappers had chosen well. The river continued through a steep valley with no signs of civilization. The rocky bluffs would have made it impossible to stop and take off across land, guaranteeing them time to travel many miles.

As we rounded a bend that hugged a towering rock face, I heard the sickening thud of a bullet against Venice's body an instant before the canyon erupted in gunfire. Before I could register what was happening, a bullet burned into my shoulder. Snipers peppered the canoe as I rose to go to Venice, already slumped forward, a bloodstain growing on her back. Before I could take a second step, it felt like someone hit me in the head with a hammer and everything went blank.

EPILOGUE

Ashley blotted her eyes with her sleeve. I worried that maybe I'd shared too many gruesome details with my granddaughter, but I just couldn't stop talking.

"It's a miracle I lived. The bullet that creased my head missed killing me by an inch, and I was hit in three other places. I always figured the good Lord saved me to take care of Teddy and your mother ... I was lucky an Indian family had a cabin nearby and heard the shooting ... I have no memory of the days after that ... I wasn't even able to go to Kansas when they buried Venice next to her father."

"I had no idea."

"I've never talked much about it, and those around me didn't bring it up. We all just wanted to forget."

"How long did you stay on the ranch?"

"Not long. I suppose I knew I'd be leaving when I decided to have Venice buried on the Bar G ... I don't even remember making the decision, but Luke took care of everything. I don't know what I would have done without Luke and Sarah ... I'm to be buried next to her."

Ashley frowned.

"I'm still not sure I did the right thing. I've regretted it many times. Teddy loved it out there, but I think he wanted to get away too ... back then anyway."

"And Uncle Ted died in World War II?"

"Saipan ... Hamburger Hill. Your uncle was a hero."

"What about Robert?"

"I don't know. We lost touch. Last I heard he was in Texas ... Melissa married again and is still up in Springfield as far as I know, but I haven't spoken to her in years."

"Did you sell the ranch?"

"No, I let Sarah and Daniel run it after that. I signed the deed over as she was dying of cancer so she'd know her children would get it. Daniel lived out there alone for years. I went out and visited a few times. The boys are there now, with their wives and kids. Dolly died in a car accident about ten years ago. I still get Christmas cards from Charles ... you've been out there; you just didn't know it. We've camped on that same gravel bar that I spent my first night on the river as a boy."

"Really?"

The screen porch squeaked open, and Maggie came out and sat with us. I saw Venice in her as I always had. "You okay, Daddy?"

"Of course."

"So what happened to the Bar G?" Ashley pressed.

"Annie's still there. Luke continued to run it. He had a heart attack a few years ago."

"Did you sign it over to them?"

"No. I still own it ... for now ... but I think it's time to pass it on."

"To Annie?"

"No dear. As of right now, the Bar G is yours."

"What!"

"All I ask is that Annie be allowed to remain in the house. She knows all of this is coming. She's been an angel through it all. You'll love her."

Maggie draped an arm around her daughter, tears flooding her eyes, as Ashley stared in wide-eyed silence.

"Your brother will get the money. He should be happy. There's a considerable amount. But I always knew you were the one who would appreciate the land for what it is and take proper care of it."

"I don't know what to say."

"There's nothing *to* say. It's always been yours, really. It just takes a bit of maturity to own something so important."

Ashley shook her head in slow motion, trying to grasp what was happening.

"I suppose we should go out and introduce you to the Bar G."

"I'd love that."

"There it is," recalling the first time I came over that hill.

The trees that lined the drive were now huge. It was like traveling through a long cave. And there in the light at the end of the tunnel stood Annie. We embraced gently, holding on without speaking. Ashley eased slowly around the hood of the car like a nervous little girl.

"Oh James!" Annie gasped. "She looks just like Venice."

They hugged.

"It's *so* nice to meet you." Ashley said with her palm on her chest.

Annie's smile couldn't have been kinder. "I'm so happy you're finally here, darling ... come in," she waved, and led us up the steps.

We sat in front of a blazing fire.

"Forgive me," Ashley began. "Mrs. ..."

"Annie, dear."

"Annie, okay ... I'm just a little overwhelmed."

"It's all right. I certainly understand. I'm just glad to finally get to meet you."

"I thought we might do a little hunting while we are here," I said.

"So you hunt." Annie turned to Ashley. "That's wonderful. Your grandmother loved to hunt. She was well known for her shooting ... the boys still keep dogs and manage the place for bird hunting."

At dinner, I suffered the first pangs of sadness since we'd arrived. It felt lonely in the big room with just the three of us at the end of the same long table where I had dined with so many loved ones so many times. Annie filled us in on the latest news of the ranch, stopping suddenly with a reassuring smile. "Don't worry dear, it's all taken care of until you are ready to get involved."

"Involved?"

"If you want," I said. "I know you have your journalism career and all."

"Do you think you would move out here?" Annie said. "It would be so nice to have you here."

"I don't know ... it's all so ..."

Annie patted Ashley's arm. "I'm sorry, dear. Take your time. The place is fine as it is, but there's plenty of room in this big old house for all of us, if you can stand an old lady's ways. Y'all just enjoy your hunt and your time together while you're here. There's plenty of time to worry about all of that later."

We decided over dinner to drive up to the cabin the next morning and spend a night. Ashley and I both wanted to see it.

After a big breakfast, we met a handsome young man about Ashley's age, waiting out front with a pickup packed with supplies and a pair of eager pointers in a chrome dog carrier.

"Mr. Crawford, it's a real honor." He hurried over with an outstretched hand. "I'm Adam."

"The honor is mine ... this is my granddaughter, Ashley."

"It's a pleasure to meet you Ashley." He shook her hand. "Just let me know if there is anything either of you need while you're here."

He smiled at her and took her small bag. I considered the possibility that he was simply an enterprising young man getting a good start with the new owner, but I sensed a spark between the two of them.

"Ready when you are. If you could just follow me in your pickup, we should be there in a little over an hour." He noted my surprise. "The paved road is nice, but sometimes I wished it was like it used to be, like the stories I heard of y'all going up there, with Mr. Grey."

As I drove, I shared more memories from our hunts and the cabin I hadn't thought of in years.

"And up there is where you and grandmother realized you had met before, on the orphan train?"

I loved that for the first time she referred to Venice as her grandmother. I could only nod as my thoughts drifted backward. Ashley watched quietly out the window, the smile of pleasant musings reflected in the glass.

The place looked exactly the same, kept up as if untouched during my decades-long absence. As Adam released the dogs, Ashley tried to pet them, but they ran around frantically, searching the earth for scent.

"They know we're going hunting," Adam said. "They aren't interested in much petting right now."

He began to unload the truck.

"I've got this," he insisted as Ashley stepped up to help. "Y'all look around. We'll head down in a minute ... the hunting's been really good."

I followed Ashley out beyond the vehicles where she stopped to admire the view. There were more little white specks in the distance, houses and silos that hadn't been there decades earlier.

"Do you own all of this?"

"I used to ... now you do."

She shook her head in disbelief.

"We'll be ready to head out soon," Adam called out a reminder to get ready.

He ushered us inside. Ashley glanced around the room as if she was seeing ghosts.

"Ashley, we'll put you in the bedroom." Adam pointed. "She stopped and gazed in from the doorway for a moment before going in and changing.

When we met out front dressed for the hunt, Adam started to the north. The dogs took the cue and raced past him.

"Adam, let's hunt back this way." I pointed.

"Best quail are down in that draw," he said. "There's always a couple of coveys. Usually some pheasants too."

"We're on more of a sentimental journey today."

He nodded and blew his whistle to redirect the dogs.

It wasn't long until they came on point.

"Good job!" Adam cheered as Ashley knocked down a bird. She beamed when Adam took the bird from the dog and showed it to her before depositing it in his vest.

We walked three abreast with Ashley in the middle.

"So how long have you been on the Bar G?" I asked Adam.

He looked over at me a bit puzzled. "My whole life ... Annie's my grandmother."

"Really? She didn't tell me that."

"Maybe she was ashamed." Adam laughed. "I was up at K State long enough to get a degree in agriculture, but I came right back as soon as I graduated. I love it here. I can't ever imagine leaving." He sounded a bit sad.

"Why would you ever leave?" Ashley asked.

"Oh, you never know." He shrugged.

The dogs came to another point. We got in position and Adam stepped in to flush the birds. This time we downed three quail between us.

"Nice shooting!" Adam said to Ashley. "I guess that's just the legendary Crawford shooting."

"Just lucky." She shrugged.

"I know better than that. Crawfords are famous for two things, good shooting and beautiful women."

Ashley's blushing even embarrassed me a little.

"Let's head down and let the dogs get a drink," Adam suggested.

"We'll meet you on that high point over there." I pointed.

We hiked up a long grassy hill that allowed a view to the west as far as the eye could see.

"Wow." She sighed.

We stared out on a vast rolling prairie, lost in our thoughts. After a few minutes, I turned and looked back at the very spot Venice and I picnicked on our honeymoon, and for an instant it became real again, my darling wife, seated on the blanket, smiling up, reaching for me, and I felt the vigor of a young man's yearning, and something deep within was as perfect as it had ever been, without a trace of sadness or regret or pain.

When a chilly breeze brought me back, I realized Ashley was studying me.

"Is this the place?"

I nodded, barely.

"And you're thinking of her right now?"

"Just like I do every day."

About the Author

Steve Brigman says when he went back to school in his mid-thirties, he really wanted to study creative writing, but that required a foreign language. Armed  with a journalism degree, he launched a newspaper career as a cop reporter, rising to managing editor in eight years. But he just wanted to write, and left the newsroom to become a full-time freelancer, writing magazine and newspaper feature stories, and the popular newspaper column: "Out in the Ozarks." In 2008, a collection of his writings came out in the funny and adventurous, *Somebody's Gotta Do It*. He's been decorated with dozens of writing awards, including a 1999 Press Club of Dallas Katie Award and the 2005 Missouri Conservation Communicator of the Year. Along the way, Steve spent three years producing the popular fishing television show *Bass Edge*, while hammering out the beginnings of *The Orphan Train*. He's currently busy editing his next novel and researching yet another. His wife of 39 years, Kathy, is his inspiration, along with Maggie, his muse who lies dutifully at his feet as he taps every keystroke. Together they enjoy hiking the hilly trails and floating the beautiful streams near their home in the Missouri Ozarks.

CPSIA information can be obtained at www.ICGtesting.com
Printed in the USA
BVOW08s0949161016

464924BV00005B/263/P